Here & Now

Gayle C. Edlin

ISBN-13: 978-0-9909736-0-7
Printed by CreateSpace

Cover design by Fred Dye (freddye.com)
Original photography by Gayle C. Edlin (gcedlin.com)

For the love of land, strong women, and story.
May we each find our sanctuary.

1: Arrival

Thunder grumbled again, its rhetoric louder and increasingly malcontent, while Lila wrestled with the too-tight, old-school cattle gate. As much as she adored A. B., she was frustrated with him now. She'd come to rely on A. B. for loosening the gates, though the real problem was Adam Spencer's stubborn refusal to upgrade this particular bane of a gate. Really, it was an alleged gate, more part of the fence than it ever should be if it even once desired to act as it was purportedly designed to do.

"Dangit, A. B.!"

Lila could picture A. B.'s gnarled grin, easily capable of sustaining itself in the face of Lila's and far stronger invective. As a short, sweaty curl slid from the feeble grasp of her baseball cap, Lila gave in to the inevitable, with one last, futile shove against the impenetrable gate.

"Fine! I'll get the pulley already!"

Another rumble of thunder rippled through the air, moving with tangible volume and force, as certain as that of the wind.

In truth, Lila was more angry at herself and the weather than A. B., or even the near-mythological Spencer. In the decade since she'd purchased the land on the other side of this gate, she'd come to know this third and final gate as difficult at best. She'd devised a pulley method for dealing with the problem whenever she arrived at the gate after Spencer tightened it and before A. B. could loosen it. She had to use her pulley more often than not, but this time, the impending storm had made her hopeful in spite of experience and she'd foolishly tried to force the inflexible gate rather than dig her pulley out of her truck.

That weathered A. B., too, would have to struggle with this particular gate was of no comfort to Lila, even though she was substantially shorter and less muscled than the rancher who had sold her this property. She had a good three decades of youth on A. B., but youth had no impact Lila could see against taut barbed wire and anal-retentive neighbors like Spencer.

Or on storms.

The storm was speaking thunderously more often now than not, and the winds were rising rapidly. Lila needed to open the gate, drive through, close the gate up again behind her, and make her way through the swaying, waving grasses ahead a good 300 yards to a small grove of hawthorns before she would have any possibility of protection. Here on the knoll with the recalcitrant gate, she was dangerously exposed.

Wind swirling around her, Lila yanked the pulley and her gloves from the hastily-piled supplies under the cover of her truck's topper. Normally, she would be better prepared than this— and she'd wait for decent weather to come to the cabin, too—but there was very little "normal" in Lila's Wyoming pilgrimage this time.

As Lila wrapped the pulley around the gate and its attending fencepost, the dizzying, buffeting wind finally selected a direction and shoved Lila, hard.

"Oh!"

Looking up, Lila saw the haze of diagonally-driven rain perhaps a mile or so away now, but nearing at a ridiculous, frenetic pace. In the split second that she watched, leaning into her effort and drawing the pulley tight before wrenching the upper ring of wire over the gate post, lightning struck. The hit seemed to be right on top of the hill ahead where her cabin stood, though the thunder did not follow immediately, proving the proximity of the lightning was an optical illusion.

If only A. B. had gotten Spencer to agree to the quick-release gate!

Lila had received a break in the price of the property when

negotiations with Spencer stalled, but she had thought then—and certainly thought now, with a storm breathing hard and right in her face—that the cost reduction wasn't worth what a new gate would have been. She'd never even met Spencer; she'd only heard A. B.'s stories.

There was little time now for recollection, let alone for recrimination. That the lightning wasn't literally on top of her didn't mean that it wouldn't be soon, and certainly the storm was practically here. Lila extracted the heavy post from the lower rim of wire that guarded its base, dragging it just far enough out of the dwindling, two-track roadway so that she could drive her Toyota pickup truck through. The wind continued to smack, tasting the truck with a very large, rough tongue, as she threw the vehicle into gear. Driving through the gate was the easiest part of the entire process!

Raindrops began to add to the abuse of the wind as Lila returned to the gate and struggled to position the fence pole and pulley properly. In her haste, she nearly trapped her pulley underneath the wire as she finished securing the post. Icy cold, surprisingly hard dollops of rain stung her arms and cheeks, driven by the force of the wind to behave more like thrown projectiles than mere droplets of rain.

Lila managed to complete her task before the full force of the rain reached her. Inside the relative safety of her truck, she set the windshield wipers into their highest speed and engaged the four-wheel drive. The clay-like soil here in northeastern Wyoming would turn from slick to thick with little provocation from rain. While it might be short-lived, this storm still had the potential to make muck out of the ill-defined road ahead.

Creeping the truck towards the hawthorns through the now-torrential rain, Lila was aware of a distinct lack of the peace that usually washed over her at this point in her journey. She would like to blame the storm, but it wouldn't be fair and if she believed anything about herself, Lila firmly held that she did her best to be unbiased ... at least once the urgency of an emotional situation had passed.

No, Lila's unease had far more to do with the stress that had led to her impromptu journey to the cabin, and the unusual lack of planning that she'd put into the trip this time. She sighed, wheeling the truck next to the hawthorns in the dip of gulley they inhabited, and then pulling forward just enough to put her and the truck on the upside of the gentle slope. She put the truck in "park" and turned off the engine; she had lost a bet against man today with her attempt to open the gate without mechanical aid—Lila was sure she had even worse odds against nature.

Still, she was hopeful that even as strong as the storm was at this point, it wouldn't last long. Wyoming weather was capricious at best, and while storms that blew up here on the edge of the Black Hills could be mighty, they didn't tend towards longevity. Even in her haste to escape what others held to be "civilization," Lila had stopped long enough to check the weather, and so she was aware that thunderstorms had been given a 60 percent chance of occurring but also that these storms were said to be held in scattered locations.

Scatter somewhere else already, would you?

Tired from the long day's drive as well as from the last push to rush through the lengthy, bumpy road—spotted here and there with clusters of curious cattle—Lila sighed. The sound of her breath huffing out of her body was swallowed whole by the smacking raindrops on the truck, and on the aluminum topper behind it.

She had to wait out the rain unless she wanted to drench her clothes, bedding, and food. Lila hadn't taken the usual precaution of packing everything into plastic bags. She hadn't even pre-packed her backpack! She didn't need to crane her neck to see the chaotic mound of supplies in the bed of the truck; she knew that the

4

evidence of her hurried, raw need to escape was written clearly in everything from the still-bagged groceries to the heaped box labeled "Wyoming"—the box that was supposed to stay in her apartment after she carefully packed up the things that accumulated in it prior to every trip.

The frustration of the past week built to the point where it finally wrung a tear out of Lila, and that inaugural tear sparked a rash of ready followers.

While in no way competing with the deluge outside, Lila's fierce shower of tears was nevertheless substantial. With memories of responsibilities both minute and significant replaying as a sloppy montage in her head, Lila let go in private the way she never would in public. Although she still felt that the peace she sought was a long way off, this was a beginning ... a release of her own personal storm, the one that rebuilt and recurred with increasing, disturbing frequency.

If I could just stay here!

The thought brought no solace, intertwined as it was with the intrinsic fear that doing so would be a permanent solution to both Lila's curse and her blessing.

Damned if you do, damned if you don't.

That's how A. B. would put it, if he knew—she "heard" the thought with his low, slow drawl. A laugh caught in Lila's throat and briefly superseded her tears. She hadn't actually spoken to her old friend to let him know of this trip, leaving only a hasty message on his answering machine instead; she'd visit A. B. as soon as she felt able.

Rain continued to fall at an impressive rate, but there was little thunder left to advocate for an extended weather event. Lila even thought she could see hints of crystalline blue in the western sky, where it was visible through the rain and the limited shelter offered by the hawthorns. The windshield was now coated in a haze of condensation, and between this and the rivulets of rainwater, Lila had increasingly limited visibility.

Still, the smudges of blue inspired more encouraging thoughts of reaching the cabin during the dwindling daylight hours, and so Lila scrounged a pack of tissues from her glove compartment, wiped her streaming eyes, and blew her snuffle-y nose. When she tucked the wad of tissues into the plastic trash bag on the floor, a whiff of tuna escaped. She'd had a tuna sandwich for lunch, hastily assembled from her stash of supplies, and a packet of mayo purloined from a convenience store. Normally, Lila would have ditched the detritus of her journey before heading into the cabin; this was but another reminder that there had been very little even in the vicinity of normal on this particular trip.

Though she was feeling less "better" than more "tolerable," Lila savored the humble improvement in her mood. It was less effusive than the pervasive odor of tuna that still hung in the air of the truck, but it was there. Lila duly gave credit to her release of emotion as well as the limited time offer of the rain; each was, in its way, cleansing.

As she continued to wait out the weather, Lila began organizing the day-pack on the front seat next to her, carefully separating the rubbish of the journey from the snacks that were still unsnacked upon, and tucking away the sundry items that she'd wrenched out of the hastily prepared pack in search of the snacks during her drive. It wasn't a complicated task by any means, but it was involving enough for a few more minutes, and by the time Lila finished the chore, the rain and wind were reduced to muttering where they previously howled.

She'd not noted the time when she'd turned off her truck, but when Lila turned it back on to defrost her windshield and more definitively check the tenor of the sky, she guessed a good 30 minutes had passed. She might still be able to unload the truck today, but since tomorrow's weather forecast was more favorable that today's, Lila was more inclined to carry only her day-pack—

with its "vitals:" munchies, medication, and underwear—up to the cabin today and put off the hard hauling until morning. The usual slew of cabin-opening chores awaited her, and she was already exhausted!

Yes, the bulk of the sorting and carrying would just have to wait.

Decision made, Lila pulled the keys from the ignition and tucked them deep into the front pocket of her jeans. She secured her cellular phone in a small, zippered pocket of the pack and regretfully left her laptop on the front seat, not bothering to tuck it underneath the faded blue towel that typically served as its sunshade. She would be back for it in the morning, after all, and in spite of the deceptively open Wyoming sky, night was not far away. Lila spared the sky one last, cursory glance, but the storm clouds had already peeled almost entirely away, leaving an unthreatening smattering of stragglers in their wake.

With one arm hooked underneath the shoulder strap of her day-pack, Lila slipped out of the truck, shaking the branch that the door bumped into and loosing a heavy sprinkle onto her head and front as she did so.

"Whoops!"

Well, at least she hadn't skewered herself on one of the thorns. Lila shook her head, and the sweaty curls that had escaped during her bout with the gate flicked across her skin—not rough, but not tickling as they were when dry and fresh. It didn't bother Lila, who had long ago realized that daily shampoos were not as nice for her hair as the ads on television would have her believe. She was actually looking forward to the rare washes that she would have at the cabin—the rarity made them more enjoyable, and the natural oils in Lila's hair made it more manageable between washing.

This is good. I'm thinking about my hair and not ... not ...

Lila bit her lip and slammed the truck door hard, lifting the handle to check the lock out of habit rather than necessity.

Raccoons might, she supposed, learn to enter the cab of a truck, but she hadn't ever seen one on her property, though she had seen a badger once. No, in Wyoming, Lila locked her doors from reflex rather than any actual need; the reflex would fade by the end of her trip.

Lila jammed her cap more firmly on her head and shouldered her pack. She patted her pocket, feeling the bulk of the keys and hearing their muted, metallic response assured her that she was almost ready to begin her trek up the hill to her cabin. She clipped her pepper spray to the waistband of her jeans, having forgotten her belt, and tucked her shirt in just along that spot where the clip might otherwise scratch her skin during the hike. Lila hadn't seen a mountain lion near the cabin, but she was alone here, and that made her cautious.

That, and she had seen the tracks of a big cat along one of the old logging trails a few years ago!

Lila spared a thought for her shoes, which would surely be drenched in the rain-wetted grasses, but her hiking boots were somewhere in the melee in the back of the truck. She decided she could find the boots tomorrow. Besides, if her shoes weren't dry by morning, she had another pair in the cabin. Better to just get to the cabin, she reminded herself again, and start to settle herself; the things Lila needed to settle were, after all, far less complicated, even if they were just as disorganized as she was.

It's overload. There's too much in my head, too much in my thoughts. It's not mine and there's just too much of it.

Too much in my memory that's not mine.

Lila bit her lip again, harder this time, and jostled the branches of the nearest hawthorn once more as she moved resolutely past. One of the spiky limbs caught her cap—not enough to rip it off but just to tip it up at a ridiculous angle—and Lila had a flashing glimpse of the would-be flippant thorn, almost an inch long and honed to a viciously sharp taper. She pulled her cap down and continued on.

While she didn't linger thinking of the woody needle that might have pierced her skin, Lila did long for the respite that the pain might have brought from the chaos inside her mind. It was stronger than her reflexive lip-biting, and would last longer. Pain was one of few efficacious methods of stopping the overload of memories in Lila's mind, but it was a dangerous tool.

"You can't injure yourself out of this, Lila!" The memory of Kristen so many years ago and the distress in her eyes when she'd found Lila cutting—anguish which had throttled Kristen after Lila had sobbed out her reason for self-abuse—"You have to find another way!"

Lila swallowed hard, the recollection of that awful scene and Kristen's unwavering support then and since causing a lump that had not lessened in the years since it first formed. Kristen was the kind of friend anyone would feel lucky to have, but in Lila's case, "lucky" was far too tame of a term; sharing her secret with Kristen had undoubtedly saved Lila's life.

The hill ahead seemed to pull itself up, posture-perfect, making it more imposing as Lila approached. Her feet began to squinch in her shoes—a musical, squeaking sound—that while subtle, was dramatically at odds with the abundance of Wyoming solitude around her. The pines, still too many yards ahead for their wind-driven speech to reach Lila, beckoned while the grasses leaned with the wind and rustled together, producing their own version of communication.

Lila remembered a short snippet of a long movie she'd seen as a child, peering over the couch behind her parents long after she was supposed to have been in bed. Set in the old West, with a specific location and title she could no longer recall, the particular scene had been both disconcerting and memorable for Lila, as a female character lost her battle for sanity against the voices she heard in the prairie wind and the rigorous demands of her life there.

On the heels of this memory, Lila also recalled that she had not snuck out of bed for a long time after that.

Unlike the character in that movie, Lila found the wind, trees, and grasses whispered comforting sounds. That she could not understand these long speeches gave Lila solace rather than pushing her to the brink of madness. It was but one of many dichotomies of the human experience that would fascinate Lila— perhaps enough to make a study of it—if only she could tolerate the presence of other people and their cherished, booby-trapped baggage for more than a few months at a time.

Months. Ha! More like weeks now. How long until it's days?

The remaining clouds were still spitting rain at random intervals, but once Lila reached the pines and could hear the nuances of their unintelligible conversation, the penchant of the clouds for temperamental expectoration was forgettable. Even the clashing sound of Lila's sneakers didn't seem quite as abrasive when she was within the protective embrace of the pines.

The ground was somewhat drier under the canopy of evergreens and their mesh of needles. The groundcover, too, was a sparser sort here; though still much in evidence, it was not as sodden as the grasses through which she'd already trod. Lila navigated around a particularly lovely sego lily, its cup-like blossom heavy with collected raindrops, and felt an anticipatory smile tugging at her lips. She looked forward to exploring to see what flowers were in bloom this year; Lila always found something new on her visits to the cabin, no matter when exactly she arrived.

Although she'd increased her visits to the cabin over time, Lila was still enough of a lowlander to need a rest on her way up the hill. Rain or no rain, she needed extra breaks today, and paused three times on the short, steep slope to catch her breath. She'd been exhausted to her very bones before beginning this excursion, so it was no wonder she felt particularly run down, pushing herself up the embankment to her cabin, driven by need.

On the third stop, with the chimney-pipe turret of her proverbial castle nearly in sight, Lila took an extra moment, inhaling as deeply and slowly as her pounding heart would allow. She let her eyelids drift downward and tried to focus not on the portion of her journey that remained, but instead on the vitality of the venture—of finding and restoring her inner peace.

Lila's heartbeat was resounding in her ears, tattooing its heightened rhythm against her temple, at her wrist, and most profoundly, of course, in her chest. She felt an occasional irregularity—what she perceived as "skipped" beats were, her doctor told her, actually extra beats—and reminded herself that Dr. Hamilton had assured her that these deceptive pauses were benign, and she could minimize the impact of her fear by remembering that.

And by breathing deeply.

Dr. Hamilton had diagnosed Lila's most recent physical manifestation of her mental turmoil as "anxiety." It was a term that still made Lila want to laugh—which wasn't conducive to improving her breathing. She shifted her shoulders slightly under the disproportionate weight of her small pack and tried to regulate her breath again: deeply in, deeply out. Anxiety, too-tame word though it was for the attacks Lila experienced with the onset of arrhythmia, was heightened by shallow breathing. Shallow breathing was, in turn, exacerbated by anxiety, and the vicious circle felt more like a tightening noose than an escalation that could be altered.

Lila was still struggling to master the technique.

The irregular beats of her heart were just the latest bodily problem triggered by Lila's mental anguish. Dr. Hamilton couldn't know that, of course, but when he linked it to anxiety, Lila knew. It wasn't that Dr. Hamilton was wrong—about this or any other treatment he had prescribed, and Lila appreciated his efforts to treat both medicinally and alternatively. But Dr. Hamilton did not understand the full extent of the underlying problem, and therefore couldn't do more than treat the symptoms of each outbreak ... never tying together the threads of depression, anxiety, self-harm, and obsessive/compulsive behaviors that comprised Lila's true condition.

And why should he? He'd never believe it, anyway.

A sigh escaped Lila's labored, careful breathing and she adjusted the straps of the day-pack before beginning the last push to the cabin. A sudden burst of motion ahead and to the left made her heart leap again—from a more natural anxiety trigger this time, at least—and as her eyes sought to track the blur from the initial sound, Lila realized it was a mule deer. That the deer's own heart was surely as off-kilter as her own would not comfort the deer, but Lila found some relief in the sharing, and her initial startlement ebbed quickly.

Just after the deer vanished into the trees, Lila's small clearing and her subtle cabin came into full view. She'd designed her cabin carefully with Lou, Kristen's construction-expert husband, providing the technical know-how and workable plan. This cabin was very clearly a utilitarian get-away, and yet, it included all the comforts of home within its compact walls.

Well, most of the comforts of home. The outhouse was situated some distance away and was not visible from this angle of entry.

To anyone but Lila, the cabin might resemble a squat, square bug more than a pristine escape. Especially now, with the shutters still up, shielding the windows with the same metal that covered the sides and roof of the cabin, there was no break in the monotony of gray. Even the door was covered in it! But Lila knew better; unlike the monstrosity Spencer had recently built—Lila thought of it as the "Taj Spencer"—Lila's Wyoming home was built to blend in rather than stand out. She lived here only occasionally, and she didn't particularly want to advertise the fact to the casual trespasser, should one appear, hoping instead to disguise her Wyoming home as an unassuming structure, perhaps used for hunting.

Lila skittered through the trapezoidal pine fencing around the cabin, remembering how Kristen, Lou, and she had laughed and enjoyed the fence-raising so many years ago. She bumped her pack and reached out to one sun-bleached beam for balance, feeling not the slightest hint of electric remembrance in the touch, despite the preciousness of this fence—of every piece of metal and even every nail—in the cabin to her. It struck Lila as fundamentally unfair that she could not tap into her own powerful memories with the same power that she could absorb those of others, if the item she touched were valued enough.

For Lila, in spite of the inherent and abundant personal value of this cabin and everything in and around it, her memories were just ... her memories, plain and straightforward, faded here and there under time's harsh lighting.

Unfair!

At the front door, under the protection of the roof of the small, open porch that provided a bit of shade on hot evenings and a solid shield from rain in a downpour, Lila extracted her keys and opened both locks. She pulled the door open, and it seemed to fight her for just a moment, as unwilling to part as parched lips, even for the cool drink of fresh air that it was about to taste. But the moment passed, as it always did, and then the cabin was breathing in the rain-cooled evening air.

Lila had to drop her pack and dig out her flashlight, for the cabin would have no power until she set out the solar panels and connected all of the wires according to the diagram she had made when Lou had showed her the process. She'd want to remove at least the eastern shutter, to circulate the air through her sleeping area, and of course she'd need to get the propane flowing to the refrigerator so it would start to cool down.

There was a lot to do, and when Lila located her flashlight, she inhaled deeply once more and then pushed past the screen door and into the cabin to do it.

2: Settling In

Lila woke abruptly just as the star-studded Wyoming sky was beginning to brighten. The light from the lone, unshuttered window above her bed seemed hesitant to enter the room, not quite reaching the far wall—a wall that was actually more near than distant. Lila's toes, peeking out from the end of the light blanket she'd tossed over herself, were chilly, having absorbed more of the brisk night air than the rest of her. But while the shutters were off this particular window, Lila had barely cracked it open in anticipation of just this kind of crisp morning.

She hadn't slept well. She sighed, tucking her toes back under the blanket and flexing them as was her habit. She stretched out her legs next, and worked her way up her body, extending muscles along the way until the point where she would typically fling her arms over her head; she couldn't do that within the compact confines of this bed. Instead, Lila stretched her arms straight up, reaching for the high bunk over her that was so seldom used for guests that she usually stored her pack there instead.

Despite the difficult, unsettled night, Lila knew she wouldn't be able to get back to sleep now. For one thing, she needed to make a morning pilgrimage to the outhouse! For another, while she could no longer count on delicious slumber starting with her very first night at the cabin, Lila could count on her insomnia refusing to be placated during daylight hours.

Even such limited daylight as this!

She sat up slowly, her 40-year-old back protesting the abrupt change in mattress support. Fragments of her disheveled dreams clung to her like baby possums to their mother, tiny claws digging in more painfully than her lightly protesting muscles could endure without complaint. Still, it was a better situation than what had driven Lila to flee to her Wyoming haven—she would count herself lucky indeed if the remains of her toss-and-turn night were nothing more than bits and pieces.

Lila had thought to dig out the backless sneakers that served as cabin slippers—"mules," she thought they were called—and was glad of it. She had her flashlight ready, of course, but it was always an adventure sorting through the myriad Rubbermaid tubs and metal canisters for her in-cabin staples. She'd never had rodent invaders inside the cabin, but when a structure sat unoccupied for any stretch of time, there was always a fair risk of such, and insects could, of course, breach even smaller cracks than the mice. Anything that might be considered food or potential bedding by a bug or animal trespasser was packed, tucked, and sometimes crammed into plastic or metal safe-keeping in Lila's absence.

As Lila exited the cabin, the screen door squeaked a morning greeting; the heavier outer door opened without comment. Outside, and around the corner towards the outhouse, the wide open bowl of sky demanded a catch in Lila's breath ... and it got one. The brightest of the stars were still outshining their competition, but the rising sun would soon make a mockery of their efforts. Still, in this lingering twilight, the sky was beautiful, and seemed to Lila to be more continuous, more whole than in more populous parts of the world.

More alive.

"More alive." Lila whispered it like an affirmation. Perhaps that was just what it was.

It hadn't been long enough since her last visit here for the trail to the outhouse to have rebounded entirely, but there were still a few grasses standing tall enough to tickle Lila's ankles and calves as she passed. The plants were damp with dew—the previous day's rain long since and greedily absorbed by both the dry ground and air above it—and when Lila looked down, she could see the dew glistening across the tips of her sneakers, too.

What has it been, just six weeks?

Her cure was not lasting as long as it once had, and Lila continued to stew over the reduction of her resilience as she returned from the outhouse to the cabin, stopping here and there in the ever-brightening light to examine different plants along the way. At first, a two-week visit to the cabin would restore Lila's ability to return to the world for a year! The last time she'd been to the cabin, Lila had stayed for nearly a month.

And now she was back again, less than two months later.

Inside the cabin, Lila tucked her flashlight between her teeth and removed the screen from her "kitchen" window. She craned her neck to shine the light down and out so she could see to detach the ingenious latches that Lou had devised for the shutters. This wouldn't be much of a stretch for A. B., Lila thought, straining to reach across the counter with its small, embedded propane range top. But A. B. stood nearly a foot taller than Lila's paltry 5' 7" and there was also a substantial difference in wingspan. The thought made her smile, such as she was able with the flashlight held just so.

I should get one of those head-lamps. For next time.

While it was a good idea, it was not reassuring to think of her next trip to the cabin just as she was starting her current seclusion. In addition to a decline in duration, the buffering effect of Lila's Wyoming retreat, too, had diminished. The residual buzz of valued things, charged with memories of those who cherished them, echoed through Lila—a vibrating sensation she typically felt in a distant and vague way, like a mosquito in an otherwise still room. But it pounded now, penetrating Lila's flesh all the way to the bone, it seemed, and while removing herself to this isolated locale provided some relief, there was not the true cessation of experience Lila had once known.

She could still feel the tattoo of the stories embedded all around. Miles of Wyoming emptiness did not seem to provide the insulation they once had.

Lila realized that even though the kitchen window's latches were opened, she was still leaning over the stove, hands outstretched and balanced along the window frame. She swallowed hard, struggling to return herself to the task at hand, and forced herself back into motion. There were two other windows to open, shutters to secure, and solar panels to set up. Then Lila had to bring her supplies up to the cabin and get everything stowed away. And ...

Oh!

"I forgot to text Kristen last night!"

Light or no light, contacting her nearest and dearest friend to ensure Kristen of Lila's safe arrival at the cabin was of utmost concern. The flashlight transitioned from her mouth to her hand and Lila fairly flew into the bedroom, where her cellular phone was still tucked into the pocket of her jeans. She flipped it open, relief flooding her when she saw that it still held sufficient charge for the task at hand—and dismay when she saw that she already had one or more messages awaiting her.

The message that appeared was, indeed, Kristen's, "u forgot again didnt u. lou says go so im omw."

Lila groaned and collapsed on her bed, clipping the top of her head against the upper bunk as she fell backwards.

"Ow!"

She hadn't struck her head particularly hard, but the solid 2x4" under-structure of the bunk was generally unconcerned with severity of force; it upheld its solidity against any attack, regardless of strength. Lila rubbed at the smarting spot, but found neither rising lump nor a trace of blood, so she hurried outside to the southwestern edge of her small patio where the signal was usually best and quickly pecked out a response.

"I'm so sorry!" Unlike Kristen, Lila couldn't give up proper punctuation or capitalization, even for the sake of urgent texting. "I am fine! But if you're still coming, are you bringing tea?"

Lila sent the message, and couldn't help the small smile that blossomed underneath her still smarting scalp. She could feel it in her lips, yes, but even in her eyes.

Even in my heart.

It felt good to smile—to smile for real, without need for affectation or on account of expectation. Kristen was a force of nature, despite the fact that she purportedly didn't much care for "bugs and sweat and other nastiness." And Kristen never seemed annoyed by Lila's absentmindedness upon her arrival in Wyoming. Nor did Kristen refer to the phenomenon as "inattentively crying wolf" ... although that was how Lila thought of her too-frequent memory lapses.

At least I remembered to tell her I was leaving!

Back at her apartment, Lila had a list of people to notify when she headed West, and Kristen topped it. Why she didn't have a similar list here at the cabin ... well.

"I guess that's just what I'll make after I finish getting these shutters opened," Lila murmured, slipping back into the cabin and setting her phone on the counter. Her stomach rumbled loudly, startling in its intensity, and she amended her plan accordingly.

And after breakfast.

Since most of Lila's supplies were still sitting in her truck, breakfast consisted of little more than a couple of cereal bars and an orange that was slightly the worse for wear after its journey up the hill in Lila's day-pack. The orange was still sweet and juicy—it was just uneven in consistency: firm across its undented plains, and then soft-to-mushy in the valleys that had been created in collisions with other items in the pack. One of the bars, too, was irregular and disfigured, but Lila ate it anyway. She'd need the energy to bring the rest of her supplies up to the cabin, and to start hauling water, too.

Water had been Lila's main extravagance here. The land, of course, had cost her dearly, but having the water collection tank checked and cleaned out, and the cabin built—including the outhouse—had also ratcheted up her tab for her Wyoming escape. Lila had, in fact, lugged water up the hill during her first few visits to the cabin due to her uncertainty of whether the underground tank and associated water lines were "good enough" for human consumption. A. B. had developed the spring years ago, and only to feed a small pond, which he used to attract wildlife for hunting.

But that very first trip, when Lila had nearly made herself sick by too-severely rationing her drinking water, had convinced her to get the tank inspected and cleaned out. She'd been pleasantly surprised by the report on the condition of the entire system— absolutely suitable for human consumption—and the hand pump, which went directly into the tank, cut her water-hauling distance down to a mere 150 yards ... and 150 mainly level yards at that.

After opening the rest of the shutters and consuming her deformed breakfast, Lila pulled a notepad from the plastic tub inside her desk drawer and wrote three words: "CALL KRISTEN FIRST!" Then she abandoned the notepad in plain sight on her desk and went to the open closet next to the door to extract the solar panels she would use for charging her phone, laptop, and other miscellaneous electronics.

Like the shutters, the solar panels were another of Lou's innovations. Lila felt a stab of guilt, thinking of Kristen driving four hours up from Casper to check on her, after all she and Lou had done and continued to do to help Lila with the cabin. That they would willingly do more—for Lila or, indeed, anyone else in the world—and not think twice about it did nothing to reduce Lila's persistent concern at being a burden to them.

It was a thought that arose in Lila's mind frequently, and her ability to reason it through was hampered by her current, agitated mental state. She sighed and returned to her current task, lifting first one and then the other unwieldy solar panels from their dark corner and moving them out into the light.

The sun had not quite cleared the hill behind the cabin, which was not actually anywhere near the top of said hill. Rather, the cabin sat on a neat, level step along the way to the true peak, which was a strenuous half-hour's hike beyond. "East and Up" was how Lila referred to that particular trek, one that she made often on her visits to the cabin, because it was hard work and hard work lent itself to both a lessening of her symptoms and to better sleep.

Tomorrow. Kristen will be here today, so there won't be time. But I'll go East and Up tomorrow.

Lila maneuvered the first solar panel out the door and leaned it—still encased in its patchwork quilt of duct-tape and much-used bubble wrap—against the cabin, near the southwest corner. The grand old pine to the slight-northeast blocked a fair bit of morning light, but Lila found that having two panels along the south-facing wall suited her needs admirably. Even an overcast day would not hamper Lila's ability to charge anything she wished, for Lou had outfitted her with two large cells to store the solar panels' collective power, and Lila had made a habit of every-other-daily alternating between the two.

Once both panels were safely out of the swinging, squeaking screen door, Lila set about locating the two folded-back pieces of duct tape on each panel that marked the side she opened. Bubble-wrap was in scarce supply out here in the hills, and so Lila tried to reduce the amount of damage she did when she pulled apart her makeshift wrapping, extracting the panels for use.

"There you are!"

Lila gently tugged the first panel's duct-taped opener apart. She'd seen a magazine blurb somewhere recently that had featured a stunning array of stylish duct tape: everything from animal print to "Hello Kitty." If she had a roll like that, finding the opening to these cushiony casings would be a snap. Besides, it would be a fun addition to her quiet, isolated space here, and as a bonus, it wouldn't cost much money, either.

I'll have to add that to the list.

When the solar panels were unwrapped, all that remained for Lila to do before they would begin the magical process of converting light to power was to connect the cords from the panels to the storage cells inside. Lila stood and tipped one panel forward carefully, reaching for the small box behind it where the cords were stored. She'd removed the lock and lid earlier, but had not unfurled the length of cord coiled inside.

Always one step off, aren't I?

Fortunately, Lila knew with the ease of practice exactly where the cords were, and flicking them gently with her fingers was all it took to send the carefully-wound coil into a degenerative spiral outwards. She clipped the two cords to the solar panel labeled "#1" and then connected the two panels in series.

As she headed back inside, Lila caught her reflection in the mirror above the bedroom dresser and stopped sharply, staring. Under the riotous curls—a gift she received after every toss-and-turn night—her face looked almost ... relaxed. Not quite, no, but it was a steep step up from the visage that she had seen just yesterday morning when—almost panic-stricken with the force of her need—she'd determined to go to the cabin without even a day to prepare.

Lila sighed, realizing she was doing that a lot today, and turned away from the mirror to the interior of the cabin. Her sigh shuddered as it was propelled out, and the hands Lila lifted to the coil of cords inside were shaking.

"I'm not better yet," she muttered, the sound of her voice bitter—steeped too long and carelessly, like forgotten tea. And she wouldn't be truly better, not for awhile.

Still, she had begun to heal.

Again.

Lila unwound the interior length of cord. Unlike the outside coil, there was no protective box inside; when Lila left the cabin, she simply curled the inside coil on the counter near the wall where it passed through and left it there until she returned. Caulk held the cord to the narrow drill-hole through which it passed, and ensured that not even the skinniest of spiders would slink into the cabin along its length.

The thought of spiders reminded Lila of Kristen's impending appearance. Kristen had always abhorred spiders. One day when she and Lou had been helping Lila erect the cabin, a spider had managed to get into Kristen's hair—Lou figured the spider had gotten into Kristen's baseball cap during the night—and she hadn't found the thing until the end of the day when she'd been working a comb through her sweaty, tangled locks, and had pulled out bits and pieces of a rather large spider.

The memory tickled Lila's funny bone now, just as it had then. Kristen had been disgusted and irate; Lou, pragmatic and sarcastic.

"Really, Kristen? You didn't think we'd run into any wildlife outside?"

"'Wildlife?' Lou, it's not 'wildlife,' it's a fucking spider! IN MY HAIR! Ohhh, and I thought I just had an itch. I bet that horrible thing bit me before I killed it—oh my GOD, Lila, I must've killed it when I rubbed my head ... I rubbed spider parts into my SCALP, probably its ass glands, for Christ's sake—and ... "

At that point, Lou had dryly observed that it likely wasn't anything "Head and Shoulders" couldn't cure. Kristen had soundly smacked him in the chest and while Lou retreated to check on a few things for the next day, Kristen had gone on to enumerate to

Lila the many trying and time-consuming ways in which she'd avoid spiders for the rest of her living days.

Her plans consisted primarily of shaking out articles of clothing and inspecting them inside and out before putting them on her body.

"And avoiding what is laughably referred to as 'The GREAT Outdoors,'" she finished.

Of course, at that point in time, Kristen could hardly have known that Lila's escalating problems would compel her past her loathing of spiders, sweating, and reduced proximity to flush toilets on an almost routine basis.

A flush of guilt rode the wave from Lila's neck to her forehead so distinctly that she felt she could have pinpointed its exact location as it progressed. Others might blush when embarrassed; Lila—in addition to her principal sensory distinction—blushed when she felt guilty.

But she would enjoy seeing Kristen, regardless of the circumstances. While not her oldest friend, Kristen did hold the distinction of being Lila's dearest. She and Lou were the only people other than Lila herself who knew about Lila's ability to sense personal histories from valued or otherwise important objects. It didn't much matter what the thing was, although Lila had observed that porous items such as wood didn't seem to conduct memories as well as solid things like metal; if it was somehow important to someone, Lila knew when she touched it.

Lila checked her phone, noted the time, and decided she might be able to work in a trip or two down to her truck before Kristen arrived. Kristen reliably sent a text when she reached the first cattle gate, where she'd park Lou's truck and hop on her mountain bike to complete the rest of the journey. Despite her purported aversion to sweat, Kristen loved to ride—as long as the rides began and ended with "civilization."

"But how will you rescue me on a mountain bike?" Lila had

asked on one of Kristen's earlier visits, where she'd chastised Lila severely for not remembering to text her on arrival.

"Rescue you? I don't need to rescue you! We both know you're fine. Except as 'sensitive' as you supposedly are, you never seem to remember your best friend when you get out here!"

The old jibe was always reassuring, even if it was ridiculous. Lila had to wonder if her apparent inability to "remember" to call Kristen when she reached the cabin was less a problem of memory than it was a problem of loneliness. It sounded like something Dr. Hamilton might say or more likely, Julie, Lila's on-again-off-again therapist.

Maybe I should start seeing Julie again when …

But Lila shook her head even before the thought could complete itself. What would be the point? If she wasn't going to tell Julie the real problem, going to appointments hardly seemed worth doing.

And she wasn't going to tell Julie. If she did, she'd sound really crazy!

Lila tucked her cell phone—she was still clutching it in her hand—into her pocket with her keys, clipped the pepper spray to her belt, and picked up her snakebite kit to carry along. Usually, these items and a small roll of toilet paper would accompany her on hikes in a fanny pack, but since she'd be hauling her big backpack up the hill first, Lila would carry them down the hill today and then add them to the pack for the trip back up. Maybe on the second trip, she'd want the fanny pack, but … but she was procrastinating, and wasting the coolest hours of the day, too.

Resolute, Lila drained the last of the water bottle she'd carried in last night and headed out the door. She could pump water when she returned; a cool water reward would be motivating enough by then!

It wasn't actually the snakes or other wildlife that concerned Lila when she was staying at the cabin. Sure, she had her bite kit and pepper spray, but one of the nicest things about the wilderness in Lila's estimation was the way both she and the critters respected each other's personal space. Lila was big enough not to be seen as prey by most anything out here, and she didn't act as predator, either. Therefore, she kept to herself and the animals kept to themselves; as long as she didn't step right on a snake, she was unlikely to provoke it, or anything else.

On the other hand, it would be easy to sprain an ankle or even break a leg. Lila slowed her pace as she began to zigzag down the steepest part of the trail back to her truck. This was the sort of misfortune Lila actually concerned herself with, and unlike the compact snakebite kit or handy little vial of pepper spray, she could hardly carry a splint with her everywhere she went.

Well, technically, she could. Lila now had in her cabin arsenal of first-aid supplies the neat plastic splint with Velcro straps that Kristen had used two winters ago when she'd fallen on the ice and twisted her ankle. It was, however, too large for Lila's fanny pack, and despite the fact that she felt injury was a bigger risk than animal or snake attack, she also felt silly carrying it with her on her hikes.

"Ridiculous," Lila grumbled out loud, trying to silence her rambling thoughts with the sound of her voice. Somewhere in the trees to her right and just ahead, a squirrel began to chitter.

"Agreeing with me? Or have you got your own issues?"

Lila managed to complete the rest of her journey in silence, except for the smacking noise of her shoes against the soil beneath her feet, and the occasional slice of the snakebite kit in her hand brushing against a sagebrush plant when she approached her truck. It was a neat noise, in fact, and after the first accidental sound, Lila made an effort to swing the kit into the taller sagebrush along her way.

At her truck, she opened both front and back to allow the still-brisk morning air to circulate, and positioned herself sitting on the truck's tailgate. From here, Lila could reach most of the truck simply by reclining backwards and stretching this way or that, and so she did, packing and arranging her burden very carefully, despite the brevity of the hike. It would be heavy, as she had everything from canned juice—which would not be making the trip all at once—to foil packets of tuna and various pre-bagged mixes of her own creation.

Lila checked the cooler and found that she still had a respectable amount of ice. She'd get the cooler's contents on the next trip, then, giving the cabin's propane refrigerator just a little more time to work up a good chill. When she finished packing, Lila had at least another pack's worth of supplies in her truck. She really hadn't planned this trip well ... or at all.

One thing's for sure: I won't go hungry!

Lila reached for a mesh bag of clothes and towels up on the shelf next to the sliding window at the front of the truck's topper. She hooked one of the bags straps with two fingers and tugged it forward as she rocked back up. As she did so, her snugly stuffed pack wobbled slightly from where it was propped up next to her. Lila abandoned her grip on the mesh bag to arrest the pack's movement, and the mesh bag flopped forward off the edge of the tailgate and into the dirt.

"Crap!" Of course, it would be the clean things that ended up in the dirt. Still, better the clothes than the computer, which she'd also get on her next trip to the truck.

It was a tribute to the parched Wyoming soil that it had swallowed yesterday's rain so greedily and thoroughly that Lila had to brush dust off of her laundry today. She took comfort in the fact that the clothing was still cleaner than it had been when she'd packed it out, and gave the bag a firm shove to entice it to stay on the tailgate while she shouldered her pack.

After her pack was secure, Lila glanced towards the sun, reliably working its way up and across the breadth of the sky. She frowned. It would be tricky to time her journey such that she was at the truck when Kristen arrived, but Lila's computer battery was fully charged, so she could work while she waited. Not that she currently felt anywhere near the capable, crafty storyteller others held her to be, but then again, she never had.

Lila grabbed the mesh bag where it squatted, slightly squashed on the edge of the tailgate, and tucked her snakebite kit inside. This load was a heavy one, alright, but it wasn't far to the cabin.

It's just UP.

That it was. But part of the appeal of this property was its untouched, unspoiled terrain. Lila took great comfort not only in the resounding spaciousness of her land, but also in that it was so pristine. So she determined, early on, to leave her truck near the southwest corner so as not to detract from the beauty—the wholeness—of her refuge with mechanized trails ... inasmuch as was possible, Lila tread lightly on her land, leaving only her home and her footprints to mingle with those of the non-human inhabitants.

Better get on with it, then ... the footprints, that is.

She shut the truck back up, leaving the windows in the front generously cracked to keep the interior cool and perhaps to disperse a bit of the eau de tuna that still lingered there. In broad daylight, Lila didn't have to worry that any of the resident wildlife would make a push into her truck in the time it took her to trudge up to the cabin and back.

She checked her phone one more time to be sure that Kristen was not breaking any personal speed records on her trip from Casper. Finding only the ever-increasing hour and minute of the day, Lila shrugged her shoulders up and down, settling her pack into just the right position, and proceeded to add heavy footprints to the lighter ones she had already made.

3: Visitors

Despite her initial, dilatory progress in retrieving her vast cache of supplies, Lila made good time once she actually started hauling. She paused at the cabin only long enough to wipe the sweat from her face and neck and drain one of the juices she'd just brought up, and then she was off again, back down the hill so as not to leave Kristen waiting.

As she cleared the trees on her second walk down to her truck, the wind was beginning to pick up, ruffling the tops of the grasses and sagebrush and whispering sweetly to the flowers scattered across the ground—flowers as preponderant on the earth as the stars had been in the heavens last night.

Pristine beauty had been the furthest thing from Lila's mind when Kristen had introduced the idea of a Wyoming escape. Kristen and Lou had been living in Casper for three or four years then, and Lila had finally been to visit—what she'd seen driving along I-90 and I-25 had not given her the greatest appreciation for Wyoming's landscape, though she certainly did value the dearth of people.

"Oh, you just haven't looked close enough," Kristen groused. "You're not going to see wildflowers when you're going 90 miles an hour down the interstate!"

"The speed limit is 75, Kristen."

"Whatever. I know you. You need to get out and walk around ... then you'll get it. You'll love it here; we just have to find you the right place!"

Of course Kristen had been right. What looked at 75+ miles per hour to be nothing but stubby sagebrush as far as the eye could see was, upon closer inspection, an ecosystem as unique and wondrous as any other. And here on the fringes of the Black Hills, there were the additional aspects of that world pouring into the rest and blending just right—a soothing cocktail of nature to satiate Lila's desperate thirst and parched soul.

Lila stopped for a moment, catching a glimpse of periwinkle blue in an open scar of soil near her feet. She peered down at the soft petals, rippling around like a parachute with which children play, lifting it up and running underneath. The petals of the flower—she thought she remembered it to be western blue flax— had separated as one unit from the rest of the plant, unceremoniously ripped from the apex of the structure.

With one finger, Lila flipped the pale curtain over, revealing its more color-saturated side. Yes, it was the blue flax, and now that she was looking, there were fragments of several others lying about, probably torn away yesterday during the storm.

I'm not the only fragile thing out here.

The truth of it stabbed at Lila as she straightened, leaving the floral parachute that had caught her eye in the dirt, though she stepped carefully around it. This wasn't the first time her Wyoming "safe place" had served her a dreary side-dish of reality, but somehow, even unsavory epiphanies were less bitter here. Perhaps regret evaporated into the dryness of the air, or was sucked into the soil as readily as rain.

A bird trilled somewhere nearby and although Lila cast her gaze repeatedly in the direction of the sound, she saw nothing. She wasn't as good with birds as flowers, though she had come to know a few of the avian denizens here by their songs. Unlike flowers, birds could scarcely be plucked and studied for identification, and although Lila prided herself in her attention to detail, most birds remained evasive, flying away well before Lila had an opportunity to study them carefully.

It felt good—SO good—to be present in the moment again,

without the overlay of someone else's emotional story interfering in her own experience. Lila resumed walking more slowly, reveling in the snippets of sound and flashes of color around her. Where she once noted nothing more than sage green and dirt brown, she now saw a near-complete spectrum, although the primary colors at present were dusty green, periwinkle, and gold.

Ahead, Lila's truck was an awkward splash of silver in the waving sea of earthy shades. She approached it tangentially where it squatted next to the vein of hawthorns that stretched up the hill in the draw. The air was beginning to simmer, heating gently at the behest of the morning sun, but it could approach stifling by afternoon if clouds did not arrive again to temper it. And then there was the possibility of another thunderstorm. Lila wasn't sure of the forecast; it wouldn't typically concern her much now that she was at the cabin, but she didn't want Kristen to get caught out on her bike as Lila had been trapped in her truck yesterday.

Of course, Kristen could travel quite quickly by bike, and while not a Wyoming native, she could have been for all of attention she paid to the capricious constitution of weather and road construction alike, so ...

A crinkling sound, plasticky and purposeful, caught Lila's attention as she neared the truck. It was slight, almost unobtrusive, but it most certainly did not fit into the native soundtrack of Wyoming. The irregularity of it sent a chill up Lila's spine despite her exertions. She slowed her walk to a hesitant two-step and trained her eye on the cab of her truck, as it seemed that the sound originated there.

The windows, lowered just as she had left them, were undamaged, so whatever was rustling around in the truck could not be particularly large, but Lila pulled the pepper spray out of its pouch at her waist nevertheless. She held it as one would hold a rock, though, since the buffeting wind this morning could not be relied upon to keep a stinging spritz of the stuff out of her eyes, too, should she attempt to use it on The Thing inside her truck.

Lila considered circling around the truck to put the wind at her back, but the apparent lack of size of the intruder held her dread in check with curiosity, and so she continued to sidle nearer the truck. She could almost see down inside when a flash of mottled fur and shiny metal near the steering wheel startled Lila enough to make her jump and gasp. But where she might have otherwise screamed simply on account of the precipitous appearance of the cat in her truck at the driver's side window, now the sight of the disheveled thing made her begin to giggle instead.

If last night's foil tuna packet—empty enough by Lila's standards, but still strongly scented and apparently perfect for licking by the cat's—in its mouth had not been enough to set Lila off, the sticky tab from a pack of wet wipes attached firmly to one ear certainly would have been. Lila clasped her free hand over her mouth to muffle her gasping laughter as the cat regarded her, wide-eyed and horrified into immobility.

Lila stepped back a few paces, not wanting to threaten this inadvertent feline comedian. The cat—still frozen in place by the shock of her appearance—was thin, though not heartbreakingly so. Its eyes were the only thing that moved as it tracked Lila's reversed progress, front paws leaning against the edge of the driver's side window at such an angle that Lila could see the pink tips of toe pads there.

"Come on out of there, kitty," Lila said, softening her voice to a near whisper. "I have things to do, you know."

The cat, now well-informed, still did not move from its ungainly stretch—the prelude to a leap-and-scramble through the window, Lila was sure. However, the ear to which the stray adhesive flap was attached began to twitch, as the cat registered its continued interference in this altogether uncomfortable situation.

Where Lila had previously abandoned the idea of moving to the passenger side of her truck, she now reconsidered it. True, both windows were open, but the cat was clearly on its way out of the truck; perhaps her presence at the passenger side would inspire it to move again, and finish its raid on Lila's trash.

While not excited at the prospect of turning this scraggly garbage thief loose with its bounty—litter could blow for miles under the impetus of a strong Wyoming wind—Lila didn't want the cat to make her truck its home, either. And yet ... what was a domestic cat doing so far out in the hills? While virtually free of the hazards posed by roads, there were plenty of predators that would surely threaten a small cat like this one.

Lila fished her phone out of her pocket and checked the time. There were no messages, but she could definitely expect Kristen at any moment.

"Well, kitty, I'm not going to stand here in the sun the whole time."

The plastic affixed to the cat's ear flickered with another twitch.

"Fine. I'll just have to deal with you making me a litterbug by association."

Lila began to move to the left, walking in an arc that, while wide and graceful, left no doubt about her eventual arrival at the passenger side door of the truck. The cat, its pseudo-earring flashing in the sun with each flexing muscle, tracked her progress with its eyes, and when it had to, began to turn its head, too. It traced Lila's progress for far longer than Lila imagined that it could stand to do so, but eventually, the cat did have to resolve what was happening.

When the cat turned back to the window it had been facing and leaped, its motion was so fluid that Lila scarcely registered that the cat had to squirm a little to get through the gap at the top of the window. Once through, it slip-leapt down the glass of the window and out of Lila's line of sight. Still thinking of the trash, Lila hurried back towards the driver's side of the truck, and caught a glimpse of the white/tan/orange/black beast bounding into the hawthorns just up the draw.

Staring after the cat, Lila shook her head at the oddity of her unexpected adventure. She was still clutching the pepper spray, she realized, and so she put that away and then stepped up to her truck to survey the damage. The cat had obviously rummaged through her trash, but aside from the tuna, there had been nothing particularly messy in it. Lila extracted a spare bag from the side-pocket of the truck door and, after rolling both windows all the way up, made short work of cleaning the cab.

With order—such as it was—restored, Lila still had plenty to do while she waited for Kristen. She started by organizing a pair of reusable, canvas shopping bags in the back, packing the rest of what she expected to carry to the cabin today carefully inside. There would still be some juice and a few grocery items in the truck, but with the canvas bags, cooler, and her computer, she'd have all of the vitals.

Lila had prioritized the two canvas bags, too; if Kristen couldn't carry the one of the bags up with her, Lila would take the bag that contained more food than water. If Kristen could carry a bag, well, then Lila would take the heavier bag with the water and enlist Kristen's help with the bag that contained more goodies than mass, like dried fruit and—Lila's and Kristen's favorite camping treat—dehydrated ice cream.

With her packing complete, Lila sat down on the tailgate, and powered up her laptop. She supposed she could try to work a bit, even if it was still early in her recovery from "civilization" and all of its emotional landmines. Besides, Murphy's Law or one of its corollaries would surely dictate that just the simple virtue of starting to work would trigger Kristen's arrival!

It didn't, though, and Lila spent an uncomfortable 20 minutes staring at her latest novel, reading and re-reading the same page without making any headway on the changes that her editor had requested. This was the most difficult part of writing for Lila. Because she knew—truly knew—how the real story had progressed, even a fictionalized account was uncomfortable for her to change in any substantive way ... it felt like lying.

But RayAnn wanted changes, and RayAnn was going to get changes. Lila gave herself a little shake and refocused on the page in front of her.

"Helloooooooo!"

Of course. I just wasn't sufficiently frustrated for Murphy to work his magic sooner!

Lila slapped her laptop shut, looked up, and spotted Kristen in the distance. She was still coming down the last hill towards Lila's property, and would soon be out of sight behind the rolling hills between her current position and Lila's. And she was walking? That was odd, even if it did explain the delay.

Lila abandoned her computer and pulled herself up to stand on the corner of the tailgate, one foot on the bumper. She waved vigorously, and was rewarded with a waved reply of equal enthusiasm.

Contact established, Lila lowered herself back onto the tailgate and tucked her computer back into its neoprene sheath. RayAnn and her edits would have to wait, but Lila wasn't afraid that the delay would be costly.

"I don't know where you got the idea that you're slow," RayAnn had told her on more than one occasion. "You're one of the fastest with writing and editing that I've ever worked with!"

Now that Kristen was near, Lila relaxed somewhat. She leaned back against the lighter canvas bag—buttressed by the heavier bag behind it, which pushed up against the wheel well of the truck—and closed her eyes. The sound of the wind, funneling through the side windows of the truck, was delicious, like divinity candy for the ears and skin. Shaded from the sun from the knees up, Lila was almost comfortable enough to nap, if sleep could be summoned only by physical comfort. And if Kristen wasn't mere minutes away!

Still, it was an oddly comfortable spot, cushioned by dried strawberries, prunes, and freeze-dried ice cream that she was probably crushing to a fine, messy powder. Lila was not troubled enough by the prospect of crushing the ice cream to move. She had plenty of spoons at the cabin, after all.

Lila listened to the wind and imagined where Kristen would be in her trek by now: coming up over the last rise? Stepping neatly across the fence with her enviably long legs and heading down the hill to where Lila was waiting? Lila peeked through the fringes of her lashes and saw that her visualizations were premature. She pushed forward off of the tailgate and walked towards the border to give Kristen a proper greeting.

As Lila approached the taut barbed-wire fence, she spotted Kristen easily and waved again. With a grin and return wave, Kristen broke off from the two-track and angled across Spencer's field on a direct line towards Lila. Kristen was trespassing by doing this, of course, but with the bitter battle against Spencer's gate fresh in Lila's mind, Lila would not fault her friend. It was all she could do not to do a juvenile little dance as Kristen approached—it was so good to see her again!

"Hey, stranger!" Kristen unslung her own day-pack, its compartments sagging loosely without much to fill them. She passed the pack over the fence to Lila and positioned her hands between barbs to force the fence down a bit in preparation for straddling her way across it. "I see the Good Ol' Bastard makes fences just the way he makes gates ... tight and tricky."

"Yeah, he re-did this one last year, I think," Lila replied, and then Kristen was over the fence and wrapping Lila into a fierce hug. "Oh!"

Tears reared up into Lila's eyes with the ease of Kristen's embrace. Lila had become so sensitized to the dangers of personal contact—granted, not with people but with the things they might be carrying—that she avoided it wherever possible. Even handshakes had become a hazard Lila preferred to avoid, lest the power of someone else's attachment to their rings or other ornamentation leave Lila overwhelmed with unexpected force and incapable of explaining her reaction.

But Kristen knew. Kristen understood. And it was such a relief to hug and be hugged again that Lila began to sob in earnest.

"Oh, sweetie." Kristen hugged her tighter, and thus invited, Lila dropped Kristen's pack and let her own arms make their way up in a return hug, crossing Kristen's back first, and then moving up to her neck.

And suddenly, a tingle of awareness rushed up Lila's left arm from her hand, raising the hair on her arms and shoving her unceremoniously into Kristen's cherished memory of the gold necklace she wore ... the one that she'd tucked into her shirt but which Lila had just brushed with her hand.

"Lou! I love it! Oh, god, but it's too much! Shouldn't we be saving for ...
"

"Kristen, will you shut up? After all we've been through, I want you to have it." Lou grasped her wrist and pulled her into an irresistible hug, toppling over onto the bed with her on top of him, sending her into a fit of giggles in spite of herself as he cushioned her fall. "There will be plenty of time to save for college. Now's the time to celebrate."

Lou reached around behind her neck, fastening the necklace into place and snagging the charm on her chin as he did so.

"Lou!"

"Sorry." He sounded anything but as he tugged the stylized outline of mother and child into place. "I'm just so glad we've made it this far. So glad we're out of the first trimester and on our way to our own baby!"

"Oh, Lou." Kristen framed his grizzled face with her hands and planted a passionate kiss on his mouth, leaning into the kiss with the full force of her love for him and their unborn child backing her.

37

Lila staggered from the force of embedded emotion, pulling her hand from Kristen's neck as if from an electric fence—with effort, despite the galvanic energy of the memory which was as painful for Lila as it was wonderful for Kristen.

"Lila? What ... " Understanding dawned on Kristen's face even as she took a step backwards herself, her hand reaching up towards her neck. "Shit! My necklace! Oh, SHIT, Lila, are you okay?"

Lila shook her head, then nodded, then shook it again, her mouth curving into a smile in spite of the anguish of tears that continued to pour down her face.

"Kristen! A b-b-baby! I'm s-s-s-so happy for you!"

Kristen was digging in the pack that Lila had dropped on the ground, and emerged with a half-finished scarf, which she hurried to wrap around her neck, knitting needles dangling from her back like giant, misplaced earrings. She grabbed Lila again in a hug, but made this one shorter.

"I'm sorry; I'm an idiot! I thought it'd be enough to tuck it into my bra—I didn't think about my neck!"

Lila shook her head, wiping at her streaming eyes. Kristen, with one more worried look, unwrapped the scarf and put it back into her pack.

"It's okay. I'm okay."

"Really?"

"Yes, I will be. I am! Oh, Kristen, are you okay? And the baby?"

"Oh hell, yes. Finally yes! We're at 14 weeks as of yesterday."

Lila grabbed Kristen's hand and squeezed it hard. Kristen and Lou had suffered three miscarriages in as many years. Lila hadn't been sure they would make a fourth attempt at a pregnancy.

"I'll take the necklace off," Kristen began, moving to do just that.

"NO!" Lila shrieked, then gulped and lowered her voice. "No, Kristen, don't. You deserve this ... you and Lou! Don't, not even for me."

Now I've done it.

Lila scrunched her eyes shut against the tears that were threatening to overflow Kristen's eyes and choked on a laugh. "Don't you cry, too," she warned, injecting as much scold into her tone as she could. "Not after that show with your scarf—very funny, by the way."

Kristen didn't attempt to stifle her laugh, though it was burdened with the power of other emotions.

"Aren't we a dopey pair? Come on; I see your truck's open. Aren't you unloaded yet?" Kristen tapped Lila's shoulder playfully as she shouldered her pack.

"No, but shouldn't you—in your delicate condition, I mean—take it easy?" Lila knew full well what Kristen's response would be when she asked, but she was counting on it to lighten the mood further.

Kristen snorted.

"I'll let you take the heavy bag, if that's what you're getting at!"

"Really?"

"Yes, really. Lou told me I'd better start milking this for all it's worth. So to speak!"

"Well, good. Because after giving you such a scare, I ... "

"Stop it, Lila! If anyone's at fault here, it's me ... oh!" Understanding lit Kristen's eyes and she shot Lila an admiring glance. "I see what you did there. Just like back in the day—we both screw up, we both apologize, and ... "

"And we both shut up!" They finished the old chant together.

"As long as you can't feel my necklace now?"

"No." The word escaped on a heavy sigh before Lila could hide her relief. Kristen laughed. "I think because it's new. It's strong, but it doesn't reach very far."

"It's been bad, hasn't it."

It wasn't a question, but Lila answered it anyway.

"Yeah."

They arrived at the truck and Lila was glad for the distraction.

"Here." Lila passed the lighter canvas bag to Kristen, and set the heavy bag and cooler on the ground for herself. She slung her computer bag over her shoulder and shut the tailgate of the truck, but paused before closing the topper. The chaos that the back of the truck had been reduced on account of what Lila had packed up to the cabin, but upon reflection, there were still places that a small cat could hide.

"What?" Kristen asked, as Lila continued to hesitate.

"Do you see a cat anywhere in there?"

"No. Wait, what?"

"You'll never believe what happened to me this morning."

"Apparently, it involves a cat."

"However did you guess?"

"I'm a little psychic."

Lila had to laugh at that.

"Well, just let me poke around here quick, just in case ... "

Though Lila sprung up on the tailgate and jostled boxes, rustled bags, and shifted her possessions hither and yon, nary a cat was roused from the remnants of her belongings.

"Alright, I guess I should've believed your psychic vision, then," she said, backing out of the truck and shutting it properly. "You should let me know if you see my hiking boots, too, because I haven't been able to find them, either, and ... "

"This cat you mentioned," Kristen said, her voice sounding oddly hushed. "Was it a calico?"

Lila's motions were arrested from her progress towards picking up the bags she'd set aside, and her head jerked towards Kristen. Kristen was looking back towards the fence-line, and when she noticed she had Lila's attention, she pointed.

Lila had trouble spotting her furry nemesis, but Kristen's arm did not waver and after a moment, Lila's eyes resolved the waving grasses to the south and slightly in front of the fence. The cat was, indeed, crouching there, next to a large sagebrush plant. It appeared to have divested itself of the annoying sticker that had so plagued it earlier.

"Litterbug," Lila muttered, shaking her head.

"I really need to hear the whole story before I can comment. And this!" Kristen hefted her bag, shaking it a bit. "This is lame. What's in here, air? Exercise is not a problem, you know! Give me the computer at least."

"No way, mama!" Lila pulled back from Kristen's reach. She stepped around the truck and started towards the cabin. Kristen followed.

"What about your little friend?"

"Are you kidding?"

"What's a cat going to do for food out here?"

Lila snorted.

"Well, it started with a little tuna from my trash."

"How did it get in your ... oh, so it was in your truck? No wonder you were looking all over for it, and the whole time it was sitting over there, watching you! And laughing."

"How does a cat laugh, Kristen?"

"Are you kidding me? You know Nero and Hercules. You know they laugh!"

"I know they plot and plan. I don't know that they laugh."

"They absolutely laugh. They also snicker, giggle, chortle, and occasionally snort, like you."

"Nice!"

"It's still watching, you know. I bet it follows you home, and then you'll have to keep it."

"Maybe it'll follow you home, Kristen! All the way back to Casper."

"Well, I do think you should invite it in, if it comes up to the cabin. Hard environment out here for a little kitty like that."

"You are such ... a sucker for cats." The incline of the hill was enough that it was beginning to wear on Lila. "I'd think ... as often as I'm out here ... I'd develop a little better tolerance for altitude."

"Wuss."

"Bite me. Did you ... bring my tea?"

"You know, I did! You're lucky that Lou and I were down in Denver just a few weeks ago, so I got a bunch from Mountain Mavericks."

"I have got ... to get there sometime."

"Maybe you should take a little rest."

"Shut it!"

"No, you shut it. You're the lowlander—you need your air."

"Fine."

Though their conversation stopped for the rest of the trip up to the cabin, the friendly banter had been a wonderful restorative for Lila. Despite the surprise attack of Kristen's necklace, Lila felt better than she had in a long time, and it buoyed her spirit far more than the mere oxygen that her lungs struggled to draw out of the thinner air of the Black Hills.

As they climbed the last rise, Kristen spoke again.

"I hope you don't think you're off the hook on this cat story. I'm dying to know what the hell happened!"

"Absolutely! I'll ... tell you all about it ... just as soon as you ... hand over the tea."

Kristen laughed.

"Deal."

4: Interruption

The tea Kristen had brought was a decaffeinated green, dense with a sweet mango infusion that delighted Lila with its scent and flavor. She brewed the tea inside the cabin while Kristen visited the outhouse and then carried two of Lila's three lawn chairs out to catch the shade that fell from the pine along the eastern side of Lila's lawn—an area delineated not by cropped grass but rather by the fence that bordered it.

Despite the rising heat of the day, the breeze was cool and they were quite comfortable there underneath the pine, whose each and every needle flirted with the wind. The waves of air tossed branches up and down, scattering the shade they cast so much over the length of time that Lila and Kristen talked that eventually, Lila had to walk her chair to the other side of where Kristen's sat.

"Always picking the best spot for yourself, aren't you?"

Kristen dismissed Lila's faux-grumble with an airy wave of her hand.

"You know, while you're up, you should make the pregnant lady more tea."

"I can do that." Lila picked up her own cup and started back to the cabin. "You got that at Mountain Mavericks? It's wonderful!"

"I did, and I know." Kristen sounded only a little smug as she extracted herself from the embrace of the lawn chair and followed Lila inside, barely escaping a slap from the screen door on the way in. "I actually have a few more varieties, one with—oh, hell, those exotic grapey things you're always going on about ... what are they called?"

Lila grinned, taking the forgotten cup from Kristen and preparing to heat another batch of water.

"Goji berries?"

"That's them!" Kristen leaned against the counter, placing one hand atop her barely-there belly with exceptional care. "I haven't had any morning sickness—not any!—and sometimes that scares me, because you know I had it every time ... before." She rubbed her belly, her touch as tentative as her words now. "But then I think, it's good, since none of those ... "

None of those survived.

Lila cleared her throat, bidding the unspoken words to remain so.

"But! I also can't remember shit these days, and the doctor says every time how great things are going, and I have to pee all the time, so! So, be right back, then! Again!"

And Kristen turned brightly away, letting the screen door slam rather than tap in her haste to make for the outhouse.

Lila turned back to her tea kettle, understanding even without the benefit of feeling Kristen's memory through her necklace. Waiting for a pregnancy to "stick" in their long battle for a baby had worn down both Kristen and Lou, despite their outward determination and apparent patience. Kristen had cried over the phone to Lila after each loss, her resilience slipping more each time rather than stabilizing as she preferred most people to believe.

Lila wiped her own eyes, straightened her spine, and dragged her focus back to the decrepit tea kettle, which was beginning to wobble on its stove-top pedestal. The kettle had been a "land-warming" gift from A. B., and she'd deflowered it in campfires at first so that it was now a blackened beacon rather than a silvery one. The dent Lila had added to its base after dropping it onto a rock the very first time she used it gave it a tendency to tip as it approached boiling.

But it gave a cheery whistle when the water boiled, and Lila had loved its full-bodied curves from the start.

I really should give A. B. another call ... or go see him after Kristen leaves!

Lila poured the water, watching the tea as it flushed from the infuser inside the clear cups she'd procured specifically for the purposes of brewing tea. Though Lila had been unaware of it before she'd converted to tea-drinking—one of Dr. Hamilton's suggestions to ease Lila's multitude of stress-related woes—tea came in an astonishing array of colors in addition to a full spectrum of flavors. This tea doubtless inherited its ruddy orange from the mango branch of its family.

"It's a ridiculously good smell, isn't it?" Kristen said, re-entering the kitchen just in time to catch Lila in the act of fairly snorting the fragrance.

Straightening, Lila answered with a grin as broad as the one Kristen wore.

"Thank you so much for coming!" Her emotions, Lila realized, were as volatile as her rocking tea kettle, which was catching residual heat from the burner where Lila had returned it. She gave herself a moment to return to simmering as she made a show of transferring the kettle from the stove to the triangular chunk of native shale that served as a trivet.

"I'll get the tea if you get that bitch-slapping door of yours," Kristen offered.

Lila forced a smile of thanks. Kristen understood, of course; they were well versed in each other's sensitivities, and knew when subtle deflection was better than blatant comfort.

"Can you stay for lunch?"

"I thought I'd stay overnight, if that's alright with you."

"Of course! That'd be wonderful!"

"I'm not taking the top bunk, you understand," Kristen said, settling herself in her chair. "Not with this belly."

Lila smirked, knowing that the increased possibility of spiders in the rarely-used space rather than pregnancy-related girth was behind Kristen's insistence.

"I suppose that's okay. Just this once."

Kristen rewarded Lila's dry tone with a snort.

"Smartass."

"Naturally!"

They sipped their tea almost in unison.

"Perfect!" Lila pronounced, even as Kristen shook her head.

"Still too hot." She lowered her cup and sighed, looking around with obvious pleasure. "It's been awhile since I've had a chance to stay overnight!"

"It has."

"Have you been lonely, Lila? Being up here so much?"

"No. No, not really. You were right—this place is perfect. I know I can get to a main road within a half hour, even if the roads are lousy. But I know no one is going to just stroll by, so ... " Lila shrugged her shoulders, letting the movement fill the void her silence created.

"But you still haven't named it?"

Lila gave Kristen a stern look.

"Kristen, I don't know why ... "

"Lila, this is *Wyoming*. You name your land in Wyoming! Come on!"

"You haven't named yours!"

"For Christ's sake, Lila, we live in town!"

"Only a true Wyomingite would refer to the largest city in the state as 'town.'"

Kristen rolled her eyes.

"It's the second-largest, and only a true out-of-stater would refuse to name a place as awesome as this!"

"I'm not refusing to name it! I just ... I don't have the perfect name yet."

"Jesus, Lila, it's been ... well, you've been here long enough."

"I don't know why you keep harping on ... "

"Then I'll tell you! The year you built the cabin, Lou and I—
okay, I—decided to build you—well, technically, Lou built it—a-a-
a ... shit, those things that go over the main road, on the way in to a
property." Kristen gave up searching her baby-clogged mind for
the appropriate word, set her cup of tea down on the ground
beside her, and etched in the air with her hands.

"It goes up like this, then across the top, and that's where the
name is."

"Oh! An archway?

"Yes! I guess. That doesn't sound quite right. Whatever! We
made one for you ... for this place."

"I ... you did?"

"We did. And ever since, Lila—ever since—it's been sitting on
our lawn or in our garage, just waiting for a name."

"That's so sweet!"

"Yeah? Well, it was sweet. Now it's in Lou's way, and he said
surprise or no surprise, you're getting it this year. So you'd better
come up with a name!"

"Wow, no pressure there."

Kristen laughed, reaching down for her tea, and then
screeched, flicking her hand and rising out of the lawn chair
sharply, as if levitated.

Lila watched Kristen sprint to the cabin, leaving an
impressive—almost visual—string of profanities in her wake.
Kristen did not break her stride in movement or word at the
cabin's door, either, dashing inside as if the hounds of hell were in
pursuit.

Lila stood, stepping around Kristen's chair, and looked down
at the singular Daddy Long-Legs spider that was maneuvering its
way from the handle of Kristen's abandoned cup to its rim. It
wasn't a particularly large spider, but from its position, Lila could
guess the nasty shock that Kristen had just suffered.

"So do you want your tea?"

"NO, goddammit, I want to BLEACH MY HANDS!"

"Way to waste good tea, there, Spidey," Lila commented, brushing the spider from its perch and carefully dumping the cup away from where the spider landed. Kristen would probably rather she dumped the still-hot tea over the spider, but Lila couldn't bring herself to do it.

"I don't care if you drown that hairy beast IN the tea, but I'm not drinking out of that cup until it's washed!" Kristen yelled, echoing Lila's thoughts. Looking up, Lila saw Kristen standing in the entryway, scrubbing furiously at her hands.

"Wasting my antiseptic wipes over a spider, Kristen?"

"Why don't you have any bleach?" Kristen shot back in return. Her smile was crooked, but it was back, and so Lila answered it in kind. Kristen opened the door for her as Lila approached. "Nice of you not to laugh outright! I know you wanted to."

"Nice of you to play doorman! Though I am carrying your cup."

"Not mine anymore! Contaminated." Kristen shuddered. "Where's your wash water? I'll boil it for you."

"I haven't actually been to collect any water yet, but ... "

"You haven't? Why not?"

"I did just get here last night."

"True, but ... "

"But I always fill a few gallon jugs every time I leave so there's no rush when I return. In the corner over there."

Kristen followed Lila's nod, and then stepped to the side so she could see around the large wood stove that squatted on its brick hearth.

"Oh, I see! Good idea keeping them in a tub. Where'd you get that thing? Are there two of them? Looks pretty sturdy—be good for prepping meat during hunting season."

"Yeah, there's two; I stacked them for now, but it'd be just my luck to have one of those jugs spring a leak, you know. I got them somewhere online."

Kristen snorted. "Not much help!"

"Not at this very moment, but I have my receipt in e-mail so I can get you a URL later!" Kristen brightened at this information.

"So Lou's got an elk tag again?"

"He does. And it'll be wonderful, because he'll go for a young one, but even so ... elk's a big animal. I'm not looking forward to processing that sucker."

"Fill the freezer?"

"Most likely! If he goes for antelope and deer, too, we'll probably have to spring for a second one."

"'If?'"

"Exactly. I told him we should just go ahead and get another freezer. He's hoping for a sale, but it's getting closer and closer to hunting season ... I don't see a sale happening." Kristen shook her head at Lou's intractability. "So how about a quick trip to the pump?"

"Sounds good to me. I always feel better after I make sure there aren't any cattle tracks around—then I'd be worried enough to boil the water."

"Don't you do that anyway?"

"Usually. But you've seen Spencer's fences, tight as ... "

"His ass."

"Really, Kristen! I was going to say, 'tight as a drum.'"

Kristen snorted.

"Yeah, well, I bet his ass is tighter."

"I'm sure I wouldn't know. Anyway, yes, let me get my stuff ... " Lila grabbed her desk chair—the only true chair in the cabin, as all others were descended from creatures more likely to inhabit lawns than live exclusively indoors—and positioned it in place to access the high cabinets above the counter.

"You use those cabinets a lot?" Kristen asked, leaning against the counter and peering up at Lila. "Short as you are?"

"Thanks, and yes. Yes, I do! They turned out to be really good storage for the things I don't use every day. Lou was right on about them."

"He's right so often it's downright irritating."

"The only problem is, I don't use these often enough to remember exactly where everything is. I'm getting there, but ... " Lila closed the first door she'd opened and reached for the second.

"You need to make a map."

"That's not a bad idea. Oh, here they are!" Lila opened the clear plastic container she'd spotted, extracted the two fabric bags that she used to shoulder the heavy 3-gallon water containers, and passed them to Kristen.

"ESPRIT? Really, Lila. And how old are we?"

"I'm sure the bags give it away, Kristen. I've kept them all these years."

"Of course you have. You'd shop at Goodwill, if only you could."

"I would, too." Lila swallowed a sigh. "And now we need a couple of the big containers." Lila pulled one off the shelf and handed it down to Kristen, and then paused. "Or maybe just one?"

"Bullshit! Lila, I don't have any restrictions, and I'm not going to start slowing down yet. In case you hadn't noticed, I'm barely showing! It's not a big uphill walk like earlier."

"Kristen, in case *you* hadn't noticed, this is my property ... "

"Nameless property."

"It's still mine! And you're my guest! It would be rude for you to be hauling as much or more than me. We'll pour the gallon jugs I filled last time into the 5-gallon I use for wash water; then you can carry the two 1-gallon jugs for refills—I'll take the two 3-gallon containers."

"That's creative of you."

50

"Thank you. I'm used to carrying these myself anyway. Hence the bags." Lila grinned down at Kristen, and passed her the second container. Transparent as it was, now that she'd played the "you're a guest" card, she knew Kristen wouldn't fight her further.

"I'm still get to carry these hot bags on the way over, though, right?"

"Of course!"

"Okay, then. Where's the five? I'll start filling it while you ... do whatever hosts do. Hostesses."

As Lila was currently struggling to close the sliding door to the mid-section of the upper cabinets, she could scarcely fault Kristen's slight modification to the plan.

"In the closet by the door. Up high, though, and ... "

"I'll stand on tippy-toes, shorty."

Lila snorted.

"Fine!"

It took Lila so long to close the cantankerous door that when she finally stepped out of the cabin, she found Kristen had finished emptying the 1-gallon jugs into the five-gallon container. The container was set on top of an inverted five-gallon bucket so Lila could drain water from a slight height into the wash basin that was neatly placed beneath. All of the items were on the short bench-seat built between the porch roof's support poles and positioned furthest from the cabin, as was Kristen. She pointed to the 5-gallon container, held snug to its perch by a stern, black bungee.

"Oh, you found the bungee, too!"

Kristen grinned, holding up the pink ESPRIT bag.

"I knew you'd organize it this way."

"Predictable, am I?" Lila bent to pick up the three-gallon containers at Kristen's side.

"Hell, yes, you're predictable!"

"Well, let's get going, then."

"I knew you'd say that."

Lila led the way and they strolled rather than hurried, pausing here and there to examine flowers or interesting grasses. They did move more quickly through the ravine on the far side of the outhouse, for while mosquitoes were barely in evidence on the grassy knoll, their population was noticeably elevated in the deep woods of the ravine.

When Lila and Kristen cleared the ravine—their passage through the forest there eased by the narrow deer trail they followed—they stepped out to a remote overlook on par with any scenic one touted along the highway.

"I remember this!" Kristen said, stepping just a little further from the trees. She strained to her full height, staring out across the full openness of the land before her with a hunger that approached abandon.

"This is where you sold me on this land," Lila said, a lump in her throat as she connected with her own memory of that day. It was a powerful memory, but still not one that rivaled the experience Lila had with the potent recollections of other people, stored in their possessions.

Though Lila tried to keep her voice even, something bitter must have trickled from her mind into her tone. It drew Kristen's gaze away from the expansive vista and straight to Lila's eyes. Lila couldn't bear the sympathy at this moment, not even from Kristen.

"It's not fair, Kristen." This time, Lila kept her focus on the words, and this time, their even tenor was impeccable.

"No, it's not."

They stood for a moment, not speaking, until the inequity seemed to shift in Lila's mind from her own, private concerns to the lack of attention she and Kristen were paying to the natural wonder surrounding them.

As if following Lila's thought, Kristen sighed and tore her gaze from Lila, returning it to the elemental beauty before them.

"It's not fair at all. *I* should've bought this property."

The incongruity of Kristen's words ripped a raw laugh from Lila, and the laugh itself felt like tearing off a bandage to find unexpected healing underneath.

"But I couldn't have sold my house to finance it. Lou and I had just bought the thing, and there wasn't shit for equity in it then." Kristen turned back to face Lila, her eyes sparkling. Lila felt the residual effects of the laughter Kristen had wrought in the relaxed lines of her face and the broadening of her smile.

"Selling my house was a pain, but it was worth it." Lila shook one of the containers she was holding at Kristen. "You distracted me there."

"I did. And unfair as it all may be, it's a trick I learned from you. A good trick, too!"

"It is. I just shouldn't rely on you to make it work for me."

"Lila Dawkins? Rely on someone else? Hardly, though you really should try it sometime." Kristen pressed on and over Lila, who had opened her mouth to speak again. "No. No! You don't rely on me enough, and I came here to help you—to help you! I could've waited for your message. I know how you are. But in any case, I want to help. It's damn nice of you to let me do it sometimes."

"You're being ridiculous now." Lila didn't believe it, but she had to deflect Kristen somehow or she'd start crying again.

"Am I?"

"Yes, I'm sure of it."

"You know, I'm thinking maybe we're still standing here on account of you forgot how to get to the water pump."

Again, Lila had to let a laugh escape from the tight confines of her throat, or risk choking on it.

"Is that what you think?" Lila asked over her shoulder as she started walking again.

"It is."

"Well, then, I'll just have to show you that you're wrong."

"Maybe. But if you do and you're as obnoxious as Lou about it, then I'm going to bitch and whine all night."

"I could never be as obnoxious as Lou about anything!"

"Don't be so hard on yourself, Lila. I have confidence that you could be *more* obnoxious than Lou!"

"Gee, thanks," Lila said, her words overlapping with the sound of Kristen's giggles.

"Oh, I crack myself up!"

Because they were so close that they could have seen the steely red of the water pump if not for the poplar trees lining the gentle depression, Lila and Kristen reached the pump quickly. The pump stood, unnatural and irregular, atop an equally non-conformist cement surface, with the access hatch rising slightly on one side.

Lila's foot slid a little as she stepped from soil to concrete. She turned to warn Kristen, but it was too late—her friend had already made far more elegant transition.

"I really should hate you, you know."

Kristen grinned.

"For my stunning good looks? Or are you just jealous of my heighth again?"

"HEIGHT."

"Whatever. I know that's what you meant."

"Whatever." Lila mimicked Kristen's tone as best she could, and dug her keys out of her pocket.

"Why do you lock it?"

"When I'm here, I usually don't. But when I'm not here?" Lila shrugged. "Just being overprotective, I suppose." She pulled the chain from around the pump's handle. Released from its constrictive grip, it made a musical sound as its links bumped across the metal of the pump.

"Overprotective, huh? And yet you have no bleach."

"I have bleach."

"You do not! You? Miss Environmentally Pure?"

Lila shrugged, tucking the lock and chain into the red ESPRIT bag that Kristen held out to her.

"It has its uses."

As Lila began to pump, Kristen moved away from the spigot. Because the pump didn't have far to go—it was tapped into the tank from the spring—Lila was soon rewarded with a gushing blast.

"Do I get to at least hold a three-gallon?" Kristen asked, grinning.

"No! You are a guest, and you're pregnant, and I want to spoil you! Even if it's just a little bit and even if you fight me every step of the way."

"Then I wanna pump."

Lila rolled her eyes, but she was laughing, too.

"Fine."

With mock pomp and circumstance, the two women exchanged places. Kristen began to pump, and Lila held out a one-gallon container, rinsing it first, and then letting it fill.

"How are you doing, Kristen, really?"

"I'm good! No, I really am. I mean ... " Kristen did not pause in pumping, but Lila saw her swallow hard. "It's not like I don't worry, you know. I worry all the time. The longer it goes on, the more it would hurt to ... to lose ... " Kristen shrugged and her eyes dropped. It seemed to Lila that Kristen was letting these movements take the place of words that were altogether insufficient to the task anyway.

Lila swapped containers as Kristen kept the flow of water coming at a moderate, even flow. She needed to redirect this conversation, and fast. She searched for topics and lit upon the shirt Kristen was wearing.

"Why don't you tell me about your shirt?"

Kristen, her eyes still focused somewhere in the dirt, looked up to stare at Lila. She kept pumping but didn't speak, so Lila tried again.

"I take it this is your latest discovery?"

"Well, duh." Kristen dropped her hands from the handle of the pump and grabbed her shirt near her midsection. As she pulled out, the logo that was splashed across her shirt straightened, so that Lila could read it clearly instead of across its wrinkles.

"'Atheist Anarchy' ... nice! But isn't it a little hot for wearing black?" Lila said, and waved Kristen back to the pump.

"Not when you have great musical taste like mine!" Kristen resumed pumping, and to Lila's relief, almost giggled. "And you should see the looks I get when I wear it on Sunday."

"Don't tell me you wear it to church!"

"No. Even I wouldn't go that far! But it's a fun name, you have to admit."

Lila couldn't argue with that, not even in jest. She swapped containers again.

"Metal, I assume?"

"Progressive metal. They're not even that hard."

Now it was Lila's turn to giggle. Kristen's taste in music was legendary in its obscurity. The louder the guitar and drums, and the harsher the voice of the singer, the better Kristen liked it.

"So they're local?"

"More or less. They're out of Denver. While Lou was running the dogs in Fort Collins last time, I was down in Denver, buying tea and soaking up some culture." Kristen let go of the pump with one hand and pointed towards her shirt again.

"Didn't Pancho almost win that field trial?"

"Yes! Second place in the derby, and she was robbed, too. Some silly little golden who skirted the water took first. Explain that to me!"

"I wouldn't even try. How did Licorice do?"

"Oh, Lic. What a dumb dog she is—not that we love her any less—but seriously, she must've been dropped on her head as a puppy. She didn't even JAM. She wasn't really ready for the derby, but Lou wanted to 'get her some experience.'"

"Ah. That's it!" The final container was full, and Lila didn't even remember holding the third.

Kristen let go of the handle and moved towards the containers.

"Where's the lids for yours?" Lila asked, but Kristen was pulling them out of her pocket already, so Lila hurried over to the slouching ESPRIT bags where she'd tossed the larger lids that capped the three-gallon containers. When she turned back to Kristen, her friend was looking out in the direction of the plains.

"You hear that?" Kristen asked.

"Hear what?"

"That ... shh. Listen!"

Lila, from her position back behind the pump, tried to turn more towards the direction Kristen was indicating with the focused, slight lean of her body. Kristen turned her head, lifting her eyebrows. Lila shook her own head.

"I don't hear ... oh!" Just as she had been about to deny the noise that had captured Kristen's attention, Lila heard it, too: a motorized whine, like that of an ATV.

"Expecting more company?" Kristen inquired.

"Of course not." Lila almost snapped the words, so uncomfortable was the idea that someone would come to her property uninvited. Even A.B.—her closest friend in the area—wouldn't do that, and certainly not on an ATV! Not unless something was wrong ...

"Lila, don't worry. I know this is your equivalent of a 2 a.m. phone call, but couldn't it just be Spencer, checking his fence? Or the old guy you're so fond of?"

"A.B. rides Snapfish, his horse. And he told me Spencer uses horses, too."

"Snapfish! I knew it was something like that, but I was going to say Photobomb." The grimace Lila dragged out with effort apparently didn't cut it with Kristen, who responded by shifting back to serious gear. "Well, what do you want to do?"

"I suppose I'll have to go see who it is." Lila eyed the containers. "But let's cap these first." She put her words to action immediately, but couldn't shake the irritation edged with fear that now gripped her. "Crap!"

Kristen, following Lila's lead with the lids she held, snorted.

"Ooh. 'Crap!' I pity this fool, whoever he is, for riling you so badly."

Lila favored Kristen with arching brows and a look of as much innocence as she could muster.

"Shall we, then?"

"Only if I can also help chase this trespasser back to whatever squalid pit of hell he came from." Kristen said, her eyes glinting with anticipation.

"I'm counting on it."

5: Loss

Lila and Kristen didn't have far to walk before the scattered population of hawthorns, poplars, and assorted scrubby trees transitioned into sagebrush and grasses. The waves and ripples of the hill they were descending smoothed, too, and poured down into the plain.

Their eyes were drawn by the two converging fence-lines marking the border of Lila's property, and to the two-track road that approached the corner there.

"And there he is ... the intruder on his motorized steed!" Kristen leaned in, hissing her commentary to Lila, even though they were far too far away for the bare-headed man to hear.

"Very funny."

"Nice looking, at least from a distance," Kristen said, quirking her eyebrow when Lila gave her a stern look.

"An appraisal already? Come on! How can you possibly tell what he looks like from here?" Lila picked up her pace, wanting to get the unpleasantness of an encounter with a stranger over as quickly as possible.

"I can tell," Kristen opined, unfazed by Lila's disbelief.

The man by the gate was tall—Lila could see that much for certain. And he'd spotted them, too; he was waving.

Lila's return wave was grudging. Kristen, when Lila looked to her, was waving with blatant enthusiasm.

"Don't you start," she warned her friend. "This person— whoever he is—needs to get off my property and do it right now."

"Well, now, Lila, I don't think he's actually 'on' your property ... at least, not yet." Kristen's air quotes were as enthusiastic as any of her gestures.

"A technicality."

"But an important one!"

As they neared the stranger, Lila's skin prickled. The man had extracted a white envelope from one of the storage compartments on the ATV, and that bright, plain rectangle set off all kinds of internal alarms that had nothing whatsoever to do with Lila's sixth sense.

"What is it?" Kristen asked, picking up on Lila's rising distress. "Are you picking something up?"

"No. No, it's not that. It's ... he's got an envelope."

"What do you think it is? Jury duty?"

"Very funny. I don't know what it is, and I don't have a 'feel' for it. But I just ... I think whatever it is, it's not good."

The man near her gate was vaguely familiar to Lila, though she was certain she had not met him before. Kristen would be sure to boast about her eyesight later, too, for the man was most definitely easy on the eyes. The thoughts Lila spared for both unknown association and inevitable teasing were fleeting; she and Kristen were face-to-face with the man now. After meeting the stranger's direct, blue gaze for a moment, Lila let her eyes slide away, back to the envelope.

"Hello!" Kristen was breezy, almost indifferent, now that they were actually meeting their uninvited guest. Still, she held out her hand over the barbed-wire fence between them and the man transferred the envelope to his left hand to shake with her. "I'm Kristen Rush; I'm just visiting."

"Jake ... ." His handshake, Lila saw, was firm and quick, and he wore no jewelry—she should be able to manage this. She realized she'd managed to miss Jake's last name in her anxious consternation.

Lila held out her hand as Jake turned towards her, trying to smile just enough to quell her nerves.

60

"Lila Dawkins," she said, and then Jake took her hand in his.

It wasn't a shock of a stranger's memory that coursed through Lila in the lengthy brevity of Jake's handshake, but it was ... something. She couldn't attribute the sensation to her uncomfortable feelings about the letter in Jake's other hand, either. Pressed to speak in order to break the static in the air, Lila connected the dots in an instant and blurted the result.

"Jake ... A. B.'s nephew Jake!"

Jake smiled, and his eyes crinkled, revealing more wrinkles near their corners than Lila would have thought possible given the relative smoothness of his skin. In those laugh lines, Lila truly recognized his connection to his uncle ... but Jake's smile faded quickly, as if pulled from his face.

"Yes, I'm that Jake McCook." He paused, then ran his free hand through his hair, ruffling it even worse than the wind had. The singular gesture somehow brought Lila to the realization that as uncomfortable as she was, Jake was feeling worse.

"I'm sorry to intrude on you here, Lila, and sorrier still for what I have to tell you. But when I found your message on A. B.'s machine, I realized you didn't know."

Lila found the air diminishing around her.

Oh, no! No, not this. Not this!

Her eyes locked with Jake's, and this time, she noticed the specks of yellow in the blue, and rich sympathy overlaying it all. And Lila knew—knew with a certainty that surpassed her ability to see into the past by means of valued belongings ... the details, after all, aren't important when someone you love is unexpectedly gone.

Despite her conviction, Lila shook her head in a slight twitch of denial even as Jake began to speak.

"Uncle Angus—A. B.—passed away last week. Heart attack, they told me."

Kristen's arm came down fast on Lila's shoulders and she squeezed tight.

"I'm sorry to tell you like this," Jake said again, his voice sounding like it was traveling through a long tube to span the few feet between where they each stood, there on either side of the fence-line. "There isn't a good way to break this kind of news, but now that I'm here, in person seems just as bad as the call I got."

Lila's held-breath escaped with a catch, like it was caught on barbed wire.

"I ... I ... " Lila fought for words. She tried to focus through the flood of tears that obscured her vision to see his expression. Jake and A. B. had been deeply connected, she knew, though they hadn't always managed to tolerate each other in person.

"I'm sorry for your loss." The words seemed feeble, and Lila spoke them so low that the wind almost carried them away unheard.

Jake cleared his throat.

"Thank you. Uncle Angus was all I had left in the world. Or ... well. That doesn't matter now." Jake looked down at the letter he was still holding, and held it out to Lila. She saw now that it had her name on it, written in A. B.'s bold, blocky print. "I found this with his will, addressed to you."

The end of the envelope shook as a gust of wind played with it—the shake reminded Lila less of the living air playing with a toy than of a deadly rattler giving a warning.

Lila realized she'd forgotten her snakebite kit at the cabin. She reached for the envelope, blinking furiously. She wished she could move faster so Jake could be on his way and she could break down and cry as hard as she knew she was going to. She wished she hadn't forgotten the snakebite kit. Kristen had distracted her, she supposed.

Somehow, Lila managed to take the envelope from Jake, who again, murmured his apologies for disturbing her at her retreat and then said how nice it had been to meet Kristen and Lila. He took Kristen's hand again, shaking it firmly, and then stepping forward, reached for Lila's.

Lila tucked the letter into her back jeans pocket and met Jake's hand for another shake.

"I'm really sorry. Uncle Angus told me a lot about you," Jake said, releasing Lila's hand as her built-up tears began pouring down her face.

"H-H-He was a good man," she managed, choking on the words.

"I can't believe he didn't say anything about me," Kristen said. Her tone was acerbic, but Lila would bet she was also close to tears. She wondered if Jake could tell.

"I'm afraid not." Though his voice was somber, Lila was certain that Jake appreciated the anguish she was feeling—and that Kristen was also feeling—as sincere. She was glad, though she wondered if it seemed strange to Jake. But Jake was saying something else, and Lila struggled through the veil of loss to understand his words.

"I'll be at the house for another week, maybe longer, but at least a week. So when you're ready to pick up ... or ... well. Feel free to stop by sometime after you've read the letter."

Lila wiped at her streaming eyes, even though it seemed pointless. She supposed A. B. had left her some knickknack or other—wasn't that what people did when they died?—but Lila didn't want whatever it was. She wanted Jake to go now, so she could abandon the futile effort of holding the pieces of herself together.

"Okay," she said, just to have something to say back to Jake's almost-revelation. To Lila, her voice seemed firm enough, even if it was quiet. The tears were still flowing, but the congestion of sobs in her chest hadn't escaped yet. So Lila fought to hold on just a little longer, and finally, Jake turned to his ATV. In a few moments, he was driving away.

"Lila, I'm so sorry! I ... " But the rest of whatever Kristen had intended to say was lost to the force of Lila's release. She sank out from under Kristen's arm and settled on her knees amongst the dirt, sage, and stalks of petal-less blue flax. Behind her, Kristen lowered herself, too, and wrapped both arms around Lila, her face at the back of Lila's neck as Lila bent forward under the weight of surviving where A. B. had not.

And Lila poured out her misery. There were no spotty rain clouds here in her personal storm, no ... there were only torrents of lamentation, and wretched, gasping cries like choppy, sporadic thunder.

As vehement and eternal as it may feel at the time, no storm lasts forever; Lila's outburst, too, eventually began to recede. Lila became aware of Kristen's low murmurs and of her hands, alternately clenching and rubbing Lila's shoulders. And of the residual buzz of Kristen's necklace, which Kristen was surely keeping away from Lila's back and neck at great cost to the alignment of her own neck.

"I'm okay," Lila bit out. "I need ... I need to get back to the pump." She struggled free of Kristen's embrace and stood, brushing dirt from her jeans. Kristen sat back from her crouch, shading her eyes with her hand as she looked up at Lila. Lila registered the angle of the sun without enthusiasm.

It must be past noon.

"Let me go pick up the water," Kristen said. "I left a trail of bread crumbs," she went on, when Lila began to protest. "Come on! I know my way around."

"I know. I do, but ... I need to ... some hard work would be g-g-good for me now."

"Really?" Kristen's expression conveyed even more disbelief than her tone, which was flattened by the weight of her skepticism.

"Really. And ... don't you have to use the outhouse again yet?"

Kristen rolled her eyes.

"Now that you mention it, yes, actually. I do." She stood,

shaking her head. "Okay, I'll walk back up to the pump with you and then take myself off to your spider-infested pit-toilet, but I will NOT like it."

"You could maybe make some more tea while I carry the water?"

"Maybe I could, at that. I knew you'd like that stuff."

"Right you are."

"Of course, Yoda." But Kristen grabbed Lila's arm before she could start back up the hill to the pump. "Lila. It's okay. You're okay ... something like this, it sets anyone off."

"I know, I know." Lila hardened her voice before it cracked, and then had to cough lest all the tension in her throat reduce her speech to inaudibility. She started off up the hill so quickly the Kristen had to scramble to follow her. "It's just ... A. B. is—was—oh! He was just so strong! He seemed like ... like he'd be here as long as ... all of this." She waved her arm at the hill in front of them, and slowed her pace before trying to talk over it robbed her of breath.

"He was unique," Kristen said. "Oh, I know it's a small word and doesn't capture how big—how fucking huge—his personality was."

"It certainly doesn't," Lila said, continuing to push uphill, trying to force welling emotion back with bodily movement.

"Lila, don't ... just don't try to NOT feel it, Lila. Promise me?"

The tears that Kristen's words conjured out of Lila this time were all on Kristen's account.

"I promise." It wasn't so hard to say the words, but Lila was well aware how hard it would be to keep that vow. Still, she wanted to reassure Kristen.

And Kristen was right. As much as Lila wanted not to feel this additional, grievous pain, it would only prolong the experience should she try to fight it. Lila's instinct was to fight—to cover and mask the pain—using one of the many, procrastinating methods that she'd discovered over the years. A. B.'s loss, smacked right over the top of the already crushing weight of sensitivity that had come with exposure to other people and the static they carried in their memory-charged personal belongings, set a new standard of fragility in Lila's overwrought mind now.

She felt like the thinnest veil of ice that forms on puddles at first frost. She felt like she could crack apart at any moment, tinkling shards released to drown in the stagnant water underneath. She felt like she was dissolving, fading, decomposing.

Yes, I want to NOT feel this.

But not feeling wasn't an option, especially in this case. A. B. was a part of the landscape of Wyoming to Lila; she visited him every time she came to the property—sometimes several times. For all the difference of years and circumstances between them, they were never at a loss for conversation, and it was good conversation, too.

It *had been* good conversation.

No, not feeling wasn't an option. But having a capacity for emotion hardly seemed a blessing under these circumstances.

Kristen walked with Lila the rest of the way to the pump in silence, but Lila felt her support nevertheless. At the pump, Kristen tapped Lila's cheek gently, scooped up the two one-gallon jugs despite Lila's protest, and turned to walk back to the cabin.

"Damn you for the comment about the outhouse, Lila!" The snippy comment was delivered with a water-sloshing wave and a grin, and Lila tried her best to smile back.

Beside the pump, with the ESPRIT bags slumping as if they, too, were exhausted, Lila's eyes wandered—unwilling but unerring—into the distance, down the hill towards the road below. How very wrong it seemed that everything looked the same as it had before she'd learned of A. B.'s death!

Everything feels different. Everything IS different! How can it look the same, smell the same? How can this be the same world it was when A. B. was in it?

These thoughts—"normal" though they might be—were getting Lila nowhere. Kristen would be making tea, and Lila's stomach rumbled, signaling the banality of hunger. It was lunchtime, and there was still water to be hauled.

And there was a letter to be read. The thought sent Lila's heart racing; what if the letter had fallen out of her pocket? But as quickly as the idea had sparked panic, Lila reached back and found the letter, still tucked into her jeans. She pulled it out, held it in her hand, and stared at it, as if by doing so she could divine something about it. But the envelope was only paper, and as such, could barely carry any hint of what was written inside.

Besides, A. B. surely couldn't have valued this letter. Lila felt her eyes filling, and blinked them hard and fast, refusing to cry again in spite of it all. A. B. wouldn't have valued this letter, but despite the message it carried, Lila surely would.

This is the last time I'll ever hear from A. B. Ever!

Lila traced her name, scrawled there across the envelope in letters that must be an inch tall. Her first name only, for A. B. had told her that she was the only "Lila" he had ever known.

"Not a Western name, then, is it?" Lila had asked, knowing by that time that A. B. rarely traveled outside county lines.

"Guess not. But you're a Western gal now, Lila, no matter if you live here a few days a year or every day. No one could doubt it. Once Wyoming is in you, it stays there for as long as you breathe."

For as long as you breathe.

No, this wasn't helping at all. But if there was one lesson Lila had learned over the years, it was that when thoughts overwhelmed, action calmed.

Lila turned her attention to the patiently waiting water, setting one bright green container into each of the maligned, color-clashing ESPRIT bags. There was a smudge on the side of one of the containers, so before shouldering the bags, Lila wet one hand under the pump and rubbed at the smudge until it smeared, and then disappeared. Unbidden, an apropos notion came to mind ... Lila had read somewhere that while life was uncertain, there was an absolute quality to the cleaning process: a stain, when sufficiently scrubbed, could always be eliminated.

"Well."

Kristen was surely on her second cup of tea now, if not her third. Resolute, Lila shouldered each bag in turn, settling the water near her hips. It sloshed slightly, becoming rhythmic as Lila established a slow, easy tread.

The beauty of her surroundings did not penetrate the barrier of disassociation that now separated Lila from the world around her. She walked back to the cabin barely glancing up, staring a fixed distance of 10 feet or so in front of her. It was only as she began to climb the rise out of the ravine that Lila's line of sight raised—an natural result of the landscape's incline rather than by Lila's design. A movement there on the edge of the ravine stopped Lila in her tracks.

It was another deer, this one a white-tail. The deer's ears twitched, and it turned its head slightly, searching for the movement and sounds that Lila's progress had been making. Unlike the deer she'd encountered the previous day, they stood today in mutual mesmerization, Lila and the deer, until the deer finally turned and flashed its namesake tail, dashing out of sight long before the sounds of its passage ceased.

"Well!" Lila said again, and this time, she had some feeling behind the word.

Rounding the corner of the cabin, Lila saw that Kristen had moved the chairs from underneath the big pine to below the porch roof, just outside the cabin door. The outer door was propped open, letting what mid-day breeze there was into the cabin through the screen door, and Kristen was sitting in one of the chairs, knitting.

"You should learn to knit," Kristen said, not looking up from her task.

"So you've said. Repeatedly!" Lila lowered her ESPRIT-branded burdens, setting them next to the bench.

"Don't you want those out of the sun? I can get the door in a few more stitches."

"Okay."

As Lila waited for Kristen to complete her alleged "few" more stitches, she took the time to rotate her arms from the shoulders. Though not particularly stiff from hauling water, Lila did tend to soreness in her shoulders and neck due to all the hours she spent working on her computer.

"You're scaring him," Kristen said.

"What?" Lila's attention was immediately arrested, if not her arms.

"The kitty. You're scaring him!" And, her row finally completed, Kristen pointed with the knitting needle in her right hand.

Lila turned to follow the direction of the needle. Kristen was only just pointing, without extending her arm at all, so Lila surmised that the cat was closer than it had been before. And it was, just on the other side of Lila's fence, back toward the humans as if it had been about to flee, but head turned to observe. Seeing that it was now being subjected to scrutiny as well, the cat's tail twitched.

"I think he's actually been socialized."

"How can you tell?" Lila kept her voice low, following Kristen's example.

"Well, he's here, isn't he?"

They both watched the cat watch them for a few moments, and then Lila turned her head back to Kristen, who had resumed knitting.

"What would I do with a cat, Kristen?"

"Don't be a dope, Lila. You could use a cat—or a dog, but hey, the cat's practically volunteering—same as you could use knitting. It all helps ground you in the moment, and I know you're all about that!

Besides," Kristen added, "what is he going to do without you?"

"Oh, so now it's my responsibility?" Lila found herself resentful, but the churlish edge to her tone surprised her.

"Of course not. You can just let him wander out here until a cougar or raptor picks him off."

"What?"

"Shh! You know nature. And that's not a very big cat."

"But what would I ... what would I do for a litter box? Don't boy cats spray? And what about shots? What would I feed him?"

"You've got that classy spare tray you showed me earlier, and if you don't have sandy soil somewhere on your property, I would be shocked. Shots and neutering—which generally stops the spraying, if he does any—can certainly wait until you're ready to go to town, and whatever you feed him would have to be better than whatever he's been managing on since he was abandoned."

Kristen looked up, grinning sideways at Lila.

"Don't you think it would be nice to curl up with a cat at night? You loved on Nero every night when you visited us."

"I ... well, maybe, but ... "

"Anyway, don't worry about it now." Kristen's tone turned brisk. "He's gone again."

Startled, Lila jerked her head back in the direction of the cat, but it was true; where the cat had tentatively stood before, only grasses and the occasional wildflower remained now. And Lila was assaulted by unexpected concern for the little three-colored cat. She channeled it into disgruntlement with Kristen.

"You planned that," Lila accused.

"What, I lured the cat here?"

"You purposefully got me upset about him leaving."

"I did what?"

"Kristen, I swear ... "

"You can't muster a decent curse in the most dire of situations, Lila. I, on the other hand, am the master of the fucking curse."

Lila laughed, and it felt good.

"Okay, you win, and I tell you what—if the cat comes back again before you leave tomorrow, I'll take it as a sign and try to make friends ... maybe even consider letting it into the cabin."

"Fair enough." Kristen folded her knitting and tucked it into her backpack. "I haven't heard your stomach swear, either, but mine is cussing up a storm. Have you got a plan for lunch or," and she pulled a familiar box out and shook it at Lila, "should I make this glorious mac-n-cheese that I packed in to surprise you?"

"I'll make it," Lila said. She reached for the box, but Kristen snatched it away. "You're a guest!"

"Oh, HELL no! You only get to use that once, and you blew it on six gallons of water. You want the comfort food? Then let me make it for you!"

Lila threw her hands up, giving in to the elemental force that was Kristen.

"Will you still hold the door for me while I get this water in?"

"I suppose," Kristen said, managing to make it sound like an immense favor rather than something she'd offered to do. She threw in a long-suffering sigh for good measure, but it didn't take much to see that she was continuing to do what she could to distract Lila from her loss.

Lila cleared her throat, willing herself not to sabotage that effort, and pulled the two containers from their respective bags, meeting Kristen and her boxed treat at the door.

"About time," Kristen drawled.

"Yeah, yeah." Lila settled the larger containers in where the smaller ones had been and cocked her head, appraising the size of the tray. "Isn't this ... "

" ... a little big for a litter box?" Kristen completed the thought, even as she reached for the cooking kettle, standing at the ready on a second slate trivet. "Yeah, maybe. Again, if you need to, you can get something more suitable when you go into town. And clean this one with ... "

Lila saw where this was headed, too.

"Bleach does have its uses," she agreed. "Okay, enough about the cat for now."

"I need some water here," Kristen demanded, holding the empty kettle out to Lila. "But what about a name for your little friend?"

"Oh, yes, I should've filled a couple of the smaller containers before bringing these monstrosities inside, but, yes." As she spoke, Lila was adjusting the cap on one of the containers, attaching the spout that stored inside for transport. She hefted the container onto the counter and waved Kristen in to hold the kettle underneath as she tipped the container to pour.

"What about a name?" Kristen asked again. "That's enough water."

"Kristen, I haven't managed to name this place in ... lots and lots of years. What makes you think I could possibly name a cat in one day?"

"You name characters all the damn time, that's what!"

"That's different."

"The hell it is," Kristen said, lighting the burner underneath the kettle. "Here we go."

Lila slid the heavy container of water back from the counter's edge with a half-hearted shove, and frowned at Kristen.

"It is different," she insisted. "People—characters—have regular names, like John and Jane. But cats and dogs, they have creative names ... how could I possibly come up with something to compare to Nero or Licorice?"

"You can name that cat John if you like, you know. No rules about that! You can even name him Jane, but the other cats will make fun of him. Like in that horrible country song that Lou's so fond of, 'A Boy Named Sue.'"

"How do you know that's a male cat, anyway?"

"Are you kidding me?"

"No, I didn't ... "

"They're called balls, Lila. Didn't you notice?"

"Actually, I didn't." Lila would have made an excuse for her eyesight, but Kristen's lips were twitching, and so Lila found herself laughing instead.

Kristen laughed, too, before turning back to the kettle, already simmering on the stove.

"You really need to pay attention to the details. And get me a spoon already!"

6: Houseguest

Thunderstorms were forecast again for the following morning, but it was early morning indeed when a crack of thunder shocked Lila awake. She felt the residual tremor from the lightning strike pass underground and over her body—an uneasy wave in an uncalm sea. The rain drummed down in a frenzied, staccato pulse against the roof above Lila, and she wondered if Kristen regretted staying the night; it could be a long, mucky walk out for her when daylight finally arrived.

"Lila," Kristen said then, her voice coming not from the bunk below Lila, but instead from near the screen door.

Lila rolled on her side, craning her neck around the edge of the wall, though she didn't expect to see anything in the darkness. But Kristen had picked up one of Lila's battery-powered candles, and it shed an eerie, red light over her where she stood next to the door.

Before Lila could ask the obvious question, a more distant thunder strike was answered from the porch with a terrible, terrified yowl that rose and fell and plucked at the hair on the backs of Lila's arms with its sheer, obvious distress.

"What the ... oh! The cat?"

Of course, the cat.

"Yes, it's your fuzzy friend, and he's scared out of his crazy little mind. I think he's under one of the lawn chairs. Can I let him in?"

"If you think he'll come ... " Lila began, and no sooner were the words out of her mouth than Kristen was opening the door. The door's squeak was lost to yet another wallop of thunder and

Kristen yelped as the cat apparently streaked over her feet on its way to shelter from the storm.

Lila sat up, realizing that she hadn't exactly seen the cat in the dim light cast by the candle Kristen held. The darkness inside the cabin was thick and unresolved, but the cat's rapid passage shifted it in a hazy sort of way. If Lila had followed the path of distortion accurately, the cat was now somewhere deep underneath the bottom bunk, nestled between the storage boxes there, or perhaps putting them purposefully between itself and everything else in the world.

Another yowl—albeit not as loud or drawn-out as the one before—from somewhere far below confirmed Lila's sense.

"Shut the big door, please," Lila said, climbing down to join Kristen. "And quit laughing."

"I shouldn't. I really shouldn't, the poor cat! But ... Lila, it's ... " Kristen's laughter crescendoed, rising far above the continuous drone of the rain. "It's your sign!"

"What?"

"You said, if the cat ... before I leave ... " Kristen dissolved again, and then made a feeble attempt to muffle her giggles with her free hand.

"Give me the candle," Lila said, reaching for it. "I've got a vanilla one around here somewhere that'll shed better light."

"Just take my flashlight," Kristen said, scrounging it out of her day-pack, which was dangling from a hook on the wall. "Wait. You're not going shining for cats, now, are you?"

Her tone gave Lila pause.

"I suppose not. Not while the storm is going, anyway. I will check the time, though."

"It's about 3:30," Kristen said then, handing over the candle instead of the flashlight. "I checked when I first woke up."

"Can you get back to sleep?" Lila ruffled her hair, knowing her own answer to the question.

"I doubt it."

Thunder boomed again, and was met with another desolate feline cry.

"I sincerely doubt it," Kristen amended.

"Cocoa, then?"

"Cocoa!"

Lila took the enthused exclamation for agreement and stepped sideways around Kristen to precede her into the main room of the cabin. The pomegranate candle cast a strange, dim light around the kitchen area, and lightning added flashes through the windows above the counter and to the west.

"Take the desk chair, Kristen," Lila offered, setting the pomegranate candle near the sink. "There's a candle or two over there, too."

Kristen turned on her flashlight to look, while Lila added the green light of a pine-scented candle to the mix.

"Oh, I see! These are great. Where'd you get them?"

"Menard's, actually."

"I remember Menard's!" Kristen said. "Oh, I'd love some of these for Christmas, hint-hint! What other scents do they have?"

"Honestly, I don't remember, but there's a lot of them." Lila finished filling the tea kettle and carefully lit a burner on the stove. "I should check my propane levels. I'll probably need a new tank soon."

"You check before I leave and I'll get Lou to bring a new tank when he comes up for turkey season."

"Fall turkey? With an elk tag to work on?"

"Oh, you know Lou. He lives for this shit. And actually, it's not ... "

"It's not what?" Lila asked, turning to see what had stopped Kristen in her verbal tracks.

There's not much that can do that.

The steady downbeat of rain seemed even louder to Lila as she waited for Kristen to respond. Kristen dropped her eyes from Lila's and fidgeted with her wedding ring.

"Well, what I thought was that it's not—don't take this the wrong way—the way Lou has to go hunting isn't really all that different from the way ... from the way you have to come here."

Now it was Lila's turn to pause, wordless and stunned.

"Different causes entirely, I'm not saying it's not different, but it's still a pull—a drive—that he really just has to answer, you know, and ... Lila, don't look at me like that!"

The tea kettle began to raise its voice, and Lila hurried to attend to it.

"Lila?"

"Oh, Kristen, I'm not offended. Don't think that. I just ... I don't think of myself being ... this sounds stupid. But I don't think of myself being like anyone else. It's ... nice, to be similar to someone else." Lila's hands ceased adding cocoa to the cups in front of her and fell to her sides.

"That's not stupid, stupid. That's human. Here, let me." Kristen bustled over to stand next to Lila and waved at the cocoa. "You sit."

"No, you're a guest."

"A bitchy guest, too! Sit!" Kristen's voice was firm to the point of undebatable. Lila smiled as best she could and retreated to the desk while Kristen mixed the cocoa.

"No chunks in mine, Kristen."

"Heathen. Chunks are the best part!"

"Gross."

Kristen handed Lila her cup and took a seat on the stool along the far edge of the kitchen counter.

"As special as you are, you're also not that unique, Lila."

"That makes no sense whatsoever."

"Yes, it does!" Kristen raised her hand when Lila would have objected again. "No, listen. You've got a certain super-sensitivity, yeah, but think of Lou and hunting again. People are driven by all kinds of things they can't necessarily explain. Yours just happens to be the way you can pick up memories and emotions from things." And Kristen pulled her necklace out of her t-shirt. The pendant caught the light of the various candles around the room and concentrated it into a few bright flashes before Kristen tucked it back into her shirt.

Lila took a careful sip of her cocoa and thought about it. After due consideration, she spoke.

"The rain seems to be lightening up."

Kristen, who had been watching Lila intently, rolled her eyes in disgust.

"Jesus Christ, Lila! I'm serious here!"

"So am I, Kristen. And you're right. You are! But it still doesn't help me ... how am I supposed to function? I get overloaded faster and faster." Lila set her cup down slowly, though she wanted to slam it hard against the counter. "Do I have to live out here all the time?"

"Would that be so bad?"

"Are you kidding?"

"It's not like you have to sell a house again, Lila. And I know you told me the cell phone service out here has improved a lot in the past couple of years."

"Yes, I really don't have to stand outside to send and receive texts anymore, though sometimes I still do ... but it's still hard to sustain calls and I'd probably have to go into town to send my manuscripts to RayAnn. Besides, winter's no picnic here, and I don't have wood, and I do like the solitude, but ... even at 40, aren't I a little young to be a hermit?"

"I'm not saying it'd be easy, Lila, but I do think it'd be better than this ... this constant rollercoaster you're riding now!"

"That's pretty clichéd, Kristen."

"Well, it's a damn good thing I'm not the writer here, then, isn't it?"

Lila laughed, and raised her mug again.

"I'll drink to that."

"You've got to get rid of these meatball mugs," Kristen said, holding hers next to the nearest candle. "Trane? What's that?"

"It's an air-conditioning company or something, I think. Don't knock the mugs. I found them in my apartment when I moved in."

"Free is good, Lila, I get it. But I guarantee you can find something prettier than this!"

"Not for free!"

"Close enough to free to make no damn difference!"

Again, the familiar banter was restorative ... almost as much so as the cocoa.

"Will you be able to go back to sleep now?" Lila asked Kristen, after they had both drained the last of their cocoa.

"Me? I'm going to have to pee again in very short order. I think it's less about the baby pushing on my bladder or whatever and more about getting me trained for my future of sleepless nights." Kristen's lips quirked as she patted her belly, but Lila could see that all joking aside, Kristen was still a long way from believing she would safely deliver this child.

"It's going to be fine, Kristen."

"Of course it is!" Kristen cleared her throat, and then lowered her voice. "Maybe you'd better spare some attention for your other guest now, though."

Other guest?

Lila's eyes left Kristen's and drifted towards the entryway. The single cat's eye peeking out from around the corner of the wall that divided living area from sleeping area was reflecting far more light than Kristen's necklace had.

"He's definitely been around people before, Lila. I'd even guess he's lived inside. I wish you could use your powers to tell me

79

his story!"

"It doesn't work like that."

"I know. And I probably don't want to know who abandoned this sweet little guy, anyway. I'd want to smack them around for doing it!"

"What am I supposed to do, Kristen?"

"Got any tuna?"

"Not at my desk, but there's some in the tin down under the stove."

The cat stuck its head further out around the corner, revealing a second brilliant eye.

"I can't get that out without scaring him back under the bed," Kristen said, pursing her lips. "Well, I can probably hold it a little longer. Let's see what he does."

"How long will it take him to actually do something, then?"

"Your guess is as good as mine!"

"I hope he comes straight over to you," Lila said. "Nero and Hercules could use a new brother. And that would solve everything!"

Kristen shook her head, and the sharp motion arrested the cat's paw, stopping its ever-so-slight forward motion.

"Like hell," Kristen said, after the cat had resumed his delicate movements. "Two cats and two dogs is quite enough! And Lou wants to get Lic pregnant!"

Lila's tight-held laugh escaped as a cough, which seemed to concern the cat, though the sound didn't give the cat pause the same way Kristen's head-shaking had done.

"Rephrase, please."

"Oh please. You know what I mean. The man's hell-bent on breeding the bitch again, even with me knocked up already!"

"That'll be fun! Diapers and ... what was it last time? A plastic kid's wading pool taking up most of your living room for Licorice and her pups?"

"Don't remind me! Besides, this cat is for you. How could it not be, after raiding your truck and following you home?"

"It followed both of us, Kristen."

"It's all you. You'll see, Lila. Mark my words—you'll see."

Lila heaved a sigh. She was beginning to believe Kristen already, in fact. The cat had only glanced at Kristen when she had moved; the rest of the time he'd been creeping steadily towards them, his eyes had been trained on Lila.

What the heck am I going to do with a cat?

"Famous writers always have cats, anyway. Don't they? Hemmingway did, right?"

"You're going to make your case based on one famous writer?" Lila asked, arching her brows and sparing Kristen a glance. The cat was now sniffing around Lila's socks.

"I only need one, if it's a good one. Hemmingway is like a trump card, see?"

The cat tipped back on its haunches and stretched upwards, sniffing. One paw stretched out and placed the lightest of pressures against Lila's shinbone as the cat leaned into his investigation.

"I think he likes yooooooou!" Kristen drawled.

"How could he be so skittish before and be just fine with touching me now?"

"I expect the storm pushed him into action. Even if he is nervous about human contact, it's way better than getting stuck out in a storm like," Kristen paused, listening. "Like the one that just passed. Besides, he's a cat. Cats do weird shit. Scientific fact!"

Both of the cat's front feet where now resting against Lila's legs. The cat paused in its olfactory investigation, and looked up at Lila. Without prompting from Kristen, Lila slowly stretched out one hand towards the cat. The cat met her offer with a few more tentative sniffs, and then leaned forward, rubbing the side of its face against Lila's hand.

"That's it! He's marked you as his own! Oh, Lou's gonna shit when I tell him this!" Kristen could barely restrain her glee, and the cat spared her a fleeting glance before retreating to Lila's side, putting Lila between him and Kristen.

"Come on, Kristen. I've seen your cats. They'll 'mark' anything, up to and including their food bowls."

"You want me to come back next weekend? No, not next weekend—I told Lou I'd go to another damn trial with him—the weekend after, then ... I could bring all kinds of stuff ... carrier, litter box, some kibble—oh! I can get him a collar and tag if you can possibly come up with a name!" Kristen snorted, making it clear that she retained a zero-confidence level regarding Lila's ability to provide the cat with a suitable name.

"Okay, I can't wait any more—I gotta pee! Where's my flashlight?"

After pointing Kristen in the correct direction, Lila glanced down again at the cat, who continued to observe the proceedings from the shadows at her side.

"What have you gotten me into, cat? And what have you gotten yourself into?"

They stared at each other. The cat did not blink, but it did concede the battle and scurried under the desk when Kristen banged her way out of the cabin, the screen door slapping shut behind her.

Despite the small size of the cabin, there were plenty of good hiding places for a small cat, Lila thought. She stood, moving slowly out of consideration for her unexpected feline guest, and carried the cocoa mugs to the sink. Lila poured another batch of water into the tea kettle and fired up the stove again.

He'll want to hide from this, too. How many times a day do I use this tea kettle?

Well, cocoa cups couldn't wait; the sugar would attract ants. But the end cap on the tea kettle's spout—the one that produced its whistle/shriek—that didn't have to stay on. Lila stuck her index finger through the ring at the tip of the metal cap and twisted it off, setting it on the shelf behind the stove.

That should help.

Turning, Lila saw the cat had advanced just far enough out of his under-desk shelter to watch her again. It seemed to Lila that he was shedding his multi-layered coat of fear more easily as time went on. And despite the many complications posed by the addition of a cat to her conflicted life and erratic schedule, Lila hated to think of what dangers the cat would face out in the wilds, all alone.

It's not good to be all alone.

As much as Lila needed her solitude, she didn't want it—not as much of it as she was getting these days, anyway. The more she thought about it, the more a cat seemed like the perfect companion … generally quiet, reasonably unobtrusive, and fuzzy.

Fuzzy is always good.

"Though I don't actually know that you're soft, do I?"

The cat did not respond to Lila's question, but he did take a moment to scrub his upper chest—as far up as he could reach—with a tongue that would have made Gene Simmons proud. Lila giggled at the comparison, which brought the cat's eyes back to her. They were orange, she realized, a deeper shade than the spots of orangey fur the cat had, and oddly lovely.

They were regarding each other steadily—perhaps they were each debating the pros and cons of adopting one another—and then the cat's eyes jerked off Lila, alighting on something behind her. A moment later, Lila heard the sounds of Kristen's return.

"Try to not let the door slam this time!"

"Ooh, fancy!" Kristen said, entering the cabin much more carefully than she'd left it. "I would've said, 'Try not to let the fucking door slam.'"

"I really never can decide which is right," Lila confessed, stepping away from the stove to peek at the cat, who was still crouching under the desk. "Expletive deleted, of course."

"Of course. Wouldn't you know which is right?"

"You know I wouldn't. I'm a writer, Kristen, not a grammarian."

"You're a geek."

"Agreed. But geekiness does not imply any special insights into sentence structure."

"I see your point. But that's about all I see ... it's just barely starting to get light out there." Kristen yawned without trying to minimize it, and the yawn seemed to consume her entire face.

"Maybe you can get a little more sleep after all?" Lila asked, reaching to turn off the burner. The tea kettle was barely starting to steam, but that was good enough for dishes.

"Maybe I can, at that." Kristen yawned again. "Yes! I think I will try."

"Me and the Mister will be as quiet as mouses."

"Oh, come on! That's pure butchery, there. And bullshit."

"Unless you've fully converted to Mom-mode, I expect you can still sleep like a rock, the same way you did when we were kids."

"I tell you, Lila, my powers of unconsciousness are not what they used to be. But! I can still sleep through the sounds of Lou snoring, so I figure I can sleep through whatever you and kitty-under-the-desk there can come up with. As long as there's no more storms, that is."

"Go on, then! Prove it!"

"Yeah, yeah." Kristen waved, heading into the bedroom and closing the light door behind her.

"Good thing we had the doors open before, kitty," Lila said. She poured just a little water into her wash basin and added a few drops of soap. "We might not have heard you crying in the rain."

"Oh!" Lila turned back to the cat, who was still watching her from his position under the desk. "Did you know there's a song by that name? By ... hmm ... Whitesnake! Sorry. You probably don't like snakes, do you? Rhetorical question."

Lila made short work of the dishes, and when she had completed her clean-up, she found that the cat had settled down onto his haunches. He still looked ready to run if so much as a butterfly provoked his sensibilities, but Lila realized even as she thought it that she understood that feeling all too well.

"It'll get better, kitty. Oh good grief, Kristen's right, you are going to need a name! I canNOT call you 'kitty' all the time. Woefully unimaginative."

The cat blinked, and then dropped his gaze.

"It won't be so bad, I swear. Well, probably. Listen! I just thought ... I do have some deli ham in the fridge! We'll have to start you off easy, though. Just one piece." Putting her words to action, Lila moved towards the refrigerator, crouching with the vanilla candle to make it easier to see inside. "No lights in these tiny fridges, cat."

Ham in hand, Lila returned to the counter and reached above it for the clear plastic tub that contained bowls.

"You probably want some water, too. I've got an old camp kit with a smaller, flatter bowl that'd suit you better, but this will work for now."

Lila poured water into a bowl and tore one slice of ham into bits.

"I should've just used a knife. Ugh." She washed her fingers in the still-warm remains of the dishwater. "It'll be light soon. I'll do a better job cleaning up then."

This time, when Lila turned back to the cat, he had advanced from his shelter. Lila searched the floor, scanning for a cat shape, and found him practically under her feet. He stretched up from his back feet, placing one front paw on Lila's leg as he had before, and Lila saw his nose twitching.

"Yes, this is for you!"

She lowered the food and stepped back. leaning against the counter, as the cat approached with rapidity born of raw, demanding hunger. He made such short work of the ham that Lila wished she'd metered it out more slowly.

"Did you even taste that?"

The cat was making the softest of smacking noises as his long, rough tongue shot out again and again, wrapping this way and that around his mouth, gathering every available minute particle of ham possible.

"I suppose I could name you Gene."

The cat began to wash behind his ears.

"No? Well, that's all I've got for now, cat. You'll have to try harder to inspire me ... do something that involves neither shrieking at the top of your lungs or ... that tongue of yours!"

As the cat still made no reply, Lila went on.

"I can see you're not ready for a drink just yet. Let me move that somewhere out of the way ... " Lila surveyed the confines of her cabin, in which there wasn't much in terms of out-of-the-way places. "Over here by the wall for now, I guess."

The cat recoiled—though not far—when Lila picked up the bowl. She could feel the weight of his watchful gaze as she stepped away from him, and finally placed the bowl on the floor next to the stacked trays Kristen had coveted. As the bowl touched the ground, the cat sprinted towards Lila, slowing the last few steps and sniffing.

"What? You think I magically conjured more ham out of thin air? I wish. That'd spare me a few trips to town."

Lila wanted to pet the cat; she could have, he was within reach now. But it didn't seem fair to lure the cat in with ham—real or imagined—and then sneak-touch him. He was continuing to sniff around the bowl, researching every scent for some relationship to ham.

Lila became aware of pressing needs of her own and decided

to make a quick trip to the outhouse. She slipped outside, leaving the cat to his survey, though when she looked back through the screen door, the cat was watching again. Lila gave him a little wave and made her way to the outhouse. She'd waited long enough that it was not necessary to bring a flashlight.

While preoccupied on her trip to the outhouse with thoughts of where she might find some sandy soil for the cat's bathroom needs, on the return trip, Lila's mind had begun to wander again. In the absence of focused thought and under the soft sounds of her passage through the grasses, Lila had the abrupt impression of something ... something ...

As she came to a sudden stop in the grasses, the stillness of the morning washed over Lila in unceasing waves, moving past her to the horizon. In the wake of the calm and the cessation of her forward movement, she understood what it was.

The feeling was not strong, but it was there. Lila turned her head from side to side, but couldn't find a convergence—there was no direction she could discern from which the tingle came. It was not strong enough to overwhelm nor direct enough to resolve, but it was distinctly around her.

Here? What could possibly be HERE that someone loaded down with their memories?

Lila could feel hysteria tickling along the edge of her awareness of the as-yet undefinable object, and she choked it down with reason.

Somebody could have lost something along a road. Or stopped to rest in their car! It could even be Spencer or some ranch hand, getting up and heading out to move some cattle.

It was hard to shake the tickle once it started, but Lila had enough to concern her now. Kristen, the cat, the letter ...

The letter.

Lila began moving towards the cabin again, her memory of A. B.'s last letter to her—still unopened—crushing both her perceptions and her panic like a rock coming down on a bug. She'd resolved to wait until Kristen left to read the letter, but her self-imposed timeline was no comfort. It almost seemed worse to have a plan!

Last words ... last words from A. B ... .last words from A. B. ever.

This wouldn't do. Kristen needed her rest and the cat—well, the cat probably needed rest, too. If he could rest, after getting caught out in a storm ... it occurred to Lila to wonder how wet the cat had been when he'd entered the cabin. Wet enough to leave footprints, yes, but ...

Had he been under the shelter of the porch all night?

Lila didn't spot the cat immediately upon her re-entry into the cabin. She waved her fingers through the tepid water still leftover from washing the mugs, and dried them on a towel depending from a hook between the windows.

This isn't any different from insomnia. I'll just get some work done and soon, Kristen will be up and ready for breakfast.

Resolute, Lila turned off a couple of the candles on the kitchen counter and walked to her desk. But there, she stopped again, held from her path by something that had never happened to her before.

Her desk chair was, in fact, already occupied. Curled tightly along one side was the cat, and he regarded her with those amazing, reflective eyes. In those eyes, Lila read both wariness and exhaustion.

"It's okay," Lila said, speaking without intention and surprising herself with the words. She wasn't sure if she was addressing the cat, or herself. "It's okay. I can work at the counter, too."

And Lila stretched out her hand, acutely cognizant of the fact that not only was she not, as she had thought, so very different from other human beings ... she was also not so very different from other beings, period.

The cat lifted his head as Lila neared him, his eyes flickering from Lila's face to her hand. And then he stretched out his own neck to meet her, sniffing first—the delicate movements of air tickled in a way that Lila could appreciate rather than fear—and then accepting the slightest of caresses that Lila curved around his cheek.

"It's okay. It really is."

She moved away as carefully as she had approached the cat, picking up her laptop with deliberate movements and excruciating languor. And then, Lila turned and settled herself at the counter, powering up the computer and signing in without sparing the cat another glance.

When Lila did finally look back over her shoulder some 20 minutes later, it was to find the cat sound asleep.

7: Bequest

In the days following Kristen's visit, Lila kept busy without any concentrated effort on her part, mostly on account of the cat. Though he remained nameless, he seemed perfectly content with his new accommodations, not once trying to shoot out the door when Lila exited for a trip to the outhouse; even her longer excursions—East and Up, or scouting for nearby sand sources—didn't seem to faze the cat.

Not that he ignored Lila, but neither did he greet her with meows and adoration. He had taken to sleeping on Lila's bed with her, but he settled himself near her feet rather than in reach of her hands. Nevertheless, whenever Lila found herself looking for the cat, he would be looking right at her, even when she made no sound. It was discreetly comforting for Lila to have someone around who made so few demands in return for simple presence, and it seemed to Lila that the cat shared her contentment with their arrangement.

The cat had taken to his makeshift litter box with ease, though Lila had rigged a privacy shield around it after seeing him use it for the first time. She'd have to come up with something better for a shield than the lids she'd removed from two of her larger plastic tubs and secured with duct tape. The litter box's proximity to the wood stove, too, was less than ideal, but since it was summertime, the situation was workable at present.

Kristen, before she had returned to Casper, had taken Lila to task on her placement of the cat's food and water bowls, too.

"Would YOU want to eat in your outhouse? You can't have his food and water so close to his shitter!"

"Even if he doesn't know it's his outhouse yet?" Lila had responded, for the cat had not yet used the box at that point, though he had sniffed around it.

The memory made Lila chuckle and though Lila had assured Kristen that she'd work out alternate arrangements, Kristen had insisted on settling the matter herself before she left. The cat now took his meals in the bedroom, in the space between the bunks and Lila's small dresser.

Lila was, in fact, now considering whether one of her storage tins would fit in the space currently occupied by the food bowls, and if the cat wouldn't mind jumping from floor to tin to dresser, where he could then dine by candlelight. Not that candlelit dinners were her principal motivation; Lila was instead determined to get the cat's food and water off the floor entirely, to remove the risk that she might drop a blanket onto the bowls during a restless night.

The problem with moving anything around that involved the dresser was, of course, A. B.'s letter, which was still sealed tight and lying in front of the red candle there. In spite of her earlier resolve, Lila had not yet brought herself to read the letter, dividing her focus between the cat, writing, and her recovery process. The as-yet unknown thing she had sensed on Sunday morning was still putting out prickly vibrations and while it was faint, it added another struggle to every day ... and Lila had allowed herself to push A. B.'s letter aside in her list of priorities.

But it wouldn't do. The cat was putting a serious dent in Lila's supply of canned meats and foil-packed tuna, and she didn't want him to become too accustomed to such treats. A trip into town for a cat food would be the ideal time to stop by A. B.'s ranch house. It hadn't sounded like Jake was going to be there indefinitely, and if there was something A. B. wanted her to have—much as Lila didn't want anything, particularly if it was something charged with A. B.'s memories—she really should attend to it promptly.

Although Lila had argued some version of this line of thought each day with herself, reason had yet to win over emotion. Today was Friday, and she was reaching the end of her opportunities for procrastination.

And the end of my rope.

"Surely I can come up with a better metaphor than that!" Lila spoke aloud, waking the cat from his post-breakfast nap. "Sorry, cat."

Rather than return to his nap, the cat stood, stretched, and walked the length of the lower bunk towards where Lila stood in the doorway. There, near her pillow, he sat, wrapping his tail around his body and laying it right over his toes, looking somehow regal and ridiculous at the same time.

"Are your toes cold?"

The cat stared at her. It wasn't a particularly accusatory glare—with the exception of his loud and precipitous entrance into the cabin, the cat was hardly a rude guest—but given Lila's previous chain of thought, she almost felt as if the cat were chastising her for her delay in reading A. B.'s letter.

"Pretty powerful stare you have there, cat."

Don't change the subject. Get on with it!

Lila sighed, and stepped over to the dresser. She threw the cat a baleful look over her shoulder; he caught and absorbed it as if it were nothing.

"It's not you. It's me. I am putting this off. I hate this. I hate that A. B.'s gone. I hate that I can't t-t-tell him ... tell him that I don't need any THING. I just ... oh! I just miss him. He was my friend!"

Because she was looking directly at the letter, Lila missed seeing the cat drop from the bed to the floor. She heard the soft sound in the stillness of the cabin, of course, but she was busy blotting tears with her the back of her hand now, and didn't turn to look. She picked up the letter with her other hand and found that holding it only increased the flow of her grief.

When she felt the pressure against her ankle, Lila couldn't quite believe it. She didn't jump—distracted as she was—but it startled her nevertheless. Lila looked down through her tears and found that the cat was, indeed, rubbing against her leg. She crouched slowly, wonder peeking through the curtains of her sadness, and then she heard it.

"You .... you're ... you're purring?"

It was a low, raspy purr, as if the cat had been a pack-a-day smoker, but it was strong. Very strong, in fact! Lila stretched her hand down and began to pet the cat. Not with the occasional, tentative touches she'd given before, but with a steady pressure that was meant to give the same comfort to the cat that the cat was giving to her.

The cat leaned into Lila's hand with something like abandon, pulling a smile to her face and inspiring her to scratch his cheek. The rumbling sound the cat was passing off as a purr intensified.

"Oh, you ARE purring! A funny purr, though, cat. And you DO need a name."

Lila moved from squatting to sit on the floor, managing the awkward transition as slowly as she could to minimize any disturbance it might give to the cat. He didn't seem to mind, and bumped his head up against one knee when Lila's caresses slowed too much for his liking. Lila set A. B.'s letter to her side and dedicated both hands to the cat, marveling in the softness of his fur and the depth of solace that her touch seemed to bring to the cat—and that his touch brought to her.

"There's something about touch," Lila remembered her mother saying, in an explanation for why words were not always enough or even necessary at all. "A hug, a kiss, a touch ... that says 'I care' with a profundity no words can provide."

It was another sad memory, for a car crash had claimed both of Lila's parents soon after. They'd never known why Lila had developed an aversion to touch; she'd never found the words to tell them.

Another sad memory, yes, but a more distant one. The cat's noisy approval of her present and presence kept Lila from falling any farther down that long-ago rabbit hole.

"You are a loud guy when you want to be, huh? You're as loud as thunder. Oh! That's it!" Lila brought both hands to frame the cat's face, rubbing along his cheeks and down his neck and sides. "Thunder. Your name is Thunder."

An odd name for a timid cat, perhaps, but his reverberating purr was more reminiscent of thunder than anything else Lila could think of. The name fit in her mind, and the cat seemed to concur.

They stayed in their mutual communion for what seemed like a long time, though Lila couldn't be sure of how long; her time sense had never been even as high as average, much less good. Lila eventually settled into a cross-legged stance and the cat— Thunder—stepped neatly into Lila's lap there, sprawling in a loose "C" shape. Then he stretched, yawned into Lila's face, and curled his toes as his purr began to lose volume and he began to lose consciousness.

Trapped by the languid, dozing cat in her lap, Lila realized that while she had still not managed to find time to read A. B.'s letter, Thunder was now providing the time for her. As much as Lila still didn't want to face A. B.'s final words to her, she didn't want to ruin her first real closeness with Thunder, either.

Thunder's eyes flickered when Lila worked the envelope open, but the sound of tearing paper proved no match for the power of sleep; the cat recomposed himself for his nap even as the softer whisper of the letter being withdrawn from its envelope tickled the air.

Lila transferred the envelope to the floor, holding the letter in both hands, staring at its folded mystery. And she thought of the last time she'd seen A. B..

94

"Heading home already?" A. B. had said, knowing full well that it had been the longest time Lila had ever spent at her cabin.

"Well, I do need to pay the bills. I'm sorry I didn't get to see you much this trip!"

"Ranch time is always busy time. And you'll be back. Now give me my hug and have a safe trip back East, you hear?"

The memory brought a smile, in spite of everything. Even with her typical care in avoiding touch, Lila had been so thrilled when she and A. B. had finally come to an agreement for her to buy her land that she'd launched at him and hugged him. Though she'd pulled back just as fast—feeling fortunate indeed that her lapse had not resulted in a memory "burn" of any kind—A. B. had always insisted on a parting hug after that.

"Handshake's just not as good, especially with a pretty gal like you."

Oh, A. B. ...

Bolstered by Thunder—safely tangible, even for Lila and her memory-sensitivity—Lila opened A. B.'s letter and began to read.

I hate long goodbyes. But there's something I want you to have, so here it is, wrote out all nice and neat. They aren't so much for company, but #225 sure seems to like you. You see Jake and he'll bring her over with a few friends. Spencer will help if you need fencing. It's not good to live alone. Believe me, Lila my gal, because I know.

And that was it. That, and A. B.'s unmistakable scrawl of a signature—his full name, Angus Blake McCook.

Stunned, Lila made no sound beyond the sharp intake of breath that had been all she could manage when she'd realized that A. B. was gifting her with cattle. Considering she had no fencing protecting her water supply, much less any way to winter them, she couldn't imagine what A. B. had been thinking.

Company? Goodness, A. B., don't you think I could do better than a couple of cows?

Even Spencer would be better company than cattle! Although,

considering what Lila knew of the man, perhaps not. And why would A. B. suggest that Spencer might assist her if she needed help? Lila scanned the letter, locking onto the words, "Spencer will help."

Spencer will help?

Lila set the letter down, her gaze dropping to Thunder, who was looking rather blissful—albeit in an awkward sort of way. She stroked one outstretched paw, and it retracted, curling. Inspired, Lila petted the cat's shoulder, and he rolled back into a rough letter "C," breaking his earlier, ungraceful-looking sleep-stretch.

With Thunder's comfort more visually apparent now, Lila picked up the letter and read its brief message again; there was no change in the words. A. B. had left Lila a small group of cattle, and while she could remember joking with him about #225—a bold cow, who rarely failed to approach whenever Lila was near A. B.'s fence-line chatting with him—she was flummoxed as to why A. B. would think she'd want to deal with cattle on her own. He knew she preferred only wildlife! And that she'd fenced in her cabin on the off-chance that Spencer's cattle might find some way to thwart his impenetrable fence and invade her land.

Lila snorted at the thought Spencer being willing to help with fencing. That had to be a joke.

Cattle! Really? And A. B.'s nephew Jake was to deliver them?

Jake must know. He said I should pick up ... now how would I pick up cattle?

It was too bad she hadn't read the letter while Kristen was still at the cabin. If there was ever an "oh-crap" moment, this was it, and Kristen surely would have taken the more vulgar form of that expression to new heights, embellishing it as the situation so dearly deserved.

Cattle! Lila returned the letter to the floor beside her and dedicated both hands to the soft bundle of sleeping cat in her lap. The quiet enfolding them both was interrupted only by Thunder's occasional, unintelligible murmurs in the secret language of Cat, and the more steady flow of brisk breeze outside. It made the turmoil that had erupted in Lila's mind after reading A. B.'s letter all the more apparent.

Well, now's as good a time as any to try a meditation.

Lila was far from convinced she could settle her mind, but since meditating would buy a little more time for Thunder's nap, she moved her hands from the cat to her knees and closed her eyes.

Breathe in, breathe out. Breathe in. What on earth had A. B. been thinking? Breathe out. Breathe in, breathe out.

How much does a cow even eat in a day? Have I got the grazing land for #225, let alone her "friends?"

Focus. Breathe in, breathe out. FOCUS.

Focus on ... what now? All I can think about are Hereford cattle! Hereford cattle, which is why A. B. started going by A. B. instead of 'Angus,' because he said, "Who ever heard of a rancher named Angus raising Hereford cattle?"

Crap! BREATHE IN, BREATHE OUT.

Yes, this was going to be a battle—an epic battle. Lila realized her face and shoulders were tensing, and determined that she would try a relaxing meditation, working her way from head to toes, instead of the breathing meditation. On a bizarre occasion like this, any little bit would help.

Perhaps because she was feeling so strained and therefore had a lot to work with, Lila was marginally more successful at holding her attention to this task. Though anxiety and its accessory irregular heartbeats had been Lila's most recent physical problem, these issues and many more over the years had all been manifestations of disturbance in her mind—rather the opposite of being "all in her head," in fact.

For Lila, it turned out that a thorny problem, upsetting situation, or increasing sensitivity to memory-laden things would leach right out of the confines of thought and result in everything from anxiety to general malaise to specific muscle spasms. And for muscle problems, Lila's neck was one of the most susceptible areas of her body to catching and carrying stress.

"It doesn't help that you spend so much of your time hunched over your computer, either," Dr. Hamilton had pointed out."

A head-to-toe meditation, focusing on every identifiable muscle area along the way, had been one of the things Dr. Hamilton had prescribed to help Lila "fix this, not just treat it." But even with the motivation of substantial improvement in her day-to-day condition, Lila struggled to make and take the time to make such exercises part of her self-care routine.

And how can I possibly spend a half hour or more on this if I've got a party of cows to deal with now, too?

Lila's eyes popped open, and she sighed.

"This isn't working, cat ... Thunder. This isn't working."

In response, Thunder rolled, exposing his belly, and stretched, pressing his front paws, claws lightly extended, into Lila's belly as he did so.

Thunder required care as well, but his needs—with the exception of obtaining cat food—had been surprisingly easy to accommodate. Lila stroked the cat's white belly fur, which was even softer than the rest of him.

Cows, on the other hand ...

Yes. Enough was enough. If Lila was going to get into town, stop by A. B.'s ranch to see Jake, and lug a bag of cat food up the hill before nightfall, she was going to have to get going. Now!

"Want a little tuna, Thunder?" The cat shook his head, and then worked at an itch behind his ear with one back foot. "Uh huh. I bet you'll change your mind when you see where I'm headed."

Though she tried to transfer him gently to the bed, Thunder leaped from Lila's lap, stalking away in an unlikely composite of outrage and wounded dignity. True to Lila's prediction, though he hurried back to her at the first scent of tuna, and even added a pleading little "mew."

"You're welcome! But you don't need to get too noisy now, Thunder. I like you when you're quiet, too."

The needs of her furry companion thus addressed, Lila turned her attention to hurried preparation for the trip she'd been avoiding. She piled her wallet, keys, a clean cap, the snakebite kit, and her cell phone on the counter and set the small bag of trash she'd accumulated since her arrival near the door. Because she reused everything she could—from Ziplocks, which were great for protection against rain when packing things out, to cardboard from food containers, which could be used in starting the wood stove on chilly mornings—there wasn't much actual garbage to dispose of.

She'd taken a solar shower the day before, so Lila wasn't worried about looking like she was living without running water, even though she effectively was. She did take a moment to change into clean jeans and a more fitted t-shirt than she would otherwise bother with, grabbing a flannel shirt and flashlight just in case.

"And what do we need, other than to figure out what to do with a miniature herd of Hereford cattle—Polled Hereford, if we must be specific, Thunder, and me being me? We must be specific."

Thunder retired to his observational post under the desk, watching Lila's flurry of activity with something like suspicion. Paper and pen in hand, Lila approached him slowly, and he leaned into her hand as she petted his head, and then stroked his cheek.

"You're pretty soft for a cat that's been roughing it for who knows how long! I'll get more tuna, too, but you're also going to get whatever cat food I can find at the store ... then maybe we can bulk you up a bit, boy!"

Lila then started her list, beginning with tuna and cat food, looking around and absently gnawing on the pencil as she considered what else might be needed.

"Oh! TP. Can always use more TP."

But because she'd just arrived at the cabin—and probably also because she was making this trip in a rush, with the curious and unwelcome stop at the end—Lila could think of little else that she really needed.

"I could see if I can find the vet in town. They must have a vet. Good grief! I wonder if they'd have a cat carrier ... no, wait, Kristen said she'd bring that next week. And she said she'd bring food, too, didn't she ... well, it doesn't matter. You need something now and we'll just work it in with the occasional tuna."

And so Lila concluded her list with "check vet" and "Jake/cows." The final note drew a sigh from Lila, reminding her of both the finality of the loss of A. B. and the oddity of his note.

I should bring A. B.'s note, too.

It felt strange leaving the cabin, knowing Thunder was there and would be there when she returned. He'd come out of his spot under the desk before she left, and made himself comfortable on her bed. The occasion had seemed to Lila to demand some sort of statement, but all she could come up with was, "Okay, then, I'll be back soon. No parties!"

Ridiculous.

The walk down to her truck was not as easy as usual. Even with gravity assisting—as it always did—the descent and the near-necessity of cat food as a draw, Lila's own resistance to the mission ahead was at a peak. Once she was in the truck and through the first gate, she supposed it would get better; then she'd be committed, as it were. But now, when turning around would be simple and quick ...

Lila's concern about damaging the two-track road on the way out to the highway was the first of her excuses to be eliminated. While the rain had been heavy at her cabin, it was patchy in its coverage; the high plains pastures she drove through, while still puddled in certain areas, were hardly flooded. In fact, now that she was paying attention and not racing against a storm as she had been on the drive in, Lila noticed that one of the ranchers who used this road had done some work on it: three previously problematic spots had been filled in with crushed rock.

Down off the hills and onto the prairie, Lila's thoughts were interrupted by an awareness of something missing. The niggling tickle/itch of the mystery thing that had been gnawing at Lila since the night of Thunder's arrival was much less here. Almost at her truck when the realization struck her, Lila stopped and turned in a circle, "listening" with all her might. Yes, there was a definite reduction in sensation here.

It must be somewhere on the other side.

And then the cattle shot back to the front of the line for attention in Lila's mind, and despite her reluctance to move forward: through all the gates, into town, through the store and its customers with their unknown land-mine hazards of attachment to things, the vet, again, presuming there was one in town? Yes, in spite of all that and Jake, too, Lila really had no choice. She had to do something about A. B.'s cows.

My cows!

Oh no they're not! There must be a way to ... but A. B. wanted ...

Lila snorted in disgust, wishing yet again that she'd become better practiced in meditation so she could stop the onslaught of stray thoughts racing through her mind. Action was the only alternative for her at present, though, and so enough was enough.

Resolute, Lila unlocked the truck, threw her supplies and trash inside, and then rummaged underneath the bag of trash where it landed on the floor to locate her gate pulley. Then, without further ado, she turned on the ignition, threw the truck in gear, and began to drive.

Spencer's stubborn gate, of course, wasn't more than a block away from where she'd parked, and even though it was still obstinate, Lila found it much more manageable under clear skies than it had been under stormy ones. Back in the truck, she started the slow, steady crawl out to the "real world," moving across the next eight miles along barely-there tracks, to clear tracks with deep crevasses of ruts, and finally to a dirt road that almost looked like an actual road.

It was a gradual transition that aided Lila's own passage from a safe place of her own creation into a less hospitable realm, where strangers and their unknowingly shared baggage strolled around, spewing their own sacred stories onto Lila with an inadvertent touch.

And sometimes, whispering at her even before that touch.

The problem wasn't so much the actual memories that Lila picked up on contact with something charged with another person's memories—those experiences, for Lila, were intense but short-lived, like a shock from an electric fence. But over time, the tingling, prickling static that built up with the buzz of passages all around her, that was what eventually got to her ... it was a constant throbbing that built up and up until it became a tower, leaning and ready to crumble, making Lila's "usual" tension seem like a relaxing spa vacation.

Her week in the cabin hadn't been long enough to dampen the background noise, Lila found, but she felt better than she had on her arrival. As she approached the narrow highway that led to town, Lila looked both ways for traffic as was recommended. Finding none, she grinned: a busy day in Wyoming was still that much safer for her than a busy day elsewhere ... and low population density was all it took!

With the interstate running through the town Lila was heading towards, there was still plenty of opportunity for her stress to rise. As always, Lila wondered how many people in that fast-moving—if low-volume—human stream were as she had once been, eager to pass through this area on their way to somewhere else. It had once seemed bleak and somewhat desolate, Lila knew, but now it was her haven, and she saw it with new eyes.

There was a pronghorn antelope atop the ridge to her right, and a herd of cattle in the field to her left. The greener, thicker grasses that led up to and beyond a lonely cottonwood at the far end of the field bespoke a stream, even though Lila could not see it from her vantage point. And up ahead, swooping in great, arching strokes, a large bird was etching patterns across the sky—the wide open, breathless blue sky.

Lila leaned into her seat, letting the back of it and headrest take some of the stress she was already envisioning. How busy could the grocery store be at this time of day? True, it was Friday, but it was barely 1:00, so Lila didn't expect to encounter a rush. Still, it was difficult not to anticipate disaster, since past experience was still the best indicator of future performance.

Nice. Now I sound like an ad for mutual funds.

Perhaps, Lila thought as the truck crested last hill before town, that was why A. B.'s letter had struck her so hard. Yes, it was his last letter to her, and of course that was a large part of her unease, but then what she had read had seemed so out of character for A. B., particularly since he knew she'd wanted safe drinking water for herself when she'd bought the property!

It wouldn't take too much to fence in the area below the water tank; it's close to the property line. But I'd hate to park in poop.

Lila snorted at the thought, though the sound was lost to the ragged, staccato pulse of her tires passing over the cattle grate just before the stop sign.

"I am NOT taking those cows! Not even #225. Not happening!"

A rust-bucket of a truck turned, passing in front of Lila as she waited to make her own turn. From the look of the burly face under the cowboy hat inside the truck, Lila was embarrassed to understand the ferocity of her words must have been written on her face. She recovered quickly enough to lift her first two fingers from their position atop her steering wheel, greeting the man in a more hospitable, suitably Western way, but did not see if he responded in kind.

8: Determination

The sun was low on the horizon by the time Lila got back to the cabin. When she opened the door, Thunder streaked away to hide under the desk, but once safely there and seeing who had entered his adopted home, he returned and began sniffing through the bags Lila had set on the floor.

"Yes, I've got food for you, too, but let me get some extra light in here ... because I need a drink."

Thunder seemed content enough in his investigations, so Lila wasted no time in obtaining her seldom-used camping lantern from its corner of the front closet. The lantern was an older model, but had the virtue of being self-contained in its own plastic covering; Lila liked the added security that provided for when the lantern wasn't in use.

The whoosh of the lantern being lit didn't faze Thunder, but he regarded the sudden brilliance of the room with suspicion, and didn't seem to care for the hiss of sound as the lantern settled into a steady burn. Eyes narrowed and tail lashing, he stalked from the main room, leaving Lila to unpack his cat food and her other supplies alone.

It was just as well. While Lila had enjoyed a surprisingly easy excursion through the grocery store, she had been unprepared for her unsettling experience at the veterinary clinic.

And it wasn't even a trip down someone else's "Memory Lane" that got to me this time!

Lila set the lantern on her desk and bent to search the recessed shelves underneath the kitchen counter for the tin that contained her cache of liquor. It was dark enough outside that shadows inside were multiplying like rabbits, even faster in this space than the rest of the cabin, so Lila had to get back up and bring the lantern into better alignment.

"Oh, there you are."

With the unassuming tin canister covered with frolicking blue ducklings extracted and moved to the counter, Lila once again settled the lantern back on her desk. As she did so, her eyes fell onto her silent, folded laptop and she frowned.

Not tonight.

No, not tonight indeed.

RayAnn is going to be ticked!

But she wasn't, not really. The tale Lila was fond of telling herself in order to motivate extra work was ringing as hollow as a broken promise.

Lila opened the canister and unwrapped one of the two solid-but-elegant glasses from inside. The bubble wrap took up more room than it might seem it was worth, but for Lila, the vitality of protecting these glasses—the ones she could remember her parents using on only a few, distinctive occasions—was worth it. Besides, she didn't particularly care for hard liquor, so didn't need too much extra room in the tin.

Lila loaded the glass with all of the ice from the tray inside the refrigerator's barely-there freezer and then chose her parents' favorite gin from the ducky tin. As rarely as she drank, she even more rarely drank the gin—Lila preferred light, sweet wines—but as she had described bleach to Kristen, Lila had conceded that gin, too, had its uses.

The gin splashed into the glass, slithering with viscous tenacity over the ice cubes in a shimmering cascade. Lila saw that her hand was shaking, and her heart took a break from skipping over beats to sink.

Just what I don't need. Something else that freaks me out!

Despite her tremors, the gin was in no serious danger of

splashing outside of the confines of the glass. As soon as it reached the level Lila deemed "adequate but safe," she recapped the bottle and returned it to the tin. It nestled in beside the remaining glass and the unopened bottle of bourbon that A. B. had given her a year ago at Christmas. Lila withdrew her focus from the bourbon quickly and registered that the gin was nearly half-gone.

Should've gotten more gin!

Discouraged at the thought that she might be drawn to drink so much—and so quickly—Lila still took a moment to add gin to her "next trip" list. Then she hurriedly returned the canister to its station on the shelf, grabbed her gin glass with both hands, and dropped into her desk chair.

Lila sipped the gin gingerly, wishing she could feel its taste as smooth, the way her father had referred to it. Lila found that the pine-y flavor scratched her palate in the first mouthful, but then the slight scent of the gin would reach her and she would relax into its familiarity—the specialness of it, the comfort it exuded. That the power of the gin was in its connection to her parents rather than inherent to the gin itself was not lost on Lila; indeed, it was one of the reasons she chose to drink rarely.

It would be too easy to rely on this. Far too easy.

Lila had read that scent was perhaps the most powerful of the senses in its ability to connect with exquisite precision to memories and the emotions tied to those memories. It was one of the things Lila found so ironic about her own touch-sensitivity: here was this acknowledged, scientific fact linked to scent and instead, Lila connected deeply with remembrances through physical contact.

Lila found scent to have little direct specificity—no individual experiences came to mind as she swirled the glass in front of her, deliberately inhaling the tangy fumes that emerged. Nevertheless, the smell of the gin did seem to have a laser-lock on the unrefined intricacies of the emotional well-being that, in Lila's mind, was tied to those special celebrations during which her parents clinked this very glass to its mate, laughed, and drank of this very brand of gin.

As the tension Lila was carrying began to dissipate, the scene at the veterinarian's office replayed in her mind. It was an uneven playback, fast-forwarding through where she'd introduced herself to the receptionist/assistant and explained about Thunder. Though harried-looking and obviously busy—the phone rang twice before the woman behind the desk had been able to complete so much as a single sentence addressed directly to Lila—Dottie had been welcoming and encouraging, all over the din of various animal sounds.

"Picked up a stray, did you? We'll get him in soon, then, and give him a good once-over for you. Now where is that appointment book? Don't worry, it's not always this crazy around here, and hopefully won't be for long, oh! And here's our assisting vet, just in the nick of time ... "

Then Dottie had waved to someone behind Lila and when Lila turned, the last person she would have expected to see was standing there, his smile slipping only a little in his own startlement.

"Lila? What are you ... can I help you? Dottie?

"Just a sec, Jake, and I'll get Mrs. Grady and her little yapper Muffin over there in to a room and we'll all be happier, Muffin included!"

"It's about time!" The owner of the yapping dog had sniped, huffing as she hefted the feather-weight dog and her not-so-insubstantial self out of the chair in which she'd been waiting.

"Right this way, Mrs. Grady, and we'll get Muffin a little snack after his shots, how would that be? We got some new biscuits ... "

Lila shook her head and took a long draught of gin, remembering Jake's brilliant eyes and the smile that had reached all the way up into them, seemingly just for her.

She groaned at the memory of bumbling through an abbreviated version of Thunder's arrival under Jake's steady return gaze, even though he surely must have had plenty to do. Lila had realized it just as Dottie bustled back into the room, waving at Jake again.

"Bud's out on a ranch call, Jake. Would you mind giving Muffin his immunizations? He's not a young dog, that one, but he's blessed with a strong set of lungs for his age. For any age!"

And Jake had disappeared, with apologies to Lila and assurances that he would come visit her and Thunder in person on Saturday. Lila turned back to Dottie feeling dazed by the speed and unexpectedness of the meeting, and it must have been printed in block letters all over her face, too.

"He's a doll, isn't he?" Dottie had asked with a wink. "Why didn't you say you were A. B.'s neighbor? It's good to finally meet you, and this way you'll get your new kitty all checked out in the comfort of his own home."

Lila groaned again, and held the glass and its dwindling burden of gin and ice against her forehead. When she looked up again, Thunder was back at his post next to the bags from the grocery store.

"I didn't even remember to talk to him about the cows, Thunder!"

The thought was heavy with despair, and Lila could imagine Kristen laughing at the incongruity. Kristen would say that Lila shouldn't be thinking about the cows, anyway; she should be thinking about Jake, and how gorgeous he was.

Kristen would've pushed A. B. at Lila, too, if she'd thought Lila found him halfway attractive.

But Kristen hadn't lived through the aftermath of her parents' sudden deaths with a controlling boyfriend who'd taken advantage of the situation to advance himself and become a controlling fiancé. Kristen hadn't managed to break off one bad situation and then follow it up with another poor choice ... the light, open relationship Lila had eventually rebounded into after Stuart had landed her with Pete, and Pete had been a practicing womanizer.

"Fuck Peter. Not literally. Peter-Peter-Goddamned-Cheater!" Kristen had said, when Lila told her about breaking up with Pete because of his repeated faithlessness. And then Kristen had called Pete on Lila's phone, listened as he began to "explain" himself to Lila—he thought—and then drowned him out by shouting her objections to his behavior, disdain edging her rage like serration on a wicked blade and profanity making up the bulk of her dissertation.

"Hot damn, better than therapy any day!" Kristen had said when Pete finally gave up, and hung up.

Lila swirled the gin in her glass as Thunder watched quietly from across the room.

"What's wrong with me?"

Lila hardly expected an answer to her question, but Thunder couldn't even hold her gaze. He was already on to staring at the hypnotic glow-hiss of the lantern behind and to the right of Lila.

Thunder's thrall reminded Lila of how much she liked to blame hypnosis for her long relationship with Pete. When she'd first discovered Pete's faithless ways, she'd thought she could "fix" things, and Pete even attended couple's therapy with her. He'd done all the right things and said all the right things, mesmerizing Lila with hope. But before too long—before she hoped too much—Pete got back out and found himself another girlfriend on the side, and another, and another ...

Since Pete, Lila hadn't had more than the occasional date here and there. Since Pete, Lila had flatly decided that she wasn't capable of judging a good man from one who would try to subvert her as Stuart had, or would walk all around and then right over her as Pete had.

"I mean, what's next? I don't need to take this game to Level 3 to see it stinks."

Worst of all—and Lila drained the last of her drink as she

thought it—worst of all was the fact that Pete had been the single most attractive man Lila had ever seen in her life. She'd been flattered by his attentions and fallen easily into the spell he was so frequently casting. Oh, Lila had found Stuart appealing, too, but Pete? Pete had been movie-star gorgeous; Pete had been enticing like gravity was enticing ... it just radiated from him in irresistible waves.

"Hungry, Thunder?" Lila propelled herself out of the chair with unnecessary force and her movement finally broke the spell the lantern had cast on the cat. "I got you both kinds of dry food that they had, Purina and ... oh, some other stuff in a bag. But it's good, I bet. You can try both tonight!"

The grocery store hadn't had any pet food bowls, but it didn't matter, as Dottie had wrangled Lila into purchasing a set from the veterinary office. That woman was wasted on office management, Lila thought; she should've been in marketing. Even without knowing that Thunder didn't have his own food bowls, Dottie had made a grand case in favor of the clinics bowls.

"They've even got our clinic name, clinic number, and emergency number right on 'em! I'll just get you two, then, I will." Dottie had sealed that deal with a wink and a grin.

"It didn't occur to me to think you might want your own name on these, Thunder. Oh, shoot, I should probably wash these before you eat out of them?"

Thunder didn't seem to care one way or the other, but stepped forward to wind his way around and through Lila's legs.

"Flirt."

After giving the matter much more consideration than it was due, Lila set the new bowls by the sink and went to fetch Thunder's makeshift dinnerware out of the bedroom. She added a small plate from the kitchen to the old set and soon, Thunder was facing two samples of dry cat food. He did not seem enthused by the experiment, and sniffed each sample carefully.

Lila, on her way to fetch fresh water, was waiting in the doorway to see which food Thunder would select first. The idea that he might eat neither had never occurred to her.

"Listen, mister. A week ago you were scrounging a tuna packet out of my trash just to lick day-old leftover juice off of it! You can't go all ... all ... all ... PRINCESS on me and get picky now!"

Thunder had turned his head to look at Lila at the opening of her part-tirade/part-sermon but he turned back to the food long before she called him a princess. As soon as she stopped speaking, Lila heard delicate crunching sounds and peeked around the cat to see which food Thunder had started eating.

"Purina then? Good. And, umm, sorry for calling you ... well. You're very manly, for a cat."

Layered over her slight but definite gin buzz, Lila found that embarrassment at potentially insulting the cat who'd chosen her far more than she'd chosen him wasn't so bad. She refreshed and returned Thunder's old water bowl to him and then headed back into the main room to finish putting away her purchases and find some food for herself.

The problem of what to do with Thunder's food, however, stymied Lila even before she'd worked through the rest of her purchases. As food, it needed to go into a canister or tub of some sort, but Lila wasn't sure she had any spares and didn't want to go through the upper cabinets at such a late hour, lantern or no lantern. She supposed she could let the cat food sit out for one night, but it just took one more check on Thunder, who was still crunching away, for Lila to reconsider. She emptied a plastic tub of spare blankets, stuffing them onto the upper bunk, and moved the cat food into the tub.

Shaking a finger at her gluttonous cat, Lila next set herself to stashing the extra TP in its designated, large canister, and moving her various other purchases into their assigned locations.

Not very adaptable, are you? She silently asked herself. And answered, *No, not even a little bit, really.*

Although Lila had adapted to Thunder and was even enjoying his presence. That seemed like a big point in her favor! And she'd done the best she could with her rising stress and hypersensitivity to memory-charged things, and dealt with days that were like walking through fields that might or might not be crammed full with mines, and ... Lila's stomach rumbled noisily, putting the brakes on her train of thought hard enough to run it right off its self-defeatist tracks.

The idea of cooking held no appeal, and so Lila took a baggie of homemade granola from her supplies and sat at the counter. She picked at the food, crunching away and watching the Wyoming skies—where she could see them through the pines—fade into the night. It was a slow, slow process but absorbing all the same, and Lila had all the time in the world here at her private retreat.

Until tomorrow, when the veterinarian with A. B.'s eyes would come to see Thunder. Until tomorrow, when Jake would come here. Here!

"Blast."

Lila nibbled at the granola until she'd finished its measured portion and then zipped the baggie shut and set it aside near the dishes. Dishes which she could easily do tomorrow before Jake's arrival, she figured, and absently rubbed the back of her neck with one hand. There weren't many, but it would be nice to wash them up, not to mention nice for Thunder to try out his new bowls.

With Thunder on her mind, Lila stepped around the corner and into the bedroom, peering through the murk of falling night to check on the cat. Her neck and shoulders were beginning to bother Lila in earnest now, but she still wanted to see if Thunder had sampled the second variety of cat food before she made a quick trip to the outhouse and prepared for bed.

Not wanting to disturb Thunder with the lantern he had taken offense to, Lila pulled her flashlight from her pocket and aimed slightly above the bed. She caught Thunder's squinted eyes in the low part of the beam on her second pass over the bed—he was crouching, front feet curled underneath his body so as to be invisible, near the foot of the bed.

"Hello, boy. How was dinner?"

Lila swept the light over to Thunder's dining area and found nothing, even when she stepped closer to be certain.

"You ate it ALL?"

Being a cat, Thunder of course said nothing in reply, though if he had, Lila supposed he might have said, "Duh."

"Well, then. Maybe we'll just give you a mix every day! We'll see what Jake says."

Lila stood up from her crouch and shrugged her shoulders, rolling her head from side to side. Something definitely didn't feel right. She reached up with her free hand to grasp and release the crook of her neck, wondering how she could feel so off when she'd barely done any writing. Lila took two steps towards the door before a budding apprehension gave way to full awareness.

"Damn."

Kristen would be so proud.

But Lila didn't feel like smiling. She stepped out of the cabin and began walking towards the outhouse, the hand that had been questing for tension now dangling, forlorn at her side. Sure enough, the wrong-feeling/off-ness/almost-pain gave way to buzzing in just about the same place she'd first noticed it. And it was stronger.

So distracted ... and a little bit under the influence ... but how could I not understand?

It didn't take a therapist to help Lila figure this one out. But the realization brought no relief from the dejection she felt with this mystery thing infiltrating her safe haven. The stronger the signal, the worse it would get for Lila, and this—while not much worse, yet—was distinctly on a downhill slide.

114

Walking back to the cabin with the tingling itch now more obvious than ever, Lila wanted to cry. Instead, she forced herself to hold back, and continued her bedtime preparations, carrying her supplies out to the fence and then brushing her teeth with a rarely-seen vigor that would make her surly dentist proud, if only the practice continued for more than a day. Determined, Lila added a rare flossing to her routine, giving herself extra points for so doing even as the unpleasant tickle continued to nag at her.

Perhaps the fact that Lila could sense the object more on higher ground would help her find it.

FIND it?

Lila's every instinct was to run for cover, not to seek out the cause of her increasing discomfort.

But this IS cover. This is it! There isn't anywhere else to go!

And that's when Lila felt a rush of something other than nerves—something powerful that wasn't panic. That, right then, was when Lila got mad.

Of all the things she'd ever felt or tried to quantify for herself about her gift/curse of "reading" other people's stories through their particular possessions, Lila could not once remember getting angry before today. She'd been scared, embarrassed, confused ... suffice to say, her emotions had run the gamut, but she'd never crossed the threshold to embrace simple anger.

But here she was, floss still in hand, standing under an utterly appropriate Wyoming sky—dark and overcast, with points of starlight being blotted out by the gathering gloom—and she was fast losing what little cool she had and bitterly resenting that, too.

Lila stalked underneath the porch roof and leaned back against the smooth, cool outer cabin wall. She let herself be taken down by gravity, resisting only a little to soften her seat on the boards at the bottom. There, she bypassed the cross-legged pose she typically tried to assume for meditation and let her knees stay up and askew, leaning forward into them so her elbows rested on top. And then

115

she breathed, in and out, as the distractions raced through her mind one after another—hard plastic box of floss in her hand, tickle-itch of the thing, ANGER, exhaustion, unfairness, Thunder waiting on the bed and how would she possibly sleep now, cows, RayAnn's deadlines, ANGER, dishes on the counter—through it all, Lila fought to bring herself back to her breath, aware underneath it all that this was not meditation as it should be.

And then Lila remembered an animated cartoon—Kristen, of all people, had sent her the link. The warrior, kneeling in meditation, had been irritated by a fly and sliced it neatly in half with his ninja sword. But with every slice, one additional fly had risen from each half of the former fly, and soon the warrior was beset by flies and the brief calm he'd attempted to establish in his mind was replaced with buzzing, buzzing ...

Like that thing, though it also feels like hissing—like water near a boil, or the ocean, after it crashes a wave onto the shore. Like my lantern, hissing.

If the cartoon was to be believed, the trick to meditation was to persevere throughout the annoyances, be it one little pest or an entire swarm of one's own making.

I didn't make THIS!

But in a leap of intuition, Lila reached the rapid-fire conclusion that in a sense, this truly was a storm of her own making. She didn't choose her abilities, no, but she chose what to do with them. It seemed like insanity to seek out the thing that was bothering her, but maybe she had to.

For what? So it can multiply?

Lila shook her head. The cobwebs of overlapping thought didn't clear with the gesture, but Lila did become aware of a gentle sound she hadn't noticed before.

"It's raining!"

It certainly was raining a lot during this visit. Relatively speaking, of course.

Lila's train of thought had gone off its tracks yet again. At

116

least the feelings of rage had been dampened somewhat, too ... Lila was back to rubbing shoulders with rage's little sister, frustration.

A quiet but plaintive meow drew Lila's attention to the doorway at her side. Leaning further forward, she saw Thunder standing there, his head jutting out and pushing slightly against the screen. He was quite a vision, backlit by the distant, around-the-corner glow of the lantern, but Lila's vision had adapted as she'd sat in the dwindling daylight. While there was little illumination, there was enough to reveal most things, at least in thick, murky outlines.

"Looking good, Thunder."

Thunder's neck jerked at the sound of her voice as he strained the screen further.

"Yes, yes. Nothing more to see here and my focus is miserable, even for me. I'm coming."

Thunder scuttled back as Lila entered, closing the outer door behind her. The cat stayed close enough that Lila could lean in and stroke his back, and he rubbed up against her ankles as she did so.

Maybe just one more shot of gin ...

One more wouldn't hurt, just this once. And Lila wanted another drink, if only to help her drop off into sleep. The rain was light and created a good atmosphere for sleeping, but Lila's head was still spinning from the day's events and the residual, lingering feeling of memories whispering through the air—close, but not strong enough to coalesce into anything more than buzzing murmurs.

Lila pulled out the tin and its happy little ducks again, setting it softly on the counter. Her hand shook again as she poured a layer of gin into her glass, and she set the bottle back down on the counter with more force than the motion required.

She drained her glass in a gulp that burned all the way down without any water to buffer its journey. Her Wyoming escape had changed almost beyond recognition, and in only a week, too.

9: Red Dawn

When Lila awoke the next morning, she struggled out of the embrace of the blankets with less vigor than necessity, cloudy in both mind and body but aware of an urgent need to visit the outhouse. The sky outside her window was red.

While she noticed the ruddy tones of the sky on her way to the outhouse—and also the abundant dampness that bespoke a night filled with more than the mere sprinkles she'd heard before bed—Lila did not let it captivate her even to the slight point of slowing her pace. Once her early morning errand was completed, however, Lila stepped back outside with the full intent of pointed observation, despite her lingering mental exhaustion and a physical weariness colored at least in part by last night's gin.

But the spectacle that awaited her when she left the outhouse and started back west towards the cabin demanded more than scrutiny—it wanted nothing less than awe.

It got that.

"Wow!"

Not only was the sky saturated with shades of red, but the still-rising sun was striking enough moisture in the air to produce the oddest rainbow Lila had ever seen. It was red—and red only—from the apex that jutted out of nowhere amongst the spotty low-lying clouds all the way down to the south where it disappeared into the trees, a steep arc of rosy single-mindedness.

While less washed with red than the rainbow and surrounding sky, everything Lila could see was red-tinged. Even the gray metal of the cabin was blushing, and it was quite pretty! But the inundation of the entire, visible world in red was also somewhat unnerving, particularly when Lila's awe lost its initial fervor and she began to recall the events of the night before, staggering into the haze of choppy memory that was all that remained after the second glass of gin.

It wasn't the gin that was the problem, of course. While she'd consumed more than she had in a long time, Lila had only drank enough to take her into the relatively safe terrain of mild intoxication. But while not hungover from alcohol, Lila was feeling ill effects from what she'd come to think of as a "dream hangover," and its symptoms weren't too far removed from the more traditional form, hence the name.

Lila took one last look around her, from the red, beribboned sky above to the pink-hued, soaking wet grasses at her feet. A pair of sego lilies to her left caught Lila's eye in particular, and she shivered, her chill heightened by both the crispness of the air as well as by the pink-tinged, eerie elegance of the cup-shaped blossoms.

While there was no cure for a dream hangover—short of a following, dreamless night's sleep—Lila did have plenty of work to do to try to refocus her scattered thoughts. She resumed her walk back to the cabin even as she became aware of an additional distraction ... the droning of the memory-charged thing somewhere to the south and west had increased in volume again.

Just what I need.

Earliness of the hour or not, Lila would not let herself dwell on any of it: not the red sky, not the mishmash of dream fragments, not the nattering murmur of the mystery thing, and definitely not Jake's impending visit. She did need to clean up both herself and the cabin before Jake's arrival, however, and if she could manage to get some writing done, so much the better. Once Thunder was checked out and immunized, Lila would think about the rest of it ... but not before.

Determined, Lila left the ethereal red world behind her and stepped back into the cabin, lighting candles in the kitchen area. She spared a moment of jealousy for Thunder's ignorant bliss—as he was unaware of the plan that included groping and needles for him later in the day, he had no impending concerns other than the rumble of his tummy—and gave him a petting that ran his purr-o-meter all the way up to its maximum volume.

"Let me wash your fancy new dishes first, fuzzball. It won't take long."

The red overlay was fading as the tea kettle began to whistle, and Lila made short work of the dishes. She washed and dried Thunder's bowls first, and lured him into the bedroom by tapping them lightly together. Their metallic sounds seemed harsh to Lila, but Thunder heard jewel tones in them and he trotted after Lila with his tail held high in anticipation.

"So you can figure some of this out, huh?" Lila said, swapping out Thunder's old, "informal" dining dishes with the new ones.

Thunder meowed, managing to sound both plaintive and urgent, although Lila supposed she could be reading too much into her feline roommate's commentary.

She scooped a bit from each bag of cat food and the sound of it falling into Thunder's bowl was like miniature cowbells that muted as more kibble fell over and in. Thunder leaped up onto the dresser and began to munch away even before Lila could mix the blend, leaving her to shake her head at his greed and exercise even greater care in making sure the lid was tight on the cat food's temporary housing.

"Might be you I need to worry about more than any mice or bugs!"

Indeed, with Thunder in the house, Lila thought she could probably dismiss any concern of mice at all. She'd take the blankets with her on her next trip out, and find them a new container before she returned to Wyoming.

Going back to the dishes, Lila found herself stewing over the idea of going "home" at all. How would Thunder travel? Would she have to ride with a litter box stowed on the floor of the passenger side of her truck?

It seemed a silly concern, particularly with all of the other problems at hand, and close at hand, too. Lila finished the dishes and cleaned the counter before refilling the tea kettle for a cup of coffee. She usually preferred tea, but as much as she was struggling this morning, a single cup of coffee filtered through her own, makeshift setup might be just the thing to get her moving faster.

Even if it does nothing for my focus!

After extracting her supplies from the proper tin, Lila molded a coffee filter into the cup-sized silver strainer she'd never used in her regular kitchen. The strainer fit just right into her insulated mug, and once coffee grounds were installed in its lined interior, all that was required was two or three slow pours of boiling water over the top and Lila would have her coffee.

While the coffee cooled a bit, Lila gave herself a sponge bath using the remainder of the hot water, and dressed in clean clothes. After she had her coffee, she'd wrap her towel around her neck and do a dry shampoo with the rarely-used canister Kristen had found for her. The first sip was just the right strength for Lila, though she didn't doubt a true coffee fanatic would find the flavor dulled after spending so much time sitting in ground form. Checking the date on the small, metallic bag, Lila found it was a full year old itself.

Well, I like a nice, aged decaf in the morning.

Yes, it was decaffeinated coffee, too ... more than enough to curse Lila to hell, if a coffee lover were in charge of such things.

The idea made Lila chuckle, and so it was with renewed energy that she proceeded outside to dry-shampoo her hair and then back inside to finish cleaning up the cabin. She ignored the heightened tingle of the thing to the south and west, although her behavior bespoke more of a determined snub than actual ignorance.

Maybe it was at the end of the red rainbow!

That thought was unsettling, but buoyed by her gin-fueled anger of last night, Lila was set on doing something—fighting somehow—for her sanity in this, her sanctuary. At least there was only one object chattering at her, albeit in an increasing loud voice; Lila found a split-focus, as she sometimes experienced in a crowd of people, to be an even more exhausting experience.

Something buried, maybe, coming to the surface?

That made sense. The cashiers in the grocery store—all two of them—had been complaining of the rains this season being unusually heavy, and the apparent storm last night and red rainbow this morning only furthered the charge as far as Lila was concerned. In light of these salient weather points, something that had been interred and was now getting washed out of its grave, perhaps on a steep slope like the ones downhill from Lila's East and Up walk, would certainly fit the bill of Lila's current distress.

... getting washed out of its grave ...

A grim comparison indeed, even if it was a singular object of some sort rather than something on an actual body.

Lila shook her head, as if all it took to dispel mental turmoil was a physical gesture. She checked her cell phone for the time and saw that she still had at least two hours before Jake's arrival, though Lila somehow thought he would be prompt.

"Well then, Thunder, I suppose I'd best get some work done?"

As if in agreement, Thunder—who had been washing up near the entryway following his breakfast—yawned broadly and turned back towards the bedroom.

"Fine. Go take a nap, then. You'll earn it later today."

Lila settled into her desk and started her computer, gazing out the window at the world outside, which had returned to normal coloration. There was nothing out there to hint that mere hours

122

ago, the entire landscape had been cast in otherworldly shades. Nothing visible, anyway.

Lila opened the window a crack, letting the sounds of wind and birds trickle in through it, and remembered the cartoon warrior again. Frowning at her abundance of distraction even in the face of her determination, Lila set a timer on her computer to arrest her work 15 minutes short of Jake's predicted arrival and forced herself to withdraw into her novel.

The timer was on account of the scene that Lila was working on—an intense and deadly encounter for one of the characters. In Lila's experience, emotional or violent parts of a story were either the easiest or the most difficult to write. In either case, however, they were absorbing and Lila knew that she could lose track of time without an electronic aid. It was just a question of whether she would be plodding along, feeling every word was an effort, or flying by on an ecstatic high with words flying off her fingertips as fast as she could type them when that timer went off.

It was to her credit, RayAnn always said, that Lila's prose was enthralling—both to Lila and her readers. What RayAnn didn't know was the one thing that made Lila feel as if the story was really "hers." It was a distinction only Lila knew, for she hadn't even shared it with Kristen: the parts of the book that were sparked by what Lila had sensed from someone else's embedded memories were not the parts in which Lila was most engrossed as she wrote. Yes, Lila had felt emotions beyond herself and knew things she shouldn't know, but the parts that she imagined and embellished— the parts that led to or from the snippet Lila had secretly absorbed—these were the stretches of story in which Lila could truly lose herself.

This was a vital delineation to Lila, allowing her to call herself a "real writer," even though parts of her stories were based in a reality she ought never to have known. And unlike many things in her life, her ability to embellish before and after some fragment was something of which Lila was absolutely confident. She'd even discussed it—albeit in non-specific terms—with a few other writers at a conference RayAnn had insisted she attend; they'd all copped to inserting some level of reality into their writing at one point or another.

"Just never to the point where that asshole ex-husband of mine can actually recognize himself," one particularly loquacious woman had said, after a long and rambling soliloquy on the subject. "Not that he's ever read a damn thing I—or anyone else—has written. Illiterate bastard.'"

Another writer at the table had prolonged the discussion after Lila had tentatively raised it, hoping to draw just this sort of reaction from her compatriot; the first woman had vowed not to speak of her ex that day, and by doing so, had obligated herself to purchasing the next round.

Lila snapped back to her computer, smiling at the memory. The smile faded as she found she'd reminisced ten minutes away already.

Not being so involved in my writing today, am I? That rat Dave is going to have a hard time getting murdered if I keep this up!

Dave did not prove to be difficult to murder, at least not in a story. His physical appearance was very loosely based on the "asshole ex-husband" Lila had heard so much about in that he was attractive, albeit in a disturbing way, but the bulk of his non-physical characteristics made his muse seem positively delightful by comparison. Lila had him messily dispatched and his body dramatically discovered well before the timer went off, and it practically made her crow with glee.

"Whew!" She silenced the alarm with a swift tap and then shook her head. "Glad that's over!"

And glad indeed that she'd been able to work with that memory-charged siren singing constantly in the background. Lila shook her head again, this time vigorously enough to set her curls flopping.

Lila's fingers flew through the Alt+F+S key series that would save her work even as she leaned slightly forward to cast an experienced eye out the window. The sky was gloriously clear and the temperature had not inflated significantly as of yet, so she should be good to go.

"Be right back, Thunder!" Lila gave the unsuspecting cat a gentle stroke across his head and back before slipping out the door, shutting it carefully behind her and latching it from the outside. Lou had added this modification as a precaution against high winds tearing at the screen door when Lila was out for a walk or some such thing; Lila had never imagined she might be using it to help keep a cat inside when she was in residence.

A cat who was about to be examined by a visiting veterinarian who also just happened to be A. B.'s nephew.

Pangs of loss tore at Lila as she started along the trail that would lead her to the gate near where she'd parked, and where Jake would soon be waiting. For all the tears she'd shed for A. B. already, Lila knew she was nowhere through mourning her wild-yet-dignified friend.

But not more, not now.

No, not now. Lila straightened her back and blew out a deep breath over the erratic thumping of her heart. Now held enough to focus on, that was for certain: between Thunder, Jake, the increasing chattering of the object somewhere out there, and even the unmourned, newly dead Dave in Lila's latest novel. She should have been working on edits, but edits required more focus than she could possibly muster just now. And it had been exceptionally satisfying to kill Dave's character. Lila even looked forward to the aftermath of the death, which she rather thought she'd attend to promptly.

And then go "treasure-hunting" this afternoon or tomorrow morning, when the weather was right.

Lila didn't see Jake at the gate when it came into sight, but she kept up her pace anyway. She assumed he'd be driving the ATV again, but she had no real way of knowing and she wouldn't hear him approaching if he happened to be walking, or riding a horse.

The ubiquitous Wyoming wind was picking up as the land was leveling off, making waves out of the grasses around Lila and she loved it. She'd spent some time recording both the sight and the sound when she'd first purchased the property, trying to capture the way she felt when she was standing—as she was now—in the middle of the grassland ocean, but the ability of her camera to encompass such vastness was nothing near the reality of submerging herself in it.

"Helloooo!" Lila's attention was jerked right out of the moment by Jake's drawn-out greeting. She waved back, correcting her path towards the gate where Jake was now standing.

"Good morning," she said as she got near enough to see the ATV parked deep in the grasses along the fence where it sloped downhill from the gate's position. "I got blown off course a bit there—didn't see you!"

"The wind does have that effect, doesn't it?" Jake remarked, his easy smile causing Lila's heart to skip for another reason entirely from its earlier acrobatics. That smile ... so like A. B.'s! "Though I haven't always liked the sound, myself."

"No?" Lila added an upswing to the end of the word, a gentle question, but Jake just shook his head.

"I feel like I'm intruding." Jake reached over the fence and handed Lila a small bag. "Would you ... ?"

"Sure, no problem." Lila took the bag and then watched as Jake grasped the nearest worn fencepost with one hand, and barely bent the top wire with the other to cross it. "And you're not intruding at all. I can't tell you how much I appreciate you coming all the way out here to my Unibomber shack to check on my cat."

My cat? Well, yes, I guess Thunder's my cat now.

It still sounded odd, even in Lila's head, but Jake's next words demonstrated that he was focused on another phrase she'd uttered.

"'Unibomber shack?'"

Sadness and humor struck Lila simultaneously, and she ducked her head into the wind as she turned, clearing her throat with a light cough and hoping it sounded of dust stirred up by the wind rather than a knot of remembrance.

"Oh yes. And this way, sorry! You can see the trail better when we get into the trees. A. B. called it that, didn't you know? Kristen's husband, Lou—you met my friend Kristen when you ... well, you met her—brought it out here in pre-assembled sections on a flatbed. A. B. took one look at that and said, 'What are you building, then, a You-nee-bomber shack?'"

Jake chuckled then, and Lila turned to look, her own mouth crinkling in response.

"Yeah, that sounds like him. Just like him, in fact."

"He dragged it out like that. Three distinct syllables, 'You-nee-bomber.' Though I suppose it should be four, really."

And I shouldn't be focusing on comparing my home to a terrorist's hideout.

Lila caught herself just short of coughing again, which was good, since she didn't want to develop yet another nervous habit.

"It was such a shock," Jake said, his tone purely reflective. "When I got the call that he was gone, it was ... ."

Lila blinked back tears.

"I'm sure."

"We were close. Even though we couldn't be in the same house without getting into some kind of argument, we were close in all the ways that matter." And then Jake cleared his throat, and Lila spared a glance over his shoulder, even though they were just getting to the steepest part of the hike back to the cabin.

"I know," she said, catching his eyes.

Not from any object, either. Lila knew from the A. B.'s words and the way his wrinkled face had smoothed whenever he'd talked about Jake.

Jake smiled. A slight smile, but a true one.

"I thought I'd know. When he ... when he passed away. I thought I'd be able to feel it, somehow. I didn't really believe it until I was making the arrangements with Max."

"Max?" Lila was drawing a blank.

"Max Huxley, from Huxley Funeral Home. He and A. B. were good friends."

"The Shepherd."

"What?"

Again, Lila looked over her shoulder.

"If Max ... Huxley, did you say? ... is a pipsqueak of a man with the biggest handlebar mustache ever seen outside of Texas, then A. B. introduced him to me as 'The Shepherd.'"

"That's an accurate description of Max," Jake said, his voice now as dry as a typical Wyoming summer. "But I've never heard him called that."

Even though the hike was getting to Lila by this point, she felt obliged to explain.

"I sometimes decide to come out to my cabin on ... well, very short notice, let's say, but I always want to let A. B. know when I'm out here."

"He trespassed," Jake interjected. "Even after you bought the land."

Lila laughed at that, even though it made her even shorter of breath.

"Ah, I'm not used to the altitude yet," she explained with a gasp, waving her hand in front of her face but doggedly continuing to move up the slope to her cabin. "But yeah, A. B. trespassed when it suited him and I didn't want either one of us to keel over from shock if he happened upon me while I was ... well, while I was out here and he wasn't expecting me."

128

Lila bit her lip and quickened her pace, in spite of the altitude. She'd been about to say that she didn't want A. B. to ride onto her property while she was taking a shower, which she did outdoors here.

"Fair enough."

"Yes! So I arrived unexpected and decided to make a quick stop at A. B.'s just before going out to my cabin. I knocked on the door, and this tiny man with his tremendous mustache answered A. B.'s door, obviously three sheets to the wind ... "

"As A. B. would say."

"Right. And when he yelped, 'It's a WOMAN!' A. B. staggered up behind him and roared, 'That's no woman, that's Lila!'"

What started as a guffaw behind her degenerated in an instant to an outright giggle. A deep, masculine giggle, but a giggle nevertheless.

"And then?" Jake asked, when his mirth had passed and Lila remained silent.

"Well, then A. B. introduced the miniature man as 'The Shepherd'—which makes sense now, actually—and they invited me in to share what they advertised as a 'mighty fine whiskey.'"

The path was starting to level out again, and Lila paused, turning to face Jake, who nearly collided with her, his grin again splitting his face.

"Ah, whoops!" Lila took a step back, hurrying to finish her story. "I declined. I'm a lightweight, and I don't much care for whiskey. And there's my cabin!" She brandished her arm in the general direction of the cabin. "If you squint, look sideways through the trees, and know where to look, that is."

Jake was doing just that, in fact.

"I think you'll have to continue to lead the way," he said finally, admitting defeat.

"I'm glad. I wanted it to be hard to spot."

"Privacy is hard to come by."

"It can be." Lila started off again. The buzzing was louder as she came up the ridge. Maybe this could help her track down the object, if ...

"Nice!"

Jake's voice cut through Lila's tension-filled planning and she started, immediately hoping he hadn't seen. She forced a smile which grew more easily when Jake moved next to her, glimpsing her cabin for the first time. A. B., too, had been impressed when he'd finally seen the assembled structure, not commenting on the smallness of the place but on how neatly it fit into the small clearing, how it seemed to belong there.

"Home away from home!" She said aloud. "And I have to thank you again for coming out."

"Not a problem," Jake said. "I make more house calls for large animals than small at ... well, at my usual practice, but it's nice to get out and about in any case. Particularly to help a neighbor."

"We are neighbors now, aren't we? While you're here?" Lila smiled at him, though her smile slipped a little. Acquiring this neighbor had come at the cost of losing A. B., and Jake wasn't here to stay, at least, not yet. Judging from his own smile's deterioration, Jake was thinking the same thing.

"I miss him, too," Lila said simply, and caught Jake's hand with her own, giving it a quick squeeze. She didn't do this without thinking; Lila had learned to be careful with touch, lest she inadvertently contact a special watch or piece of jewelry. But as before, Jake's hands and arms were bare of such trappings.

After a moment, she pulled her hand back and turned to the cabin door.

"Would you like to meet your patient?" she asked.

10: Searching

Thunder was not eager to meet Jake, though not for lack of Jake's trying in that smooth voice of his that sounded like it had been coated in melted butter. Thunder had shot underneath the bed so fast that Lila wasn't sure he'd even actually seen Jake.

"I didn't even think. Kristen is going to bring me a cat carrier, but I never thought I'd need one while Thunder was still in the cabin!"

"I'm not in a hurry, Lila, don't worry about it. We can wait him out." Jake gestured to the high stool Lila kept near the kitchen counter. "May I?"

"Oh yes, please. Would you like something to drink? I have water, of course, also tea and coffee, and I have some juice ... "

"No, thanks." Jake seemed well at ease and so Lila finally admitted defeat, seating herself at her desk and trying to keep her mind in the moment. It had been a long time since she'd had someone new in her cabin.

"A. B. loved to talk about you," she finally said. "He was so proud."

Jake froze, his movements changing from easy fluidity to ice in an instant. His voice, when he spoke, was suddenly rough.

"What?"

"He talked about you, all the time. Not what you were doing, but who you were. Dedicated, determined ... " Jake seemed stunned and Lila paused before adding, "Sometimes wild."

Jake half-smiled at that. He coughed, and his voice was back on its way to silkiness when he spoke again.

"For all we rubbed each other the wrong way when we were together, I knew. I knew he was proud. I was, too."

Lila couldn't think of anything to say to that, so she nodded.

And then noticed the memory-charged mystery object again in the absolute silence that followed.

The stress must have shown on her face—and she wouldn't be surprised, given that she was the worst poker player she knew—because Jake's reflective expression shifted.

"It's so quiet," Lila whispered then. It took a lot of effort, because she practically wanted to shout, to drown the thing out.

Now it was Jake's turn to nod.

"One of many great things about Wyoming," he said, his smile returning in full. "Must be ideal for you!"

Still caught up in the buzzing of the thing, a mosquito she couldn't find to silence, Lila failed to follow Jake's train of thought.

"Oh, as a writer? Of course. Yes, of course." Flustered, Lila determined to get herself a drink, regardless of what her guest needed at this point. She slipped over to the refrigerator and selected a bottle of water.

"Good work!" Jake said in impossibly gentle tones as she turned back to her chair. Again, their conversation seemed to stutter for Lila, but when she looked at his face, he was looking past her. She followed his gaze.

Thunder had poked his head out around the corner.

"The sound of the refrigerator must have drawn him out," Jake said.

Lila took a long draught of her water before responding.

"I did feed him tuna a time or two. What should we do now?"

"Just sit back down." Jake kept his voice sweetly soft and Lila was pleased at his focus on calming Thunder.

Lila moved back to her desk, striving for deliberately casual and wondering how good of an actor one needed to be to fool a cat.

"Hey, Thunder! Come on, boy, it's okay."

Thunder's eyes flicked from Jake to Lila and back to Jake again.

"He's not buying it yet. Talk to me?" Jake said, his tone questioning even as his words were commanding. He turned away from Thunder to look directly at Lila, his eyes smiling along with the rest of his face. "Did you always want to be a writer?"

"Yes," Lila answered, shaking her head. And laughed as Jake's expression turned purely quizzical. "Yes and no, I guess. I never thought about it when I was a kid, but if I wasn't doing chores or homework, I was sure to be reading or writing."

"Seems like writing was your vocation from the start, then, even if you didn't know it."

"I guess." Lila wasn't entirely comfortable with the topic of how she became a writer, Jake's voice notwithstanding. He seemed to be determined to caress Thunder with his tone. "How about you? Did you always want to be ... " Lila shot a glance at Thunder, who had advanced only slightly from his previous, half-hidden position. " ... a v-e-t?"

Jake caught his laugh before it fully escaped and shook his own head. "Yes. I didn't run my own animal hospital or anything, but I always liked watching Bud—he was the "young vet" then—when he came out on a call."

"And now you work for him?"

"With him, he'd be quick to say." Jake sounded like he couldn't believe the turn of events himself. "Just temporarily. I'm in practice with another vet in Billings, but when ... well. Bud needs the help and I need the distraction."

Thunder's footsteps, while delicate in the extreme, were clearly audible in the silence that fell between Lila and Jake. Thunder reached the stool Jake was sitting on without wavering in his deliberate, stalking pace and raised himself up just enough to sniff at Jake's boots.

"Hi there," Jake said.

"He was much more cautious with Kristen," Lila said, thinking what Kristen might say about Thunder falling under Jake's spell and why wasn't Lila doing the same?

Why aren't I?

"Are you sure this cat is male?" Again, it took Lila a moment too long to comprehend Jake's question. The droning hum of the thing sang deep inside Lila's head, persistently embedded there despite the fact that she'd yet to see it.

Much less touch it.

"Pretty sure," Lila finally responded. "The ... external equipment ... did lead to that conclusion."

Jake snorted at this, and Thunder pulled back slightly.

"It's just that male calicos are rare. The cat needs two X chromosomes to be calico, so that means what you have here is a cat with two X chromosomes and a Y. Male, but sterile."

"Really?"

"Well, he could have some other sort of chromosomal abnormality. All of them are rare, but XXY is probably the most likely. He's not going to make you millions or anything," Jake went on, smiling at Thunder, who had resumed his nasal inspection of Jake's footwear. "But it's certainly unusual. And unless he starts spraying urine, you don't need to have him neutered."

"Huh. Well, I'm not about to sell him to a circus anyway," Lila said firmly. "Though it is odd ... it's odd, what you said."

Lila plugged her mouth with her water bottle as Jake bent forward, offering his fingers for Thunder's perusal. She'd been about to say that it was strange for two freaks of nature to wind up in the same small cabin!

After a detailed examination of Jake's fingertips, Thunder butted his head on Jake's hand. Jake eased out of his chair and after a testing stroke along Thunder's back, began moving his hands in a more purposeful way over Thunder's body.

134

"Just like that?" Lila's tone was more rueful than she intended.

"I have a way with animals." Jake said, smiling up at her. "But if you could get my bag, that'd be very helpful."

Lila was more than happy to be able to assist, even if it was tricky to maneuver her way around the impromptu exam area on her floor.

"Designed for one," she commented on her return, setting the bag down next to Jake. "The cabin."

Jake glanced around himself, as if he had not previously noticed where he was.

"It's small, alright," Jake replied. "But cozy, not cramped. Do you get visitors often?" He nodded to Thunder, and so Lila crouched down next to the pair of them and took over the task of holding Thunder to prevent an escape the cat did not seem to have any intention of making.

"Not often. Kristen comes out when she can, but I'm usually sequestered here alone. Not really by choice, but ... it can be ... necessary, I guess I'd say."

"I understand." There was a depth of meaning in those two small words, making Lila look up from Thunder's body. Jake's eyes were close, so sharp and focused on her own.

Could he really understand? Of course he couldn't.

The moment passed like a scene in which an animated character drops off a cliff ... with a remarkably long pause before gravity resumes and restores normalcy.

"He seems to be in pretty good shape," Jake said, his eyes dropping back to Thunder, who was now purring up a storm. "I'll take a look at his teeth after I give him his shots. Any sign of worms?"

"Worms?"

"I've got standard dewormer here, but if you've seen any signs of tapeworm, for instance, I'd want to give him a different medication."

"Kristen didn't mention ... worms."

"Haven't you owned a cat before?"

"No. No, I haven't. I like cats, but I just ... writing, traveling, I haven't had a pet since I was a kid. And that was a dog. Worms, really?"

Jake laughed.

"It's not that bad. And it's pretty difficult to get infected from your cat, unless you're awfully lax with your hygiene."

"I beg your pardon," Lila said, and recovered enough to put a huff into her voice when she said it.

Jake laughed again.

"Let me finish up here and we'll take a look at where he's been sleeping, and in the litter box. I saw that earlier, has he been using it?"

"He took right to it," Lila said.

"Sand is probably where he's used to going; you made the transition easy for him." Jake sounded approving.

"It's all been pretty easy. I didn't have to do much ... although, worms ... "

"I didn't see any signs looking him over," Jake said, syringe now in hand. "Don't worry too much."

"How does one worry too much about worms? No, don't answer that, I don't want to know. If you don't see any signs, we'll call it good. Though why Kristen didn't mention the possibility ... "

"She has cats?" Jake smoothly injected Thunder while he spoke.

"She does. Nero and Hercules."

"Purebreds?" Jake sounded faintly disapproving at the possibility. He delivered another shot to Thunder, who twitched his tail but did not otherwise react.

"No, Kristen just goes big with names. She got them from a shelter."

"There you go," Jake said, warming again almost instantly.

"Shelters take care of worming, and usually spaying or neutering as well. But this little guy—and yes, he does have the 'external equipment' to prove it—doesn't even have ear mites, so I have to think his chances of not having worms is decent, too. Lucky boy! Now, let's take a look at those teeth ... "

Thunder was less than enthused with Jake's brief examination of his mouth, but it was over quickly and Jake convinced Thunder to submit to a cheek scratching afterwards.

"You do have a way with animals."

"I do my best." Jake said, winking at Thunder.

Kristen would be appalled that the wink hadn't been for her. Lila grinned and stood, dusting off her hands as she did so.

I really should have swept the floor again.

"So, ahh, you said, check the litter box? What ... what do we have to look for?"

Jake unfolded himself from the floor with considerably more grace than Lila. He stepped next to the litter box with her and calmly educated Lila on what to look for to spot the presence of worms. Thunder poked his head over the edge of the box during the lecture but then bolted when Lila picked up the slotted spoon she'd permanently demoted to serving as a litter-box scoop to excavate one of Thunder's droppings.

"You know, they make special sifters just for scooping," Jake commented dryly.

Lila's laugh came out in an awkward bark, half-laugh, half-cough.

"Yes, but I had to improvise at first! And then it just made more sense to buy a new spoon for the kitchen."

"I can see that. What I can't see, you'll be happy to know, is any sign of worms."

"That's good! But you said something about checking where he sleeps, too?"

Jake nodded.

"Right around the corner, at the foot of my bed," Lila said, pointing. "I'm just going to wash up quick."

"Thunder acted like I'd lost my mind the first time I scooped his litter box," Lila continued as she gave her hands a quick scrubbing in the sink. "You should've seen the look he gave me."

"He wondered what he'd gotten himself into, huh?"

"I guess!" Lila grinned, still drying her hands as she stepped into the doorway to her tiny bedroom.

Jake was crouching beside the bed, peering across its surface.

"What are you looking for again?"

"The descriptions you read most often are that bits of tapeworm look like dried-up bits of rice," Jake said, sounding very casual about it.

"Lovely!"

"I think it's more like shreds of antique parchment paper that's been layered and baked in the sun for a few years," Jake said, standing. And then he chuckled, probably on account of Lila's expression. "Or maybe I'm just trying to impress the lady writer here. I think that's what A. B. was after, giving you the cows."

And Lila, who prided herself on her exceptional skills with words and their precise meaning, could not think of anything to say to that. It took her a ridiculous amount of time to remember to close her mouth.

Just as Jake was beginning to look uncomfortable, Lila came up with a single word.

"What?"

"The cows," Jake said, speaking slowly, as if that would help. "That's what was in your letter, wasn't it?"

"How did you ... "

"I got a letter, too, and A. B. made a point of telling me to help you with the cows. '#225 and a few of her friends?' I think he was trying to push us together."

The thought of A. B. as matchmaker had never entered Lila's

mind, but she considered it now, and clutched the towel she was still holding in both hands as she did. It made an unlikely bridal bouquet, she thought irreverently, and dropped both hands to her sides at the very idea.

Jake was watching her, one corner of his mouth quirking upwards.

"I did wonder why he'd think I'd want cattle out here," Lila said finally, still flummoxed. "I never pictured A. B. as Cupid!"

Jake laughed again then, and Lila smiled up at him, even though he now seemed a bit too close, as they both stood there in front of her bed. She came back to the present so suddenly that she might have dropped into it, almost hearing the thud of her very being impacting the timeline.

"Okay, A. B.'s nefarious scheming aside, what about the worms? Did you find anything?"

Jake's expression flitted between chagrin and amusement, with amusement taking the win in fairly short order. "No signs of them. I'll leave you a standard treatment, just in case, but it looks like Thunder's lucked out in a lot of ways."

"Is that weird?"

"A little, I'd say. But maybe he hasn't been on his own for long."

Thunder slipped into the silence that fell between them and leapt up on the bed, emitting tiny snorts as he inspected its surface with his nose.

"Looks like he's doing his own check," Jake said.

"I wonder what A. B. would think of him?" Lila said, rather suspecting he'd be pleased. "Other than how nicely he fit into the scheme?"

Jake grinned.

"That'd probably be all A. B. needed to approve," he said, smiling, and Lila smiled back at him. She figured she looked just as sad underneath her smile as Jake looked underneath his.

It really should have been an uncomfortable situation. Lila wasn't about to fall into A. B.'s scheme, despite Jake's good looks and apparent openness—he didn't seem to be disappointed that she wasn't falling into his arms, after all—but should-have-beens aside, Lila found A. B.'s plotting almost sweet.

Though it did make her wonder when he'd written the letters.

"Was your letter dated?"

"No," Jake said, shaking his head and then moving forward as if he intended to ease past Lila—not a simple task, given the small space of her home and the smaller confines of the bedroom. She stepped around the corner to let him navigate more easily. "He could have been plotting this for years."

"He certainly could have!" Lila agreed, moving back into the kitchen area and finally ridding herself of the towel on which she'd dried her hands to aridness. "Although probably not too long. #225 is ... well, what? Maybe six years old?"

"I have no idea." Jake heaved a sigh as he stood, his bag in hand. "I don't know what I'm going to do with the ranch, either."

He looked so disconsolate just then, Lila felt a wash of sympathy.

"Would you want to come back here to talk ... and for dinner?" Lila said, mindful of her plans for an afternoon of searching for signs of the thing that continued to mutter away, despite the abundance of distractions.

Jake's expression gave nothing away, and Lila hurried on.

"Unless that's too weird. Like my cat, I mean." She smiled, hoping it made her words and her offer more appetizing. "I'd suggest Mavie's, you know, in town, but I don't really ... well, I don't eat out much."

Especially not when her ability to endure the buzzing of memory-heavy objects she'd be likely to encounter in a public place was at a low point. At least the annoyances here were singular, as far as Lila could tell. And maybe, just maybe, she'd be able to find that thing yet today!

Jake was nodding and smiling again now.

"I'm good with the weird I've seen here so far. Seriously, it sounds like a great deal for me. I'm not that much of a cook," Jake said. "But I could bring a little something, at least. Rolls? Maybe some wine?"

"That'd be great!" Lila thought again that she should be feeling some trepidation, maybe making sure that Jake knew that all she was offering was a friendly ear, but all she really was feeling was ... content. He was A. B.'s nephew—that made him feel almost like family.

Family!

Lila cleared her throat. "About six o'clock?" That should give her enough time to conduct her search, and then clean up and assess her options for dinner.

"Six it is." Jake nodded. "I can find my own way from the gate."

After a light lunch, Lila strapped on her fanny pack, slathered her exposed skin with sunscreen, and headed out to find out the thing that had infiltrated her property. She still couldn't fathom what it was, but she knew that it wasn't far away. The grating, insistent background noise in Lila's mind had seemed to escalate after Jake left the cabin, probably on account of the fact that without Jake there, she had only Thunder for distraction. And he was a good distraction, Thunder, though he didn't speak beyond purrs and the occasional meow.

Finding the memory-laden object was Lila's priority now, and perhaps because she'd spent far more time evading chattering objects than locating them, she found herself struggling with the process. The noise in her head would get louder for awhile and then softer; she'd backtrack to try to find it getting louder again only to then discover the clatter dropped off no matter which new direction she tried.

She went up and down the various ridges of her property, and the actual surface area was much larger than the nominal acreage she'd purchased. Lila felt that she was covering every inch of the land, though of course she wasn't. She hadn't gone East and Up, for example, but that was only because she felt quite strongly that the thing lay somewhere South and Down. Regardless of her approach, however, she just couldn't seem to zero in on her target.

At one point, hands on her hips and outrage on the tip of her tongue, Lila had a flashback to watching *The Lone Ranger*—reruns of the classic series—with her parents, remembering their shared delight whenever a villain was tracked down.

"Tonto could find this thing," Lila grumbled aloud. "Though for sure he'd tell me I sucked."

In addition to losing each and every iota of her patience, Lila was fast losing the last of her resolve when it occurred to her to try something different. She found a moderately-sized boulder in the shade of some pines and flopped on top of it. After finishing the last of the water she'd brought with her, Lila leaned back, closed her eyes, and regulated her breathing.

It seemed to take a long time for her frustration to ebb and for the whispering of the pines to fade into the background of the object of Lila's quest. Behind the relative darkness cast by her eyelids, Lila strove to focus only on the noise generated by the unknown thing. And then, as her concentration deepened, Lila envisioned a convergence ... a point of origin ... a single trail leading to ...

She sat bolt upright.

"The map! I need the aerial map!"

Lila had to laugh at her herself then, and she did. Here she'd gone off all determined and focused, and then attempted to get mystical. In the end, all she'd gotten was sweaty and dirty. But then again, if she hadn't gone through the frustration and then innovation of this afternoon, it might not have occurred to her to use the map.

Which, granted, she might have thought of if she had just taken the time to actually *think*.

Lila fished her cell phone out of her pocket and checked the time.

"Good grief!"

It was almost four o'clock. And Jake was coming back in only a couple of hours!

I have to get cleaned up, again, and figure out what to cook, and I think I have to actually wash my hair, not just dry-shampoo it again, and ... The drone of the thing bubbled up between Lila's roiling thoughts.

And, if I have any extra time at all, I have to trace the map and try to figure out where that noisy thing IS!

Lila stood, oriented herself with the sun and a rock outcropping to her left, and turned to follow the ridge she was on back in the general direction of the cabin. She knew her property well and had named several of the larger rocks based on their shapes. Between those landmarks and the old logging trails that still remained, 20-odd years after A. B. had permitted harvesting of some of the trees, Lila could find her way to almost anywhere she wanted to go.

Of course, she frequented certain areas more than others due to her own personal preference. Now that she thought about it, it made sense that the object wasn't in any of those spaces. If it were, she might have stumbled across it before, or maybe some sign that it was ...

Lila stopped in her tracks, a fragment of memory tugging at her so intensely that it almost seemed physical. Something A. B. said before she'd bought the property—she'd asked, what was it?—and his demeanor had changed like a flipped switch.

"How long have you owned this property?" Lila remembered asking.

"Since I bought it." A. B. answered, but his ready smile had vanished. Lila had thought that odd, but she'd gone on anyway.

"I saw an old house to the South. It looked like it had been burned."

"That's on another parcel of land." And A. B., who never turned away from anyone that Lila ever saw, had turned away from her.

That was it. A. B's flat delivery might have been mistaken for taciturnity on its surface, but Lila had heard immeasurable pain in the simple words; when he'd literally moved away from their conversation, Lila had no desire to follow further. There weren't many spots on her land from which she could see that desecrated homestead—now part of Spencer's empire—but putting all of the pieces together, Lila was becoming more and more convinced that the thing she sought was not only to the South, but also related to the burned-out house she'd all but forgotten.

Lila reached one of the logging trails and turned sharply to follow it. This trip to Wyoming was shaping up to be unusual in a lot of ways. Not only was she going to be sharing dinner with Jake, it looked like she would also be going trespassing on Spencer's land.

11: Dinner

"That was good!" Jake said again.

He'd been generous in his praise for the simple meal Lila had prepared, though not unbelievably so. She hadn't been concerned about the lack of complexity of the dish she'd chosen—pasta in a tomato sauce seasoned with a mix of her own creation—because she knew it was delicious.

"I'm glad you liked it. If it hasn't got pasta in it, I usually won't cook it," she said with a smile and shrug. "I like to keep things simple."

Jake smiled.

"Your place, your choice! I'm the same way about wine." He picked up their glasses, which had been unused during the meal. "Do you want to try the Riesling now? It's a good dessert wine, though this particular one isn't as sweet as some."

"Yes, I'll try it," Lila said, rising from her desk. She'd managed to turn it into a reasonable approximation of a dining table for the occasion, but it was still somewhat awkward, she realized now. "I'm not a wine aficionado by any means, but I do enjoy sampling. Just let me clear our plates out of the way ... "

In the time it took Lila to move the plates to the sink, Jake had opened the wine, which he'd brought along in a small cooler.

"I cheated," he confessed as he began to pour the wine into Lila's glass. At Lila's blank look, he held up the cap of the bottle with his free hand. "Screw-top. Simple, like you said!"

"Oh!" Lila laughed and shook her head. "Fine by me."

"You were saying that you use a lot of dehydrated foods when you're here?" Jake asked, pouring his own glass.

Lila nodded.

"Yes. With such a small refrigerator, I've had to get a little more inventive to make sure I'm not eating pasta and only pasta—not that I'd have a problem doing that, but as much fun as it would be, I know it wouldn't be good for me in the long run. So I dehydrate a few fruits and vegetables, which is nice because they're light-weight. Though I do bring in some canned goods, too."

"A. B. ... ," Jake began, and then stopped, his smile fading a bit. He restored it with obvious effort and raised his glass. "Here's to A. B."

Lila touched her glass lightly to Jake's and they both sipped the wine, which was faintly sweet.

"This is lovely!" Lila said, and Jake nodded his agreement. "But you were saying?"

"A. B. talked about you a lot, too. I don't know how I didn't manage to meet you sooner ... I did hear about you."

Lila felt her throat constrict.

"He was a good man," she finally said.

"He was. A character, too."

"That's for sure." The mist behind Lila's eyes eked out a little, but then she remembered the gates and laughed. "Did he tell you about the gates?"

Jake's expression went blank for a moment, but then awareness dawned and he grinned.

"Spencer kept tightening them and A. B. kept loosening them? Yeah, he told me. It was real cloak-and-dagger stuff the way he described it."

"I can just imagine," Lila said, the lump in her throat softened by the humor of the memory.

They both fell silent, but it was a pleasant sort of silence. An evening breeze slipped through the window and brushed lightly across their hands where they rested, Lila's on the stem of her wineglass and Jake's on the table near his glass.

"You know, I can't remember the last time I had these out." Lila said, lifting her glass again.

"You don't drink much wine?"

"I don't drink much at all, really," Lila said. "But every now and again ... but anyway, these are pretty glasses, and I was thinking I should use them more often. I could use them for water!"

"Why not!"

This time, Lila's smile was entirely for Jake. She felt like the smile on his face was directed right at her, too. It was easy, friendly ... almost comfortable..

"So. You inherited the ranch."

Jake's smile folded in on itself, flattening, like origami in reverse.

"Yes, and I don't know what to do about it. I'm not ... this land ... " He heaved a sigh. "This land doesn't have the hold on me that it did on A. B., but I know he wanted me to have it."

"You wouldn't have to decide right away, would you?" Lila asked, even as Jake began to shake his head. "You could lease out the land ... "

"Not unless I sold off the cattle, too," Jake pointed out.

"Oh, that's true." Lila frowned that she hadn't considered that point, and stared accusingly at her nearly-full wine glass, as if the missing sips were at fault. And then she almost laughed. "Yes, I suppose even if you offloaded #225 ... "

"And some friends!" Jake said the words with her.

" ... on me tomorrow, it wouldn't make that much of a dent in A. B.'s herd."

"No; that much I'm sure of," Jake said, and his grin now was rueful.

"And you really think he wanted to try to ... to get us to ... ?" Jake was nodding, looking quite serious, but even as she tried to entertain the idea, Lila's thoughts stumbled over an unexpected flaw in that logic. "Then why did he tell me Spencer should help me with fencing, too?"

"What?" Jake nearly spit out the wine he'd been sipping.

"My letter ... hold on, now how did he put it exactly?" Lila rose, wine glass in hand, and retrieved the letter from her bedroom. "Here," she said, holding it out to him. "Go ahead, it's not long."

Lila slid back into her seat, setting her wine back down without tasting it further, her eyes locked on Jake's face as he read A. B.'s last words to her.

"'Spencer will help if you need fencing,'" Jake said, shaking his head and setting the letter down between then when he finished reading. "Well, I don't know, Lila! This makes my idea about A. B. wanting to throw us together seem silly. He told me to see Spencer if I didn't want to try to keep up with the rest of the cattle ... something to that effect."

Jake frowned, his eyes falling to Lila's letter and then slowly floating back up to her face. "I thought it seemed like he was pushing me towards you, but now it seems like he wanted all three of us to get to know each other, for whatever reason."

"That certainly knocks the romantic aspect out of the picture," Lila said wryly, trying to lighten the mood, but Jake seemed lost in disconcerted thought.

"It does that," he said belatedly, and gave her a tiny quirk of a smile. "And there wasn't a letter for Spencer."

"Oh!"

They both stared at Lila's letter then, as if it were the third person in the unusual triad that A. B. had apparently been attempting to form.

"Think we're reading too much into it?" Jake said, breaking through the trance.

Lila tipped her head, considering.

"I have been known to do that," she said. "But A. B. wasn't one to do or say things without a reason, either."

"That's true," Jake said, grimacing. He leaned back in his chair suddenly. "I remember once, when I took off with the truck to go to a party—I couldn't have been more than a few days over 17 at the time, because A. B. had just started letting me use the truck, with permission—and he came after me on horseback."

Lila could already envision it.

Jake shook his head, chagrin flowing off every movement. "He never did say how he found out, but he got to the site almost faster than I did, because he went cross-country, and I'd barely cracked open a can of beer when he showed up. And all he said was, 'Jake, you can call yourself a borrower or a wronged man all you want, but you take my truck without asking again and I'll report it stolen and tell them my brother's boy was the one that did it.'"

"That seems a little harsh," Lila said. "And he said this in front of everyone you knew?"

Jake nodded, but he was smiling a little.

"The girl I wanted to impress more than anything was there, too. It made me angry, but it made me think. A. B. could've done a lot of things and I would've been able to convince myself that he was the one in the wrong, but he just said what he'd come to say, held out his hands for the keys to the truck, and then left me with his horse."

"He left you with his horse?" Lila repeated.

"Yes. And I rode home without so much as finishing that one beer. I realized I was doing just what he wanted. I knew Falcon could probably find his way home without any direction from me, too, but I found the idea of being responsible for one of the horses a lot more terrifying than being responsible for the truck."

"As A. B. intended," Lila said, nodding now herself. "Because of your affinity for animals."

"Yes, and yes again. And all that to your point ... A. B. says and does things for a reason."

"So he wants each of us to talk to Spencer. Do you think it's just what he said? For fencing and for unloading the cattle?" Before Jake could speak, Lila went on. "I don't think it is. Because I don't want cattle, and I certainly don't want Spencer making more gates I'll have trouble opening!"

"Well, I'm pretty sure I don't want cattle, either," Jake said. "Maybe I'll talk to him."

"Have you ever? Talked to him, I mean?" Lila asked.

"No, actually, I haven't."

"Neither have I," Lila said, and it sounded more like an admission when she said it, like something she should be sorry for. She wasn't sure why.

"Well, this is weird," Lila said, before she could censor the thought. Jake was in agreement with her, though.

"It certainly is," he said, and raised his nearly-empty glass to her half-full one. "To A. B., again. The man can still make us think."

They fell silent once more, sipping their wine and each reflecting, Lila supposed, on their own internal dialogues.

Jake finished his wine and poured himself a smaller, second serving. He held the bottle out towards Lila, asking without words if she would like some as well, but she shook her head.

"Did you know A. B. read all your books?"

Lila, who had just been raising her glass, set it back down with a little thump. The wine swirled about haphazardly, not unlike the thoughts in her head at the moment.

"No?" Jake smiled.

"No! I sent him a signed copy of *August's Feint* when I bought this land, but he never ... he never said a word. I certainly didn't know he'd gotten the rest! Are you sure ... "

"There's about ... ten? Maybe a dozen of them, and someone read them, I can guarantee that," Jake said firmly. "There was one—I don't remember the title—something about a light? A beacon, maybe? It was pretty dog-eared, that one."

Lila shook her head. She had exactly a baker's dozen books to her name now, and it sounded like if A. B. didn't have them all, he did have the bulk of them. "*A Paltry Beacon* wasn't well-received at all, but I always liked it. I wonder what A. B. thought?" Her voice faded as she realized she'd never know, even with her special abilities. Paper was not conducive to retaining memories.

"I don't take much time for reading," Jake said, sounding apologetic. "When I do, it's usually something related to work."

"It's all related to my work," Lila said. She had to force her smile a little.

"I suppose it is at that. It must be something, being able to make up stories in your head."

Because the truth was somewhat more complicated than that—complicated, and convoluted—Lila could only nod. It was, indeed, "something."

"It can be," she said at last. "Right now, I've got a new story I'm involved in, but I'm supposed to be editing a different piece for RayAnn—my agent—and it's a constant struggle to force myself to do that, instead of working on the new story." She laughed. "I'm mostly working on the new piece."

Jake smiled.

"What I like most about veterinary medicine are the animals, of course, but also that the field is always changing. New ideas, new techniques. You'd think I'd be up for the challenge of the ranch, but I just don't know."

"It didn't come to you … in a way that's easy to accept." Lila chose her words carefully, skirting the word "death," but she and Jake both knew it was there. "That alone has to make it more difficult to handle."

"I'm sure that's part of it. I know I'm fortunate that I can take some time away to think about it, although while I do, I'm missing out on meeting the new vet in my office at home."

"Billings, right?"

"Yes, Billings. And you? Somewhere east, I take it?"

"Wisconsin," Lila said. "A little town on the Mississippi you've probably never heard of and most people can't spell. Trempealeau."

Jake grinned.

"I don't even want to try to spell that. French, is it?"

"Yes. There's a mountain—well, not like the mountains in Wyoming, but they call it Trempealeau Mountain—and it stands in the water. I think that's where the name comes from, something about the mountain with its feet wet? I should know this, but I mix up the Native American stories with the ones from the French explorers."

"You haven't had that much wine!"

Lila chuckled at that.

"I don't need that much wine! It's a thing I have, along with an inability to learn how my car works. I mix up historical facts in my head. It makes RayAnn's job that much harder, fact-checking and such."

"Now that sounds like a handicap for a writer."

"It depends. It means I need a good editor, yes, but it also means that my characters can be more believable, in a way. People don't get all their facts straight in real life, either, so they shouldn't always in novels." Lila eyed Jake closely. He seemed to be listening, but she wasn't sure.

"Hmm."

In the silence that slithered between them then, a rumble of Thunder's namesake spoke up, distant but firm.

Jake bent forward to peer out the nearest window. "I'd better get back if I want to beat the weather."

"I don't think I've ever seen it rain this much out here!" Lila said, rising to help Jake collect his cooler and the light jacket he'd brought along. Whether his escape was opportunistic or timely, she decided, didn't really matter. It had still been a good evening.

"It's unusual for sure. In fact, I don't think it's rained this much since ... " Jake's voice trailed off then, and Lila saw his lips press firmly together before he turned towards the door. Whatever he'd been about to say was clearly and irrevocably stopped.

"Thanks again for dinner," he did say, surprising Lila with a hug that was delivered too quickly to be construed as anything significant, no matter what A. B.—or Kristen—might have wished. "And for the 'food for thought,' too."

And then Jake was gone, with distant thunder continuing to mutter. Lila stood on the porch for a moment, listening to it, and listening to the whine of the memory-tied object intermingling with it.

"We're all out here talking to ourselves," she observed quietly.

But not for long.

Lila stiffened her spine and stepped back inside.

Her glass was, perhaps prophetically, still half-full. She picked it up and sipped it slowly. Thunder clattered again, closer than before, perhaps, but not appreciably so. But the sky was distinctly darkening, bringing premature shadows into the cabin. Lila finished the wine too rapidly, knowing she was doing so, and then turned slowly in restitution.

The dishes awaited.

The next sound of Thunder was a meow, and the hollowness of the sound was likely due to the fact that he was somewhere under Lila's bed again. Regardless of location, the hunger in the cat's tone was unmistakable.

"Thunder! I forgot to feed you!"

Lila reassigned the dishes to a lesser status of importance— dishes would be used to such downgrades, if they had any sensibilities whatsoever—and hurried to scoop Thunder's supper for him. He poked his nose out from under the bed but did not scamper out, so Lila crouched and slid the bowl towards him.

The metal made a scratchy sound as it moved across the wooden floor of the cabin, but Thunder didn't flinch from that. He must have felt safe enough from his namesake in his little den underneath Lila's bed, for he began to munch away at his meal.

"Weird little cat," Lila said, giving the top of his head a quick petting. "Lucky little cat, too."

Natural light in the cabin was now dwindling as fast as water running out of a drain. Between the approach of the storm clouds and the setting of the sun, Lila's candles were fighting a losing battle. Not needing to get into any dark corners this evening, Lila turned on a small, battery-powered lantern and determinedly approached the dishes. Twice as numerous as usual, they demanded completion before bed.

It had been a nice evening. Interesting, too, with all the intrigue that A. B. had set in motion. The man was seeming more and more like a master manipulator, and the thought had Lila smiling slightly as she filled the tea kettle with water to boil for washing dishes. Her smile faltered only a little when she paused in front of the window above the sink and "heard" the buzzing of the memory-intense thing more strongly there. It was distinct and annoying, apparently penetrating the glass of the cabin's windows more easily than its walls. Lila felt her jaw, neck, and shoulders tensing in response.

Tomorrow. Tomorrow, she would do something about it.

Although ... now that she was thinking about it, that aerial map might still come in handy. Lila turned away from the stove, trusting it to work on the water she needed to wash the dishes, and slipped back into the bedroom.

"Sorry to bother you, Thunder," she murmured. Of course, the box she needed was the seldom-used one in the back.

Lila wrestled her flashlight from where it had gotten stuck between the mattress and wall, and then knelt on the floor to peer under the bed. Thunder blinked when she shined the light in his eyes.

"Don't worry. I just need a box ... " Lila moved the light away from Thunder, shining it through the gaps between the neatly-aligned plastic boxes under the bed. "Aha! There it is."

Thunder seemed determined to hold his position, so Lila shifted the box blocking her target carefully, so as not to further decrease the size of the narrow tunnel between boxes that the cat was occupying. Lila extracted the dusty container and replaced the box that had blocked it just as the stove brought the tea kettle to boiling.

The cut-off shrieking of the tea kettle when Lila arrested its call let the ominous rumbling outside take center stage in the night's erratic symphony again. Lila cast a sympathetic glance in the direction of the bedroom; this certainly wasn't the quiet evening Thunder would have ordered if he had been in charge.

She transferred the box from the counter, where she'd briefly abandoned it to deal with the tea kettle, to the desk. Since she'd cleared off the desk in order to press it into service as a dining room table, she had plenty of room to unpack the box there.

She forced herself to do the dishes first, though.

Once that chore was resolved, Lila moved to the desk and soon located the aerial map with her property lines neatly delineated. She opened the map to lay it out in its entirety; this took some doing, since it had been several years since she'd packed it into the box with a few seldom-used reference books, spare notepads, and an "emergency" roll of fluffy toilet paper. The folds of the map were in full-on rebellion at having to unfurl.

While large, the map was old enough that it didn't show Spencer's new, ungainly home and its lone outbuilding located over several intervening ridges in the relatively distant Southeast. But the burned-out remains of the old house Lila had spotted when she was scouting her own property did appear. And while she couldn't be totally sure, Lila was more confident now than ever that she'd felt the thing more strongly in areas that aligned, unblocked by hills, with the ashes of the old home.

The dim shadows outside that had not already been overwhelmed by the setting sun and advancing clouds faded entirely into blackness while Lila pored over the map. She knew her property well, but by feel rather than by latitude, longitude, or whatever fractions thereof were represented on the map. Still, there were two stretches she knew she'd walked during her hunt today and they were both neatly aligned with the scar on the map that denoted the remains of the burned house.

"Ugh!" Lila ran her hands through her curls and shook her head over the map. She could trace straight lines with her fingers over this map all night but she wasn't going to know for sure until morning. There was just no way.

The storm appeared to have drifted slightly north, with nary a drop of rain to splatter against the metal roof of Lila's cabin.

"Thunder! Get your furry butt ready to come out from under that bed!"

Thunder did not dignify Lila's feeble witticism with a reply, but Lila did hope the diminishing sounds of atmospheric disturbance would help soothe his nerves. It was lovely waking up with a warm body next to her own again, and Lila was fast becoming enamored of the experience.

When she returned from brushing her teeth, Thunder peeked around the bedroom corner and greeted her with a low-toned "meow." Lila imagined he didn't want to wake the noisy storm gods outside again, and found herself charmed when Thunder followed up his quiet greeting with what she would have sworn was a wink.

Yes, she would have sworn thus if Thunder hadn't immediately sat down to scratch at the eye that had twitched with one back foot.

"It's been a long day, cat ... let's get some rest."

Lila turned off the mini-lantern and the candles in the kitchen, almost—almost—not minding the ongoing whine of the thing she was going to search for tomorrow.

To search for, and to find.

In fact, she was almost excited by the idea. Not that it would be a cure, of course, because objects didn't just stop "talking" to her after she touched them. But they generally were reduced to distant, tolerable whispering—as if, having been truly heard once, they experienced some kind of relief.

It was the one facet of Lila's gift/curse that she could appreciate in an extrinsic sense, that there was a balance to it. In exchange for enduring the generally intense memories stored in an object, the volume of that object's story was reduced substantially. If only it wasn't so hard on Lila to absorb those memories in the first place!

"If only ... " Tears sprang to Lila's eyes and she scrubbed them away with one hand while patting the space next to her with the other, hoping to summon Thunder.

The breeze teased its way through the open window, soothing and sweet, but hardly enough for comfort.

Ifs were futile sprouts, choking the substance of reality like weeds crowding a garden. And further, a waste of time! It was hard enough to see things as they were—and in Lila's case, the way things were was inescapably woven into the fabric of the way they currently existed—without clouding the scene with "if only," too.

Movement near her feet, a "thud" muted by the bedding, brought Lila back to the moment. She drummed her fingers again, and felt Thunder's movement as he stepped towards her, signaling his arrival at her hand by bumping his head up against her skin.

"There you are." Lila scratched at the cat's fur, tentatively at first, and then with vigor as Thunder leaned into her. His purring, which began in a low-pitched rumble, soon escalated into an outright raucous sound.

With Thunder humming in the tune of his people at Lila's hand, his happiness clear and present, and the distant-near thing calling out to her with the unbearable weight of whatever memories it harbored, the idea of balance again struck Lila. She faltered in her ministrations to Thunder, and he butted his head against her once more, leaning forward so far that he flopped down out of his crouch into a sprawl beside her.

"Sorry, boy," Lila whispered, and rolled slowly towards the cat, so as to give her left hand a break. Thunder accepted the change in position and resumed his purring.

Somewhere out there, the thing that was summoning Lila continued to bray, unaffected by anything so capricious as human hands and their tendency to tire. And even as Lila's eyelids grew heavy—she thought more on account of Thunder's close proximity and that crazy, endearing purr than anything else—she realized that this, too, was another sort of equilibrium.

Human beings had, after all, brought this thing to life, somehow imbuing it with their stories. And it was going to take a human being's touch to dampen the siren of powerful memory.

It was going to take Lila's touch.

12: Trespassing

The day started well enough. Lila breakfasted early, texted Kristen, and proceeded to work on the aftermath of Dave's death in her novel, even with the mystery object buzzing in the background.

Though the first round of storms had missed the cabin, the next had hit full-on in the middle of the night, so Thunder was a bit bleary-eyed, having flung himself out of pleasant slumber back underneath the bed when round two struck. He'd stirred himself for breakfast along with Lila, and then retired to nap in the fuzzy sunlight that struggled through the cloud-heavy morning sky to barely warm the bed. Lila tested the grasses on her first trip to the outhouse and found them to be cloyingly damp, so she determined that she would write some more while she waited for the traditional, arid magic of Wyoming to reassert itself.

And that, Lila thought, was the turning point in the story of her day. The next chapter of her novel turned from straightforward to convoluted and her thoughts from clear to murky. After making a mess of a beginning and then stewing over it for far too long, Lila eventually decided to take a break. But then she'd elbowed her napkin too close to the propane burner of the stove while heating water for tea. The resulting smoke and flame scared her, but not to the degree that her initial shriek terrorized Thunder.

After the inadvertent napkin fire was safely extinguished and Thunder metaphorically peeled from the ceiling—how high could her new roommate jump, anyway?—Lila found herself confronting shaky hands and a brain that was just as jittery. She was too traumatized to return to crafting a compelling scene anytime soon, particularly a scene that had become problematic. What difference did it make if she got a little wet around the ankles on her quest? The thought was like an adolescent's shrug, cocky and daring.

Reality was a wet blanket, almost literally. Lila was soon thoroughly soaked from toe to knee and although her legs were hardly model-proportioned, the drenched distance was both impressive and oppressive. The abundant remains of last night's storm soaked through denim, socks, and tennis shoes. Further, the leftover rain that clung to the nearly-luxuriant flora was cold! And as a final indignity, Lila didn't realize she'd left her cell phone in the cabin until she was nearly at the southern fence-line of her property.

"Oh for the love of baby bunnies," she scowled, checking her pockets again. She even pulled the snakebite kit out of her fanny-pack, but her phone remained stubbornly absent.

She was so close to Spencer's terrain! In spite of her absolute code to carry her cell phone with her everywhere she went, Lila was loathe to return to the cabin, particularly since the hike was uphill from here. She cast a glance back over her shoulder—her trail through the scruffy plants that were growing so prolifically with continued rains was visible as a dull smear against the shiny dampness—and shook her head, turning back to the fence-line ahead.

No.

Lila was going to find this thing and "hear" its story, putting as near a full stop as possible on its intrusions into her cabin life, and get her recovery back on track!

The irritating vibration of the thing was definitely increasing. Lila took a deep breath and slogged forward, her wet feet squeaking inside her shoes. Time and proximity were raising the "noise" to a level that would soon be impossible to ignore even if she were a master meditator, which she was nowhere near. The escalating yammering was wearing on Lila like a blasphemous chant, here in the place that had always held so much peace for her.

She found a low spot along the fence and grimaced at the necessity of rolling underneath, but as hard as Spencer worked to keep his gates snug, she knew his fence-line would be pristinely taut as well. The ground beneath was not nearly so conformist, and so when the gap between the lowest line of barbed wire widened over a natural dip in the soil, Lila slid off her fanny-pack and slipped below the fence without further hesitation. Fortunately, she didn't transfer near as much water onto her back and shoulders with this quick maneuver as she had onto her lower body with her long hike. Once she'd safely traversed the barrier, she rebuckled her fanny-pack.

Now that she'd crossed from her own, well-traveled territory into Spencer's range land, Lila found herself scanning the horizon in spite of the fact that there weren't even cattle to be seen, much less any people. It was probably just as well that she was out and about relatively early today, saturated plant-life notwithstanding. Lila hadn't spent a lot of time observing this particular stretch of land, but she thought the herd tended to move through this area later in the day rather than earlier.

Picking her way towards the line of hawthorns that ran along the draw, Lila sifted back through her memory, trying to isolate views that incorporated the burned-out house. As she recalled, it was somewhere to the left of the hawthorns, so she'd need to cross the dip of land where the greenery was at its most flamboyant.

A sliver of remembrance bit into her consciousness as she walked; she thought she'd heard or seen on a map that there was a spring somewhere in this draw. Lila would want to cross sooner rather than later if she wanted to avoid additional water issues.

"Though how I could get any more soaked than I am now ... "

Lila snapped her mouth shut and stopped, eyeing a promising space empty of hawthorns ahead. It was flush with deep grasses that swayed lightly at the command of a soft breeze. She needed to stop talking; sound could carry out here, and she was, after all, trespassing. A. B. took pride in his unauthorized trips hither and yon, but Lila was a newbie.

And Angus is gone now.

Lila gasped. The thought was hardly revolutionary in its content, but the fact that it wasn't hers—and that she had yet to touch the object to which the memory fragment was tied—was unprecedented in Lila's experience. Never had she had such clarity of someone else's thought without touching the object to which it was connected.

The nattering noise in her mind was becoming slightly more coherent, now that she considered. The thought about A. B. had shot out of the murmuring like a chunk of debris ejected from a tornado, and it left Lila stunned, her heart racing and her mental "ears" cocked, alert for more. But there was so much roiling about, whispers and shrieks overlapping, and noise crackling over it all ...

FIRE!

Lila swayed almost as much as the grasses just ahead of her, doggedly making her way forward despite fear grabbing at her like prickly burrs, tenacious and painful. Driving the fear was the fact that the memories, still largely amorphous, were connecting with Lila before she connected to "their" object. That she still didn't know what was calling her was also unsettling—like an earthquake was unsettling—but Lila's desire to end the memory maelstrom still trumped her rising terror.

Although how much more she could take, she did not know.

On the other side of the draw with its hypnotic grasses, moving with a wind Lila could no longer hope to hear over the wretched tsunami of stored, remembered debris, she crested the edge of the draw and then she saw it. It was a rusted shape, roughly rectangular in structure, and tipped slightly to the right, standing somewhat centrally in the burnt-out shell of the old house. Time and weather had reduced what the fire had not taken entirely, but neither had appreciably damaged the old stove.

One door was missing from its front, the other was hanging open—gaping and off of one hinge, in fact. The open door was wedged there against some other detritus, and memories were gushing out of the open maw of the stove like demons fleeing a doorway to hell.

Lila kept walking towards it, while the memories tied to it continued to flood out at her, volume increasing while time both speeded up and slowed down simultaneously. It felt like moving through fog that was as thick as it looked, only there was nothing visible in her way. And it sounded like an outdoor rock concert, minus the music, with words and shouts and emotions dancing frantically around, crashing into her, knocking against her so hard she staggered.

I ... I haven't ... haven't even ... touched it.

Lila's own thoughts were being pulverized, superseded by force. Instead of the instantaneous transfer she typically experienced on touching an object, she found this one behaving more like an active participant, summoning her as much as she was seeking it. It was more of a connection than it ever had been; indeed, Lila looked at her outstretched hand as she crossed the house's foundation and didn't have the slightest idea how long she had been walking like that.

It was the act of entering the house that finally tapped something still cognizant in Lila, behind the torrential memories that were not her own, underneath the overlapping thoughts, flattened somewhere below the smiles and screams that desperately longed for understanding after years of isolation.

The stove wasn't the only valued object ... the house itself had been treasured, for a time. All of it: the house, the stove, the open stove door ... all of it was missing something that held even more intact memory. The missing stove door, *that* was what was calling to Lila ... more than the stove itself, more than the house.

Even as she realized the stove wasn't the biggest problem, Lila's choppy forward motion at last stopped and she touched the stove, right on its top.

She screamed with the force of what it told her. Screamed until she couldn't breathe, couldn't see, couldn't hear ... couldn't fathom what had ever compelled her to come to this place to hear this horrible, three-sided story.

And then, as bluntly as the cliché, everything went black.

When Lila came back to herself, she was lying in the shade of some hawthorns. A black fly was biting her right hand, and when she raised her left hand to swat it away, she found herself moving more slowly than she could reasonably expect, given the immediacy of the situation.

"Lie still," a man's voice snapped, his voice low but his tone urgent and irritable.

Lila gasped, and struggled to do the exact opposite of what was being demanded of her. Again, her body did not seem well-connected to her brain, fumbling in a feeble way that—if movement had a scent—would reek of molasses.

"I said, lie still!" Hands grabbed her shoulders from behind and pressed her firmly down into the cool dampness of soil and grass. Lila caught only a grim expression underneath the brim of a cowboy hat before the man moved out of her field of vision.

"Who are you?"

"Spencer. Adam Spencer. This is my land you're on."

"Oh!" Lila was grateful to feel appalled, to grasp the awkward calamity of her situation. "Lila Dawkins."

"I figured. What I don't know is what the hell you're doing on my land. And whether you're going to die while you're doing it."

Lila fluttered her hands up against his, which were still restraining her.

"I am so sorry, I'll ... I'll explain everything, I promise, but ... would you come around where I can see you?"

The grip on her shoulders did not relax.

"Only if you also 'promise' to stay lying down." From Spencer's emphasis, Lila thought he wasn't going to put much stock in any oaths she made.

"I do." And that sounded altogether wrong, so Lila tried again. "I promise."

"Fine." His agreement grudgingly given, Spencer—she couldn't even bring herself to think of him by his first name, her mind still reeling with what the stove had disclosed, not to mention this man's angry demeanor—released Lila's shoulders and sidled into full view. He stood outside the shadows of the hawthorns, backing up until Lila could see him without craning her neck too badly.

Then he said, "So explain."

Lila swallowed hard, the fingers of her now-itching hand slipping down to her waist, reaching for her water bottle, finding nothing.

"I suppose now you need a drink first?" Spencer clearly wasn't going to agree that such a thing was necessary, but Lila nodded nevertheless.

"This better be damn good," Spencer said, his curt words edging on a snarl, and he stomped back behind Lila and soon dangled her fanny pack with its liquid side-bottle in front of her.

"Thank you!" Lila reached for it and was relieved to see that her trembling was already lessening, and her hands were responding more quickly to the demands of her still-reeling brain.

"Had to get it off to get you lying down," Spencer snapped, moving back to where he'd been standing before. "Tuck it under your head if you must, but do NOT try to sit up yet."

"I won't, thanks." Lila flicked her glance back to him as she tugged her water bottle loose and followed his suggestion.

He was every inch impatient, his body language all aggravated tension from his boots to his hat. Lila forced her eyes more quickly over the expanse of muscle in between, but could still tell that it was as taut as one of his fences, and she fleetingly wondered if he'd carried her to the hawthorns.

She supposed he had.

She cleared her throat and directed her gaze to the water bottle, which seemed to have an inordinately long expanse of threading on its cap. With deliberate effort, Lila decided that, dressed as Spencer was, there was also a horse somewhere nearby—so much for her notion that morning was a good time to go exploring.

Lila sipped her water carefully, finding it still deliciously cool. She could not have been out of her senses for long, despite the rawness of her throat. She shuddered, remembering again what she'd learned inside the shell of the house when she'd touched the stove, and jerked her gaze back to Spencer.

"I am so sorry," she said, diving with desperate determination into an explanation she had yet to formulate.

"You said that already," Spencer replied. He did not relax, his voice did not soften, but Lila felt that he was relieved that she was aware and speaking coherently. She must have been in quite a state when he'd found her.

"I was out for a walk—I'm a writer and I take long walks, especially when I'm stuck on a project—and I saw the old house through a patch in the pines on my property ... "

"So you do know you're trespassing."

"Yes, and I can't apologize enough for that. I also can't explain how sorry I am that I didn't bring my cell phone with me. My best friend, Kristen Rush—she lives in Casper—she insists that

166

I do because I'm prone to ... to violent migraines, and ... "

"Migraines. You're going to tell me that you were screaming bloody murder for ten minutes on account of a fucking headache?"

Lila felt her face flush with anger and embarrassment, and welcomed both.

"Migraines go far beyond 'headaches,' and they most certainly do ... mess ... with one's mind." Now it was Lila's voice that carried an edge. She lifted her chin slightly when Spencer's eyebrows quirked upwards at her careful avoidance of profanity.

"I don't need an education on migraines," he said, without appreciably reducing the bite in his voice.

"Apparently you do," Lila shot back, tempted to throw her water bottle at him.

If I thought I could hit him ... Lila cut off the thought and pressed on with speech.

"But that's beside the point. The point is, I had a ... an attack, I couldn't see or hear through it, and anyway, I had no way to contact Kristen or anyone else because I forgot my phone at my cabin."

"What do you have to do after one of your 'attacks?'" Spencer said, arms still crossed in front of him. He hadn't needed his fingers to frame the last word with quotation marks; he could do that with the power of his grating voice. "To recover?"

"Rest." Lila realized her entire body was tense, and relaxed her neck in particular, letting her lumpy fanny pack bear the full weight of it. "I have to rest."

"Then why would you have to call anyone?"

"Because I said I would," Lila snapped. "Look, you call Sheriff Hoffman, press charges if you want, I don't care. In fact, I'm sure I've earned it, so go ahead, by all means. But would you just stop making this ... this *situation* ... worse than it already is?"

Spencer's eyebrows had advanced so far upwards during her short tirade that Lila wondered if it were possible to pull a muscle in one's forehead. Her immediate concern about whether she'd pushed her luck too far was alleviated when those elevating brows dropped just as she stopped talking.

"I damn well would have called 9-1-1," Spencer said, the tiniest hint of a wry smile quirking one end of his mouth then. "I forgot my cell phone today, too, or I'd've called the minute I rode up and saw you there. Screaming," he added, the edge of his smile vanishing.

Lila shut her eyes against the tears that welled up in an instant. The stove, the fire, the missing door ... but she didn't want to think of that now—she *couldn't* think of that now. She looked back at Spencer, then down to take another draught of water.

"I haven't been careful," she said, allowing truth to help her flesh out her lie. "I haven't been getting regular sleep, or staying hydrated the way I should. That helps a lot with my attacks." Of course, what helped more was escaping memory-laden objects and their intense stories, but she couldn't tell this angry, irritating man that.

"Are you going to promise to do better there, too? Are you going to stay off my land?"

Anger surged into Lila, pushing her heart to skip a beat, and her abused muscles to tense. But she took a breath before speaking and was proud to have her next word come out evenly, if not calmly.

"Absolutely." She did not clarify which of the two questions she was answering.

Their eyes met and held, and Lila was shocked to see that Spencer's eyes were a stunning hazel, rich with color and texture. Her next breath caught in her throat, but when she dropped her eyes and saw his mouth was now forming a smirk, she let it go in a rush.

"In fact, I'd be happy to get off your land right now," Lila said, "even if I have to crawl off of it."

"And I'd be happy to arrange a more comfortable departure."
Spencer stepped forward and stretched out a hand to her. "Don't
be too proud to refuse my help; you did promise to take better care
of yourself."

"So I did." Lila knew she sounded petulant now, but she
didn't much care. Why on earth would A. B. have wanted her to
meet this man? He was insufferable!

Lila set her hand in Spencer's and let him pull her up to her
feet. He was not a terribly tall man, she saw when she was
standing, but he was still taller than she was. And he was watching
her with an uncomfortable intensity, so she tried to free her hand.

"No," he said. "No, I'll see you back to your place." And he
whistled three shrill notes.

"What?" Lila was flabbergasted. And her hand felt hot,
trapped in the steadiness and strength of his. "I'm fine, I ... "

There was a snort, and then a horse trotted around the curved
line of the hawthorns, stopping very close to Lila and Spencer.

"That may be," he said, conveying doubt if not outright
disbelief with his voice rather than his words, "but Sunny and I will
see you safely back, and that's final." Spencer brushed the horse's
face gently with his free hand, and then tugged lightly at Lila's,
which he still held with his other hand. "You can ride sitting in the
saddle, or you can ride tossed over it. I don't really care which; I
just need to get on with my day."

"You ... I ... "

"You're a writer, aren't you? You must be able to come up
with a few more choice words than that."

Lila closed her gaping mouth so quickly she nearly bit her
tongue. She probably should bite her tongue, to prevent herself
from using it to say something entirely inappropriate!

"Fine," she said finally, and fought the urge to stomp her foot
when Spencer laughed out loud. But he finally let go of her hand.

He stood there next to his horse—had he really said its name was "Sunny?" and how could he look like the Marlboro man and still have such a sweetly-named horse? maybe it was "Sonny"—and Lila realized he was waiting for her. He heaved a sigh as it became obvious that she had no idea how to proceed.

"Haven't you ever ridden?"

"No."

Spencer shook his head.

"I shouldn't be surprised. First things first, you should probably put that absurd little pack back on ... " He waited while she did, and then pointed toward the stirrup. "Grab hold of the saddle horn and put your foot in the stirrup ... no, your other foot, unless you want to ride backwards ... "

Lila was thoroughly flustered by the time she was sitting in the saddle, and became even more so when Spencer mounted the horse behind her. To be in such close proximity to such a thoroughly unlikeable man, especially in her current state of mind was just too much. Particularly when he wrapped one arm around her waist.

Lila was tremendously thankful for the slight barrier of the fanny pack. The situation was already unpleasant, but without that small addition of breathing room ... but why weren't they moving?

"Where to?" Spencer said, answering aloud the question Lila hadn't yet asked.

Lila couldn't help the groan that escaped her. Spencer clicked his tongue and Sunny obliged by moving forward at a gentle pace.

"I'll just head for the nearest gate. Maybe when we get there, you can explain where I need to go next."

"The gate is far enough," Lila managed to say through her gritted teeth.

"No, I don't think it is. But don't worry. You might have trespassed in my house, but I'll stop at the door of yours."

"What? You'll stop at the gate! There's no comparison between that ... that shell of a house and my cabin! You don't live in that house. You never lived in that house, James built it for Nell ... oh!" Lila caught herself, too late.

"What do you know about that house?" Spencer said, the edge of his voice even sharper than before.

Lila turned to try to glare at him, but her timing was unfortunate and on the way she got a direct glance at the house itself with its skewed, sentry stove. She wrenched her gaze forward and away, aiming at the fence-line in the distance, scanning for the spot where she'd scrabbled underneath.

"What do you know about that house?" Spencer was not going to be deterred.

Lila sighed. Again, she tried to stay as close to the truth as she could. "I'm a writer. I imagine as much as I know."

Spencer had nothing to say to that for several minutes, for which Lila was grateful. Just when she was beginning to relax and even dare to hope that they'd make it to the gate in silence, Spencer spoke again.

But not about the fire.

"I don't have much time for reading."

Too busy building monstrous homes into the sides of mountains and tightening your cattle gates? Lila squashed the uncharitable thoughts in favor of a vaguely civil comment about ranching being a lot of work.

"It is. Between that and funerals, I've got pretty much nothing in the way of downtime."

Aghast, Lila wondered if Spencer's mention of funerals was a jab at A. B.

"Funerals?" She made it into a question.

"My step-mother and then her second husband."

"Oh! I'm so sorry."

"Don't be. She didn't suffer. Can't say the same thing for him, living with her all those years."

He had to be doing this on purpose, Lila thought. Nurturing

her sympathy one minute, crushing it in the next. He probably never even had a mother! Or a step-mother, either. Unreasonable though the idea was, Lila clung to it like a child holding fast to her security blanket.

"And then A. B.," Spencer said, sighing, and Lila shot right back onto the provoking roller-coaster of emotion. Because Spencer sounded ... sad.

"Did you even know him?" Lila couldn't help asking.

"I did. I knew he was loosening my gates, though I never caught him at it. I knew he was trespassing on my land, though I never caught him at that, either. I knew he had a weakness for a good whiskey and I knew he'd take me to the cleaners if I ever took him up on that game of poker he always offered. But I wish I'd done it anyway."

Now it was Lila who had nothing to say, and she said it all the way to the gate while her thoughts raced and circled, tripping and stumbling. She tried to remember anything specific A. B. had ever said about Spencer and could only think of jabs about the man's cattle gates, and the oversized home he'd built upon purchasing his parcel of land from A. B. And now that Lila thought about it, she wasn't sure that it wasn't all just talk, even teasing.

"I miss A. B." She said it without intending to, and stiffened when it slipped out, bracing for Spencer's rejoinder.

But all Spencer said was, "He was a good man."

Then they were at the gate, and when Sunny stopped, Lila moved. She wasn't, however, fast enough to escape Spencer. His free hand joined the one that hadn't shifted from her waist.

"Slow down," he said, when she bristled. "Just go slow. I don't have time to cart you in to town to see the doctor."

"You don't need to 'cart' me anywhere," Lila said, and while she did move her legs carefully, aligning herself to slide down Sunny's side, she whipped her head around to glare at Spencer. "Now let me go."

172

Spencer held his hands at Lila's waist long enough after that for it to become uncomfortable, and his eyes were locked with hers, too. Lila didn't waver, not wanting to see if he was starting to smirk, because she would not give him the satisfaction. After what seemed like far too long, Spencer moved one hand, bringing it up slowly between them.

He wasn't going to ... surely he wouldn't ...

When the curve of his movement took his hand up to his hat, he touched it lightly, tipping it towards Lila, and then nodded.

"Go ahead, ma'am."

And Lila almost laughed at the absurdity of it all—almost, except for the nearness of him, the smile in his eyes that was far kinder than what she knew she'd see if she glanced down at the hardness of the rest of his face.

"Thanks," she said, without inflection. Then, as she leaned and started to slide down Sunny's side, she added with as much attitude as she could, "SIR."

The snort Lila heard must have been Sunny's, because the laughter was all Spencer's.

13: Turmoil

It was all Lila could do not to scream again when Spencer insisted on following her up to her cabin, Sunny—who was, indeed, female—trailing easily along behind him. Watching him easily open the gate that gave her such trouble was almost as maddening, but this insistence on seeing her home ... that was the limit.

"We'd be there by now if we were riding," Spencer observed, just as they were approaching the final uphill stretch.

It didn't help to know that he was correct. Lila gritted her teeth hard to avoid snapping at him, and heard him chuckle behind her back.

"You pull your shoulders up to your ears when you're angry," Spencer said when he'd finished his laugh. "You're going to give yourself neck problems doing that."

"Once you ride off into the sunset, I'll be back to my sweet-tempered self in no time, so don't you worry about my neck."

"Sunset? I must have missed the part where you invited me to stay for dinner," Spencer drawled. Lila found herself becoming exhausted, not only by the climb, but by the additional strain of trying to keep her shoulders down and relaxed.

"You can't miss what I don't offer."

"That's what you think."

Lila pushed forward, trying to increase her pace in spite of the angle of incline ahead. Between the "download" she'd endured at the burnt-out house this morning—a home she now knew had been built by James for his bride, Nell—and Adam Spencer's grating presence, Lila was at the deep end of her nearly-dry pool of reserves. A fact which was made increasingly unpleasant by Spencer's persistence in trailing her back to her cabin!

Fortunately, the cabin was just now coming in to sight for Lila, and Spencer spoke up a moment later, letting her know that he'd spotted it as well.

"Now *that's* a cabin! A bit small, maybe, but great location."

Lila squinched her eyes shut for just a moment, and then popped them back open, not stopping in her progress towards the security directly ahead.

"Thanks," she said, though she knew the tone of her voice was not particularly grateful. Well, the tone of Spencer's voice was not particularly complimentary!

And now I've regressed into a teenager, Lila thought, annoyance flushing from every pore not already dedicated to anger. She realized her shoulders were inching up again and forced them back down.

At the gate to the cabin's yard—before she could catch her breath or change her mind—Lila turned sharply to face Spencer and he nearly walked into her.

"Oh!" Lila gasped, not expecting to find him following so closely. Spencer dropped Sunny's reins and reached out with both hands to steady Lila as she wobbled.

"I'm fine," she said, raising her arms slightly in hopes of shrugging Spencer off. It didn't work, of course, and he was staring at her again with that peculiar intensity that seemed to be his trademark.

Lila tried to catch her breath.

"I'm fine," she said again, and it came out more steadily. Spencer let her go, but only with his hands ... his eyes were still holding her as tightly as ever.

"I live in Wisconsin when I'm not here." The explanation was part obligation, part desperation ... would anything make this man go away? "I'm just not used to the altitude."

"Hmm." He was clearly unconvinced, and behind him, Sunny tossed her head, as if to support his disbelief.

"Thanks for ... well, for helping me," she said, while inside her head, the teenager Spencer had revived shouted, *GO AWAY!*

He turned away long enough to retrieve Sunny's reins and then grabbed Lila with those gold-flecked, green orbs of his once more. Caught, and held, like he was applying some sort of hypnotic ray, and it raised the fine hairs on the back of Lila's neck ... *that look.*

Spencer took one step forward, close enough that Lila could feel the heat of his body, hear the fabric of his shirt when it moved with his arm as his free hand came up, passing far too close, just as it had when he'd tipped his hat to her at the gate.

He tipped his hat again, and his eyes narrowed as he grinned.

"My pleasure, ma'am."

"You've got a funny way of showing your 'pleasure,'" Lila said, and then—of course too late then—thought better of her words.

"Do I? What would be more appropriate?" Spencer asked, and though the words sounded rhetorical, the deliberate movement of his head towards hers was anything but.

Lila found her mind fluttering, though neither flight nor fight came into the fray ... just a flurry of confusion. And so Spencer brought his lips down to hers and kissed her without challenge. It was not the sort of kiss that Lila could mistake for anything but teasing—at least, it didn't start out that way. But in direct opposition to the levity of its first application, that kiss sparked in an instant, flaring to full blaze out of its gentle, jesting initiation.

It happened like stumbling hard, like going over the edge of an unseen precipice. Lila was annoyed when Spencer first touched her but before it could even sink in that she hadn't pulled away, she found herself not only not distancing herself, but actually pressing forward. She was kissing him back! Like frozen butter in a microwave, seeming to go all at once from solid to puddle ... from icy cold to snapping hot.

Not that Lila was thinking in writerly metaphor. Now, in the unexpected passion—yes, passion—of Spencer kissing her and her kissing him, Lila wasn't thinking at all, but was fully immersed in emotions just as powerful as those she'd experienced earlier in the day.

Just as powerful, but much more pleasurable.

If Sunny hadn't shifted, knocking the pair of them with her head, there was no telling how far that kiss would have gone. Spencer's eyes were as piercing as ever as he drew away from Lila. Both of them were breathing audibly. The scent of him was all around her, and all over her! Lila noticed they each took a full step back but didn't know how they'd managed to time that maneuver any more than she knew what had just happened with that kiss.

That kiss!

Oh, no.

Yes, she did know. That kiss ... that was attraction, pure and simple. Just what she did not need!

Judging by the expression on Spencer's face, it was just what he didn't need, either. He searched her face with those flashing green eyes, his smirk noticeably absent. Lila stared back, knowing her expression must be the feminine mirror of his own, very masculine astonishment.

Then she blinked.

And just like that, Spencer relaxed into a stance so languid, Lila could almost believe she'd imagined the past minute or so.

That kiss!

"Better?" Spencer said, the hands that had pulled Lila against him when their kiss had deepened now brushing lightly against his horse's head.

Meddling horse.

There was no proper response to this sort of situation—a

pinnacle of consternation if there ever was one—so Lila forgave herself for the derogatory mental slight against Sunny.

"Thank you," she said, uncomfortably aware of the huskiness of her voice. She cleared her throat, and as Spencer's recurrent smirk broadened, Lila angled her head ever so slightly towards at Sunny. "Your timing was quite good. For a horse."

Demonstrating her excellent sense of timing yet again, Sunny blinked, and Spencer's grin faded. Lila's budding triumph was so certain that she tossed her head a little, flinging her curls into impudent bounces.

Spencer laughed, turning away and mounting Sunny in a movement so flush with male fluidity that Lila's chagrin shoved her triumph aside, toppling it over into a sloppy heap.

Spencer tipped his hat to Lila for the third time that morning and rode away without another word.

Lila inhaled shakily, exhaled in a huff, and turned on her heel to open the gate. At least she was finally rid of Spencer ... if not the memory of that kiss.

His kiss.

She made it through lunch before the teariness set in. It was understandable, she told Thunder—whose eyes had widened impossibly while his ears tipped at all sorts of angles when Lila had started sniffling—because the day had been stressful enough without Spencer. But trying to interact with Spencer after just enduring the horrific memories revealed by the stove at the burnt-out house had ratcheted Lila's emotional strain to a level she'd never previously experienced.

She made a cup of tea with tears leaking out of her eyes, then carried the tea outside and around the corner next to the propane tanks where she'd set a lawn chair.

"Interact!" A poor euphemism if there ever was one.

But Lila would not think about that kiss; she flat-out refused to think about the way Spencer had ... and she had ... she flat-out refused to think about "that kiss." She needed to sort through what had happened today before Spencer had arrived to muddle things up in her body, and to further the confusion in her mind.

Lila had felt faint before when coming out of a memory-induced transfer. But she'd never actually blacked out, even when she'd touched an earring that had been given to a woman by the man who later killed her. Lila shuddered slightly at the recollection of that event, and her involuntary movement sent a corresponding wave through the cup she was holding. Since the tea was still too hot to drink and the cup was full, she set the tea down beside her chair and leaned back to think while it cooled.

"Here it is, Nell!" James' form was hazy as he entered the room, his outline blurring into the lanky structure of his body, softening it.

"James! It's beautiful!" Nell spun around in the empty space, standing on the stones that would one day hold the wood-burning stove. Joy poured off of her as she turned, glowing and sparkling, as if she were living glass in a sunbeam. "I love it. I love you!"

She threw herself into James' arms, holding him tightly as they kissed, but then they broke apart.

"What was that? Was it ... ?" James dropped his eyes to Nell's belly, which was ever-so-slightly rounded.

Nell laughed, water trickling into a hidden pond, out of the reach of any light. She was happy, yes, but she was also nervous.

"It was. You can touch him—or her—if you want."

The shady layers of the man Nell had once loved shifted again. He started to pull back, but she reached out, taking his hand in her own. He let her bring it to her belly. To feel their child moving inside her.

He seemed transfixed.

"It's going to be all right, James. We're going to be all right." Nell

seemed sure of it.

But James wasn't sure. Though he loved Nell, James wasn't sure at all of her love for him.

He wasn't even sure this child was his.

Lila almost knocked over the tea when she reached for it. There was so much wrong with the memories she'd accessed this morning. This had been the least of the bunch, the most mundane, and it was still gravid with emotional undertone. Lila would be willing to bet that James had some kind of mental illness. At the very least, he was carrying an overabundance of conflict inside himself, severely compromising his ability to love.

And Nell would die at his hands, Lila knew. Even though it happened decades in the past, Lila was sick to her stomach with her special knowledge of things to come in the convocation of memories she'd found at the stove.

James was not a solid figure in any of the scenes Lila had been caught up in. There was a cloudiness to him in the memories, a shifting, partial obscurity that meant that difficulties had tainted Nell's memory of him. Although in this case, "difficulties" was hardly sufficient to describe the impending disaster of the fire.

Among other things.

Lila forced herself to sip her tea as her stomach rebelled again. She hadn't gotten much clarity about the fire. The stove, as strong as its containment of memories had been, was not the main source of the chatter Lila had been picking up. It was the missing stove door that was the main conduit ... the door Lila wanted to avoid, but needed to find.

It was still baffling to Lila, because while the stove door was still hidden somewhere—somewhere in alignment with the house?—the stove could not have been buried; the stove had obviously been standing in that burnt-out house all along. It flew in the face of Lila's notion that the then-mystery thing had been coming to the surface while its chatter had been getting louder. She rubbed her forehead with the heel of her hand. She wasn't feeling well at all.

It was supremely frustrating, having made the decision to seek out the memories that were reaching her in spite of her having not yet reached them, to find that there was still more to be done. Lila sipped her tea again and leaned back into her chair, trying to think of another situation in which she'd found a lesser part of a memory-related relic. This was worse than the proverbial zebra running amongst a herd of horses ... it was like an invisible zebra accompanying horses through fog.

Lila sighed, or would have, but on the intake of her breath she realized she could smell propane. It was faint but distinct, and her gaze sharpened as it was pulled to the tanks that powered the cabin, sentries standing to the left of where Lila was sitting now.

A leak?

That couldn't be good. Lila got to her feet and approached the tanks, setting her nearly-empty cup of tea on the sill next to her bedroom window, which was on the same side of the cabin as the propane tanks. She waved her hand around the tanks in the various places where the connections were located, from the tank towards her nose, but couldn't seem to zero in on the smell. In fact, she could barely smell the odor at all when the wind gusted.

She'd have to talk to Lou about this, though. He'd want to replace connections, or tighten them, or something. She wondered if he'd be able to talk her through the process so he wouldn't have to travel up to the cabin, taking time away from work. Lou was in construction and summer was extremely busy for him; weekends were not exempt from rush jobs, of which Kristen told her there were many this year.

Lila stepped back, moving the chair and her tea as far away from the propane tanks as the current shade on this side of the cabin would permit. She sat back down and picked up the tea, determined to finish the cup before she lost her patch of sun-protection. The cabin wasn't quite square with the North-South axis—a fact which had clearly bothered Lou but did not faze Lila—and as a consequence, she couldn't count on the sun's path over the course of the afternoon to add to her current comfort zone.

What else could she pick out of the sloppy amalgamation of memories the stove had shown her? There was another man in Nell's life, that she knew. And James would turn to alcohol to deal with his perpetual uncertainty in Nell and the child she bore, a fact that would ultimately culminate in the drunken confrontation that would kill Nell.

"You LIED!" James shouted, his voice not only ragged on the edges, but mutilated all the way through.

"James!" Nell was sobbing, her full skirts cascading over the enormity of her pregnancy now. She held one arm pressing against her side, just behind her hip, stretching out the other towards James. "James, please!"

But James ignored both Nell's verbal and physical pleas.

"You lied to me then and you're lying now! You're a cheat and you're a whore!"

"James!" Nell seemed to shrink, her body curving around that hip, away from James, as he approached her with menace oozing out of every indistinct edge of his body. His fists were clenched, his rage amplifying with each step.

And then, out of Nell's skirts, came another cry.

"MAMA!"

Lila's grip on her now-empty tea cup was white-knuckled, and it was a struggle to set the cup down again as she folded over, wrapping her arms around her knees. That memory was tied to Nell's second pregnancy, and the idea of a tiny child witnessing such a thing was miserable to the point of nauseating.

It was too much. A much-loved home, a stove loved to an extreme not only for its beauty but also its nurturing capability—Nell had baked everything from bread to Thanksgiving dinner in and on that stove—and a deadly fight and fire were overlapping and churning even in the present time, in Lila's mind. She had never had so much to filter through, and such highly-charged material, at that. It was almost as if ...

Although the day was warm, and the shade in which she was seated was comfortable, if not precisely cool, Lila was abruptly chilled from the nape of her neck to the tips of her toes. It was almost as if the memory was personal, like her parents' wedding rings, which Lila had refused to touch for years after their deaths, but which could to this day bring to mind a hazy mishmash of their wedding and anniversary memories whenever she dared to try.

But she didn't know James or Nell! No, she didn't, but she might know someone else connected to their story, Lila realized, and that notion forced her even more tightly into her chair-supported near-fetal position.

If not the children, she considered, perhaps the other man in Nell's life. She gasped, remembering the first thought that had connected clearly with her when she'd made her way to the house this morning.

And Angus is gone now.

A. B.! A. B. was involved in this somehow!

It was too much. It was far too much.

Lila stood up as if rocket-propelled, and then dropped back into her chair as a wave of vertigo tackled her.

"Mrrt?" Thunder's meow, clearly questioning, drew Lila's unseeing stare to the window of the cabin, where he was stretched up from the bed, pushing his nose against the screen. The cat sniffed at the air and then sat, his mouth half-open, as if tasting whatever he'd smelled. He dropped out of sight and Lila heard the sound of his feet hitting the cabin floor, running out of the room.

"It's too early for supper, Thunder!" Lila called. She sounded like a late-night 70s-show radio host, her voice at least one octave below its normal register. Had she really been crying all this time? The tightness of the skin on her face would seem to support the notion, seconding the wrongness of her voice.

"Well."

Lila cleared her throat, dumped the remainder of the tea, which had long since gone cold, and stood more carefully.

"Maybe I should do a load of laundry or something."

Though the idea was physically unappealing—her laundry drum was small, and hand-powered, too—it was as far and away from sorting out Nell's burdensome memories that it practically seemed like a trip to an amusement park. And so Lila went back into the cabin to sort out which items of clothing could most use a cleansing.

She forgot all about the wispy odor of stray propane fumes.

Meow!

Lila woke up with the stove door serenading her like fingernails on a chalkboard, but it took her an inordinately long time to realize that what had woken her was not the memory-laced noise in her head or the dim light from the not-yet-risen sun, but the stench of propane in her bedroom. She tried to sit up but the whirling of the room—so dramatic, it was as if Lila were caught in an extra-large washing drum—made sitting impossible.

More powerful than dizziness and nausea, though, was fear. With near-terror as her catalyst, Lila slid herself over the edge of the bed, keeping her head low and trying to master her shaking limbs. It took a significant amount of focus, and she was reaching for the screen door's handle before she thought of Thunder, or remembered that she'd heard him meowing with an urgency that had almost thoroughly blended into the stove door's nightmare siren.

"Thunder!" She threw herself back towards the bedroom and

suffered wretched dry heaves for her efforts. With no sign of the cat on either the bed or the floor near it, Lila could only hope he hadn't crawled underneath the bed again. She certainly didn't dare to try to search underneath at this point ... she needed fresh air—a lot of it—and she needed it as fast as she could get it.

Thunder had meowed, hadn't he? Lila was sure he had, but then again, she was stuck in a shifting, unstable world where propane made up part of the atmosphere. Maybe she'd only dreamt the sound?

"Meow!" No, that was real enough. Lila was certain now. She peered across the dim light of the kitchen, and finally spotted the cat.

There, on her desk, she saw the cat's silhouette, saw the flash of his eyes when he looked at her, and then turned quickly away, ducking his head around the clear barrier of the window pane. He peered around the glass where it tipped into the room in its open position, now staring at something outside.

And breathing the freshest possible air in the cabin.

"Lassie! Did Timmy fall into the well again?" Lila called. Despite the weakness of her sally—and the stupidity of wasting her precious breath on it—she was somewhat reassured by the fact that she could think clearly enough to complete a sentence, even a silly one.

And she was intensely glad to have Thunder with her.

The nausea was unrelenting but the air through the screen door was chilly, and the ill wind that had blown it directly into her bedroom last night was beginning to shift. Lila made one more journey to the bed before exiting the cabin, dragging her sleeping bag behind her.

She hoped Thunder would have the good sense to stay by the far window.

Outside, Lila gave in to the pressure roiling in her gut and threw up, though she expelled only the slightest bit of liquid. She tested her ability to stand, but didn't make it off of a tentative, one-kneed position. The vertigo was confounding in the extreme! Before dragging her sleeping bag around to lie underneath the window near which Thunder perched, Lila managed to crawl to the propane tanks to shut off the main valve to the cabin.

She wasn't sure it would help, but she doubted it would hurt.

Lila also took one of the two bottles of water that she'd left outside near her front door—for easy cooling overnight, without further straining her tiny refrigerator—and then made her way through the lightly-damp grass to the far side of the cabin. She was fortunate it wasn't raining, not that she'd let any amount of rain drive her back into her cabin right now.

"Mrrt?" Thunder was still at the window.

"It's okay, boy," Lila said. She stretched one arm up, and Thunder bent, sniffing in her direction, though of course she couldn't reach all the way up to the window's edge. "At least, I think it will be okay, once things stop spinning."

Lila positioned her sleeping bag just far enough from the window that she could see Thunder there without lifting her head and tucked herself in. Then she remembered the water and carefully raised herself up on her shaking elbows to drink. She hoped to drink half the bottle, but her stomach resisted the notion, so she had to content herself with just a few sips.

When she laid back down, the full horror of her situation struck, and she turned onto her side just in case she threw up again.

It's okay! I'm okay! Thunder's okay!

The wind caressed her curls, then ruffled them as it picked up its now-redirected pace.

She wasn't sure she could sleep at all, with everything tipping and bending around her, a vortex of uncertain ground. Not to mention inside her, where her innards were in an uproar of near-open rebellion. Lila wished she could prop herself up somehow, but there was no way she was going back into the cabin for a pillow at this point.

Except maybe for Thunder. Lila opened her eyes, and for a moment, thought he had abandoned his post at the window. But no, there was an ear, lower and further down than she expected to find it ...

"Ha! Clever boy." It didn't look comfortable, but Thunder had managed to tuck himself in between the window pane and its screen, laying on his side against the glass where it tipped into the cabin. The window would be strong enough to take it, Lila was sure, and she could try to rest more easily now.

"Stay there. Stay!"

Thunder didn't meow a response of any sort, but Lila almost thought she could hear him purring. She took some comfort from that, and closed her eyes against the turmoil that leaking propane had wrought.

14: Reparations

"What in the hell?" It was Spencer's voice.

Lila groaned. She'd slept, she knew. Maybe she was dreaming now? She dreaded opening her eyes ... trying to sit up while Spencer was watching her was a truly appalling notion. He couldn't really be here, could he?

Of course he could.

If the encroaching presence of Spencer inspired Lila to crawl deep within her sleeping bag, concern for Thunder provided the opposite impetus. As soon as the thought of Thunder occurred to her, Lila opened her eyes and searched the window. She was just in the nick of time, and saw part of Thunder's flank and tail before he disappeared from sight.

She noted gratefully that the window and cabin supporting it were firm and unwavering, as was everything else in her immediate field of vision, with the exception of the grasses around her. The wind was agitating those, as the hurried sound of boots approaching Lila was aggravating her.

Lila raised herself cautiously to her elbows, and when that went well, she turned to see Spencer ducking through the sagging Ponderosa pine fence that surrounded the cabin, Sunny grazing unconcernedly behind him.

"Get off my lawn!" Lila said, unpleasantly aware of both the rasp of her voice and residual shaking of her limbs. She was hungry, she realized, though the nausea had not completely dissipated. At least the spinning had!

Spencer had stopped in his tracks when Lila spoke to him, yet he looked anything but motionless as he stood there, anger surging off every tense muscle in his body.

"Dammit, woman! Two days in a row?"

"Two days in a row what? You're the one trespassing now!"

They glared at each other, and Lila suddenly realized how she must look. Not only disheveled and ill, but possibly transparent in her worn tank top, which was fully exposed as she sat there, her sleeping bag pooled around her.

Well, she wasn't going to reach for the cover of the sleeping bag now, even if Spencer did start to smirk.

Not that he was smirking. At least, not yet.

"Two days in a row I've found you collapsed or near it," he said finally, adjusting his stance to one less obviously broken out of mid-stride. "I came up here to make sure you were all right after your ... migraine ... yesterday."

Had that really happened only yesterday? Lila felt the weight of the events of the past 24 hours crush her. And Thunder!

"I'm fine. And you have to go. I have to check on Thun ... on my cat."

"Your cat? Does it get migraines, too?"

On top of being sick to her stomach, hungry, possibly dehydrated, and beginning to twitch from the mental strain of listening to Spencer, Lila allowed herself to be goaded into answering honestly.

"I have a propane leak in the line somewhere by my bedroom. I woke up last night smelling the fumes, and ... wait! What are you ... don't!"

But Spencer had started moving again when Lila had gotten to "fumes" and he was inside the cabin before she could wobble her way to her feet, the screen door slapping shut behind him.

The wind breezing over her backside took a moment to activate Lila's sense of propriety, in spite of the fact that Spencer was now inside her cabin. Belatedly, she sank back down into her sleeping bag, because she was wearing nothing on the lower half of

189

her body except for her underwear.

Please let this be a bad dream.

Her head throbbed, as if the migraine she'd concocted yesterday had been conjured into existence today, but Lila supposed it was a residual effect of inhaling propane. Kristen would have her head for not calling Lou immediately about the issue ... if Lila's head didn't explode in the aftermath of her forgetfulness, that was.

"Cat's fine," Spencer said, his face appearing in the window above her. "Hungry, I guess, but fine."

Lila met Spencer's eyes just as Thunder launched a vocal complaint somewhere in the background.

"You shouldn't be in there," Lila said.

"I don't smell any propane," he responded. "Except a hint in the bedroom. The cat won't go in there at all."

"His name's Thunder," Lila said, thinking that this conversation was beyond inane, even under the circumstances. "And I meant that I didn't invite you in."

Spencer half-smiled at that.

"I don't need an invitation. I'm no vampire."

Lila dropped her eyes then, and clutched a handful of her sleeping bag with delicately quaking fingers. She could not think of a reasonable response to this ridiculously unreasonable situation.

"Tell me where I can find something for you to eat," Spencer ordered, sending Lila's stomach into another tumultuous roll. "Something mild. A slice of bread?"

"There's bread on the shelf above the wood stove." It was an effort to respond politely when Lila wanted to scream, but he was right ... she needed something to eat, or at least, to nibble on.

"I see it."

Lila listened to the gentle, plastic sounds of the bag rustling as a slice of bread was separated from its compatriots. After a few seconds, the noise penetrated the functional part of her brain enough to prompt her to glance about for her water bottle. She managed a few sips before Spencer made his way out of the cabin and back to her.

"Here." His voice, uncharacteristically mild, startled her as he sank into a crouch in front of her. He held the bread out to her in slow motion, and she took it in kind, brushing his steady fingers with her own shaky ones as she did so.

"I hope you don't make a habit of this kind of drama," Spencer said then, ruining the moment with the acidity of his tone.

"And I hope you don't make a habit of this kind of acrimony," Lila snapped back. She rued her response immediately, and felt her face flush with guilt. Caustic or not, intrusive or not, Spencer had been helping her two days in a row now.

Rescuing her.

She tore off a small piece of the bread and shoved it into her mouth before daring to look into Spencer's face. His smirk was back, but it was wryly tipped.

"I do, actually. I've been told I'm as corrosive as battery acid."

Lila couldn't improve on that comparison—at least, not in her current state—and so she said nothing, but continued to eat the bread and wish that Spencer would go away. She had enough on her metaphoric plate as it was, recovering from propane inhalation putting up with the continued nattering of the stove door ...

She froze, awareness funneling into a tight focus as she realized that the only sounds around her were purely audible. The stove door was silent!

"Are you feeling sick again?" Spencer asked, fluffy solicitousness under a thin glaze of annoyance.

Lila shook her head, casting about for the first excuse that came to mind.

"Thunder," she said, her voice too loud by design. Thunder obligingly answered her with a querulous meow. "Would you mind ... feeding him?"

Spencer's sparking green eyes had that same look he'd given her when she'd explained her screams of yesterday as a migraine, but he nodded. And he kept his eyes locked on hers, wariness supplanting what little concern Lila had been able to find earlier.

"Where?"

She told him where to find the food and Thunder's bowls, and asked him to feed the cat on the desk by the window. And then she continued to pick at the bread and drink more water, listening to the surprisingly pleasant sounds of Spencer moving around in her cabin, preparing food for a now-raucous Thunder.

And nothing else. There was no itch-tingle on the back of Lila's neck, no fragmented memory calling out to her from a mystery location, no more hinting at what previously had been lost to time.

Why was she searching for any of it? Didn't she have trouble enough as it was?

Lila managed to finish the bread before Spencer reappeared, his boots marking his metronome-even pace across the dirt and grass back to her. The nausea had all but disappeared now, so Lila was left to blame only Spencer's presence for the flustered state of her stomach. She looked up at him when he stopped in front of her.

"Do you know how to check the connections?"

"What?"

"On the propane. I see you shut off the main valve. Do you know how to check the connections, to find the leak?"

Lila shook her head.

"I was going to call my friend for help."

But Spencer was shaking his head, and holding out his hand to her.

"Come on. I'll show you."

Dumbfounded, Lila stared at Spencer's outstretched hand as if it were a rattlesnake, coiled and ready to strike. As it might as well be, in her pantless state.

"I ... "

"It's not a big deal. We're neighbors."

And Angus is gone now. Lila remembered the wretchedness of Nell's cry, but the pain she was feeling now was all her own. To defuse it, she again resorted to the truth.

"I'm not wearing pants," she said, and when Spencer laughed outright, she raised her voice to cut through his mirth.

"Why did you keep tightening the gates? If you knew A. B. was just going to loosen them up again?"

Spencer's laughter ceased as if turned off at its source, and his lips pressed together tightly, thinning with applied force. He tipped his hat back a notch and turned to direct his gaze and most of his body to the north, giving Lila a view of his back and only the slightest profile of his face. He kept staring that way for so long that it began to seem to Lila as if he would never answer her, or move, perhaps ever again.

She finally concluded that he was waiting for her to go get dressed.

"Oh! Why didn't you just say so?"

Spencer chuckled, but still didn't move.

Lila stood slowly. She continued to feel weak and uncertain, but she wasn't physically wavering, as far as she could tell. Spencer might as well have been turned to stone where he stood. That was an impossible standard, but Lila was glad she felt as if she could pass a sobriety test at this point. That was enough for her.

For now.

Lila grabbed the sleeping bag and wrapped it around her, though not for warmth. She eyed the sun's position in the sky as she hurried into the cabin, judging it to be no later than 10:00, and possibly earlier. She'd never been a good judge of time.

Inside the house, she spotted Thunder washing up. He was sitting on the chair in front of the desk, which suited Lila fine.

Spencer might have been able to detect a lingering odor of propane in the bedroom, but Lila couldn't, and that, too, was reassuring. She dressed quickly, but carefully, and picked up the other water bottle from its post near the door when she went back outside.

Spencer remained where she'd left him.

"At first, I tightened the gates because that's how I wanted them. After A. B. made a habit out of loosening them up, I tightened them because it was fun."

He turned to Lila after he finished speaking, his bland expression giving no weight to his words, but also taking nothing away from them.

"Fun for you? Or fun for A. B.?" Lila had to ask.

"For both of us. A man needs work to do, but it's not a chore if there's an element of fun."

"A. B. was loosening the gates for me," Lila said. "You wouldn't put in the quick-release gates when I was buying the property, so A. B. said he would help."

Spencer frowned, but that expression began to break apart almost as quickly as it formed, a visual representation of resolving confusion.

"There was a lawyer involved," he said, his expression clearing entirely. "My step-mother's attorney. I have my own representation now."

He didn't need to fill in the details. The distaste he'd expressed earlier for his step-mother extended quite obviously to her attorney.

"It should never have gone through lawyers anyway." He shook his head slowly. "I'll put in the quick-release gate handles. I've been planning to for awhile now. But the business with A. B. distracted me."

"Don't feel obligated."

"I don't. I've already bought them."

"Oh."

194

"Do you have liquid soap? Detergent or dishwashing soap—either will work." Lila felt her expression wipe itself clean, like a whiteboard being erased. She sorted out the topic change just before Spencer clarified it himself. "Let's find that propane leak of yours."

It was a surprisingly simple process. Apply a soapy solution to the suspect areas and wait. Spencer did turn the propane back on, of course, but that was it. When it appeared, the slight froth was something of a letdown for Lila.

"That? That's it?"

But Spencer was nodding.

"The way the wind was coming last night, and the way your cabin is situated, it wouldn't take much. Your bed's right under that window!" He glanced away and pointed, and when he turned back, he seemed to have gotten closer than he was before.

"The wind was strong and out of the east last night. Nothing unusual, not like ... " Lila let her voice trail off and stood, determined to put some additional distance between her and Spencer. She wrenched the main valve closed again. " ... not like the rest of this summer."

"What's unusual about this summer?" Spencer demanded, standing with her.

"The rain, of course." Lila was able to answer after the barest pause.

"Of course."

"And meeting you. You and Jake McCook! I never met either one of you in all of the time I've owned this land."

"I travel a lot. Traveled a lot."

"Why?" Lila was interested in spite of herself.

But Spencer wasn't about to satisfy that curiosity. Instead, he extracted a cellular phone from his pocket.

"I think I have this very connector," he said, tapping the source of the leak lightly with the phone. "But if not, it's a common enough piece. I can bring it by this afternoon."

He framed a photo of the propane system's problem spot and took a picture before Lila could protest. Belatedly, she did so anyway.

"You don't need to do that!"

Spencer shot her a sideways glance.

"But I can, and I will." His tone implied that his statement was inarguable, and it made Lila bristle.

"There's no need!"

Spencer ignored this. He snapped off the cover of his phone, and took a second photo, holding the phone's cover even with the faulty connector for a sense of proportion.

Lila crossed her arms in front of her chest, willing herself not to stamp her foot. Spencer finished his photographic efforts and eyed her with amusement.

"Did you fight A. B. about the gates, too?"

"Of course not."

"Why not?"

"Because A. B. was ... " Lila's voice caught. "A. B. was always kind. It was his nature."

"And it's not mine." Spencer didn't phrase it like a question, so Lila didn't answer him ... not aloud, anyway.

"I left you to scream in a burned out house one day, and to deal with a propane problem you couldn't fix by yourself the next. That's what gave away my unkind nature."

Chastened, Lila found herself blushing again. And although she felt the rightful appeal of delivering an apology, she gave in to wrath instead.

It was easier.

"I knew A. B.! I don't know you."

"And if you don't want to know me, that's fine," Spencer said, stepping closer, and then veering to Lila's side just when his nearness would have otherwise made her frantic. "If you want to continue to lie about what happened to you yesterday, if you want to push me away because I'm not A. B., that's fine, too."

He was walking away now, and Lila followed him long enough to be sure that he was going to leave the yard, to finally leave.

After crossing through her fence the same way he'd done before, Spencer stopped and turned back to Lila with that same mocking smile that she'd originally dubbed a smirk.

That "smirk" now seemed as self-defensive to Lila as her current rage, but she shook that thought off as best she could, sending her curls bobbing. And making her wonder just how awfully disheveled she looked, yet again.

"Yes, I will be back," Spencer said, misinterpreting her movement. "You can keep your secrets. In good health, though, I hope."

He whistled for Sunny, who nibbled one more mouthful of the apparently delicious grass on the far side of Lila's fence, and trotted over to him. Spencer stepped easily into the saddle, his movements purely liquid as always, which didn't account for the way his turned back seemed to be towards Lila for the longest time.

Once astride Sunny, Spencer turned to Lila again, his expression grim. She stared back at him, aghast at the situation, her behavior, the horrible timing of the propane system in its failing, Spencer's very existence, and the state of the world in general. She supposed her expression was now more like a cornered animal, but she couldn't imagine what she could do to correct it.

Spencer tipped his hat to her, the movement gentle in spite of ... well, in spite of everything. The courtesy of Spencer's deliberately conscious action robbed Lila of the unconscious ability to breathe. She didn't notice she was holding her breath, though, until Spencer wheeled Sunny away from her.

Nor did she realize she had raised her own hand in farewell.

Lila's initial reaction after Spencer's departure had been to undertake a mad and rapid search for the stove door since she knew he would not return for some time, but that fleeting notion had died a quick death when she remembered she couldn't sense the accursed thing. In the absence of the possibility of continuing her stove door quest, Lila's hunger, thirst, and other bodily concerns commanded precedence.

Indeed, she was sure she couldn't have managed a demanding hike even if she tried.

Of course, being unable to heat water, her dining options were limited. She settled on a pack of tuna spread over plain bread, and Thunder approved her choice so intensely that after slipping him a small morsel, Lila scurried outside to finish her half-sandwich in peace.

The food did much to improve her mood, though her stomach still wasn't entirely settled, so she used her empty water bottles to attempt some sun-tea, made with a ginger-lemon tea of which she wasn't entirely fond. However, Kristen swore by the stuff to settle the stomach, so Lila always had some on hand.

While the tea was soaking the sun's rays, Lila trekked to the pump to obtain some cool water, so as not to have to open the refrigerator and lose whatever remnant chill remained inside it. She drank as much as she could stand, and then dragged her sleeping bag back underneath a tree—she had a spare bag, so would use that one inside until she got this one washed again—and had a nap in the shade there.

The wind, which had picked up as the day progressed, finally woke her by repeatedly tickling her with her own hair. Lila scrubbed at the side of her face absently, with the slow awareness of waking from sound sleep, and then began rubbing at the back of her neck, which itched abominably.

When her perception awoke fully, it was with an almost audible snap, and Lila flew up off the sleeping bag.

"The door!" She could sense it again, and it was violent in its volume. But so was her bladder's need for attention, and so Lila set out for the outhouse.

Afterwards, she carried the sleeping bag to the fence and tossed it over the top to catch more of the blustery breeze. Lila was sticky with sweat herself, and the heat seemed to be rising still.

The buzz of the stove door was so strong, Lila could not pick out the slightest echo from the house, but she felt that the general direction was the same for both. She groaned, remembering Spencer's parting comments to her, and knowing she was going to trespass on his property again made her feel even worse about her own outburst.

She supposed she could blame it all on how she had been feeling—on having been slightly poisoned by her propane system—but Lila knew there was more to it than that. She leaned into the sleeping bag where it rested on the fence, careless of adding additional sweat and maybe a stray tear or two to the bag's burden.

It was her attraction to Spencer. Spencer! Not Jake, who certainly seemed like a more sensible choice, at least from what Lila knew of him at this point. But no. Spencer's piercing eyes and lean form were ... well. Attractive is what they were—what he was. And Lila didn't trust attraction, not anymore. She didn't trust Spencer; not in spite of what he'd done to help her, but because of it! Pete had been solicitous, too.

Spencer is not Pete.

No, Spencer was not Pete. Unlike Pete, Spencer wasn't made of pure irresistibility by any means. Lila thought about all of the things Spencer had said the first day she met him—*yesterday? Really, only yesterday?*—and it suddenly occurred to her that Spencer had been pushing her away as much as she'd wanted him to, right up until ...

That kiss.

So he felt it, too. And instead of being afraid of it as Lila was, Spencer was emboldened by it. It was an awful thought, and it competed fiercely with the nattering noise of the stove door. Lila groaned aloud, lifting her face out of the now-stifling sleeping bag's folds and bringing her hand to her forehead.

"Don't tell me, let me guess ... another migraine?" Spencer asked.

Lila laughed. It was a sound tinged with hysteria, but she had to laugh at his timing. Between Spencer and the door, Lila began to doubt she'd survive the summer with any semblance of sanity intact.

"You have ... " she began.

"Impeccable timing," he finished. He slid off the saddle in his usual graceful motion, but Lila directed her vision towards Sunny instead of Spencer's lean frame.

The horse winked at her. Although Lila could only see one of Sunny's eyes and rationally knew the "wink" was more likely to be a blink, she had to admit that a wink would fit into this ridiculous scene perfectly.

Spencer strolled over to Lila, tugging off his gloves as he did so. He pulled something out of a front pocket of his jeans and held it up. Through the clear plastic of the encasing bag, Lila could see the brassy sheen of her new propane connector.

"Had to go into town for it after all," Spencer said, tossing the bag to Lila. She fumbled to catch it, and barely succeeded. "But Lowell had just the thing on hand in hardware."

Spencer reached for the fence and started to duck under it, but Lila seized all her courage and brought her own hand down on his. And froze as the noise of the stove door turned off in her head as if by a switch.

It's not the propane ... it's HIM!

When she touched him, Spencer arrested his movements, straightening and facing her, those green eyes wary but direct as always. And in spite of the turmoil Lila was feeling in realizing that Spencer's touch was what negated the buzz of the stove door, she had to finish what she'd started.

"I'm sorry." Lila got the two words out, and then gulped for air, feeling Spencer's inexplicable yet inescapable appeal through her fingertips. An appeal far beyond the incredible ability his touch seemed to have in silencing the mental chatter of memory-laden objects.

Her awareness heightened in the sudden quiet of her mind, Lila moved her hand, weaving it through air that felt thicker than normal and into her curls, which were getting downright greasy. Spencer said nothing, so Lila tried again.

"I'm sorry. I'm normally self-sufficient and some would even say I'm lucid, at least from time to time, but I haven't been that ... with ... with you. And I don't want to be rude, but I can't talk about it. I just ... I can say I need my solitude to ... to be able to interact with ... people. I can say that. I need to ... to ... "

Lila shook her head, her treasured words unreachable, unusable. She raised both hands to her head this time and nearly bashed herself in the forehead, because she was still holding the metal connector in one hand.

She shrugged in surrender, meeting Spencer's eyes again. This was going nowhere fast. Lila dove right at the bottom line.

"I would like us to be on good terms ... as neighbors."

Spencer raised his brows at that.

"I'd like us to be on good terms period," he said. He rested both forearms on the top of the fence, his hands overlapping. They were lightly tanned in spite of the gloves he was holding in the top hand, the skin just a little darker than the gloves, in fact. Toned in color by the sun and in texture by the wind and hard work, Lila thought she had never seen hands so very appealing before.

Jerking her line of sight back to Spencer's eyes, Lila searched them for hidden meaning. Spencer had his secrets, too, she decided, considering that straightforward gaze.

Straightforward-seeming gaze. That's what it was. But not devious. Not secretive, or so it seemed to Lila in a chaotic instant of clarity. Just holding his cards until the proper time to play them.

Telling herself it was only a formality, not an excuse for a touch she had refused to seek for too long, Lila held out her right hand. Spencer met Lila's hand with his own and they shook on it. Spencer's dead-on stare twinkled as their hands separated, a look that Lila recognized as mischievous. She thought he might follow the handshake—during which she'd felt more than agreement and knew he had, too—with a tip of his hat, and he did.

It was the slightest touch of his finger to his hat, the barest dip of his head towards her. It was distinct, but whispery ... like something he might do in a crowd and Lila would still know it was something just for her. Oh, how she'd like to write all of this off on account of the propane!

She'd like to, but she couldn't.

And maybe, just maybe, she didn't even want to. Door or no door.

15: Planning

"Kristen, please, I ... "

Lila pulled the phone back from her head as Kristen let fly with another vituperative soliloquy. A slight chuckle drew Lila's eyes to trace the only non-violent sound that had reached her ears since she'd answered Kristen's call. Sure enough, Spencer was watching from his post at her propane system. He'd showed her how to replace the connector, as promised, and had just started giving the entire setup a soapy review when Kristen called.

Lila pressed her thumb over the phone's speaker and dared to say, "She's got a real way with words."

"And the lungs to deliver them effectively," Spencer said, amusement coating every word.

Lila turned away from him again and moved to the edge of the fence, striving for privacy that just wasn't available, not with Kristen on a rampage. Lila wanted to watch the final leak-check, but she wasn't going to have that opportunity—at least not without Spencer savoring the full flavor of one of Kristen's diatribes.

" ... GOT to take better fucking care of yourself!" Kristen was raging when Lila dared to bring the phone near her ear again. "Why didn't you call me right away when you woke up sick? What if you hadn't woken up, Lila, what the hell then? Who else could I put in the will to take care of my baby?"

Her voice broke on the last word, and then Kristen's rant devolved into sobs barely strung together with profanity. It was shocking enough for Lila that she felt her heart skip a beat.

"Kristen! Kristen, don't cry! It's okay! I'm okay, and so is the propane system, it's ... oh, Kristen, don't!"

"I need ... you have to ... I ... SHIT! ... fucking hormones!"

As Kristen fought for control, Lila felt the wretchedness of the morning descend again, shattering the fragile peace that she had started to enjoy as Spencer had capably and deliberately walked her through replacing the connector.

"Here."

Lila snapped her head in Spencer's direction. She'd not heard him approaching through Kristen's meltdown, and here he was, almost right next to her, one hand reaching for her phone.

Wordlessly, she handed it to him. He looked the phone over briefly, and then pressed the speaker button. Lila winced as Kristen's current choking cry was amplified.

"Hello?"

Just like that, Kristen fell silent. And the silence stretched long enough for Lila to think to count it out in her mind.

1 ... 2 ... 3 ... 4 ...

"Who is this?"

"Spencer."

"And who THE HELL is that?"

"I'm Ms. Dawkins neighbor."

"In which direction?"

Spencer caught Lila's eye and grinned.

"West. And South and East, too, actually."

"I thought so. You're the asshole whose gates are too tight."

"Kristen!" Lila was aghast.

"Well? Isn't he?" Kristen was unrepentant, but at least she'd stopped her disconsolate lamentation. "And you, Lila, should tell me when I'm on speaker phone. You know I hate speaker phone."

"You're on speaker phone," Spencer said. The acid in his voice, Lila noticed, didn't reach his eyes. "And you are ... ?"

"Kristen Rush. Listen, you really fixed the leak? You're sure?"

"I was about to leak-test the system when you called."

"The whole thing, now, including the stuff inside the cabin?"

"Kristen, I ... " Lila couldn't let this continue.

"SHUT UP, Lila! Every damn connector and every fucking pipe is the same age. I have to know you're safe!"

"The whole thing, including the parts inside," Spencer said, making the words a promise with the firmness of their delivery.

Kristen's sigh was so deep that it seemed as if the dancing Wyoming wind itself was affected, gusting in rapidly changing directions just as the sound came through the speaker.

"Okay. Okay then. But Lila, you call me tonight, and you call me tomorrow, first thing. FIRST. THING!"

"First thing tomorrow, Kristen." Lila said, throwing up her hands.

"And tonight!"

"And tonight."

"Okay."

And Kristen hung up.

Lila took the phone from Spencer's still-outstretched hand.

"You don't have to ... "

"Why don't you do it, then?" he suggested.

"What? You're testing me now?"

The crinkles at the corners of Spencer's eyes were oddly alluring. Formed more by sun than laughter, Lila still suspected, they were like the beams of light that cut through an overcast sky ... beckoning, magnetic ... and hopeful.

"Not exactly," he said. "At least, there's no grading involved. Just practice, if you want it."

Lila nodded with unnecessary vehemence. Unnecessary, that was, for her agreement to the task—necessary to break the spell Spencer was casting on her. And whether he knew it or not, he was most assuredly practicing some form of witchcraft—or would that be warlockcraft?—on Lila.

"I do. I mean, that's a good idea. I don't know enough about the propane system, I can see that now. I should have been more careful last night. I noticed the smell yesterday afternoon; I just forgot about it ... I wasn't myself, I ... well, I forgot about it. And I shouldn't have."

Realizing she was babbling, Lila snapped her mouth shut and dared a glance back at Spencer's face. The sun's rays had faded around his eyes, but he was watching her, attentive as any bird of prey Lila had ever seen swooping above.

She cleared her throat, and it sounded exactly like the absurd, nervous attempt at diversion that it was.

"Let's get started then."

Spencer only nodded in answer to Lila's statement, which had come out sounding much more like a question. And in contrast to Lila's bobbing head motions, Spencer's agreement was direct and sure.

After Lila's bumbling tests had been completed—and though she was sure that Spencer had suggested she redo the segment underneath the stove on account of her inexperience, she had been too cognizant of the fact that she'd had to get on her hands and knees to conduct that portion of the leak-test—Spencer had left almost abruptly. He'd said something about needing to get Sunny back to the stable and left without even tipping his hat.

Lila was appalled by how forlorn she'd felt at that unusual departure. Although how she thought she could determine a normal exit after knowing Spencer for a mere two days, she could not say.

Late afternoon was easing into evening now, and Lila was seated at her desk, Thunder snuggled into her lap. Her computer was in front of her, but not open, and Lila wanted to feel guilty about not working. She wanted to, yes, but emotions were indifferent at best to wishes, and Lila knew that RayAnn would just be glad she was all right after the propane incident.

Work could wait indefinitely.

And so Lila stroked Thunder, who gifted her with an intermittent yawn or purr as he alternately dozed and slumbered. The cabin was hot, but the wind was accommodating and kept the toasty air circulating at a steady pace. Lila also had the assurance of Spencer's and her own efforts that there would be no repeat issues with the propane, although she thought of sleeping outside again, just for a day or two.

Lila looked at Thunder, who was relaxed in a loose "C" shape in her lap, one paw covering the tip of his nose.

"If not for you, I probably would."

The surge of affection Lila felt at the memory of how Thunder had awakened her this morning blended seamlessly into a reminder of her promise to call Kristen. It must be after 5:00 by now; Kristen should be home. Lila carefully extracted her cell phone from her pocket without disrupting Thunder too much and dialed Kristen's home phone.

Lou answered on the first ring.

"Lila! Everything okay?" He rushed on, trampling over the barest beginnings of Lila's response. "Kristen told me, and I'm so sorry. I should have been checking the system regularly for you, or showed you how to do it. Or both. Kristen! It's Lila for you!" Lou shouted the last, and Lila pulled the phone back from her head.

She hoped Kristen wasn't in another yelling mood herself.

"Lou, it was an accident, that's all. I'm fine, and the piping is fine now, too."

"That's good. I'm glad! But I'll still check it out again when I'm out hunting this fall. Here's Kristen."

And Lou—who regarded the telephone as a required tool of business and didn't much care to use the thing otherwise—then handed the phone off to Kristen.

"Am I on speakerphone again?"

"No, you're not, and if you were, you'd only be talking to me and Thunder."

"Good. I fucking hate speakerphone. Now tell me, are you REALLY all right? And I don't care what you say, I'm coming up tomorrow anyway, so you just be ready."

"Kristen, I'm fine! I really am. I was sick this morning, but I feel great now." Lila found herself crossing her fingers at the slightly skewed truth, and as Kristen launched into a lecture on the importance of taking better care of herself—thankfully at a lesser volume than she had done earlier in the day—Lila tried to convince herself that Kristen didn't need to know about the situation with Spencer.

"If you want to continue to lie about what happened to you yesterday ... "

Lila winced at the memory of Spencer's cutting words. The man certainly had infiltrated his way into her life in a mere two days, hadn't he?

"Kristen, wait."

Kristen uncharacteristically let Lila cut her off mid-sentence, and Lila floundered in the moment she had sought to create but wasn't sure she could legitimately inhabit.

"Kristen, there's a lot going on ... I need to tell you, okay?"

"Talk." Kristen delivered the commanding word with a wealth of undertones—chief among them, Lila thought, was relief.

It wasn't as hard as Lila thought to tell the story thus far. Of trespassing on Spencer's land, about which Kristen was positively gleeful, to the appalling state in which the encounter with the stove had left Lila.

"That's never happened before ... has it?" Kristen asked. Her words struck Lila as if they were a literal barrage of fists, making her understand as nothing had before how much she hid inside herself.

Even from Kristen.

"No. No, it hasn't, and neither has ... well, I'm getting ahead of myself."

Kristen was also delighted by the way Thunder had alerted Lila to the propane smell in the cabin—"Good kitty! Tell him Auntie Kristen is bringing him a whole case of tuna tomorrow!"—and also by Spencer's mysterious appeal to Lila.

"So he's hot, then? Peter-Peter-Goddamned-Cheater-hot?" She interrupted, making Lila frown and temporarily reconsider the whole honesty bit.

"No, it's not like that ... "

"Hotter than A. B.'s hot nephew?"

"Kristen!"

"Ahh. He IS hot. I can tell just by how you don't want to talk about it. It's just between us, Lila ... I won't breathe a word of it even to Lou. You know he'd be out there with a shotgun, protecting you like a bratty little sister!"

Lila laughed, doubt fading away.

"Okay, he's hot. He's ... " Lila searched her memory of Spencer for an appropriate descriptor, and found it lying right under the man's hat. "He's cowboy hot."

"Excellent! Go on, go on!"

It was Lila's rendition of Spencer's ability to put a stop to the barrage of input from memory-charged objects that challenged Kristen's significant credulity.

"You're shitting me."

"I am not!"

"Really? Touching this cowboy-hot, asshole fence tightening neighbor of yours, who you never even laid eyes on in all these years, THAT is your equivalent of hitting a mute button?"

"Really. I don't know what else to say, Kristen, I know it sounds crazy, but what doesn't sound crazy about me and the way I get histories out of objects?"

"Hell, I don't have a problem believing this shit—real life is always crazier than anything people make up, remember?—but what I don't have is any idea why you haven't chained this miracle man up to your bunk and jumped his bones already. Not that you'd need to chain him, I mean, but just to keep him at the ready, that's all I'm saying."

Indignation and amusement briefly warred in Lila's throat for a scant time before laughter won the battle. Kristen raised her voice and kept on talking.

"I'm serious! If touching the man's hand can give you a few hours of peace, can you just imagine what a good fuck would do for you? I mean, other than the obvious, which is a plus anyway, if you get my drift."

Tears were streaming down Lila's cheeks, and Thunder blinked blearily up at her, his rest ruined beyond repair. He rose, stretched, and bounded away, while Lila tried to catch her breath and Kristen continued to extol the positive benefits of Lila "getting it on" with Spencer.

"Kristen! You know I'm not like that!"

Kristen snorted. "You could be," she said then, setting Lila off again.

"Look, Lila, all I'm saying is, you could use a roll in the hay. I had my eye on Jake for you, I'll admit it, but Spencer's sounding better all the time, and maybe you could even convince him to loosen up his gates while you're loosening up his pants!"

"Kristen ... stop ... I can't ... I swear I can't ... even hardly breathe ... "

Kristen started to giggle then, and their shared laughter soared to heights raptors only dreamed of seeing. It took them a long time to come back to Wyoming soil, and although they were physically still distant, Lila felt as if Kristen were right in the room with her again.

Just as she'd promised to be the next day.

"Kristen, are you really coming up here tomorrow?"

"Damn right I am, but I can't stay over. I just have to see you for myself ... "

"I'm glad. I really am. Listen, are you up for some trespassing? I'm thinking ... maybe ... "

But Lila didn't need to say the rest out loud.

"You bet! Absolutely! As long as we don't have to wear ninja gear. It's too hot for that, even if this summer is as 'mild' as they say."

They hung up shortly after Lila reassured Kristen that no special costumes would be required for the trek she proposed, and Lila stood and stretched. Her muscles were pleasantly uncramped, unlike their typical state following a long stint at her computer. She tried to be cognizant of her posture when she was writing, but the truth was, Lila had always been more involved in the lives of her characters than in her own moment-to-moment existence.

Until recently, Lila reflected, rounding the corner of the bedroom to find Thunder curled back up on the bed.

"So you feel safe here again, do you, boy?" Lila sank onto the bare mattress next to Thunder, and stroked his fur. He yawned in her face and stretched out a paw towards her leg, flexing his claws without digging them in when he touched Lila's jeans.

"I'll take that as a cautious 'yes.'"

Lila inhaled deeply, finding no hint of propane remaining, but shuddered at the thought of sleeping here tonight. She'd kept the window shut tight since this morning, and the small room didn't seem the same without the breeze that normally flowed from the screen door behind her out through the window.

Just a freak accident! Lila shook her head. She could remind herself—literally until the cows came home—but she knew she would struggle with sleep tonight, even with Thunder to watch out for her.

Until the cows came home ...

That made Lila think of Spencer, which was just one more subject not conducive to relaxation. Lila got up and went out into the kitchen, determined to find something to make for supper. She would use her stove, by golly, and she would crack open her bedroom window the way she always did, too! She would not worry about the propane system again, and she would not obsess over a man she barely knew.

Even if that man did fill out his jeans in a singularly enticing way.

Lila set her empty kettle onto the burner with a smack that reverberated in the quietness of the cabin. She'd forgotten that she was nearly out of fresh water, what with the laundry she'd done last night. And ... she dashed outside and looked up into the rafters of the roof that extended over her porch, Lila groaned at the sight of her forgotten bra and underwear there, swaying in the breeze.

Yes. Of course. Of course it had been the red bra/panty set. And the rainbow-colored "days of the week" underwear collection.

Lila was appalled, but she knew Kristen would be rapturous. Kristen, who purportedly threw out her underthings at the slightest hint of wear, because, "You never know when you're going to need a ride in an ambulance with some adorable EMT."

Lila wondered if Kristen would now amend her mantra to include, " ... or have some hot cowboy ride up and see your laundry hanging out to dry."

This not-thinking-about-Spencer plan of hers was working out about as well as a pugilist touring a Whack-a-Mole test factory. The simile wasn't her best, Lila considered, but it wasn't bad.

"Maybe I should write? Right after I get some more water."

It was counter-intuitive—or would seem so to a non-writer, Lila supposed—but writing was a contrary muse. Lila could have all the time in the world to write, and her words would get jammed in a constricted bottleneck, unable to wend their way out. And on a deadline, when productivity was essential and one would think

212

creativity would be choked under the pressure, Lila frequently found herself working at her very best.

Now, following the incident with the propane, Lila knew nothing would be expected of her, so she figured she was likely to struggle. Except that RayAnn had no idea that Lila had been ill this morning, so RayAnn would still be thinking Lila would be operating in deadline-mode.

The mental gymnastics were silly, but Lila had found them useful in the past. Convincing herself that she had some target to hit was often a good motivator for her, and she slipped into rationalization mode easily.

It was reassuring, following the chaotic events of the day, particularly the sickening morning she'd endured.

Lila shouldered her ESPRIT bags, each holding a 3-gallon water jug, and headed for the pump. The day was winding down now, with the sun sinking into the west, using the sentry pines to cast long shadows across Lila's path, until the woods became too thick to penetrate. Lila spared a moment to turn and admire the red-gold splashes on the western sides of the pines; she loved this time of day, this enduring, short-lived light.

Emerging from the ravine, Lila paused again to savor the view. The sun, unimpeded by clouds for once this visit, was distorting as it met the horizon, appearing as a slight oval—as if the day's events had translated into physical pressure for it, too. The sunset coloration was delicate rather than bold, a fact more than made up for by the pines' wind-inspired serenade and the occasional, sharp "twang" of a diving nighthawk, feasting on insects in the dwindling light of day.

Kristen was right. Lila's Wyoming home was more than overdue for a name. But Lila, who had titled each of her novels with barely the effort it took her to breathe, was at a loss to sum up her sanctuary in a simple word or three. She turned from the panoramic view and continued on to the water pump, thoughts bubbling in her head like a watched pot ... never quite reaching a boil.

On her return to the cabin, Lila left the water sitting near the door and climbed up on the bench just under the edge of her porch's roof. She retrieved her laundry, carried it inside, and put it away before returning for her water supply.

No wonder Spencer had hurried off. The red and the rainbow! She could not possibly have left a worse selection out for her neighbor to see, unless it was the ratty old pairs she kept on hand for a certain time of month. Lila found herself chuckling in spite of it all as she prepared dinner with a little extra rice, to make up for the unexpected demands of the day.

While the rice was cooking, Lila powered up her computer and stared out as the light drained from the sky in slow, slow motion. She wondered if she'd be "powered up" again herself by the time Kristen arrived, and decided that—if her limited data set was anything to go by—yes, she would.

Although, maybe Kristen is right. Maybe I should just find a way to keep touching Spencer and not worry about finding the door.

Keep touching Spencer!

"Yes, because that wouldn't complicate anything, now would it?"

Thunder appeared, drawn by the sound of her voice, she supposed, and demanded his supper. Lila opened a small tin of salmon and added a bit to Thunder's meal, sealing the can into a zippered plastic bag and stashing it in the refrigerator. She was going meatless tonight, herself, and when the rice finished cooking, Lila added just a bit of cheese to it and dined by battery-powered candlelight.

Her thoughts flitted between Spencer and tomorrow's planned excursion, nervous butterflies that couldn't decide where it would be safe to land. Despite the fact that Kristen was planning to arrive relatively early, Lila knew she wouldn't be able to sleep well tonight. Her experience the night before and this morning had spoiled her for sleeping, and her napping throughout the day had probably not helped, either.

And so, once the dishes were done and the wind's direction checked yet again—it was holding fast to its normal path, sparing Lila the misdirected gusts that had gone past the propane tank the previous night—Lila parked herself in front of her computer and started editing the piece she'd told RayAnn was her top priority.

Two hours later, Lila stopped to take a trip to the outhouse. When she stood, she felt the familiar resistance of muscles held too long in one position. Lila tried to relax her muscles as much as possible while making all haste in the direction of the outhouse, but that was a difficult proposition. So she paused on the return trip, and when she leaned back ...

The sky, in its typical wide-open wonderment, was serving up a bonus offering of incredible beauty. The apparently endless blue expanse by day was even more stunning by night, punctuated with more stars than seemed possible—like a Facebook meme overpopulated with exclamation points, the Wyoming night sky was exponentially overzealous. Unencumbered by clouds, and rimmed in Lila's vision with the pines that surrounded her cabin, the stars were uninhibitedly exhibitionist as they released the full bounty of their brilliance.

That the light Lila was now seeing had traveled through distances so vast they bordered on the fanciful was not lost on her. She shivered, and it was not on account of the temperature, which had receded from the significant heat of the day. As Lila's eyes became more accustomed to the darkness, scores of additional stars revealed themselves to her, and she was drawn directly to the swath of concentrated star-power that comprised the Milky Way.

She'd wrapped her arms around herself without realizing it—so much for stretching, again—but when she did notice, she stretched her arms back out, as if opening up for a hug with the stars themselves. Lila lifted her face up, letting the fragile remains of brilliance generated hundreds and thousands and millions of years ago fall on her here, just outside her tiny home, on her tiny planet, orbiting her tiny star.

It was a momentary marvel, this pure, certain feeling of belonging, and Lila savored it with all of the determination she possessed.

Inspired by the significance of her bonding time with the stars above, Lila scurried back into the cabin and flipped open her laptop again. She had intended to brush her teeth and go to bed after her excursion to the outhouse, but the juxtaposition of the enormity of the night sky against her own day's experience pushed her instead to the scene that had stymied her just before her first trespassing adventure.

Not that her experience was unimportant or trivial; Lila considered, as she waited for the laptop to power up and plugged the power cord into the cabin's solar-charged battery backup to support the computer's battery, nearly spent on editing. No, what the stars above had reminded Lila was that what seems to be tantamount at one moment can be reduced to minutiae in the next.

And the reverse was also true. Lila slipped new batteries into a pair of candles and set them beside her, hoping Kristen didn't arrive too early the next day.

Dave's killer was in for some realizations of his own, and Lila was excited to see what happened next.

16: Subterfuge

Lila woke with full sun streaming in her window and a crotchety cat bumping his head against her hand where it lay in a patch of bright light.

"Thunder! What time is it?" Lila found it was hard enough prying her eyelids open; sitting up proved to be an additional challenge.

All Thunder could tell Lila about the time was that it was later than usual, which she knew, so she made haste to feed him and then checked her cell phone.

"9:30? Oh no," Lila groaned, dropping the phone on the bed and clutching fists full of scrambled curls with both hands. If Kristen had departed Casper when she planned to, she could be arriving at any minute.

Lila dressed as quickly as possible, and then flopped down on her still-unmade bed to look beyond the time on her phone. Thunder serenaded her with the modern music of his breakfast: a crunchy beat accompanied by the occasional jangle of stray kibble escaping a hasty mouthful.

"late leavin, c u >10!"

Lila released a breath she didn't know she'd been holding. She had a few minutes to gather herself and some semblance of breakfast, and to put the cabin back in rough order after her late night. But she'd still have to hurry to meet Kristen!

Lila stuffed her phone in her pocket and prepped her fanny pack with water from the refrigerator, since she hadn't remembered to set her "usual" bottles outside last night. Even in the jumble of this morning, satisfaction flooded Lila's senses—it sounded like a shout on echo, and felt like the first breath of autumn air across her skin—as she recalled her writing last night. She'd only quit when the stove door had picked up enough volume to interrupt the vividness of the storyline she'd been working on ... that had been around 3:00 a.m.

Probably a good thing the stove door got through to me, or I wouldn't have gotten any sleep at all!

Although the stove door was part of the reason she and Kristen were meeting today, so technically, Lila supposed the stove door's penetration of her writing trance still qualified for the "not good" category.

But Lila had slept, which was most definitely good ... capital-lettered GOOD, in fact! She'd slept, she'd awoken—late though it was—and she'd not been the slightest bit dizzy nor scented anything but Wyoming air, dust, and other odors that were healing rather than sickening.

Lila added a snack-size baggie of her homemade granola to her fanny pack and patted her phone where she'd tucked it into her jeans pocket. Yes, she was ready. She'd finger-comb her hair on the walk and that would do; Kristen had seen worse. Lila waved goodbye to Thunder rather than petting him, as he had finished his food and was scrutinizing his litter box—apparently looking for just the right spot to go—and then she dashed off in the direction of the outhouse herself.

Chirping birds and the rise and fall of cattle calling to each other in the distance somewhere were the background soundtrack as Lila hurried down towards the gate. When it appeared in her sight, she worked one of the water bottles loose from its position at her waist without breaking stride and then stopped to drink greedily. Not because the downhill walk was such a difficult workout, but rather because her long, working night had left her as parched as a similar expanse of time drinking in college might have done.

Thirsty, yes, but invigorated, too. It was amazing the difference one day made! Lila tucked the water bottle back into its holster and resumed her walk, ruffling her curls with her fingers as she went, tugging here and there at the spots that felt bunched and gnarled to her questing hands.

So engrossed was she in her task that she didn't notice the man crouched in the dirt along the western border of her property until he stood, dusting off his hands in such a way that it sounded like slow applause at first. Lila jerked to a stop, eyes darting until she found the source of the sound, and caught the tail end of Spencer's vertical movement, along with the motion of his hands.

"Morning, ma'am," he called, bridging the distance between them with his voice, and without apparent effort. "Out for a walk again today?"

Lila bristled, and suppressed her outrage with effort. Spencer was spying on her now! She felt the rush of blood to her face, flagging her guilt in red on her cheeks, because of course she fully intended on trespassing.

As soon as Kristen gets here!

Lila traced the road up as far as she could see it, but didn't see Kristen anywhere yet. She counted to 10 in her mind, rushing it, but hoping the effort was worth making in any case.

"I'm expecting a visitor," she called out to Spencer then, adding, *Not that it's any of your business!* with extra vehemence in her thoughts.

"Is that right?" Spencer moved his inspection south to the next post along the fence. Lila wondered how he could make his disbelief so obvious without putting a nasty twist into his tone.

"Yes," she said. Her own voice needed some of Spencer's secret modulation, somehow, because even one word came out with a snip and irritation so clear that a child could accurately diagnose her distress, if not the exact cause of it.

Spencer dropped to one knee in the dirt again, his gloved

hands seizing the fencepost and testing its security with a couple of strategic pulls. The posts along this line of the fence were new and old intermingled, straight steel alternated in no discernable pattern with wood posts that approximated linearity at best, and mocked it at worst.

Although Lila kept moving, she was transfixed by Spencer's hands as he worked the post, and then checked the four strands of barbed wire that bisected it. What was it about his hands? They moved like any other hands, as far as Lila could tell. Encased in a second skin of leather, they weren't even directly visible, and yet ...

And yet, there was something about the man's hands that stirred a primal reaction in Lila. She found herself thinking of how those hands would be on her skin, how they would move with the same determination, but with exploratory caresses instead of methodical motions.

Good grief.

Lila grabbed for her water bottle again, and fumbled it into the dirt. When she lifted her head after retrieving the bottle, Spencer had taken his eyes off his task and transferred them to her.

"She'll be here any minute," Lila said, and it sounded like a non-sequitur because of the way her thoughts had detoured far and away from the brief conversation she'd been having with Spencer.

Spencer smiled, but the gesture didn't make it up to crinkle the corners of his flashing green eyes. He stood—refraining from dusting himself off this time—and moved on to the next post.

Which, of course, happened to be in the direction of the old house, and the call of the still-missing stove door.

"Where's Sunny?"

Spencer cast a look back at Lila that carried more suspicion than a small movement should be capable of doing.

"Gave her the day off," he said, words clipped short. "Had to bring out minerals for the cattle." He gestured back towards the road, and Lila knew the spot he must mean, about a half-mile back.

"Then I thought I'd just do a quick check and see how many of these posts need replacing."

"Oh."

It sounded legitimate to Lila, but then, she supposed it would. On the other hand, that Spencer would leave his vehicle parked out of sight ... that didn't seem so up-and-up.

"Well, I'm just going to wait for Kristen at the gate."

"Fine by me," Spencer drawled, and tipped his hat. "Not that you need my permission to stay on your own property."

Lila opened her mouth to retort and then snapped it shut. Unbidden, Julie sprang to mind, exhorting Lila to "half-smile"—"like the Mona Lisa," she'd said—in times of stress. Lila still thought the notion was too simplistic to help, but since she'd thought of it, she tried it now.

Her lips refused to bend to her will, and so she turned away from Spencer's now bemused stare, and set off to the gate.

"Shoulders!" Spencer called out, and then he laughed.

"Ugh!" Lila growled, hoping the small sound didn't make its way back to Spencer. Although the annoying man would probably do nothing more than laugh again.

"Lila!" It was Kristen, waving.

Lila groaned, but refused to look back to where Spencer was now surely watching again. She was in for it now ... between the two of them, she would have no peace, even if by some miracle she and Kristen would be able to look for the stove door now!

"That must be the hot cowboy," Kristen said, dramatically sotto-voce, when they met at the gate. "Mmm-hmm, I do believe it is."

Lila didn't reply. She was transfixed by the new quick-release gate handle neatly installed on top of a brand-new sentry post.

"What? What is it?"

"Spencer. He must've ... " Words flew out of Lila's mind like a startled flock of birds and she had to settle for pointing.

"Sweet!" Kristen said, enthusiasm as unbridled as Sunny apparently was today. Kristen flicked the clasp of unbarbed wire that provided extra security for the gate against a cow looking for a good back scratch out of the way and gave Lila a hard look.

"That's not all," she said, lowering her voice back down into the stealth range. "You're pissed! What did he do? What did he say?"

Now Lila did look, and found Spencer strolling along down the fence line, continuing his inspections with apparent single-minded focus. Lila sighed, returning her gaze to Kristen, and reached out to hold the gate post as Kristen operated the handle. An unnecessary gesture, with the smooth operation of the new device.

"He's ... it's just ... I don't know, Kristen! He's horrible, and then he's wonderful. And then he's horrible again! I swear, he's checking fences just to keep me off his property. I didn't even notice the new handle or post, I was so mad."

Kristen stepped through the gate, and took a long hard look at Spencer as Lila closed the gate and wire hook again. They both turned fully to watch Spencer as he knelt in front of his next target.

"You left out hot." Kristen said then, elbowing Lila in the side. "You've got good taste!"

"But he's an ass ... " Lila caught herself.

"Hole. Asshole, that is. Yes, so you've said. And what man isn't? For that matter, what woman isn't? Lila, just because you picked two men who had more dark than light in them doesn't mean all men are that way. Look at Lou! Man's a consummate butthead when it comes to laundry, dishes, and all the stuff a couple is supposed to share nowadays, but he's still father material!"

"A consummate butthead, huh?"

"Well, I don't want to overuse 'asshole' so early in the day. I could go with 'dickwad,' but that's so immature, and here I am, a mother-to-be, and I'm going to have to clean up my language."

Lila laughed then. Kristen had been profane before it was vogue.

"I think you'd better just settle for teaching proper use of vulgarity to your children," and Lila wrapped an arm around Kristen's shoulder and pulled her in for a hug as she emphasized the plural.

"God, that's what Lou said, only he didn't put it nearly as nicely." Kristen hugged Lila back. "Look, you're aware of Spencer's assholery early on, which is more than you were with Peter-Peter-Goddamned-Cheater. And we're never having a repetition of Stuart's bullshit, so what are you worrying about?"

Lila looked down at the ground underneath her feet. It seemed solid enough, even with the stove door's latent howling, but she was still afraid.

"I'm afraid," she admitted, and Kristen's arm tightened around her.

"Don't be. Don't! I mean, unless you're afraid you won't be able to walk for a week after ... "

Lila laughed out loud, and Kristen joined in.

"You're horrible," Lila said, when their spasm of laughter waned.

"I know. But you still love me. Why do you think you can't find a horribly wonderful man to love, too? Or at least to have a delicious, raunchy FLING with."

Lila shook her head at that, but her face was now sporting a decidedly full smile.

"Come on, now," Kristen said with one last squeeze of Lila's shoulders. "Daylight's wasting and I really do have to get back tonight."

And Kristen strode off, not arcing up the hill towards the cabin, but instead taking a direct line off the curve of the land and heading right at Spencer.

"Kristen, what ... "

"Come on!" Kristen said, turning back to Lila with a spark of devilment in her eyes. "I have a plan."

"Nothing good has ever started with those words," Lila muttered, but she followed Kristen anyway. She couldn't imagine where this scene was headed and the mystery of it—disaster though it would invariably prove to be—was no more resistible than Kristen herself.

When Spencer finally looked up, Kristen waved with enthusiasm she normally reserved for new metal bands.

"Mornin'!" Kristen called, picking up her pace and stretching out her hand. Lila hurried to watch the unfolding drama at close range.

Spencer tugged off a glove and shook Kristen's hand, already looking slightly confused. He caught Lila's eye for a moment before looking back at Kristen, who was bubbling enthusiasm for his fence evaluation. Lila somehow kept her shoulders down, but she couldn't vouch for whatever sentiment her eyes conveyed.

"I wonder, though," Kristen was saying, animation never flagging, "if Lila could take me down to the house she was telling me about, on your property."

Spencer's eyes might as well have been made of knives now, and they stabbed both Kristen and Lila in turn, although the former appeared not to notice.

"That's an interesting request," Spencer said, removing his other glove with deliberate, slow motions. He rested one forearm on top of the post he'd just examined and leaned towards Kristen. Lila kept looking at his face, but not without effort.

Those hands!

"Here's the thing," Kristen said, leaning in, too—as if about to disclose a secret. And then she did, with, "I'm an amateur photographer and I'm hoping to get into your collection."

"Collection?" While Kristen had long been a shutterbug, Lila had no idea what "collection" she was talking about.

"I haven't heard of you," Spencer said, baldly cool. "And I've heard of pretty much every artist out of Casper."

Kristen laughed, and Lila could only stare. She hadn't seen Kristen work so hard to charm a man since Lou walked into her life.

"But I have heard of you! And while I'm not in the Nic or anything," she demurred—demurred! Lila could hardly believe it— referring to Casper's art museum, the Nicolaysen, "I am up and coming. If you'd been in Jack's Coffee House this week, you would've seen my exhibit."

"Kristen! Your photos are up in Jack's?" Lila grabbed Kristen and hugged her hard. "You sneak! Why didn't you tell me?"

"It only just happened, Lila, and here I am to tell you in person!" Kristen said, her sincere smile generously highlighted with devilry. "The photos just went up," she said to Spencer. "I specialize in close-ups of western artifacts, though I do the occasional panoramic view as well."

"I don't have much photography in my collection," Spencer said, suspicion still clear in his stance, "but I'm always on the lookout for new talent. Jack's, you said?"

Kristen nodded, "Yes, for the next eight weeks."

"I'll be sure to check it out." And with a nod, Spencer turned away, sliding the shields of his gloves back over his hands.

"But the old house!" Kristen exclaimed, reaching out to catch Spencer's arm before he moved too far away.

Spencer turned back, his expression fierce and snapping underneath the shadow cast by his hat.

"Please," Kristen said, all but batting her eyes at Spencer. "The stove sounded so interesting to me. I'm sure I could get some unique imagery out of it."

"I'm sure you could, too," Spencer drawled, his eyes dropping to Kristen's hand, which was still resting on his arm.

"I wouldn't consider trespassing," Kristen lied blatantly, not moving her hand. "But I was fascinated by Lila's description of the stove. I just have to ask you to please consider allowing me to check it out for myself."

Her plea made—and Lila had found it delightful, even though it had come down to being at Lila's expense—Kristen finally removed her hand from Spencer's arm, her considered reluctance no doubt meant to boost the message that her artistic desire was overwhelming her common sense.

SOMEthing is overwhelming her common sense! Lila couldn't decide if she was honored or appalled that it was their friendship, in fact, that was inspiring this display.

Even though Kristen had been known to pull over along a stretch of roadway just to take a photo of an interesting splice in a strand of barbed wire, and probably did have an interest of her own in the stove.

Spencer remained mute and motionless for long enough for Lila to become uncomfortable again. If this ploy failed, what was next? Tea back at the cabin and periodic viewing through binoculars, to see if Spencer had left yet?

"Far be it for me to interfere with a Wyoming artist," he said finally, raising Lila's hopes only to smash them with his next words. "Just the old house, then."

"Just the old house," Kristen promised solemnly, and then ruined the seriousness of her image with a little bounce. "Lila can escort me. We're having lunch afterwards, perhaps you could join us?" she called, and Lila bit back a gasp at Kristen's brazenness.

"Not today," Spencer said, turning his back to them as he headed towards the next post on the line.

"Another time, thank you so much!" Kristen turned to Lila, all grins and either a twitchy eye or a multitude of winks. "Lila, can you take me there right now?"

"Sure, I guess. You have water?"

"Yeah, in my pack with the camera, but don't worry, I keep the camera in a separate compartment and a waterproof bag." Kristen lowered her voice now. "Did I remember right about where the house is?" She gestured in the direction Spencer was walking.

"Yes, and he'll walk right by us if he's really checking this whole line."

"Perfect!"

"Perfect? How? Come on, Kristen, give me a hint. You know I don't have your gift for strategy."

Kristen laughed at that.

"My famous writer friend envies my gift for deviousness, I mean, for strategy? This is all kinds of awesome!"

Despite repeated cajoling on Lila's part, Kristen refused to divulge her plan—if indeed she had one at all—regarding Spencer's proximity to their limited range of permissible trespassing. Lila soon gave up on the topic and when they finally arrived at the shell of the old house, she decided on a new line of inquiry.

"So tell me about this collection of Spencer's."

"You haven't heard?" Kristen interrupted her perusal of the stove in its sad setting to see Lila shake her head. "Well, it's big news in Casper, that's for sure. Your stunning example of Western manhood is a big-time collector of Western art ... and people are taking notice. Oh, this is so cool!"

Kristen stepped carefully into the remains of the house and circled the stove, examining it from every angle. Her camera, which she'd held loosely in her hands since they'd crossed the fence into Spencer's territory, came to life, clicking and zooming and aligning this way and that for just the right capture.

Lila stood back and watched. The stove door was distinctly louder here and the stove was reduced to a background muttering, like a slow-moving stream just barely within hearing distance.

"If Adam Spencer buys one of your pieces," Kristen said

sometime later, as if the conversation had not come to a full halt earlier, "other people start buying, too. It's like contagious hotness!"

"Nice," Lila mumbled, her own attention wandering as she sought the direction of the door. It couldn't be far away ...

"I love the design on the door here!" Kristen exclaimed. "Hell, I love the way there's only one door. The way it's hanging open. But this pattern ... this is really fucking gorgeous."

Lila couldn't remember the design Kristen was talking about and wasn't sure she'd actually viewed it at all. She approached the stove, stepping gingerly into the outline of the house and sidling around to see the front side of the yawing stove door.

"See?" Kristen pointed, her finger swirling over the elegant vines and flowers, stopping above a hummingbird that pointed into the very center of the largest blossom.

"It's beautiful," Lila said, and grimaced, remembering a scene that wasn't hers to know, wherein Nell had uttered the same words. Nell's memory was like a transparent overlay on the present, adding a filmy haze to the world. It was slight, but Lila found it difficult to shake, regardless.

"I'm keeping an eye out for Spencer between shots," Kristen said, her cunning smile shuttered as she watched Lila's face. "You try to zero in on the direction of the other door. Think about this pattern, maybe, and try to follow the noise trail back to it?"

"That's a good idea," Lila said, and straightened. "And you make sure you take a break for water. You haven't had to pee once yet."

"I've been holding it," Kristen said with a grin. "But thanks to that comment, I can't possibly manage another minute. Here, take this." She thrust the camera into Lila's hands and went directly towards the nearby hawthorns.

"Only for you would I suffer the indignity of pissing outdoors!" Kristen proclaimed as she walked away. "You and that amazing stove, anyway."

Lila stood still, holding the camera gingerly, as Kristen's footsteps were muted by grasses and distance. She looked down at the floral pattern, ravaged by rust and time, but still touchingly delicate, a strange beauty embedded on the heavy metal of the stove. Shouldn't the stove have melted in the fire? Lila didn't know, and supposed that it clearly "shouldn't" have, since it had not.

She slipped the strap of Kristen's camera around her neck and half-shut her eyes, but a wave of dizziness sprung them back open. Lila swallowed hard and tried to envision the other door, a mirror to its mate, she supposed, hanging in the spot where it belonged.

The thin overlay of past and present she'd experienced before returned, and stuttered, like a puzzle piece that wouldn't quite fit. Lila concentrated, thinking of her own feet secure in the "now" while her head sought Nell's heart, which had so loved this very stove, with its missing door ... a door that was somehow more special than its mate ...

"Angus!" Nell ran her fingers over the pattern of the door, following the three-dimensional vine at first and then fluttering onto the hummingbird that hovered near the top. "It's beautiful, it'll be like a garden in my kitchen! But ... but you shouldn't have." Her radiant smile faltered. "James won't ... "

"He doesn't have to know it's from me," Angus said, his youthful voice determined.

Nell's laugh was stunted.

"Who else would it be from, my sweet Angus?" Nell's hand moved from the stove door Angus was holding to his face, cupping his cheek gently. "But I love you for this thoughtful gift."

She did not add, "I wish I could love you the way you deserve," but it reverberated out of the memory as if by trumpet fanfare.

"Lila!"

Lila turned to Kristen, who was back from her bathroom break and staring at Lila with no small concern, her brow furrowed and lips turned down, even though her voice was but a whisper.

"Are you okay? Just nod," Kristen said, relief transforming her face as Lila nodded. "Good, good. We'll talk later ... Spencer's headed this way, so hand me my camera and try to not look white as fucking parchment, okay? Oh, and play along with whatever I say."

"Don't I always?"

"Yes, you've got the makings of a fine sidekick when you're not in a trance! Did you get a bead on the other door?"

Lila stepped to the side as Kristen smoothly resumed photographing the stove, and saw that Spencer was indeed striding their way, though he was still quite distant. She tossed her head, remembering Nell's unspoken words and the adoration—not passion—she held for James' younger brother.

"I think so," Lila said. "I think it might actually be down past the draw."

"I probably peed right on it. Marking my territory and all."

"No, it's not that close. It's not too far, but it's not ... " Lila clamped her lips down as Kristen shushed her.

"Remember, play along!"

"Aye-aye, Captain."

Kristen winked, but refused to laugh. She raised herself up from her crouch and waved enthusiastically to Spencer.

17: Revelations

I t had been like watching a bizarre dance, Lila thought as she and Kristen set off the slight downhill slope towards the draw. She didn't look over her shoulder, feeling Spencer's stare as if it were a physical touch.

Though if it were, she and Kristen would surely be jerked to a halt. Spencer had finally yielded to Kristen's passionate pleading, but to say that he'd given his permission reluctantly would be an understatement drilled deeper than any well.

Kristen stopped at a fencepost that stood listlessly with only one other of its brethren for company. A rusted coil of barbed wire leaned haphazardly against the first post, its once-circular shape distorted by time and gravity into a squashed ovoid with an off-center divot.

"This is prime!" Kristen exclaimed. "Lila, go stand over there," and Kristen waved one arm dictatorially towards the draw. "I've got to get this!"

As Lila took her position, Kristen circled the post, considering, coming to a position that would place the shell of the house in the backdrop of the shot.

Of course.

Kristen raised her camera and then lowered it. She cupped her hands and called out to Spencer through their unnecessary megaphone.

"Adam! Hey, I can call you 'Adam,' right?" Kristen rushed on without waiting for a reply, much as she'd done when cajoling Spencer into letting her and Lila spend more time on his land. "Can you step to the side, or go back a bit? I've got just the hint of the old house here in ... yes, that's good. Oh, even better, thank you again!"

Lila watched Spencer move slowly away, his focus splintered by the subtle rise of the land, the way he was shaking his head only notable because of how it was magnified by his hat joining in the movement. He paused for a moment, lifting his hat and running his fingers through thick hair that looked to be chafing under the restraint of the hat.

As Spencer tugged his hat back into position, he caught Lila watching him and favored her with an unsmiling glare. She raised her shoulders and then dropped them in an exaggerated shrug, and that did it, just barely. Spencer smiled that smirk-smile of his and tipped his hat.

And then he turned and walked back to the fence-line he'd been working.

Watching Spencer's back, broad shoulders tapering down to ... Lila blinked quickly, dragging her line of sight away from its destination. She didn't believe this was luck, but she didn't have time to consider what Spencer might be up to, not with the irritating cascade of memory-sound that was shrieking in her mind, storming to a summit that seemed so close that she could crest it at any moment.

Lila edged nearer the hawthorns. She felt as if she were a human tuning fork, vibrating ever louder by the demanding strikes of some unknown taskmaster who wanted to achieve an unsustainable volume.

She felt as if she would shake apart, that the seams of her body were insufficiently secured for this level of outside interference, that her innards would soon make their way outwards through fissures that had been developing slowly over the years, that she would bleed to death both figuratively and literally as the incredible strength of memory stuck in the unassuming coffin of the stove door crammed its way into a new vessel ... into her.

232

She felt ... she felt ...

"I think we're alone now," Kristen sang breathlessly in Lila's ear, making her jump. "Shit! Sorry! These trances are new, Lila ... at least, you having them when you're not touching anything is new."

"Yes," Lila said, her vocal cords churning the word out through some sort of memory-based haze inside her throat.

"And they're stronger, aren't they."

"Yes," Lila rasped again, though Kristen's tone hadn't indicated that she was asking a question.

"Come on." Kristen took Lila's arm and tucked it through her own, her voice strong despite an underlying quaver. "You need to resolve this. WE need to resolve this. Soon, before I can't take it and just haul your ass back to Casper with me."

"Don't forget Thunder," Lila said, and was rewarded with a pat on her arm and a barely-there smile from Kristen.

"That's better. That's you. Maybe you can divide your thoughts between Thunder and this door?"

"I don't know ... it's so hard to focus already ... "

"Well, then, I'll help you with division, same as back in school."

Lila almost chuckled at that.

They walked along the edge of the hawthorns, taking it as slowly as a woman of their combined ages might have done. Kristen spoke of Thunder frequently, asking questions about his habits and health, forcing Lila to answer, and then kept silent for a few minutes in between her queries. The hastily-invented process worked, too—at least, it kept Lila from sinking completely into the mire of memory.

"It's like I'm almost submerged and then I can breathe again," Lila said after a time, words escaping like gasps themselves as she explained, and Kristen looked at her with concern all but scrawled on her forehead.

"We've only been walking for fifteen minutes or so, Lila."

"It's longer than that," Lila answered. "It feels longer, anyway."

"That's what he said," Kristen said, her attempt at cheek falling flat as a rotten apple, flesh smacking against hard-packed soil.

Flesh smacking against hard-packed soil!

"We're close. We're really close," Lila blinked frantically, barely aware that her eyes were now sending a deluge of tears down her face. "This way."

She pulled with such force that she severed the bond of her and Kristen's linked arms, and when that happened, Lila plunged out of the present, sunny day and into the murky dark that follows twilight.

Plodding steps, a heavy burden, the weight of a heart broken more than once this day weighing Lila—no, weighing Angus—down, Angus tugged the body of his brother James through the draw where the hawthorns grew.

He had to finish this. He had no illusions that Nell would survive, having seen the damage James had wrought earlier when he'd shoved her towards the stove, when she'd fallen and hit her head—hit her head!—but the doctor was with her now. The doctor was with her now and the boys were with The Shepherd.

Angus had done everything he could for the woman he loved. Everything! Up to and including killing the man who had quite literally thrown away his perfect wife, his perfect boys ... his perfect life.

Angus sobbed, dropping the body near the edge of the dead ravine. The soil here was barren, desolate, the Badlands in miniature, with great gouges form by time and rain. Very little grew here.

"Lila?"

"You had everything!" Angus screamed, anguish pouring out, blood from a fatal wound. "Everything! And you threw it away. You KILLED her! YOU KILLED HER!"

He fell upon James' body, pummeling the airless chest with his fists until exhaustion weakened their blows and then he clutched James to him, stroking

234

his brother's hair, his hand coming away sticky with blood.

With blood from the exit wound of the bullet fired from Angus' gun after James had nearly killed the woman they both loved.

"She never loved me," Angus cried into the darkness of James' dead eyes, hands now framing the lifeless face that glowed eerily in the moonlight. The face of the brother he'd once looked up to, once loved as his hero. "She always loved you. And you threw that away! You threw her away.

You threw ME away."

The body slipped from his fingers, head lolling in the dirt, eyes turned vacantly toward the ravine.

"You deserved to die, you did." This in a whisper, uncertainty carrying the words, wobbly and near to dropping them.

A coyote began to howl, a high-pitched, piercing shriek that begged for an answer it would not, this night, receive.

The hawthorns behind Angus and to his side were silent witnesses, never to reveal the burden of their knowledge. The draw skirted the edge of the ravine at this one juncture, a place where James and Angus had visited as boys, playing that they were exploring the surface of the some other planet, so alien was the landscape. Angus dropped back into the jagged, uneven soil along the edge, the weight of the day and his actions weakening him at last.

He would bury his brother here, just far enough away from their childhood play-land to protect James' body from being exposed by the erosion. He'd seed the soil with wild grasses next spring; plants gave soil strength to stay put, to hide its secrets.

A faint glint of moonlight through the clouds struck the stove door where it lay at James' side, having slipped off his midriff as Angus pulled James' body along. The floral scene was marred with Nell's blood; Angus wasn't fool enough to use it to mark James' grave outright, but he did intend to bury it with James.

To mark his brother's corpse with the evidence of what he'd done.

"Lila!"

Lila leapt from the dark scene she'd been witnessing back into the sunlight, realizing that the keening sound she'd taken for a coyote was her own cries. Kristen was holding her by both shoulders, keeping her from the edge of the ravine Lila had seen through A. B.'s eyes.

A. B.!

"A. B.," Lila manage to say, cutting off the horrid sound she'd been making without knowing it. "A. B. killed James."

"WHAT?!" The question was sharp—the voice that asked it, deep.

Gasping, Kristen let go of Lila and spun around towards the hawthorns. There, Spencer emerged from the trees, his face wearing an expression black as ashes, advancing on Kristen and Lila with the tumultuous speed of wildfire.

"'A. B. killed James?'" Spencer stopped just shy of touching Lila, so close that Kristen bumped against them both when she thrust her body into the gap.

"Stop it!" Kristen was fierce in her defense, unrelenting. "Back up! Back THE FUCK up, and do it NOW."

"Tell me what's going on!" Spencer said, raising his voice but not shouting. His eyes grabbed hold of Kristen and Lila alternately, flipping between the two of them as if he didn't know where to direct the full strength of his ire. His hands were clenched at his sides, knuckles white. "I saw what was happening right up until you crossed the draw, saw how Lila here was staggering around, and now she's saying 'A. B. killed James' and you're telling ME to back the fuck up?"

Lila could not feel more shaken if she'd been physically accosted.

"Yes, I am!" Kristen said, unmoving and unmovable, her full attention now directed at Spencer, rather than Lila, who was slipping into another kind of darkness.

"Lila!"

The last thing Lila saw before she blacked out was Spencer trying to push past Kristen to catch her.

She came to in the shade, her head in Kristen's lap, her face being gently smoothed by her friend's damp fingers. The fingers drifted away, a water bottle gurgled, and then the fingers drifted back, moving in gentle contrast to the sharp words Kristen was speaking. Spencer's response was muted, but the shade shifted suddenly, flashing Lila briefly with light.

Light that contrasted with the deadly gloom of the story she'd been hearing from the stove door. Light that left as swiftly as it had arrived, bringing Lila back to an awareness of how loud the memories were that still remained in her mind. The light flashed again as Spencer disagreed with something Kristen said. Droplets of water rained down on Lila and she opened her eyes to Kristen's flashing fingers above her face.

Spencer was the source of the flickering shade she was lying in, Lila saw then, blinking frantically to focus. The stove door was panting so closely nearby that she felt that it might be just underneath ... underneath ... underneath!

"Let me go! Let me up!" Lila struggled halfway out of Kristen's lap, panic sharpening her voice as Spencer reached towards her and was slapped away by Kristen. "No! Let me up! It's here! The door ... James ... oh, let me GO!"

"We're too close," Kristen was saying, her hands shifting under Lila's back as Lila moved, hastening from restraint to support. "I'll help her get away. You look."

Her words alarmed Lila further, although the additional fear was small compared to the terror already inhabiting her body and mind. She therefore did not dedicate any of her limited reserves to figuring out why what Kristen was saying should frighten her, but allowed Kristen to lead her away from the ravine.

Lila was splintered between past and present, overwhelmed by

A. B.'s guilt, anger, and anguish. Kristen wrapped both arms around Lila's waist and steered her towards the draw with its steady hawthorns, murmuring in her ear that everything was going to be all right, that Spencer understood, that she'd had to tell him ...

The words finally penetrated the haze of distant/near memory, and Lila stiffened, her shaking, scattered being coalescing under the bright light of the present day, stabbing her like a butterfly on a specimen board.

"'Tell him?'" Lila said then, seizing a small segment of Kristen's words and repeating them back numbly. "You TOLD him?"

"And he understands," Kristen said, her eyes running scared even though her voice held its ground. "He believes. Now sit down in the shade and drink this."

"You told him?" Lila dropped as if the ground had retreated under her, causing Kristen to gasp and hurriedly crouch at her side.

"I'm sorry, but I had to. You just ... you collapsed, Lila! He was going to pick you up and move you, and I knew that would sever the link ... drink this. Please, just drink this."

Lila took the water bottle from Kristen's hand but ducked as Kristen tried to touch her cheek.

"Lila!" Kristen packed a mother's guilt into that word, and Lila's fear and confusion about Kristen telling Spencer her secret skidded into worry for her friend.

"Kristen, you ... are you okay?"

"Me? Oh god, yes, I'm fine ... oh, Lila, yes, I'm fine, the baby's fine, and I wouldn't have told Spencer anything but you ... I couldn't think fast enough when you passed out and I ... "

"Shh." Lila shoved the water bottle back at Kristen, her hand continuing to shake as she did so. "It's okay ... I ... " And then they were both crying, hugging each other, and Lila was whispering in Kristen's ear even though there was no need, "It was the worst thing I ever saw, Kristen ... A. B ... .he was my friend! And he killed

... he killed ... "

"I found it!"

Spencer's shout drove a wedge between Lila and Kristen, prying them out of their loose embrace with force, causing both to gasp.

"Breathe, Lila, and drink the water."

Kristen had to steady the bottle to get it to Lila's lips without covering them both in water. In Lila's head, the background noise began to raise in volume, escalating like a summer storm that appears as a foreboding thunderhead in the distance. Spencer was kicking at the earth, opening a larger window for the stove door to shout its tale.

The maelstrom is always more impressive when it's on top of you ... or in this case, under your feet.

Lila hardly realized she was moving, didn't know what happened to the water bottle. Kristen was attached to her side like a conjoined twin, supporting her, screaming words at Spencer Lila couldn't hear, wouldn't understand if she did.

Spencer got larger in Lila's field of vision even as his visage dimmed, fading out almost entirely when she finally sank to her knees in the dirt beside him on the edge of the ravine.

The ravine that had advanced significantly over the years, exposing bone, too, underneath the leading edge of the stove door that lay on top of James McCook's body, a subterranean tombstone being unearthed by time and the elements, in spite of A. B.'s efforts to camouflage the area with greenery. The shield, the sentry, the once-loved stove door that had been warped in its use as an inadvertent implement of death was now revealed.

Lila put both hands on it, absolution in her posture but not in her mind ... or in the rush of terrifying memories.

James and Angus fighting, Nell attempting to intervene. Nell, her head bloodied and misshapen where it hit the stove door when James pushed her away. Angus, rising from the floor where he'd fallen in shock when James had shoved Nell, like a frantic, lost wraith. James, falling back in horror as he realized what he'd done.

Angus, with nothing more in his mind than saving Nell, even as he realized she surely could not survive this massive injury.

Two little boys, one dark-haired, one fair, standing by the stairs while James sobbed insensibly and Angus hurried Nell out to his truck, then came back for the boys.

Angus standing, boys in his arms, their three tear-stained faces wiped clean of emotions, left destitute, listening to the sounds of a broken man begging for forgiveness from an indifferent god.

Beneath his shattered heart, Angus was beginning to nurture a rage so absolute, not even a divine intervention could suppress it.

Lila exploded back into the present like a child grabbing an electric fence with both hands. Spencer had scooped her up, shattering her link with the past in spite of the fact that she'd been touching the stove door.

"I don't care!" he was saying, surely loudly, but still sounding to Lila as if his voice was coming from far away instead of right under her ear. She willed her arms to come up and wrap around Spencer, one at his waist, the other across the chest that vibrated when he spoke. "She might as well have been seizing for all the shaking she was doing! It can't be good for her. How long has this been happening to her?"

All my life. Lila thought it, but let Kristen do the talking for her.

"Her whole life," Kristen said, sounding as tired as Lila felt. "But it hasn't been like this. It's never been like this."

Spencer carried Lila for a distance that seemed significant to her, though she couldn't possibly estimate it. She wanted to tell Kristen to shut up for a minute and have something to drink, to make sure she was taking care of herself and the baby. She wanted to tell Spencer to put her down ... no, she didn't want to do that, but Lila was sure for some unfathomable reason that she should do

240

that.

She wanted to go back to a time when A. B. had been her much loved friend and not the man who murdered his brother for killing the woman they both adored.

"She's crying again," Spencer said, when he reached the deep shade of the hawthorns. "Or still. Dammit, when does this stop? You said she'd come out of it when I ... "

"That's what she said," Kristen said meekly, no hint of a joke in her voice this time.

Lila chuckled. It came out raspy and uneven, but it was clearly a laugh.

The atmosphere charged with activity as Kristen searched for water and Spencer tried to set Lila down. Her refusal to release him—something she'd surely be embarrassed by later, she realized dimly—forced him to sit with her still in his arms, and resulted in her curling into him to keep her head against his chest, where it had been when he carried her.

His heart beat rapidly, his skin smelled of clean Wyoming air, dust, and hard work. And he was warm in a way that didn't add to the rising temperature of the day, but complemented it instead, particularly here in the shade.

Lila would hang on a little longer, keep herself isolated from the jarring imagery her eyes were sure to provide for just a few more moments.

"Lila, here ... " Kristen pressed a cool water bottle against her cheek. "Drink some, please."

"You first," Lila said, opening her eyes then. Kristen's face swam into clarity, charging through the time warp that had enveloped Lila so thoroughly it still lingered, like a terrifying dream even in the pure light of day.

"Okay, but then you!" Kristen took a long drink from the bottle and pressed it back insistently towards Lila's face.

With a sigh Lila was amazed she could produce, having been

breathless to the point of airlessness for much of this strange morning, Lila lifted her hand and head from Spencer's chest. The absence of his heartbeat in her ear was shocking ... frightening.

Lila did her best to force an even rate of air in and out of her lungs, alternating it with water to her empty belly as she was able. She felt incompetent at this simple task, lost in a strange land with only these two people, this unlikely pair who knew what she could know with a touch.

Spencer's hand at her hip squeezed as Lila attempted to sit up straighter, and she pressed against his side with her own hand in return, finally bringing her eyes to meet his, so near. He'd lost his hat, she thought inanely, and his eyes were familiar in a way beyond her own experience, sitting like green gems in the paleness of his face, his dark hair a squashed, unfamiliar mess revealed when his hat had come off—when had he lost his hat?

Was he afraid? Was that the spark she saw now?

Frightened green eyes, rumpled dark hair ...

Knowledge stabbed Lila like an attack, puncturing the slight equilibrium she'd been determinedly striving towards.

"You're James' son," she said. As if she had a choice to speak the truth that was now so obvious.

"What?" Kristen and Spencer spoke the same word together, not quite in unison but in a stuttering stereo.

"You're the older boy. You were there. You saw the fire." Something flashed behind Spencer's eyes, more than fear this time. He started to pull back from Lila but she dropped the water bottle and threw herself against his body, starting to shake again. "A. B. tried to burn the house down but when he came back and found James lying outside ... he ... it was hazy ... but I know he buried James here. He was responsible for ... ... I think he shot James in the head!"

Spencer's chest heaved underneath Lila's head and she caught a glimpse of Kristen's horrified face before she shut her eyes tight

242

again.

"You didn't see that," Lila said, striving to provide comfort though she doubted her ability to do so.

"Yes, I did."

Lila wanted to pull away, to let a gasp like Kristen's propel her away from the horror she heard too clearly as truth in Spencer's words.

"You must've missed that part," Spencer said, his words controlled but the grief, shock, and anger behind them too powerful to be restrained entirely. "I hid in the truck, rode back with him, without him knowing. I thought he was going to my mother. Not to this house ... not ... "

"I-I-m sorry," Lila managed, her words being swallowed whole underneath Kristen's cry of, "Oh, no, no!"

"A shot is quick. It was more than my ... than that man deserved. I didn't know it was A. B.. I could've thanked him."

"Thanked him?" Now Lila did move back, scrambling into Kristen in her haste to extract herself from Spencer's touch.

How fast things could change.

He stared at her as Kristen's arm slid around Lila's shoulders, the slighter familiarity of it replacing the unusual heaviness that had been Spencer's embrace.

"He killed the man who killed my mother, didn't he?"

"But ... "

"But nothing. There's no point in excusing murder because of relation." Spencer's eyes flashed, whatever fear Lila thought she'd seen there utterly obliterated now. "I should have realized ... A. B ... .but I called him 'Unky.' I didn't remember his name." He laughed, and it was a shattered sound. "Didn't remember his name, but I remembered that night."

"You have a brother. It's Jake."

"So I gather." Spencer stood slowly, not bothering to brush the dust off this time. His face became shadowed as he moved into the path of the sun. "I have to go."

Kristen shifted, but Lila caught her arm with one hand before it left her entirely, willing her not to interfere. From the silence that ensued, Kristen got the message.

Spencer's gaze dropped from its track over their heads down to where Lila and Kristen remained in the dirt.

"Can you get home?" He asked. "Both of you?" His eyes moved from Lila's to Kristen's and back again.

"Yes," Lila said, and squeezed Kristen's wrist until she huffed, "Of course."

"Can you?" Lila asked, arresting Spencer's gaze just as it began to drift.

"Yes," he said, distracted but clear. "Thank you."

Those green eyes locked with her own again then, flaring with a special vibrancy Lila felt all the way to her core.

It was too much. She looked away first, and spotted Spencer's hat stuck into the side of a sagebrush plant.

"Your hat ... " She pointed.

"Thanks again." Spencer's boots sounded impossibly loud against the soil as he strode away. He put his hat back on and stood, facing at an angle away from Lila. She found that she was holding her breath, waiting to see if his farewell would be considered or propelled.

Was it all too much? Lila wondered. It felt like too much. It felt like an overload that would drive Spencer away from her forever.

But Spencer looked back at her once more before he left, and though he did it without smiling, he did tip his hat.

18: Taking Chances

"I'm going to have to leave soon."

It was the fourth time Kristen had said so, and despite her exhaustion, Lila smiled.

"Okay," Lila said, just as she had each time Kristen had remarked upon her not-so-imminent departure. "I'm fine. You can go whenever you need to. I understand; you have to work tomorrow."

"Oh, the hell with it. We both know I'm staying over. I just need to call Lou; he can tell Danielle I'm knocked up or something." Kristen extracted herself carefully from the chair and stalked off towards the outhouse.

"Reception's not so good over there!" Lila called after her, knowing that Kristen was likely only making yet another pregnancy-enforced pit stop before placing her promised call to Lou.

Kristen's response was flippant, in a single-fingered sort of way, confirming Lila's suspicions and pulling a pained grin from her. The rigors of the day had left even her face feeling exhausted.

Lila leaned back in her own chair, fingering the rim of her tea cup, which had been empty for some time now. With Kristen staying over, she should make another trip to the well, and try to decide what to make for supper.

Lila mulled over the question of dinner at length, feeling the breeze caress her gently, her thoughts entirely her own now. It was a luxury few people had to ponder, she supposed, the fact that your thoughts were yours and yours alone. At least she was enjoying a respite now, though she couldn't help but wonder if the stove door would have more to say once the residual effects of Spencer's touch wore off. He'd broken the link during the transfer, after all.

A distinct snort made Lila jump up into a posture reminiscent of a salute as she instinctively shaded her face with her hand to look to the west, the direction from which the sound had come. Spencer was dismounting from Sunny by the fence there, and Lila gulped, an effort to swallow the lump that had formed in her throat at the sight of him, backlit by the afternoon sun.

As Spencer ducked through the fence—one hand protectively on his hat—Lila settled the tea cup on the ground next to her and hurried to fluff her hair with her fingers. She felt as flighty as a teenager facing that special boy in her life, as exhausted as an old woman who had just buried her partner of many years.

Today is one of those days that just keeps on giving.

"Hello," Spencer said as he neared Lila, and to Lila's great surprise, he pulled off his hat and ruffled his own hair.

"Hello," she responded, ill at ease with the banality of his greeting. "Would you ... would you like to sit down?"

"Thanks, yes, I would." Spencer sat in the chair Kristen had so recently abandoned. And sat there, silent, fingers of one hand lightly drumming against the hat he held in the other.

"Are you okay?" Lila said, uncertainty inspiring her to break the silence.

"Me?" Spencer looked at Lila with clear frustration.

"Who else?" She frowned. "You had a lot to absorb today." Spencer took a breath, perhaps to speak, but Lila pushed over his unspoken words as concern overwhelmed courtesy. "I'm sorry, I know it's ... I mean, I realize it's unbelievable ... well, it doesn't matter. You seem to believe it, which is good, I guess, but the fact that A. B. killed James ... your father ... I just don't ... "

Lila fell silent, words and the ideas she'd hoped to express with them jumbled in a hopeless pile-up in her head.

246

You'd never know I get paid for my excellent grasp of the English language.

She said that, too, since it was the one coherent thought left to her and then dropped her eyes under the continued intensity of Spencer's stare.

"Maybe you, that's who else," Spencer finally said, and Lila, frowned, eyes lifting, not understanding. "I don't understand ... " His words mimicked her thoughts, but his exasperation was incomprehensible to her. Spencer's hands flew apart, one carrying the hat, and that somehow made his gesture seem all the more expansive. "I don't understand, and I wouldn't believe—couldn't believe—if I hadn't seen you do it. What you felt was all over your face as you saw it, while you were touching that door, and I knew it was real. I knew."

Lila drew in a breath, heart starting to race, and Spencer reached out, covering Lila's hands, which she had knit together, a white-knuckled clasp in her lap. He drew back just as suddenly.

"Why does my touching you break your ... trance, or whatever it is?"

"I ... " Lila waved her own hands in the air, as if ineptly trying to catch a fleeting notion. "I don't know. I honestly don't. It's never happened to me before."

"Never?"

"No." That Spencer's touch affected her in other ways she kept to herself, hands back to clenching, holding that secret tightly.

Though given the way she had clung to him in the aftermath of the memory transfer, she supposed "secret" was debatable.

"Well. Anyway, you obviously know what happened to ... to James," Spencer said, spitting out the name, "just as if you were there ... so like I said, YOU, that's who else you should be concerned with." His eyes flashed like a homing beacon, his voice softening. "But here you are, concerned about me."

"I ... I'd be concerned about anyone who went through what

you did," Lila said, and Spencer raised his brow.

"There's nothing special about me, is that what you're saying?"

Lila almost smiled as Spencer's words lengthened in a drawl. He was putting on that blasé facade that had come into their earliest conversations so frequently, but she knew it now for what it was.

"There's nothing special about this?" Spencer leaned in towards Lila as he said it, and she saw out of the corner of her eyes that the back of the lawn chair he was sitting in tipped up as he stretched. "Nothing at all?" Spencer asked, his face now so close to hers that Lila held her breath, waiting, hoping ...

When Spencer started to pull back, his eyes twinkling wickedly at the answer he'd obviously read on her face, Lila sighed and leaned forward herself. Maybe, after all they'd gone through together, everything disconnected and connected ... maybe it was enough to take a chance.

Lila found herself wanting this chance with a keenness that bordered on desperation.

"There might be something."

And then Lila kissed Spencer, hard, momentum carrying her forward as she pressed into the kiss. He leaned into her, catching her, and tumbling them both into the sweet grasses under them, knocking his hat free of his hand as his arms swept around Lila. Their clutching embrace was distinctly mutual, its intensity forged and strengthened by reciprocated longing.

This kiss was everything its predecessor had been and more, and Lila lost herself in it, lying on top of Spencer, their legs intertwined, their bodies melting together as if already joined into one flesh.

An indiscreet cough, half-heartedly repeated, broke the spell woven by crushing lips and roving hands.

"So, I'm leaving now," Kristen said with forced cheerfulness, grinning down at them.

"I thought you were ... " Lila began, and then snapped her mouth shut.

"Staying? Oh no. I couldn't possibly. Aside from wanting to see how the photos turned out, I have to work tomorrow, Lila, you know that!" Kristen's already wide grin nearly split her face as she turned her attention to Spencer. "Hello again, Adam! The ground's a good choice, by the way; Lila's chairs really aren't comfortable. But the bed's not bad!"

"KRISTEN!"

Lila felt Spencer tighten his grip on her waist, though she hadn't actually made a move to pull away. He craned his neck to look at Kristen.

"Room enough for two," Kristen added cheekily, prompting Lila to swipe at her ankle—out of reach, and Lila wouldn't want to pull her down anyway. Probably. "Though Thunder might have something to say about you staying over."

"Thunder didn't seem to mind me," Spencer managed to interject as Kristen took a split second to inhale.

"That's right, you've met! Excellent, and you get points for doing well with cats, or at least, the cat that matters right now. Alrighty then, I'm off. No, don't get up, I know my way back. You stay right there, both of you stay riiiiiight there." Kristen turned to go, jaunty as a sailor returning to port after a long stint at sea, and then turned back, waving her hand vigorously. "So long! Farewell! Ta-ta! No pun intended."

No pun intended? Lila spared a glance downward and saw that her shirt was gaping open, making more than evident the fact that she'd discarded her bra upon returning to the cabin. She sighed dramatically as Kristen laughed, practically dancing as she bounded back towards the cabin.

"Kristen, you're incorrigible!"

"I know! But you love me anyway. Bye!" Kristen snatched her

pack from its position near the cabin door, cooed to Thunder inside, and set off merrily back towards the outhouse, opening her cellular phone as she bounced away.

"Lou? Yeah, I know, reception is bad, but listen, change of change of plan—seriously, just listen to this, it's worth it—and you will NOT believe what I just saw, except ... " Her voice was snatched away by a gust of wind and did not return on account of increasing distance.

Lila's eyes returned to Spencer's face just as he turned his bemused gaze to meet hers.

"Is she always ... "

"Always!" Lila said. "And then some."

"You don't know what I was going to say," Spencer protested, in a voice that was nothing like a protest.

"It doesn't matter," Lila said, her attention fast returning to the decadent feeling of Spencer's body underneath hers. "She's all that, always, and then some but right now I don't want to talk about her."

"What do you want to talk about?" Spencer asked, caressing Lila's cheek with one hand as his other hand slid underneath her shirt to press against the small of her back. Sensation condensed at that innocuous point and from there, rushed through Lila's entire body.

Lila lowered her lips to just above Spencer's, her brazenness unleashed as much through her own determination as through the slow, sultry movement of Spencer's hands.

"I don't want to talk," she said, imagining that the soft breath that carried her words must feel like another sort of caress and hoping Spencer would speak, too, so she could find out for herself.

She also hoped that he wouldn't speak at all.

"Is that right?" She was right: Spencer's words felt delicious, so close that she could literally devour them.

"Yes."

"Yes." Spencer's hand, firm against her back, began to rove upwards; the hand that had cupped her cheek moved down along the side of her neck, traveling a path of thrilling seduction with deceptive laziness.

For a long time after that, there were no words at all ... only the scent of crushed grass, the touch of Wyoming wind and sunlight on their bodies, the taste of each other's skin, and the sounds of desire answered in unity.

"Are you cold?" Spencer asked, one arm cushioning Lila's head and the other pressing gently just underneath her breasts.

"Cold? No." Lila was, in fact, well-protected by Spencer's body where it curved around her own. "Wind's dying down a bit anyway, isn't it?"

"Seems to be."

They lay without speaking again until the sharp sound of Sunny nipping the grass on the other side of the fence drew cumulative pieces of Lila's attention away from the warm pressure of Spencer wrapped around her.

"Can you stay?" She asked, her daring heart skipping a beat, yearning for his affirmative answer.

"The night? If Sunny can stay in your yard, yes. If you want me to, yes."

"Do *you* want to?" Lila lifted her head, turning it towards him as much as their positions allowed.

Spencer groaned and kissed her cheek, shifting with her until he was able to kiss her fully on the lips.

"Hell yes," he answered then. "As long as I don't have to sleep on the ground. I'm not as young as I think I am."

Lila laughed lightly at that.

"Neither am I." She framed his face with her hands. "I still think of you as 'Spencer,' is that odd?"

Something crossed behind Spencer's eyes, though he didn't let it touch the slight smile on his lips, which he pressed briefly to Lila's before sitting up.

"I never liked 'Adam.' Only my step-mother called me that." He reached for Lila's shirt, handing it to her with deliberate slowness. "Do you really have to put this back on?"

Lila caught her breath, thinking more of what she could do than what she could say.

"I don't have to leave it on ... for long."

"That works." Spencer dipped his fingers into Lila's curls after she took her shirt from him, tugging lightly at the tangled mass. "Your hair ... "

"It's a mess, I know."

"God, no! Beautiful-wild is what it is." What seemed for a moment like a form of hypnosis flared into desire and Lila wasn't sure if she entered into Spencer's arms just then, if he pulled her, or if they simply materialized into the embrace.

A meow that bordered on a yowl followed closely by a snort from Sunny was what separated them some timeless time later.

"Yeah. So. Chores first." Spencer shook his head as he said it, with one regretful caress for Lila before he turned away to find his jeans.

Lila watched him as much as she could, needlessly unbuttoning the shirt that had slipped over her head so quickly when they'd undressed each other. She put her shirt back on the traditional way so she didn't have to take her eyes off of Spencer's broad shoulders, so she didn't miss a single second of the way the early evening light was falling against both the skin that frequently saw the sun, and that which was most often hidden.

When she met his eyes, she saw him watching her the same way, and the heat of his gaze made her shiver.

"Are you cold now?" he asked solicitously, holding her panties now.

Lila pressed her lips together, but couldn't stifle their upward motion.

"Still no. You?" She tried to make the question sound innocent, since she could see that being chilled was not at all what afflicted Spencer.

"No, not really." He tugged his jeans into position, turning slightly from Lila to complete the process, which drew a giggle from her. He stepped into his boots without any appreciable balance problems, and picked up his shirt, turning the crumpled ball over in his hands before tossing it back to lie near his hat.

"In fact, I don't think I need that just now," he said, lips curving up at the corners, eyes sparking like flint above fresh tinder.

A giggle escaped Lila before she could stifle it, and as Spencer sauntered towards Sunny, she slipped into her shoes and stalked to the cabin, wearing her panties but carrying her jeans.

"Unfair!" Spencer called after her, and this time, Lila laughed outright.

Inside the cabin, Lila fed Thunder quickly. As she was refilling his water bowl, it occurred to her that Sunny was going to need water, too.

"Now what can we use ... oh!" Lila thought of the old metal bucket she kept in the cupboards above the kitchen area and positioned the desk chair to retrieve it. She was just reaching for the bucket when Spencer entered the cabin.

"Completely unfair," he said, looking up at her as she stood on the chair. Lila smiled, obscurely shy now, and handed the bucket to him.

"For Sunny, for water?"

"Thanks," said Spencer, setting the bucket on the cabin floor and moving to spot Lila as she got ready to jump down from the chair.

"I'm fine," she said, clasping only one of Spencer's outstretched hands, the strange modesty that had afflicted her atop the chair still clinging to her with clammy tentacles.

"Fine? You're incredible!" Spencer stepped forward and lifted her, holding her at her hips. He slid her down his body until her feet reached the floor—which she found to be no more stable than the chair, at least, not with Spencer so close. Their eyes locked for a moment before Spencer bent his head to press hot kisses against Lila's breasts where they peeked out of the "V" of her shirt.

Lila gasped, clutching Spencer's shoulders, arching her back and then wavering she bumped into the chair behind her.

"I've got you," Spencer all but growled, pulling her closer still, pressing his hips into hers as he seared her skin with the brand of his mouth.

"You take my breath away," he said when he finally lifted his head again.

"Well, the feeling's mutual," Lila said, running one finger over Spencer's lips. He caught her hand and kissed its palm, sweeping Lila up in yet another raw rush of passion.

"Water, you said?" Spencer asked, his words coated thick with regret as he pulled back from her.

"Yes, a hand pump, past the outhouse ... there's a trail ... "

"Maybe I should douse myself while I'm there," Spencer said, picking up the bucket.

"Maybe I should come with you?"

"No, I've got this. And I'll hurry."

He turned to leave so quickly that Thunder skittered back from the corner of the bedroom where the cat had been spying on them.

"Sorry, boy!" Spencer leaned down and let Thunder sniff at his fingers for a moment before continuing on his way.

Lila stepped past Thunder into the bedroom as Spencer's

boots tattooed the boards on Lila's deck before shuffling into the grass beyond. She bent and peered across the bed through the window, watching as Spencer passed the outhouse and disappeared into the trees beyond.

"Mrrt?" Thunder popped up in the window, head turning this way and that, as if to see what Lila was looking at.

"I hope you don't mind, Thunder, but I don't think there's going to be room on the bed for you tonight. Unless ... have you tried the upper bunk?" Lila swept Thunder up and transferred the startled cat to the upper bunk, earning a scratch on her arm for her efforts. Once his feet were back on something solid, however, Thunder took to sniffing around the space with interest. Lila shifted the cat's bowls to the corner of the dresser, to allow him room to jump down when he was ready.

When she turned back to the bed, she noticed what she'd somehow managed to overlook earlier: Spencer's hat and shirt, sitting on the pillow nearest the wall. He'd folded the shirt, though somewhat haphazardly, and the hat was sitting askew atop that. The sight of Spencer's clothing there, on her bed, was shocking.

She'd never had a man in this bed, she realized. Not once since the cabin had been built had any man lain here, except for Lou, when he and Kristen had laughingly demonstrated that the bed was, in fact, well suited for two.

"Doesn't matter," Lila had said, blunted by the disaster of Stuart, not yet knowing that Pete would be worse. "I won't be sharing this bed."

Life had a not-so-funny way of turning absolutisms on their heads, Lila thought now. She shook off the doubts that swarmed in her mind like blood-lusting mosquitoes. Doubts were not something she wanted to focus on now. Not now, with Spencer shirtless and working the pump to bring water to Sunny. Not now, with Spencer's shirt and hat here, offering Lila the perfect costume change for a night she knew already would be powerful enough to embed into an object, if only she could do that with memories of her own.

Now was a time for action, not doubt.

Lila slipped out of her shirt and into Spencer's, setting his hat on top of the hair she'd still not combed, and then scurried back into the kitchen area to wait.

She heard Spencer's return through the open kitchen window, eavesdropped on his gentle murmurs to Sunny and the sound of him removing the saddle, his hands brushing across Sunny's back afterwards. She wanted to peek, to add the visual aspect of him as he tended to the horse, but she kept her gaze directed across the room instead, so her first sight of him entering the cabin would be of him seeing her.

Her, sitting in the chair, wearing his shirt and his hat. Staking what was undeniably a premature claim, she knew, but then again, she wanted to mark this night as hers and his alone, in spite of anything else.

In spite of *everything* else.

Lila waited, the sounds outside permeating the cabin like a lake's waves lapping up against its shore. Although she was filled to overflowing with sensation, charged as strongly as any object she'd ever encountered with emotion, she also felt as if she fit—the perfect puzzle piece for once—here and now. It was unexpected because although the cabin was her sanctuary and she was used to being more comfortable here than anywhere else, she never expected to feel that with Spencer here ... with Spencer here with her.

How was it possible to feel both at ease and tense? To be both enervated and electrified?

She waited, letting the feelings wash over her. She thought Julie would be proud, and then Spencer pushed through the screen door, dismissing Julie and the rest of the world from Lila's thoughts.

256

He froze when he saw her, and she raised a slightly shaking hand to tip his hat to him, her smile all her own. She'd been right: watching Spencer's face light up was purely delicious.

He crossed the length of the cabin in quick strides, wrapping his arms around her as she stood up into his embrace, kissing her with a thoroughness that Lila met and attempted to raise. The hat was forgotten and fell at some point, but like the proverbial tree, made no sound—at least, not that Lila could recall later.

Later, when they lay together on her bed, hands still roving over each other but now in the gentleness that follows passion, Spencer chuckled.

"There's a spy in here." He pointed up, and Lila leaned across his chest to see Thunder, peering down from the upper bunk.

Thunder cocked his head at Lila and disappeared briefly, then leaped down from the bunk to the dresser, and then to the floor. He dashed out of the room at high speed.

"I need to get him some toys," Lila mumbled, lowering her head to Spencer's chest. He feathered his fingers down her spine.

"Does he always travel with you?" Spencer's voice was amplified, overlaying the steady beating of his heart.

"Never, actually." She propped herself up to look at him, tracing his cheekbone with one finger. "I found him—well, he found me—just last week."

Just last week? That was incredible.

"He must've been around people. Maybe abandoned, though."

Lila nodded, drifting her hand down to press against his chest, watching as he inhaled sharply at her touch.

"Jake thought so, too."

"Jake?"

"I still can't get over it—he's your brother."

Spencer said nothing, and Lila realized his hand at her back had stopped moving. She looked up and found him frowning, brows knit fiercely together.

"When did you talk to Jake?"

Lila tipped her head, considering, and wondering if she was reading too much into Spencer's reaction. Given her experience with Stuart, however, she didn't think so.

"When he gave me ... " Lila swallowed hard, and felt Spencer's hand at her back soften, begin moving again, soothing. "When he gave me the letter from A. B.—the letter to be delivered when he ... died."

Spencer lifted his head from the bunched pillow underneath and kissed Lila's forehead.

"And when he came here to check Thunder. He's a vet, did you know that? He's filling in at the clinic in town."

"I did not know that." The words were clipped short, but Spencer's hand continued its gentle, fluid motion, and so Lila put her head back down against his chest.

"Funny," she said, "I didn't know any of you boys—you, Thunder, or Jake—when I left to come out here. I was ... I guess I don't know you well yet, but ... I do know you, somehow." She pressed a kiss against Spencer's skin, peeking up at him then. He was still not fully engaged, but he met her gaze with his own. "Anyway, I was in sorry shape when I came out here."

"What do you mean?"

Lila sighed.

"It's hard to explain, and I've never had to, not since I told Kristen. I ... it's like I can't hold it all, after awhile, all of the things other people remember so strongly. I get to a point where I've picked up so much that I'm ... it's like my brain is overflowing, and I get anxious. More than anxious. I have trouble sleeping. I can't function well in crowds—I can't do that ordinarily, but it's worse ... I've abandoned my cart in the grocery store, I've had to pull over when I'm driving, I've gone to the emergency room, thinking I was having a heart attack."

258

"Shh." Spencer cupped her head with his hand, smoothing her hair at first, then lightly plucking at a curl, then caressing again. "I understand."

"Do you?" Lila rose up on her elbow to stare at him. "Do you really? Sometimes I feel like such a freak, I just ... "

"Stop." Spencer pulled her to him, kissed her in a way that left no possibility of speech, and then lightly bit her lower lip when he pulled slowly away. "You're special. You've got more on your mind than yourself and that's a rarity no matter how it happens, but the only way you're a freak is that you're freakishly amazing."

Lila stared at Spencer, marveling that she'd ever considered him annoying—but no, he could most definitely be annoying! But he was amazing, too. And Lila found herself close to tears, being confronted with yet another dichotomy, this one wrapped into such an appealing package.

"You're just saying that to get into my bed." She tried to say it lightly, but Spencer rubbed her cheek with his thumb, taking the tear that had escaped Lila's burgeoning eyes out of its track as he did so.

"No, ma'am," he said, his words breezily light in the darkening room. "First, I'm already IN your bed, and second, I don't say what I don't mean."

Night was falling hard around them now, the day that had, at times, seemed eternal now revealing itself to be nothing more than ordinary ... at least in terms of duration.

Lila started to shift away from Spencer's chest, but his arm around her tightened.

"Stay." His voice was a barely there whisper, his heartbeat seeming to increase when he said it. "If you're comfortable, stay right here. Please."

Lila pressed a kiss against Spencer's collarbone and this time, his heart definitely sped up. She wanted to make sure he was comfortable, too, but instead she allowed herself the incredible luxury of drifting off to sleep, serenaded by the strong rhythm of Spencer's heart under her ear.

19: Rough Edges

When Lila woke, dawn was extending tentative fingers across the sky, exploring the puffy clouds that drifted by and flaring them with reluctant light. Spencer's body was curved around her own as it had been after they had made love outdoors ... had they really made love outdoors? And then again—and again!—in her bed? The sensual soreness of her body attested to the fact, but Lila was still astonished.

It was another first for her. Several firsts, really.

"You're awake early." Spencer spoke softly in her ear, and then traced the edge of it with his tongue, sending wonderful shivers down Lila's spine.

"You're insatiable!"

"And you're not?" He chuckled. "Actually, I have to step outside."

"Thank goodness. I need to make a trip to the outhouse myself."

"Guess we're both only human after all," Spencer said, sitting up slowly. Lila started to do the same but found the pressure on her foot was Thunder's head. She laughed lightly, bending forward and stroking the cat, who yawned in her face.

"I tried to show him the upper bunk," she said, slipping between the dual obstacles of Spencer, standing beside the bed now, and Thunder, who remained in a curled up ball, head extended even after Lila slid her foot out from underneath his baleful gaze.

"He'd obviously rather sleep with you, not that I can say I blame him." Spencer kissed her, and then groaned. "God. Go! Go, or I'll never be able to do what I need to do."

Lila grinned, chagrin overpowered by delight, and lifted a long flannel shirt from its hook. She shrugged into it before stepping outside, wrapping it around her like a robe, which was exactly why she kept it at the ready.

The air outside the cabin was brisk, but not bitter. Lila hurried along the dim path to the outhouse, grasses tickling her ankles as she went, barely dampening them. It hadn't rained during the night, for once, and the moisture the grasses were dabbing on Lila's skin today was more typical for Wyoming's climate.

Sunny nickered as Lila re-entered the yard, and when she stepped around to the front of the cabin, she saw Spencer lightly stroking the horse's face and neck. Sunny pressed back, seeming to nod as she did so.

"Breakfast?" Lila called softly. Her voice carried easily in the relative stillness of the air, and it likewise carried Spencer's response.

"That'd be great!"

"I'll make pancakes." She turned, glad she had a small supply of real maple syrup that she'd been saving for a special occasion— she typically made her own syrup out of dark brown sugar and water, with a touch of butter.

Back inside the cabin, Lila slipped into a comfortable long-sleeved shirt and yoga pants that she'd never once used for yoga. After her walk to the outhouse and back, the cabin seemed comfortable enough, temperature-wise, but cooking the perfect pancake was an exercise in patience and patience wasn't much for getting the blood circulating.

She fed Thunder, and just as she entered the kitchen, she heard the groan of the bucket's handle as it shifted on its hinges when Spencer grabbed it. While he headed back to the water pump, Lila selected two Ziplock bags of the pancake batter she'd prepared for her own use at the cabin. After a moment's consideration, she added a third.

It had been a long time since she'd cooked breakfast for a man.

Although, she had recently cooked dinner for Jake. That thought reminded her of Spencer's grim tone when she'd mentioned Jake the night before. It raised the fine hairs on her arms, remembering the way Spencer had stilled and the way his voice had changed, becoming withdrawn and brittle.

It was an uncomfortable blight on an otherwise delectable evening. Lila transferred her disconcertion into action, stirring the pancake batter with far more force than was required.

Spencer whistled to Sunny as he returned, setting the bucket into Lila's yard by reaching through the fence across from the kitchen window, and then turning to look away towards the South. There, the sunrise was tinting the sky pink and edging the clouds a sherbet shade of orange. It looked to be the type of sunrise Lila thought of as a "wrap-around," with color reaching all the way from the East to the West, touching every direction and sub-direction in between.

Watching Spencer at least as much as she watched the pancakes she'd started to cook, Lila almost waited too long to turn them.

Oh, I've got it bad.

Lila struggled to keep her focus on the pancakes after that, even as she imagined Spencer's stance as he continued to watch the sunrise, right down to the way he'd tilt his head.

She wondered where his hat had ended up.

The creak of the screen door announced Spencer's return and Lila jumped.

"I didn't hear you crossing the porch!" she said, in answer to his quirked brow.

"I wasn't trying to be sneaky. You must have been thinking hard."

Lila compressed her lips into a straight line at the double-entendre and handed Spencer a plate. His eyes teased in more ways than one as he accepted it.

"Too obvious?"

"Way too obvious." She slid a pair of pancakes onto his plate and gestured towards the syrup, which she'd heated on the stove's seldom-used second burner.

"Thank you." He moved behind Lila to sit on the stool at the counter, and she turned to one side to watch him.

"I don't make a habit of this, in case you're wondering."

"'This?'" Lila poured another pair of pancakes into the frying pan.

"Not breakfast, I eat breakfast every day. Most important meal and all that. But breakfast with a woman ... it's a luxury I don't get to enjoy nearly as much as I'd like."

"Funny, I was thinking much the same thing." Lila looked at him then, keeping her voice light. She knew that was a contrast to what she was saying without words.

"You don't often have breakfast a woman, either?" Spencer took a bite of his pancake. "Mmm. Vanilla?"

"Yes, vanilla. And no. I don't usually have breakfast with anybody but myself. And now Thunder."

"How long have you had him in the cabin again?"

Lila tried to count the days as she slipped a spatula underneath a pancake to check its progress.

"A week or so," she answered finally, shrugging. "I don't track time too well when I'm out here."

"I can see that," Spencer said, pointing at her calendar on the wall with his fork. "You're months as well as years off."

Lila laughed.

"No, that calendar still works. This month started on a Monday, so does the month displayed. I usually check my phone when I really need to know what day it is. Or when I need to check in with Kristen, and ... I really should do that."

While she was casting her gaze around the room, trying to spot her cell phone, Spencer stood and wrapped his hand over hers where it brandished the spatula. His touch sent a tremor through Lila that had nothing to do with embedded memories and everything to do with the indefinable "something" that was so distinctly between her and Spencer.

"Go ahead." Spencer's voice might have been coated in maple syrup for the way it slid over Lila, warm and sweet. "I've got this batch."

"Oh! Thanks." She was flustered, but she managed to release the spatula and step backwards without falling over her own feet.

Lila found her phone in the bedroom, and Kristen's most recent text—one of a dozen or more she'd sent since returning to Casper—was waiting impatiently there.

"TaLK TO ME IM DYING HERe!" it succinctly read.

"Later, I'm having too much fun here," Lila responded.

Though "fun" was an insufficient descriptor by far for what Lila had been having. She smiled at the thought, and then turned off her phone.

Back in the kitchen, Lila found the pancakes neatly plated and waiting for her. Spencer had filled the bottom of the frying pan with the next round, which was one large pancake rather than the two smaller ones Lila typically prepared. She felt his eyes bore into her as she stared at the monstrosity.

"I'm all about efficiency."

"Wait until you try to turn it!" she replied archly.

"Is that a challenge?"

"If you like." She grinned, finding this light banter more fun than she would have expected. "You know, I really didn't like you much when we met."

"I don't much like trespassers myself."

"Hey!"

"I've been known to admit when I'm wrong, however rare the occasion may be." Spencer gave her a significant, long look before raising the entire frying pan and neatly flipping the pancake midair.

"A man of many talents, I see!" The pancakes—pancake, in this instance—in good hands, Lila scooped up her plate and took a bite.

"Depends on who you ask, I suppose." Spencer let a silence fall, during which Lila could hear the hiss of the propane stove and the slight sizzle of cooking pancake. "Is Kristen really a photographer?"

The pancake turned to mush in Lila's mouth in an instant, but she forced herself to finish chewing and swallow before answering.

"She is."

"I couldn't find any record of her work online."

Yes, the mood in her cabin had altered quite distinctly. Lila stared at Spencer. His posture was more tense than it had been when she went into the bedroom, his eyes focused straight at the frying pan and not even flicking in her direction. She set her plate down and crossed her arms in front of her, fighting for understanding even as fear fluttered up, batting its clawed wings against Lila's fragile trust.

When Spencer slid the pancake onto his plate, she noted his phone next to it.

"And did you look on Facebook?"

"Facebook?" Uncertainty prickled Spencer's tone, and Lila registered it with relief, though she kept her arms crossed, protecting her space with the feeble gesture.

"Yes. Jack's Coffee House has a fan page there, where they typically introduce their featured artists. They work with a lot of unknowns, like Kristen, so they do the promotions. But they're a mom-and-pop outfit; they don't even take credit cards. They do Facebook, and that's about it."

"I hate Facebook." Spencer looked at her now, and Lila didn't

266

try to hide the hurt she was sure was written all over her face.

"I hate spying," she said, noting Spencer's slight recoil when she spat the words out. "I lived with an expert at it. He would've found the Facebook page whether he liked the site or not."

"Lila, I ... "

"I'm probably more broken than you are, Spencer. In spite of what I know about your childhood, or maybe because of it, I trusted you somehow, and if you can't ... if you don't ... "

"Lila!" Spencer set the frying pan down with a smack and extended his arms toward her, though he didn't move any closer. "You don't trust me. You're attracted to me and I'm attracted—incredibly attracted—to you, but don't tell me you 'trusted me' like I've damaged that already. Hell, we barely know each other!"

Lila laughed, the kind of laugh that sounds like glass breaking. "You've got me there."

"I want to know you. I hope you want to know me." Spencer took a step towards her then, and Lila searched his face, still trying to decide if she wanted to hold her ground or give up a little. Not that she had much room to maneuver.

Spencer was waiting, his arms starting to fall to his sides.

"I do. Want to know you." Lila sighed, dropped her own arms, and moved into Spencer's embrace. After his arms settled around her, she wrapped hers tight around him.

"And you're right. I'm pretty fucking broken. Though not as much by childhood trauma as you might think. Not the one you know, at any rate."

"Oh, Spencer, I'm sorry."

"No. I'm sorry. No wonder I seldom have breakfast with a woman, much less *this* woman." Spencer squeezed her against him, and in spite of the awkwardness and ambiguity of their conversation, Lila sucked in her breath as the length of their bodies pressed tightly together.

"Insatiable," Lila murmured against Spencer's chest.

"Only for you." His voice was tight, but passion had topped suspicion, and Lila didn't need the kiss that Spencer ravished her with to prove it. Though she did appreciate the kiss ... appreciated it deeply. "And your pancakes."

"The pancakes can wait," Lila said, and jostled Spencer backwards so that she could reach the knob of the stove to turn it off.

"They certainly can."

Spencer left sometime around mid-day, and while all Lila really wanted to do at that point was take a nap, she instead filled the sun-shower bag and hung it in the middle of a sunny stretch of the fence around her cabin.

While the shower water warmed, Lila heated water on the stove for the dishes. Afterwards, she heated a second pot for tea and then turned her phone back on.

"ill b here when you come up 4 air," read Kristen's latest text, and it made Lila smile, even with the affront of Spencer's checking up on Kristen.

They'd talked about it after breakfast—the second round of breakfasting, that was.

"I'm not like that," Spencer had said after Lila described some of Stuart's more controlling behaviors. "I'm NOT!"

"And you check up on everybody, so it's okay?"

"Well, no."

"Aha!"

"'Aha' nothing." Spencer stuck his stack of pancakes with his fork, leaving it sticking ludicrously out of the middle of the pile. "You can hardly blame me, the way she showed up so conveniently."

"She came to check up on me!" Lila grabbed Spencer's fork and helped herself to a generous bite of his pancakes. "I was about to die of propane poisoning, you know."

Instead of protesting her stealing his pancakes, as she'd intended, Spencer caught her hand and trapped it between both of his.

"Don't even joke about that."

Lila had swallowed hard, emotion coating her throat more thickly than syrup could ever aspire to do.

There was definitely something between her and Spencer. Something more than the attraction that had sent them both, heedless of the consequences, tumbling into the grass. And into her bed.

Goodness.

"I'll call you tonight," Spencer had promised when he finally took his leave. "I'll call you tomorrow, too."

"Can't you come back tonight?" Lila had asked, after she'd literally thrown herself at him.

"I think I'll probably have to meet with Sheriff Hoffman. There is a body on my land, after all. Although, I suppose ... " Spencer bent and kissed Lila's neck until she gasped. "I suppose James won't be any deader tomorrow than he is today."

That had made Lila gasp, too, though not with pleasure. And she'd caught Spencer's face between her hands.

"Please don't. Don't joke about that." The words were out before she realized that she'd almost parroted Spencer's words to her.

Spencer's eyes had flared, then softened just as quickly.

"I won't. But don't you go back down there without me."

"Wh-What?"

Those expressive eyes darkened under the brim of his hat, which they'd found in the corner beside Lila's desk.

"You weren't done when I pulled you off the door."

"I ... I ... well, no, I wasn't. Or the stove door wasn't, I guess. But I ... I can't ... "

Spencer's eyebrow had quirked.

"But you can't ... what?"

"I can't feel anything from it right now!" Lila had been agitated about that, but unable to pinpoint why. After so many years of longing for an "off" switch for the abilities that both enlightened and tormented, she would have thought she'd be elated to find one.

But Lila's emotions were nowhere near precise about Spencer's touch providing her peace ... in addition to the other, not-so-peaceful things his touch provided. She'd told Spencer that it was both a relief and uncomfortable, somehow, to be unable to sense the charged memories she knew were still waiting for release. That was true, but underneath all of that, Lila was nursing another, stubborn discomfort.

It had occurred to her that maybe Spencer knew something that he didn't want her to know. Something that the stove door could reveal. Not to mention that the way Spencer could give Lila the sweet bliss of inhabiting her own thoughts—and only her own thoughts—gave Spencer another power over her.

Lila set her tea down before the shakiness of her hands spilled it all over her.

Spencer's right. I don't trust him.

By association, Lila didn't much trust herself, either.

She called Kristen then, sending her friend into a spiral of concern when her delighted barbs were met with Lila's breathy tears.

"What did that bastard DO? I'll kill him myself, Lila, hide his carcass under James', we both know nobody will find him ... wait, I'll feed him to the dogs, that's what I'll do, I'll ... "

It made Lila laugh, and that made Kristen stop her verbal rampage.

"Oh, Lila. You're just overloaded, you dummy. You think you can absorb the triumphs and tragedies of history and then deal with a real, live male and have it all just make sense?"

"No! Well, maybe. But I think ... what if there's more to the story, Kristen?"

"So what if there's more to the story? Jesus, Lila, of course there's more to the story. Isn't that how you make your living, telling that 'more' from the perspective of—correct me if I'm wrong," Kristen added, in the tone of someone who is certain that she's not the least bit incorrect, "but I do believe that you've written each of your novels from ONE character's perspective, haven't you. And there's always more to a story than one perspective."

Lila felt the tension seep out of her, coating the air with its metallic flavor, like tea gone horribly wrong.

"Am I wrong?" Kristen asked.

"No. You're not wrong. Not that you didn't know that."

"Look, Lila, maybe it's not even Spencer, pursey, that ... "

"'Per se,'" Lila sniffed, unable to allow Kristen to slip a fake word in place of two perfectly good ones.

"I knew you couldn't stand not correcting me! See, it's not so bad! And as I was saying, maybe it's not even Spencer, *per se*, that's putting your little memory-absorption process on 'mute.' No, let me finish, it's been so long since you had a man in your life you cared anything about. You loved Stuart without reason, and he certainly didn't deserve it, and then there was Peter-Peter-Goddamned-Cheater—I said, let me finish!—and it was all about lust with that one, though you tried to love him, too, because that's what we all want.

But Lila, look. You don't know what to do with the whole package, so to speak. You really don't. And even if it's just potential for the real deal, Adam's got something that speaks to your heart and your mind—along with your naughty bits, too—

271

and it's putting you into the present in a powerful way. It's not that his touch is magic, though I'm guessing he's working some sort of magic," Kristen finally chuckled at her own sermon, "but he is bringing you 'into the moment' in a very immediate sort of way, and that's just got you all kerfuzzled."

Lila waited, but Kristen had completed imparting her great wisdom. While Lila wasn't sure she could agree, she had to admit, there was something to Kristen's notion.

"You should probably fire Julie today," Kristen said, her tone of voice unshakable.

"I probably should. All I need for therapy is you!"

Kristen crowed gleefully into the phone.

"Me, and Adam! Okay, so that's all food for thought or whatever, but COME ON, tell me about your fun."

"Kristen!"

"I'm incredi ... I mean, incorrigible, whatever! Just tell me if it was good between you before all the worries set in, okay? I need to know that. I need to know he held you afterwards."

"It was good. It was great! And he did hold me." Lila felt herself relax into the memories. "Every time."

"*Every* time? Oh hell to the YES, that is what I want to hear."

"And we talked. I told him about Stuart after he looked you up online and asked me if you were really a photographer."

"Ahh, so that's what he did. A little paranoid, yes?"

"Yes! You can understand, Kristen ... "

"I can, of course. Not trusting ME, is he? Dumbass. I am so totally trustworthy, after all, showing up armed and dangerous with my camera."

Lila sighed.

"That's what he said."

"'Armed and dangerous?' Lila, you ought to dump him for such nonsense!"

"Kristen, be serious."

"Okay. Look, yes, you guys barely know each other. But Adam's made a leap Stuart or Peter-Peter—let's make that PPGDC—never did and never could. Adam saw you in—Lila, in the scariest fucking scene I never wish to see again, you were shaking like I couldn't believe and at the same time, moving like a damn zombie, except you couldn't even speak to say, 'Braaaaaains!'—and he believed what was happening. He looked as scared as if death itself was coming down on him, watching what you were going through, but he still tried to wait it out like I told him he should. And then when he couldn't take it anymore, he caught you up in his arms like a fairytale prince—a hot*damn* cowboy fairytale prince—and carried you off."

Kristen paused to inhale, then let it out in a whoosh.

"I tell you, Lila, it was SWEET. Minus all the scary shaking and all."

Now it was Lila's turn to breathe.

"Heavy breathing, nice. Maybe I could spin out a novel someday myself?"

Lila laughed.

"Tell me, my famous author friend, what genre do you think I'd be best suited for?" It was a stock question, and Lila primly provided the expected answer.

"Paranormal romance."

"VAMPIRE PORN!"

They both laughed then, waves of healing humor lapping at the tension and eroding it as easily a sugared sandcastle.

"Did I tell you I discovered another new band?"

"'Vampire Porn?'" Lila asked, wiping at her eyes with one hand.

"Close! 'GULIBLE PENIS!' All caps, with one 'L.'"

"Good grief!"

"Go on, guess the genre."

"I don't know!" Lila was still remembering how Kristen had

"accidentally" stumbled on a paranormal romance novel in a used book store, read it cover-to-cover in a single night, and then described it in all its raunchy glory to Lila the following morning.

"Come on, you do, too. GULIBLE PENIS. All caps, with one 'L.'"

"Punk rock?"

"See? You did know!"

It set them both off again, as Kristen had no doubt intended.

By the time they ended their call, Lila was longing to answer the unknown, as-yet-unreturned call of the stove door. Determination to learn what there was to learn had returned to her in force, but because her abilities were still muted, she could not complete her inexplicable mission.

Her ungiven promise to Spencer to wait for his presence, she noted, was not much of a deterrent.

Lila sighed, connected her phone to its charger, and glanced out at the now-overcast sky. She hoped the water had heated before the clouds had thickened, and wondered absently when that happened. She'd best go shower now, she supposed, regardless of the relative warmth of her water supply.

Showering out-of-doors was one part necessity, one part decadence. Lila hadn't wanted to install a shower stall indoors, even though Lou had proposed a neat setup with a slightly-elevated shower stall in order to insert a flat tub—not unlike the one that had served as Thunder's first litter box, underneath to capture the wash-water—but the idea of losing a corner of her small cabin to a shower stall had been too much. Lila's curls responded poorly to daily shampoos, anyway, and she scarcely needed a daily shower to cleanse her body, preferring a sponge-bath style cleaning for simplicity and speed.

Although, with Spencer in the picture—if she could even think of such a daring image as herself with a new man—Lila now felt a pang of loss. With a flush of heat as a vision of showering with Spencer crossed her mind.

I wonder if I could get that shower retrofitted?

With a short chuckle for her wandering, happily voracious mind, Lila changed into her shirt-robe and scooped up her towel, soap, and bathmat. The thick, rubbery mesh wasn't especially comfortable to stand on, but it kept the pine needles off her toes. She set up her shower underneath a favorite pine tree just outside her cabin's yard and found the water to be acceptably warmish, if not a truly pleasant temperature.

Carefully regulating the water's flow, Lila shampooed her hair first, then washed her body with the remnant suds that slid down as she slowly rinsed her hair. The air was turning chilly, but this spot was strategically selected, and provided some respite from the worst of the wind, which was picking up speed in stuttering starts.

The wind reminded Lila of the time she'd spent sheltered in Spencer's arms, making her consider that an outdoor shower with Spencer would be far more lovely than an indoor one. She'd would just need to pick up a second solar shower bag. Toweling off, Lila determined to add it to her list, even as the scared woman behind the one caught up in the unexpected glory of a new love affair whispered that it was all happening too fast, too soon

Too strong.

Back in the cabin, Lila changed into clean clothes and came around the corner from the bedroom just as Thunder was finishing up behind his privacy shield.

"Oh, Thunder!" Lila was aghast at the state of the litter box, which she'd been diligently scooping whenever she noticed it needed doing. "I haven't been paying attention at all, I'm sorry!"

Thunder didn't seem inclined to hold a grudge, but Lila couldn't help thinking about Nero, the more finicky of Kristen's two cats. Nero had been known to do his business just outside of the box if the inside had so much as a single lump in it. While Lila had no reason to suspect that Thunder was going to demonstrate the same fastidiousness as Nero, she also had no interest in forcing the issue.

"I'll get this right now, boy, then we'll have a little dinner, okay?"

Lila dutifully cleaned the litter box, and determined, with a sigh, that she needed to get more sand to fill it. This train of thought made her consider that a five-gallon plastic pail, with a lid, would be ideal for storing a supply of sand outside of her cabin—she could even use the bucket as a doorstop, when the weather was nice enough to leave the outer door open. The plastic ice cream pail she had been using really wasn't sturdy enough, nor did it hold a very large supply.

"I wish you'd reminded me before I showered!" Lila told Thunder, who leaned into her caress with both abandon and a hearty purr. "But I guess you've got enough on your mind."

That reminded Lila of her list, and so she hurried to add "5-gallon bucket, w/lid" and "2nd solar shower" to it before putting her shoes back on and slinging her fanny pack around her waist.

She was out of the line of sight of the door when she heard the knock, a smile erupting across her face as she pictured Spencer standing there. But when Lila rounded the corner, plastic ice cream pail in hand, it wasn't Spencer whose frame filled her doorway.

It was Jake.

20: Stricken

"I'm sorry; you look like you're on your way out," Jake said to Lila's stunned stare.

"I was ... I was just going to get more sand for Thunder's litter box," Lila said, her powers of speech operating on only a slight delay. She noticed Jake's tentative smile had vanished, and suspected that was probably her own doing. She'd dashed to the door thinking her lover—*her lover!*—had come to surprise her, and instead found herself facing his long-lost brother.

She could only imagine how her face had looked to Jake as it changed from delighted expectation to shock.

Adding yet another wrinkle to an already disastrous—albeit figurative—ironing pile, while Spencer now knew who his brother was, Jake didn't have the slightest inkling that he even had a sibling. This realization struck Lila and chilled her in a literal sense, spiking goose-bumps up her arms.

"Well, that's just about perfect," Jake was saying as Lila's mind lurched about in a drunken stupor. "I thought I'd just drop off some supplies; a cedar-based cat litter that you might like for its scent. It's light, too, and natural, so you wouldn't have to cart it to town for disposal."

"Oh! That's ... I didn't know they made anything like that." Lila opened the door and stepped outside, taking the large bag that Jake was holding.

"You might try a mix of sand and this stuff first, to see if he'll accept it, but I figured with all the pines in the area, the scent would probably appeal to Thunder. Look, I didn't mean to interrupt, I just wanted to thank you for dinner the other night and this it seemed like a good idea at the time."

"No, it's very thoughtful, and a lot lighter than sand, I can see." Lila shifted the bag, rattling the ice cream pail that now dangled from her wrist.

The bag was, in fact, inconceivably lighter than the potential issues between Jake and Spencer, especially since Jake didn't realize he had a brother in the world.

"Yeah." Jake stuffed his hands into his pockets, gazing past Lila, along the side of the house.

"Is something ... is there anything you wanted to talk about?" Lila asked. The cat litter, light though it might be in comparison to sand, was assuming a leaden quality as the silence between her and Jake lengthened. She lowered the bag to the deck, setting the pail beside it.

Jake sighed, his eyes flickering back towards Lila as she straightened up again, meeting her gaze but not holding it as Spencer's did. Nevertheless, Lila saw more resemblances now between Jake and Spencer than she would have suspected she could, not having both brothers together. Jake favored Nell physically, and Spencer ... Spencer favored James in that regard, though both brothers had almond-shaped eyes.

Nell's eyes.

As Lila attempted to shake the chill that had clutched at her when she'd noted Spencer's similarity in appearance to his deceased, much-maligned father, Jake appeared to be wrestling with something as well. He ran one hand through his hair, much as Lila had seen Spencer do, and this commonality, too, frightened Lila in a completely irrational way.

"I don't have any right," Jake said finally, "but I do need someone to talk to. Max Huxley showed up this morning and told me I had a brother."

Whatever Lila had been expecting Jake to say, it hadn't been that. She wished she'd been able to cultivate a poker face sometime over the years, but she saw Jake absorbing her unspoken response through her expression even as the wish dropped hollow and ungranted to the ground.

"You knew." He barely breathed the words, but at least, he didn't seem angry.

"I just found out," Lila answered. It was honest enough, even if it wasn't the full truth. To forestall the question of how she knew, she heaved her own sigh, made all the heftier with her desire to keep this knowledge hidden.

"Do you want to come in?" she asked. "I'll make tea, tell you what I know."

But Jake shook his head.

"I need to get home," he said. His voice was steady, but labored, as if carrying its own load of secrets. "Not A.B.'s place. Home. It's Adam Spencer. My brother, I mean. And he knows, too?"

Lila, her throat too tight to speak, settled for a nod.

"So he knows about ... about our mother?"

That question caught Lila's remaining breath and stole it away, making her gasp as if a vacuum had been created within her lungs. She reached out, grabbing Jake's arm without intending to, the instant of uncertainty rippling out from her and moving past Jake as fast and as intense as an earthquake.

"What about your mother?"

Jake met Lila's eyes now, and she saw her own turmoil there, spiraling into his and out of control.

"She's in a coma. She's been in one since the night ... the night ... " Lila found herself nodding, and Jake seized this acceptance even as Lila let go of his arm. "Who told you? How did you know any of this?"

Lila swallowed hard but the frantic chaos in her mind was only amplified by what she saw before her now. Before her, behind Jake, approaching them both.

"Spencer." Lila almost whispered his name, transferring her now shaking hand from her side to the doorframe for support.

"Spencer? I thought you didn't know him?"

"She didn't," Spencer said, stepping onto the edge of Lila's porch floor, boots snapping hard and startling Jake into a spinning turn. "But she does now."

Lila felt lightheaded as Spencer's eyes flashed from her face to Jake's, which was now all but invisible to Lila from where she stood. Having her hand on the doorframe was insufficient to steady the precarious tilting of the world around her, and so Lila tried to focus on her breathing.

The silence lengthened between Jake and Spencer, as Spencer's gaze finally fixated on his brother's face. To say they stood like statues would be to malign the life-like appearance of fine sculpture ... the two men stood much more stiffly and less naturally than marble would have done.

Finally, Spencer took one step forward, bringing his hand up, and Lila's heart leapt in terror as a scene she'd gleaned from Nell's stove superseded itself over the live drama now playing out in front of her: a vision of James striking out at A. B., and of A. B. fighting back.

But the memory faded as Jake met Spencer's hand and shook it briefly. Jake stepped out and away from the hand Spencer tentatively raised to his opposite shoulder, though.

"It's too much. I ... this is all just too much. I need a few days. I'll call you?" He turned to Lila as he finished, and Lila registered Spencer's slight recoil at the words.

"I can text you Spencer's number," she said. "But if you need someone to listen, yes, call me."

"Thanks," Jake murmured to Lila. "Thanks," he said again, this time to Spencer.

And he was gone, moving so quickly that he could have been running, leaving Lila alone with Spencer and the storm raging in his captivating eyes.

"Did you hear?" Lila said, feeling the faint trying to force her into blackness, blinking it back and breathing deeply after she gasped out the words.

"Hear what? Are you alright?" Spencer's eyes softened, following Lila's tensed muscles from her face to her hand, gripping the edge of the metal around the doorway so tightly that it was physically painful. When Spencer reached to unclench Lila's hand, she saw that she'd cut herself against the back edge of the trim.

"Your mother," Lila told Spencer, enunciating the words carefully. "Nell. The Shepherd—Max Huxley—told Jake ... she's alive. She's in a coma, but she's ... "

And then Lila had to hurry to try to support Spencer as he fell into her, her need for air forgotten.

"It's nothing," Spencer snapped, that acerbic cover of his settling onto him with the aplomb of a superhero's cape. "You've got a nail coming out of your deck there. I tripped." And he scooped Lila up into his arms, jostling her hard against his chest as he did so. "And you've got a faint coming on, if I'm not mistaken. Did you go down to that damned grave without me?"

"No!" Lila reached for the screen door, but Spencer turned, moving smoothly in spite of carrying her, and blocking her stretch. He had her inside the cabin and on her bed so fast that Thunder had to leap out of the way as Spencer pushed Lila down.

"Lie back and relax," he said. "I'll get you some water."

"I'm fine! I ... "

Spencer's hands moved from Lila's shoulders, where he had been pressing firmly, to cup her cheeks.

"Can you not carry the weight of everyone else's trials for a few fucking minutes?" The words snapped out, bit off as if they were all vulgar, and Spencer's flashing eyes emphasized his speech.

But his hands on Lila's face were achingly gentle, and his fingers played in her curls. The sweetness conveyed in his touch reached Lila with the perfection of unmistakable clarity, a success rarely achieved by carefully chosen words.

"Okay," she whispered, covering one of Spencer's hands with her own. "But just for a few minutes."

Spencer's lips twisted up at the ends, proof positive that he caught Lila's subtle chastisement of his crassness, but the twin flames of his eyes raged on. Still, he squeezed her hand before moving to the kitchen, and she heard him murmur to Thunder, who meowed a response.

Lying down, and likely also because Spencer had dampened her abilities with his touch again, Lila found all vestiges of instability wiped clear from her body and mind. She reached for the pillows to prop herself up but, remembering Spencer's question, determined to wait for his return.

He was only moments behind this thought, and Lila was glad she had waited as she saw him taking her in. The cold heat started to seep out of his expression, and he sat next to her, holding his free hand out so she could sit—leaning against his strong frame instead of her suddenly unappealing pillows—and handed her a cup of water.

"Thank you," Lila said.

They sat together, Lila reclining against Spencer and Spencer clasping her there with his arm wrapped around her waist. The breeze flickered over them, heat draining from it as the day lengthened, but Lila found herself warmer than the ambient air temperature warranted. When she finished the water and turned her head to look at Spencer, he crushed her lips with his own, ardor surpassing any other emotions, though still tempered by concern.

"I'm fine. I really am," Lila said when Spencer drew back to look at her again. She tucked the cup inside the open window and then snuggled against Spencer's body as close as she could get.

"And you didn't go to ... "

"No, I didn't." It was hard to admit, but Lila understood the need, and so she went on, "You're right. It's too much for me to go alone."

Spencer's arms tightened around her as she spoke, and Lila heard his heart skip a beat underneath her ear. The wonder of his wordless response made her look up in surprise. Spencer met her eyes, and Lila saw for an instant an undefinable something behind them, but then Spencer kissed her again and the message of his eyes was lost.

"There's a lot of too much lately," Spencer said, pulling back after a long moment. And now it was Lila who reached up to touch Spencer's face, attempting to smooth the tension from it.

"You didn't know about Nell?" she asked. He shook his head, frown deepening.

"Why is Jake getting told about ... about our mother, and not me?" He paused, then spoke again, the effort to do so grating harshly, roughening the edges of an idea that was already coarse and jagged. "Why did A. B. keep Jake with him and not me?"

Self-pity wasn't woven into his words. Spencer's tone was unblemished by the awful import that his simple speech carried. The foundation of pain was, nevertheless, all too evident.

"Guilt," Lila said, the thought coming out of her mouth before she even considered whether or not to say it out loud.

"What?"

Lila cleared her throat and leaned back to look up at Spencer.

"If I had to guess, I'd say it was guilt," she said, trying to match the calm with which Spencer had spoken. "A. B. shot James. You said he didn't know you were there, but he must have."

"He didn't ... how could he? I hid!"

Lila pressed a hand over both of Spencer's where they were now clutching her waist.

"But A. B. took you and Jake to The Shepherd, right?"

Understanding spread across Spencer's face like a prairie fire, ravaging all available fuel and leaving nothing but charred waste in its wake.

"Of course. He would have known I was missing. He and A. B. would have been able to put the pieces together, even if A. B. didn't see me at the house." Now Spencer sounded anguished, and Lila shifted to grasp his body as tightly as he was holding hers.

"Kids always think they're better at hiding than they are," she whispered, watching Spencer intently.

Emotions flew over Spencer's face, casting both shadow and light as they crossed.

"I suppose," he said, sounding more brittle than bitter now.

"Maybe we should go see The Shepherd," Lila ventured, hoping an offer could carry her notion into acceptability. She didn't doubt Jake when he said he needed time, but she knew what Spencer needed was action. When Spencer didn't reply, but just looked at Lila with his sharp green eyes, she went on, "Max, I mean. A. B. introduced him to me as The Shepherd, so that's how I think of him, but his real name is Max Huxley. Maybe we should go see him?"

"Maybe *we* should." Spencer added the slightest of emphasis to the pronoun. An equally scant smile bloomed on his face, sparking a broader reflection on Lila's.

How long they sat there, smiling at each other, was not something Lila would have written into a story, had she been creating this one. But it seemed significant as she experienced it, a silent, shared communion coming out of yet another painful experience.

It felt important. It felt real.

A soft scratching finally penetrated the spell between Lila and Spencer.

"Oh!" Lila exclaimed, leaning around Spencer as if she could see around the corner that way. "I still have to get more sand for his litter box."

"Where?" Spencer asked, blocking Lila's escape from the bed with his body.

"Just along the ridge and down by the fence-line," Lila said. "It won't take long."

"Down the fence-line by my property, you mean?" Spencer said.

"Oh for goodness sakes, Adam Spencer! I can't get anything off that stove door now anyway! You've had your hands all over me!" She shoved against Spencer's chest and started to cross over the delicious, frustrating barricade of his body.

Spencer's arms tightened around her waist, pulling Lila tight against him again, a force as inescapable as gravity.

"I'm sorry."

"What?" Lila searched Spencer's face, so close in front of hers.

"I'm sorry. I ... trust isn't something that comes easily to me."

And now it was Lila's heart that skipped a beat, and not in a way that sent her into throes of anxiety—though rationally, she supposed it should.

"Me, either," she confessed. "But I'll work at it if you will."

"Count on it," Spencer said. They sealed their deal with yet another crushing, soaring kiss.

"Why don't you come with me?" Lila offered later, buckling her fanny pack to her waist and picking up the ice cream pail.

"Thanks, but I was thinking maybe I could start supper."

"You cook?" Lila blurted.

Spencer smirked broadly at her chagrin.

"Yes, Ms. Dawkins, I cook. It's a handy skill to have when you like to eat."

"Well, of course you can cook. I hope you can't write, though, or I'll feel completely unskilled."

Spencer's eyebrows rose, one quirking wickedly. "I think you have a lot of skills. In fact, I ... " He reached for her, but Lila danced out of his way, laughing.

"Food's in the storage tins under the counter," she said, blowing Spencer a kiss as she hurried out the door. "And the refrigerator, of course. I'll be back soon!"

"But where's the apron?" Spencer called after her, gruff voice laced tight with well-disguised humor.

The fact that she could see through Spencer's defensive veneer more and more easily kept a smile hovering on Lila's face as she traced the ridge to the point where she wanted to descend.

The path Lila chose was based on its relative ease, so she made it quickly to the grassland below the pine-topped hills. The prairie, abundantly watered this year, was practically lush, spotted with clusters of color and rippling in the evening breeze like the fur on Thunder's back when she barely touched it.

Lila made her way to the old trail along the fence-line. The land here remembered violations of man and machine long after the two had ceased to traverse it, and although neither Lila nor anyone else had driven across this particular stretch of what might debatably be called a "road" since she'd purchased the land, scars of sandy soil still lay exposed to the elements. Erosion had increased previous destruction, spreading it wider and broader than it had begun.

The advantage to Lila in this case was soft, sandy soil perfect for Thunder's needs. As she crouched in a likely-looking spot along the old two-track trail to scoop some up, it occurred to Lila that converting Thunder to the cedar-based litter Jake had brought should take priority.

"At least before winter sets in!"

In winter, Lila parked her truck near the end of the state-maintained part of the road, and put in a call to the Sheriff's office to be sure that her vehicle wouldn't be towed. She was accustomed to snowshoeing to get to her cabin, pulling her supplies in a sled behind her, but digging through the drifts that would seal this area in the winter and then attempting to chisel frozen sand for

Thunder's litter box would be out of the question.

Bucket filled to capacity, Lila stood and dusted off the knees of her jeans. She glanced out past the sinking brilliance of the sun across Spencer's land. She couldn't see the old house from this particular spot, nor feel the tug of the stove door that marked James' unmourned grave now, but Lila knew with a breathless certainty when she was aimed in the proper direction.

What else is there to learn?

She shuddered at the thought of more tragedy and turmoil, wishing selfishly that Spencer hadn't pulled her away when he did. And yet ... if he hadn't been there, if he hadn't done what he did right when he did it, he might not be in her cabin now, cooking her dinner!

And in spite of the trepidation her unlikely romantic history provoked in her now, Lila had no desire to wish away the complicated, attractive man currently cooking in her kitchen.

Her smile restored, Lila turned to negotiate the sandy embankment behind her. The steep lip of the structure fairly ordered her around its edge, but imbued with longing to return to her cabin—a place that, while she loved it dearly, had never seemed more like home than it did today—Lila scrambled right up the sheer, concave curve.

The soil slipped under her feet, making Lila move faster and work harder to reach her goal, so when she did, she was breathing hard and slightly off balance.

She was so focused on getting to the top of the slope that she neglected to pay attention to the terrain. And consequently, Lila almost fell onto the snake in front of her that sat, coiled and terrifying, on the side of a sentry sagebrush.

Her half-emitted scream garbled in her throat as Lila tumbled back down the sandy incline she'd just come up, landing in a graceless, painful heap right back where she'd started. She was half-covered in the sand she'd scooped up for Thunder and aware that she'd twisted her ankle, but terror nevertheless forced her to scramble backwards.

Lila put a good 10 yards between herself and her landing site, eyes darting left, right, and all around as she went, before she realized that she was not being pursued. Her heart beat a hasty tattoo from the inside of her chest straight through every piece of tissue and bone in her body. Her breath came in gasps, fluttering aimlessly like a bird that has just struck glass, and blackness hovered at the edges of her vision.

She made a concentrated effort to breathe more deeply, and after a moment, stood and took a single step.

"Oh!"

A shot of pain injected forcefully just above the edge of her shoe insisted upon reconsideration of her plan to walk back up to the cabin. Adrenaline had fueled her initial flight from the snake, but now, she was feeling the twist she'd inflicted on her ankle.

Lila moved slowly to a nearby large rock and leaned against it, checking her ankle for swelling and finding nothing significant. From this vantage point, she could see the snake, still coiled next to the sagebrush at the edge of the slope she'd both scrambled up and fallen down. Although the very sight of the thing sent Lila's adrenaline back into overdrive production, she forced herself to look long and hard at the snake, and its desiccated appearance gradually took the place of the nightmarish fears it had inspired ... even after its death.

Now Lila fumbled for her cell phone, and dialed Spencer's number, grateful for the ability to do so.

"Hey, you!" Spencer answered, his voice soft and smooth even as the connection sputtered with static. "Dinner's almost ready."

"Hey!" Lila tore her eyes away from the dead snake across the road and smiled in spite of the residual pain in her ankle and the still-accelerated speed of her heart.

"What's wrong?"

"Nothing," Lila said, hastening to reassure him as he picked up on her mood like a bird dog on a scent. "I mean, I'm fine, but ... I twisted my ankle and ... ."

"You what? No, I heard you. Let me whistle up Sunny and come get you."

"I was hoping you'd say that," Lila said, tension breaking in her voice even as she sighed in relief. "It's fine, I'm sure, but I'd rather not walk back up, and ... "

"Dinner will keep. I'll turn off the burner and cover it."

Now the tears started, and Lila sniffled.

"Are you sure you're all right?"

Lila nodded, and then realized the absurdity of that response.

"Yes, there was a snake, but it's dead and ... "

"I'll be right there." Spencer severed the connection almost before he finished speaking, urgency dripping from every taut syllable.

Lila frowned, lowering her phone from her ear and staring at it as if it were the source of her consternation.

"You don't know where I am!"

Whatever landmarks Lila had thought to provide to Spencer, however, were entirely unnecessary. Riding Sunny at a speed she'd not suspected the mild-tempered horse capable of reaching, he came pounding into sight, following the fence-line, as if he were conjured up for the sole purpose of ensuring Lila's rescue.

Spencer wheeled Sunny in front of Lila, casting his eyes down, around, and across the road.

"My prince!" Lila said, tears threatening again at the sight of Spencer, his stance so clearly protective.

"Where's the snake? You're sure you killed it?"

Shaking her head, Lila pointed.

"Across the road; it's already dead, and I ... oh!" Lila found herself sitting in Spencer's place as he dismounted and lifted her up onto Sunny's back in his place with movements so swift in succession they might as well have been singular.

"I'll check," he said, holding Lila's thigh as she settled into position. He gave her no time to disagree, but spoke gently to Sunny and then crossed the old disaster of the road to where the bucket had fallen.

"By that sagebrush on the top," Lila called after him. "I didn't see it until I was right on top of it, and then I just ... well, I fell trying to get away."

I could write a much better scene than this. And yet, as Lila watched Spencer stride deliberately towards the snake, she reconsidered that thought.

I could write better for my actions, but not for his.

And how long had she known this man? Lila sighed.

Spencer circled the snake warily, but his posture lost much of its tension, and Lila knew he realized the threat was not immediate.

"That must've given you a hell of a start."

"It did. What are you ... oh! Thank you!" Spencer jumped down the embankment and then turned away, retrieving the bucket and scooping up sand as if that had been his only purpose on this unplanned jaunt.

"Thanks," she said again, swallowing hard as Spencer approached, his eyes locked with hers and his swagger—it was distinctly present again—incapable of occluding the fact that he had literally ridden to her rescue.

Spencer set the bucket down and gently reached for Lila's ankle.

"This one?"

"Yes."

Spencer's warm hands slipped underneath Lila's jeans, probing her skin delicately, gently.

"Probably just a sprain," Lila offered, ruining the nonchalance she strove for with a cracking voice.

"Probably," Spencer agreed, looking up at her from under his hat's brim with eyes that were distinctly more passionate than nurturing now.

"It feels better already." Lila said.

"I'm glad. But you should be more careful, coming up a steep slope like that." Steel edged his voice, but Lila saw through that self-defensive wall.

"I will be," she shuddered.

Spencer stared at her for a hot-and-cold moment that prickled the fine hairs on the back of Lila's neck, though not in a frightening way.

"Let's get on home," he said then, turning his face from her as he bent to pick up the bucket of sand.

Let's get on home.

Lila couldn't speak, so complete was the smile that filled her face.

21: Preparations

"Jake called," Spencer said into the darkness, jolting Lila out of her light doze. Her leg felt heavy and when she tried to move it, she remembered that it was wrapped in Kristen's discarded splint. Spencer's words penetrated Lila's sleep befuddlement then and she lifted her head from his chest.

"He did?" The flickering candle was casting shadows from its position on the floor next to the bed—Lila couldn't see Spencer's expression.

"Yes. I hung up on him to answer your call."

"You what?"

"Are you going to say anything that's not a question?" Spencer softened his words by squeezing Lila tight against him.

"Well, I ... "

"I wasn't rude, if that's what you're thinking."

"I wasn't ... why don't you just tell me more about it, then?" Spencer's chuckle rumbled through his chest, and Lila smiled, realizing that her yet-another-question was the reason for it. She lowered her head to feel the last bit of Spencer's laugh. "Annoying man."

"I don't ... I never wanted a brother," Spencer said. "A mother, yes, but not a brother. I don't know ... how to be with a brother."

Lila thought about that.

"Having a brother isn't too far removed from having a mother—which you also have, by the way."

Spencer sighed, and the sound was like escaping on a breeze rather than being pushed away.

"A comatose mother. Great."

"It's not what you hoped for as a boy, I know," Lila said. "But you might be surprised at what it would mean to see her, to hold her hand." She swallowed. "My parents were both killed in a car accident—that's what I always say, because most people don't want to know the details—but Mom ... Mom was in the hospital on life support for a few days after the accident. She never regained consciousness and of course I would rather have had her whole, but ... I ... it was important ... it was good, as much as it hurt, to be able to say goodbye and believe that she could hear me, even if she couldn't answer me."

Spencer kissed the top of Lila's head, his fingers entangling in her hair.

"To tell her once more that I loved her, that was important," Lila finished, whispering the words. She blinked back the tears that edged into her eyes, blurring her fuzzy night vision.

"I'm sorry."

"It was a long time ago," Lila offered.

"Time doesn't heal wounds, no matter what people say. It just allows them time to scar over so we can get on with our lives."

"A scar IS healing!"

Spencer laughed.

"Okay, a scar is healing, but the mark stays there."

"Yes. Yes, it does."

They lay in silence for a bit, Spencer with his hand on Lila's head where it rested against his chest.

"So what did you talk about? With Jake?"

"Nothing much. He said he had business to settle in Billings, but he'd be back in a day or so." Spencer sighed. "I didn't tell him anything about ... that night."

"You can, you know."

"Of course I can ... wait ... you mean, I can tell him that you ... experienced it?"

Lila struggled to find words to explain her feelings on the subject, but Spencer spoke again before she could.

"I don't think I want to tell him that. Not now, anyway. Maybe someday, if this 'brother' thing works out, but ... "

Lila giggled.

"Oh, you think that's funny?"

"Yes, I do. I really do."

"And why would you think that?" Lila couldn't be sure, but she thought Spencer was sincerely confused.

"Because this 'brother' thing is forever. You might never be close, but you're always brothers. You're lucky, you know. At least you have a chance."

"I guess." It was a non-committal reply, but it didn't sound sarcastic, at least. "What about being your knight?"

"What?"

"I can't do 'prince,' I'm afraid. At least from what I've seen on Disney ads, princes wear tights, and you might have noticed that's not my style."

Knowing she couldn't see his eyes, Lila lifted her head and sought that green, mesmerizing gaze anyway. She caught only a glint before Spencer's hand drew her face towards his in the darkness, his lips bumping just to the side of her mouth before he corrected himself and kissed her full on the mouth, hard.

"Any chance being your knight is a 'forever' kind of thing, too?" He asked again.

"It could be." The words were out before she decided to speak them, and Lila floundered in the wake of their significance. "I mean, if you want the job. The armor could chafe. Or squeak. I don't know. It might be too much, too soon, too ... "

"Too much, yes. Too soon, maybe. Too ... what else was there?"

"Too ... I don't know!" As close as they were, as much as being in his arms made her believe that 'forever' was an actual possibility rather than a fairy-tale concept, Lila felt a surge of fear.

"I don't know, either. But that's nothing to be afraid of."

"Isn't it?" Lila whispered, her lower lip trembling against Spencer's. He captured her anxiety with another kiss, searing her fright to ash and scattering it as if it were lighter than the thinnest of embers.

Lila wasn't afraid the rest of the night.

"How long would it take?" Spencer asked the next morning over breakfast. The hash—leftover from the meal he'd prepared the night before—simply seasoned, was still delicious on reheating and Lila had just taken a generous bite.

"For me to be able to 'hear' the door again?" she asked when she was able. "I'm not sure, exactly. A day would do it, certainly."

"A whole day?" Spencer asked, brows furrowing. He deepened the severity of his expression when Lila giggled.

"I know, it's a lot to ask ... "

"It really is."

"I know!" Lila's smile dropped off her face as she considered both what she might learn.

"Hey, it's not that bad," Spencer said, covering her hand with his own. "I'm a grown up. I can handle a day without touching you."

Lila looked down at his hand, and released her fork to turn her own hand into his.

"Reallllly," she said, conjuring up her best drawl in an attempt to play into Spencer's misconstruing of her concern.

"I'm not saying it won't be a challenge," Spencer replied, squeezing her hand before releasing it. He sighed heavily. "I suppose I could take care of the ... necessary business with Sheriff

Hoffman ... to remove myself from temptation for the day."

This time it was Lila who reached out, clasping Spencer's hand. She sighed, exasperated, when she realized what she'd done, but clasped his hand in both of hers rather than relinquishing it immediately.

His eyes sparked wickedly as he brought his free hand up around Lila's.

"Yes, well, apparently one of us will have to remove ourselves from temptation," Lila said then. "It's far too easy to give in."

"Too this, too that," Spencer said, shaking his head. "You worry too much."

"You don't know the half of it," Lila said, before biting her lip to stop herself from saying even more.

"But I want to, Lila. The half, three-quarters, the whole. Remember that, will you? Hold on to that. When you're not holding on to me, anyway."

"Oh, you." Lila gave in to the relaxation of Spencer's grip on her own and let go.

They finished their meal, not touching any more, in a silence that was nevertheless strongly punctuated by the unspoken communication that they shared every time their eyes met.

"So," Spencer said, delivering his plate to the sink with exaggerated care to pass around Lila without so much as brushing against her. "23-3/4 hours to go. That's not so bad."

Lila snorted, shaking her head.

"It's awful!" She said it decisively this time, after due and considered reflection.

"Yes, it is." Spencer's opinion on the subject was clear in his voice, which was as seriously determined as Lila's.

"But we're grown-ups," Lila said, standing. She made her way to the sink as circuitously as Spencer had, though she moved slower on account of the splint. Spencer's eyes twinkled when he made a dramatically slow faux lunge towards her, causing her to giggle again.

"More or less," Lila amended then. Spencer only shrugged his shoulders before collecting his hat from the hook around the corner.

"How will you know when it's time?" he asked, settling his hat onto his head and making Lila regret their plan all over again.

"I'll feel it," she said, the hair on the back of her neck rising in eerie anticipation at the thought. "If you can leave the stove door somewhere ... well, somewhere within about the same distance as it is now."

Spencer nodded slowly, his eyes locked on Lila's. She could tell he understood that she'd phrased the idea the way she had to give him the ability to hide the stove door from her, if he chose.

"I'll put it in the hawthorns before I call Sheriff Hoffman," he said, returning Lila's gift of trust right back to her.

"And I'll call you when it's time. I hope it'll be during the day, but ... I ... it could mean a long night—and nightmares—if it comes on late in the day."

"I'll come back tonight, then," Spencer said. "I'll sleep on your porch if I have to, but I won't leave you alone, even if I can't touch you."

And as his simple words brought tears to her eyes, Lila smiled. Spencer nodded as if to seal his promise and turned to go. He took one step towards the door before turning back.

"Are you sure you want to do this?"

"It's the only way to end the ... prodding, I guess, from the door," Lila said, shrugging. "I feel like, as strong as it's been— more than any other object, the way this one keeps reaching out to me, even at a distance—it'll just keep coming back ... "

"But there's another way."

Spencer's conviction stunned Lila for a moment, but when he raised his arms, holding them open to her, she realized what he was suggesting. She tried to assume a stern expression, but laughter won out.

"You'll have to be away from me eventually," she said, shaking her head.

"For a whole day? I doubt it. Besides, maybe you could build up a level of protection, like a static charge but in a good way." He lowered his arms and, leaning provocatively against the wall beside him, winked at Lila.

"What a lovely thought," Lila said, grinning in spite of the tumult in her mind, wondering again if Spencer was deliberately trying to keep her from the stove door and then chastising herself for being so untrusting. "And I would like to test that, very much, but perhaps we could do it on the next memory-stuffed thing."

Spencer raised his eyebrows.

"There's always another thing," Lila said then, her despair so weighted in her voice that she knew that was what brought Spencer's brows back down.

Spencer took another step, this time towards Lila, but checked himself. He tipped his hat instead, and held Lila in an embrace of vision rather than of physical touch—so tightly that she shivered in response.

"Call me," he said, "and be careful on that ankle."

"It's fine," Lila assured him. "Really, I think I could take the splint off already ... but I won't! Not if you're going to give me *that* look!"

Spencer shook his head and turned away, but Lila saw his smile before he could hide it.

She slipped towards the door to watch him cross her yard, whistling for Sunny as he went. The horse nickered from somewhere out of sight and then strolled leisurely into view. She bumped her head against Spencer's arm as he reached out to stroke her face, and Lila couldn't help but wish to trade places with the horse right now.

A ridiculous thought.

"Mrrt?" Thunder leaned against Lila's leg, following his strangely delicate meow with his usual raucous purr. Lila looked down at the cat as he rubbed around her uninjured ankle, and he glanced over his shoulder at Spencer and Sunny outside.

"He'll be back," Lila whispered, bending to scratch Thunder's cheek. The fact that she was certain of her assertion bloomed inside her, comforting her in a way that the tightly closed bud of wishful thinking had never done.

She straightened, watching Spencer lead Sunny towards the gate, out of sight around the corner of the cabin, and relished the springtime of this new love, this unexpected connection with this maddening, substantial, significant man.

And then she set her shoulders and turned to do the dishes, and some writing.

In spite of the fact that her "memory mute button" was fully depressed, Lila wasn't able to engage in her work-in-progress. Although the skies weren't entirely clear—so her solar-powered battery system would not be refreshing itself as quickly as it would on a day of full sun—Lila indulged in her favorite music for focusing on editing.

As the sounds of Amy Lauren's *On Water* filled the cabin, Lila settled herself to work on RayAnn's edits to Lila's most recently completed novel. While she preferred to write in silence, Lila found it easier to edit with music surrounding her. And not just any music, but wordless, complex, nature-inspired piano! Lila had wondered if *On Water* would fail to mesh with the sagebrush- and pine-filled view out her window, but perhaps because of the unusually damp weather this year, it worked like magic.

Lila kept focused through two—or was it three?—playbacks

of the CD, the most recent release by the artist, even through
Thunder attempting to block her view of the screen with his furry
body. She lured the cat into her lap with minimal effort and kept
right on working, but eventually, Lila's own body insisted upon a
break.

She visited the outhouse first, and then did a little stretching
on her porch, noting the thickening clouds in the sky above. She
considered checking the weather, but instead checked her cell
phone, and found it bearing a hefty load of text messages from
Spencer.

"23.5 hours to go!" read the first, which Spencer must have
sent while astride Sunny.

The last in the set carried notably less enthusiasm, and
pertained not to missing her, but instead to the unpleasant
necessity involving the sheriff.

"Hoffman asked how I found the body."

Lila dropped onto her bed next to Thunder, who had
relocated when she'd gone outside, her hand around her phone
tightening. She'd not considered that aspect of the situation, and
wondered how Spencer had answered.

It wasn't a lack of trust that inspired Lila's consideration this
time, but that odd disjointing between the closeness she felt with
Spencer and how little they still knew about one another. Lila
always tried to stay as close to the truth as she could in situations
where she'd lied—or at least didn't tell the entire story—about her
strange, memory-related affinity.

She frowned, imagining how she would feel if Spencer didn't
share her sense of ethics, and then sighed as she considered
whether what she did could be construed as "ethical" at all.

"'Ethical Quandary' is a better band name than what you over-
think in the name of looking out for yourself!" Lila remembered
Kristen saying.

"What kind of band?" she'd responded, watching Kristen

through a sheen of tears.

"One that's never getting out of the fucking garage!" Kristen snapped. "Now, 'Out of the Fucking Garage,' or better yet, 'Out of My Fucking Garage,' THAT is a good band name! Angry thrash metal, I'm thinking, and not mainstream angry thrash metal, either. Something cutting-edge. Oh! OMFG! The perfect abbreviation! Imagine the t-shirts!"

Lila smiled slightly at the memory and took a moment to "listen" for the stove door's contained, inconclusive tale, but it seemed she was still well within the thrall of Spencer's touch. She dashed off a short set of texts to Kristen describing the plan she and Spencer had formulated, leaving off the mention of Sheriff Hoffman's current task, and then wrote to Spencer as well.

"I miss you."

"I'm editing my new book."

"I'm sorry I'm not with you right now."

"Nothing 'received' yet."

"I love you."

But though she typed those last three words with barely a hesitation, Lila backspaced over them so rapidly she ended up sending a blank text as her final message.

Oh, bother.

Lila set her phone on the pillow, where the vibrations of any incoming messages would be absorbed by the bedding and mattress, and caressed Thunder's head where it peeked out from underneath the dual shelter of paw and tail. He rumbled brief appreciation, paw curling in response to Lila's touch.

"The power of touch, huh, boy?" Lila said, her fingertips lingering in the softest fur just behind the cat's ear.

Back at her computer, water bottle in hand, Lila spent a long moment staring at the "sleeping" screen. Touch, something she'd strategically avoided for years ... the very thing that brought her both anxiety and struggle as well as some of the best ideas she'd ever had, ideas she'd woven into stories with the repeated touch of her fingers against the keyboard.

How incredible to think that touch could also be a relief and a comfort approaching a sacramental level, even for her, even with the problems and trials it also brought.

Lila's hand on the water bottle was growing cold, and she set it down with careful deliberation, noticing nuances of the sensations of both holding and not holding that mundane object. Duality and complexity merged in her writing all the time, but somehow, in some ridiculous way, she'd not considered how it could—how it *was*—infusing her entire life.

The totality of indivisible contradiction, of complexity merged with simplicity, of pro and con conjoined and purely inseparable suffocated Lila at that moment. Even though her breathing continued, even though her awareness remained, it was as if some universal truth—some abundant, obvious, unmistakable concept—had reached out and shaken Lila.

Its touch was both curse and salvation.

How much have I missed, trying to protect myself from feeling? What have I lost in the guise of saving what I have?

It was a heady, horrifying idea, and yet, there was a peace underlying it. Whatever happened from whatever choices Lila made, at least she'd be making them now not from a concern of whether they were "right," but out of an understanding that there would be both components of good and bad within them, as there were within all human endeavors, and all human experience.

Perhaps all experience, period.

A bird scrabbled against the wooden frame outside Lila's window, its chirps thick with its anxiety as its feet sought stability sized for small, avian toes. The ledge was unqualified to this task, and moreover, Thunder leapt onto the desk, drawn by the sounds of the distressed bird. The bird flew off, calling out its concerns in alarmed squawks that diminished in volume even as they increased in fright.

"I hope you were stealthier than that when you were living outside," Lila said to Thunder, who continued to stare after his now unseen and unheard prey. His tail lashed, and he approached the window slowly, eyes flicking from side to side. "Not that it matters now; I'll make sure you have plenty of food now."

Lila's promise drew a considering glance from Thunder. She chuckled, finding the look to be almost condescending.

"Of course you were a sneaky beast when you wanted to be, and of course you don't NEED me to feed you. But I kind of like the job, you know?"

Apparently, Thunder did know, and he bypassed Lila's hand to bump the top of his head against her chin.

As charming as Lila found the gesture, knowing it to be an affectionate one, she was glad that her time away from the computer had not only sent the screen to sleep, but had also engaged the "lock" mechanism. For his part, Thunder transitioned swiftly from loving to annoyed at the sound that was generated by his feet pressing on the keys, tipping his ears back and rumpling the fur along his spine as he backed up to gaze out the window again.

His fur was soon restored to smoothness even if Thunder didn't quite regain his equilibrium so easily.

Another thing we have in common.

"Well. Back to editing, then!"

Lila logged in and turned the music back on. She had no way of knowing how much solar battery power remained without dredging out the little tester with which Lou had supplied her. But, accustomed to the restrictions of the cabin and with the deadline imposed by the return of her ability to sense the stove door drawing ever nearer, Lila was determined to work for as long as she could.

Editing was strange business. Even relatively minor edits

could lead to major story overhauls, depending on what one change revealed. It was not unlike plucking at a loose thread on a sweater: sometimes, you could snip the thread off with just your fingernails, and other times one absent-minded tug would lead to the unraveling of the entire garment.

And Lila wouldn't resubmit the piece to RayAnn without reading it through first. Lila had crafted the story, read it, edited it, re-read it, and fine-tuned it so often she felt that she knew it all by heart. And yet, on reading it again—generally in the printed form, although she'd made use of an e-reader on occasion—she'd always, always find something else.

She'd been delighted in a moderately evil way when she'd submitted this particular piece to RayAnn for the first time. Lila had a long history of typing "taunt" when she meant to write "taut;" the two words were, for some unaccountable reason, confused in Lila's mind.

"I don't always write 'taut' when I mean 'taunt' … " she remembered trying to explain to RayAnn, only to have RayAnn dryly speak over her to complete her sentence, " … but when you do, you mean the exact opposite of what you just said."

So when the title for this piece had come to Lila as *The Taunt Line*, she'd seized it and laughed until she'd brought herself to tears.

"You're a stinker," RayAnn had said. "I had to call to say so right away, even if I didn't have to call to tell you I've got the new manuscript. I presume this is NOT another typo, but that you've somehow channeled Tim Gunn and 'made it work?'"

"Yes! Wait. Tim who?"

And then Lila had received a lecture on the finer points of fashion reality TV, which hadn't gone well at all.

Fortunately, RayAnn did find that the title worked, and moreover, she loved the inside joke.

I should check in with RayAnn.

Lila shook off the idea. It wasn't that it was a bad notion, as she did owe RayAnn a progress report, but at this point in editing—and particularly with other ... distractions ... on her mind—Lila had to beware of procrastination.

So she hunkered down over her laptop and doggedly continued working. When her mind wandered, Lila brought it so sharply back to task that she fancied she could feel it as a mental scratch.

Her stomach complained loudly some interminable time later, startling Thunder, who had tucked his front paws under himself and hunkered down on the desk next to the window. He poked his head up and extracted his front feet at the alarming sound, resembling a frightened, miniature sphinx in this new posture.

"Sorry!" Lila apologized to the wide-eyed cat, who appeared less than soothed by her words. "I'm just hungry, though."

It was well into the afternoon now, and so Lila slapped together a peanut butter and jelly sandwich before she allowed herself to gather up her phone again.

"hows it hangin? o i kill me" read the first message.

"Oh, Kristen."

Lila found only two other messages, both from Spencer. The first, apparently in response to her own blank message, was also blank.

The second said only, "Me too."

How she could feel so taken aback and yet still be sporting what could only be a ridiculous, besotted smile, Lila wasn't sure. Buoyed by her "over-thinking" earlier in the day, she sent, "Crazy, huh?"

She only got to take two more bites of her sandwich before Spencer responded.

"Yeah. Crazy wonderful."

"Exactly." Lila typed back.

She sent Kristen an emoticon denoting a grin, and then

drafted a message to RayAnn, telling her only that edits were underway. When Lila thought of how much she wasn't saying, she edited her response to add: "Could write another novel with what's been going on!"

"I won't, of course," Lila assured Thunder, who yawned in her face. "But it just goes to show the old saying is still around because it's just that accurate: truth IS stranger than fiction. And speaking of fiction, I'd better get back to those edits."

The Wyoming wind picked up outside throughout the afternoon, sending restless tendrils through the window to tickle Lila's skin as she sat, plugging away at RayAnn's directives. But Lila focused as if she'd trained for it, and perhaps she had, despite her opinion to the contrary over the years.

Maybe I could get meditating down after all! She thought at one juncture, and then shook off the idea just as quickly, interfering as it was with her revamping of one minor character, turning the man from slight and shifty to massive and brassy.

It wasn't until Lila's neck and shoulders began to protest the way she was leaning in towards the computer that she paused long enough to do another inventory of the physical discomfort she was feeling. It was abundantly obvious that the sensations were not all based in the realm of poor posture, but Lila rubbed at her neck with one hand anyway, lest the distinct, unmistakable crawling of skin be the result of a strategic spider's stalking and not a resurgence of communication from the stove door.

She leapt out of her chair as fast as her muscles would accommodate her wishes—and considering their protests, it must be later in the day than she realized—and hurried into the bedroom to text Spencer.

"It's time," she tapped out, pressing "Send" before registering the comparative darkness of the bedroom.

"6:00!" She gasped aloud, even as Thunder registered his agreement with Lila's assessment of the hour, and meowed hungrily.

"Okay, I'll feed you," Lila said, scooping up Thunder's bowl and turning just in time to see the frame of a man fill the screened doorway before her.

"About time, I'd say," Spencer said, the smile in his voice soothing Lila's startlement almost before it had time to rise into her throat. "I was starting to think I'd get drenched before you were ready." He stood still on the other side of the door, not reaching for the handle, wind tugging on his hat and the long coat he was wearing, as well as the second, slung over his arm.

"I've been parked with Sunny under a tree on the ridge," Spencer said as Lila continued to stare.

"For how long?" she managed to ask.

"As long as it took," Spencer replied after a pause, and the tone of his voice stole Lila's breath away all over again. "I told you I wouldn't leave you alone tonight and I meant it."

It was heart-melting and it was strange, but it was sincere—Lila had no doubt. She let her budding smile grow over her worries and bloom in full across her face. Spencer smiled back, echoing her expression.

"Hurry, though." He nodded towards Thunder's bowl, still in Lila's hand, sparking her into motion again. "Storm's coming."

22: Storm

The wind was blowing in earnest now, and although Sunny was standing between Lila and the brunt of its force, Lila shivered. The horse regarded Lila steadily, calm in spite of the approaching turmoil, and it brought a slight smile to Lila's lips even under the flooding sensations of the stove door. She turned to press her face against the horse's neck.

"It'll be alright," she said, more to herself than Sunny, and without any real conviction to back up the sentiment.

"I've got it!" Spencer called, and Lila looked back at the hawthorns as he emerged from their midst, holding the stove door in both hands in front of him as gently as if it were a baby's coffin.

A baby's coffin?

Lila shivered again and reached for the coat Spencer had brought for her, which was slung across Sunny's back. The horse watched, unruffled. She hadn't seemed to think it strange to have Lila ride her alone as Spencer led them down to where he'd placed the stove door.

"No lightning at least," Spencer said, looking up and to the West, where the storm was now visible as a hazy sheen, rain descending in torrents, perhaps only minutes away.

Spencer stopped a few feet away from where Lila stood with Sunny, and waited while she shrugged on the coat. He set the stove door on the soil between them, crushing a small patch of waving grass, and Lila stared at it there, wondering if she would be flattened next.

The stove door's disjointed song escalated as rapidly as the approaching storm, chattering, nattering, telling its tale, words overlapping and scenes intermingling like an all-senses included version of AM radio at nighttime.

"Lila?" Spencer spoke, his voice coming at her as if from an increasing distance. "I'll say something every now and then, like you told me Kristen did the last time. You have to try to answer me. I don't know if I can wait long enough otherwise."

Lila forced herself to nod, and looked up through the tempest of memory-driven madness at Spencer. His face appeared oddly distorted, overlaid with that of the younger version of himself that Lila had glimpsed before, and the knowledge that what she was about to experience was tied to Spencer sunk into Lila like a serrated dagger.

"Yes," she forced herself to say. And then she took the staggeringly few steps required to reach the door, dropped to her knees, and laid her hands flat against the cold metal.

"You killed her!" Angus shouted, tears streaking his face.

"NO!" Lying on the ground, one hand extended up towards his brother in a pleading gesture, James was convulsing, his body wracked with sobs, grief as palpable in the air as the stench of the burning house, burning dreams.

"She's barely breathing, she's like to be gone before morning!" Angus raised the pistol then, angling it down at James. His hand was shaking, but his resolve was not; he brought his other hand up under the butt of the gun to hold it steady. "You're a drunkard and a murderer!"

"No, no! If she's alive ... " James lowered his hand and stared at the barrel of the gun, then at Angus' face. He wavered, physically first, and then through his voice. "Angus, if she's alive, I got to see her. I have to make a ... make a ... make it right."

"Amends? There's no way you can make amends! That woman loved you more than her own life, and you can barely form a sentence, you bastard. You bastard!"

"But I'm not the bastard, am I?" The words were slurred, but they were painfully explicit. "Adam's the bastard, Angus. Your bastard. She loved you enough to bear your son, and then she tied herself to me just because I was here

and you weren't. And I wanted her, loved her, you weren't here ... but you ... "

"I never ... NEVER ... laid a hand on Nell, and she wouldn't allow it if I'd tried. Adam's your son. Yours. And so is Jake. You don't even realize what you've lost, James, but that doesn't mean you haven't still lost it. All of it."

Angus cocked the pistol then, and the sound managed to drown out that of the fire, even with the roof beginning to crumble.

"Lila. Answer me, Lila, please!"

The scene shifted, tipping, and Lila gasped.

"Spencer!" She managed, and the memory world stabilized again.

"You're a liar," James said, his expression both sullen and fearful. "Dirty damn liar."

"I am not!" Angus raged, taking one step forward, his pistol briefly stuttering from its target and then homing in again with determination wrought by the most powerful motivator of all ... hope lost to death.

"Then why'd you bring him with you?" James asked. And his gaze slid behind Angus, causing Angus to turn.

It wasn't much of a lapse, but it was enough.

Even as James launched himself up off the ground, Angus had both sighted Adam behind him and realized James' intent.

"Daddy!" The boy cried, his face lit by the fire, his eyes reflecting the incomprehensible, unmistakable scene before him.

Then Angus was on the ground, knocked over by James, the gun flying away in the force of the impact. Angus fought hard, compelled by fury and loss, hampered by grief. James, operating under his own grief, was like a wild animal, swinging madly, still under the alcoholic influence that had resulted in Nell's awful injury.

"Daddy! No, Unky, leave my Daddy alone!"

The boy's cries reached Angus, between the flurries of blows, and when he looked out between the entanglement of his and James' limbs, he saw those small hands holding the gun, knew there was no intent to harm but only mimicry, only a boy's innocent desire to protect his father at the dark end of

310

this horrible night.

"Adam, no!" Angus tried to extricate himself from James' tenacious, unreasoning grip, tried to put himself between the little boy and the father he sought to protect.

"Lila!"

Angus reached for the gun, James still pulling on his shoulders, trying to drag Angus back down to a beating that he could never deliver to his satisfaction, driven mad by baseless suspicion.

The gun went off, its aim true even though its target was unintended.

"Daddy! DADDY!" Adam screamed, flailing on the ground where he'd fallen after firing the gun. Angus swept Adam up in his arms, carrying the thrashing, sobbing child away from the fresh ugliness of yet another death, yet another tragedy.

"Adam, listen to me, come boy, you know all brothers fight!" Angus circled around the truck, away from the fire, his hold on Adam unrelenting even as his mind reeled and he struggled to process what had just happened. "Your Daddy had too much to drink, that's all, he didn't mean to hurt your Mama, or me, or ... or you ... he'll ... he just needs to sleep a bit, he does."

Adam continued to wail, but Angus kept up his monologue, pressing rough kisses against the boy's forehead and brushing back the rumpled hair when his voice failed, when he couldn't speak through the massive, formless, overwhelming destruction they'd both endured this night.

"Sleep?" Adam finally said, his young voice shattered, too. Exhaustion was rampant in his quivering muscles, now, and he clung to Angus instead of fighting him.

The night air was chilled here, sheltered from the fire's heat.

"Yes, boy, you need to sleep. This has all been a dream, a terrible dream, and none of it's real. You're going to wake up tomorrow and the life you find is going to be new, all of it."

"Lila!"

The scene skewed again, and Lila gasped, her mind lurching between past and present because of the shifting of the stove door beneath her hands.

311

"Lila, answer me, or I'll stop this!"

Spencer's voice sounded wrong, but Lila registered his distress only peripherally, fighting to keep the stove door firmly under the palms of her hands.

"It's almost done, it's almost done," she said, her own voice cracking, leaning forward so her body's weight secured the door in position.

"I know, I ... "

"Not real?"

"No, this isn't real. It's a dream, Adam, all of it. Your Mom and Dad will come get you soon and then you'll wake up. That'll be hard at first, but you'll rememb ... well, you'll find your way. They'll help you."

Angus' plan, sparked so obscurely in his attempt to comfort Adam, stabilized the longer he talked, the more he considered. The boy had just killed his own father—accidentally, unintentionally, but he'd done it—and abject terror nearly consumed Angus at the thought of Nell's beloved son growing up under that impossible shadow.

Adam was young, barely three, surely dedicated adoptive parents could help erase the dual trauma of losing mother and father! Or at least, they could eradicate the nightmare of this night.

And Angus had the very people in mind for the task.

Adam was still now, sucking his thumb, a habit from which Nell was ... had been ... working hard to wean him. Angus could not begrudge his nephew—face streaked with soot and tears—his small comfort and so he carefully eased the boy into the cab of his truck, gentleness in every small motion, love overlapping the vastness of pain.

He sat in the truck with Adam for a long time, watching Nell's dream home burn, staring at the dancing shadows cast by fire, finding the one that marked his brother's body unerringly, unfailingly. When the rain started to fall, at first in hesitant spits and spackles, then in roaring, pouring waves, Angus started the truck and drove away. He'd need to ride back out to bury James, after the fire was out, but if he didn't move the truck now, the dry Wyoming soil would turn slick and force him to walk back out with Adam, and he didn't want to do that to the boy.

Grim lines solidified across Angus' face as he drove away, the memory of this night etched down through his ribs and into his beating heart. He'd bury his brother alright, with the stove door on which Nell had struck her head.

He'd do it, and then he'd never speak of it again. And hope that Adam would never have to carry the burden that now threatened to crush Angus with its weight—its awful, immense, Atlas-stopping weight.

"LILA!" Spencer reached for her as Lila toppled backwards into the present, and she gasped when she landed on her backside, seeing his face streaked with dirt and tears, even as the heavens above then split open and began to wash the evidence of Spencer's distress away.

"Spencer!" Lila righted herself and threw herself into his outstretched arms, meeting him over the top of the stove door, feeling the slight, residual heat of memory fade instantly into the present reality of metal being cooled by healing rain.

"Oh god, Lila, I remember now. I remember." Spencer's face was buried in Lila's curls, one hand clutching the back of her head and the other clenching against her coat, pressing her body against his.

"You remember?" Lila tightened her own grip on Spencer as he fought against sobs. "Spencer! I'm sorry! I'm so sorry, but it was an accident ... you were just a child! A little boy who didn't understand everything that was happening!"

Her words wrenched a single cry out of Spencer, and it twisted and shattered as it broke out of his throat—out of his very soul—into the downpour.

Lila held him while he rocked against her, stifling the sounds of the long-delayed pain he was only beginning to process, holding onto her as if she was the talisman that could protect him now, as Angus had tried to protect him then.

Lila knew that if she wasn't, she wanted to be.

"I'm here. I'm here." She said it many times, but she couldn't think of anything else that had as much meaning, so she kept on saying it.

It was the sound of thunder that finally broke Lila's litany, sparking fear in the midst of pain.

"We have to get back to the cabin," Lila said. "Spencer, where's Sunny?"

"She's here. She'll come when I whistle." Spencer's words were flat, his tone terse, but he still held Lila as if she were the only buoyancy in a watery world.

Which, Lila was beginning to think, Wyoming was indeed becoming.

"Call Sunny now, Spencer. Let's get Sunny and go home— home to the cabin. The storm's getting worse. Sunny will be alright in the yard, won't she?"

Lila felt Spencer nod against her before he pulled his head back to look at her, a task that was becoming increasingly difficult as the storm devoured the slight, residual light of day.

"I've got flashlights, too," he said as he stood, still not letting go of Lila but pulling her up with him.

"Good thinking. Let's hurry."

They didn't say another word, but walked into the hawthorns with their arms wrapped around each other as the skies continued to weep rain over them.

Sunny materialized out of the gloom when Spencer whistled, though how she'd heard him in the din of driving rain and groaning trees was beyond Lila. Soon the three of them were making their way towards the cabin, pausing only long enough to work the gate at the border of Lila's property on their return journey.

As they entered the pines, thunder sounded again, inevitably drawing closer and vibrating not only through air but this time through the very ground underneath their feet. Lila couldn't feel the passage of the sound through Sunny's body, but she thought the horse must surely feel the tremors of air, ground, and the humans astride her.

Lila hoped it wasn't too stressful for Sunny.

The rain sounded different in the pines than it did in the open prairie, the splatting of droplets somewhat tempered by the fanning fingers of pine needles that waved greetings to the rain, and slapped against Lila's and Spencer's coats when they brushed too close to one.

Almost there.

Lila tightened her grip on Spencer's hand at her waist, and he leaned into her slightly in response.

It's going to be okay.

But Lila wondered, how much did Spencer really remember? Did he understand the sacrifice A. B. had made for him, how much he'd wanted to spare his nephew the pain that had throttled him all at once tonight?

Is it all too much?

Lila tamped down on the thought, dodging another swaying branch, just as they emerged in sight of their destination. They'd get themselves and to the shelter offered by the cabin and its porch, and then she and Spencer would talk.

But once they were inside the cabin and the storm brought the fullness of its wrath down, sending ripples through the structure with every lightning strike, rain drilling at the metal roof like a thousand crazed woodpeckers, speech seemed like less of a necessity than an extravagance. Spencer and Lila were communicating, all right, but they did all of it without the indulgence of words, using the older, truer medium of touch instead to connect, to reassure, and yes, to love.

When the palest light of morning filtered through her window, Lila woke. Thunder was peeking over Spencer's shoulder—Lila had curled herself around him this night—and he was stroking the cat's head gently.

Thunder rewarded Spencer's efforts with a purr; Lila with a kiss against his shoulder.

"How long have you been awake?" she asked. Spencer's hand paused in its slow caresses and Thunder bumped his head against the palm, urging continued progress.

"Not long." Spencer stroked Thunder, head to tail, and then turned into Lila, dislodging the cat from his edge-of-the-bed perch in spite of his slow movement. "Sorry, boy."

Lila sank into Spencer's embrace, pressing her cheek against his chest, listening to his heart's slow, steady pace.

"It wasn't your fault," she dared to say.

"No, it wasn't," he agreed.

"A. B. thought he was doing the right thing by sending you away," Lila pressed on, tipping her head back and locking eyes with Spencer. He did not flinch, and raised his hand to play with her curls. "He really felt *he* killed James because he brought the gun that you ended up with. He didn't want you to remember, not any of that, and to have to deal with the pain."

Spencer's green gaze sharpened.

"I wonder what he'd think of you having to share that memory with me now?" He spoke softly, but Lila wondered if anger or observation drove those carefully intonated words.

Perhaps both.

"Sometimes good intent isn't enough to fix a situation. Sometimes there is no fixing it," Spencer sighed, pulled Lila tighter against him, and crushing a kiss against her lips with increasing passion, until it affected every part of her body.

"But you appreciate the intent?" She all but gasped when the kiss ended.

A flicker of a smile crossed Spencer's lips then. It didn't spread over his face, didn't touch his eyes, but it was a smile nevertheless. Lila smiled back.

"I do appreciate the intent," he said. "Yours more than

A. B.'s, but yes. He tried to help me. He did."

"You could still talk to The Shepherd. If you wanted to."

"I could."

They lapsed into silence again, secure in the comfort of each other's arms. Light and sound gradually increased in the cabin, filtering in from the outside.

Mornings in Wyoming were adept at making their way inside early, particularly in a cabin without curtains. Lila had never wanted curtains, since it was her considered opinion was that they'd need to be removed every time she left the cabin, packed away to prevent rodent or insect damage in her absence.

Still, today of all days, it would have been nice to linger in the respite that sleep offered. The events of the previous day had been exhausting.

"I should see to Sunny," Spencer said finally. And then he laughed, the kind of laugh that bore no amusement with it. "I've never owned a pistol. Never wanted one, always had an aversion to them, in fact. Don't even like to hunt, though I wondered why Dad—my adopted father—never asked me to go with him. Now I know."

"Spencer ... "

"I should see to Sunny."

"Spencer!" Lila clutched him, turning his face back to hers with one hand, wrapping the other as far around his torso as she could reach. She searched his face, the dullness of the piercing, sparkling eyes she'd so quickly come to adore frightening her. "Spencer ... I love you. You're not alone in this. I'm here."

Lila wouldn't fool herself into thinking her words were a panacea. They weren't. Spencer would need time and support to process the memory that had been revealed to him ... and Lila would, too. But speaking the words now was so clearly right—not in the sense of protecting herself, perhaps, but certainly in the sense of protecting this connection she and Spencer were forging together.

The film peeled back from Spencer's eyes and he met Lila's lips with his own, assuring her without speaking that he understood, that he agreed. That ...

"I love you, too," he said, pulling back only far enough to get the words out. "I think I loved you from the moment I touched you."

... from the moment I touched you.

It seemed to Lila that there was a joke to be made there, and maybe something deeper than words to learn, too. But Spencer kissed the thought away, just as she kissed away Spencer's thoughts; they were doing and being and connecting ... and not thinking at all.

Mornings in Wyoming were made of stern, cowboy-wakening stuff, but they were not, Lila found, more powerful than the somnolence that follows passionate confessions, and even more passionate lovemaking.

When Lila awoke again, it was to Spencer's stealthy movements. He slipped from the bed, shushed Thunder with a careful serving of kibble—"Damn metal bowls," Spencer whispered to the cat. "I'm going to get you some nice, quiet plastic someday."—and the sound of her screen door opening and shutting.

Assuming Spencer was going to check on Sunny and perhaps get her some water from the well, Lila luxuriated in her bed a little longer. The air still felt cool against the exposed skin of her arms and shoulders, so she guessed they hadn't slept long. The breeze was present, but not particularly strong ... perhaps the weather would be stable for a bit.

When Lila realized she hadn't heard the sound of Spencer's

boots, she leaned over the edge of the bed and peered out through the screen door. Thunder had finished breakfast and now sat in front of the door, watching Spencer, who sat on the low bench on the edge of the porch. He was barefooted and turned sideways, with one leg up on the bench and the other resting on the porch floor, leaning against the post across from where Lila usually her wash basin, gazing out past the fence that bordered Lila's yard and plucking at a long-stemmed grass.

"Spencer?"

Spencer glanced back towards her then, and gave her a little wave. Lila waved back, and then slid out of bed and shrugged into her shirt-robe. She slipped outside to join Spencer, facing him on the bench. He accommodated her by shifting his position to straddle the bench, and Lila took his free hand.

"What is it?"

After a moment of staring down at their joined hands, Spencer raised his eyes to Lila's. Searching them, she felt reassured, but saddened, and squeezed the hand she held.

"My Dad—my adoptive Dad—was great. He wasn't much for physical affection, but he had a presence that ... well, he conveyed his love for family and friends in other ways. I don't remember my adoptive Mom well, because cancer took her when I was six, but I do remember she was a hugger." His lips twitched into a smile. "I don't just mean she hugged me, either. That woman would hug anyone she thought needed it, and she'd hug as a greeting, too."

Lila smiled back.

"The stove door," she said, feeling Spencer press her hand harder as she began. "It's okay ... I just wanted to say, I got an impression from the stove door—from A. B. into the door—about the couple he wanted to adopt you. He liked the man, and liked him a lot, but he really thought the woman was perfect, in terms of nurturing, I mean."

"I think she must have been," Spencer replied. "And I think

Dad must've been perfect when it came to refocusing me, because I swear, even though I knew I was adopted and remembered bits and pieces about the fire, I didn't remember a thing about ... "

This time, it wasn't enough to squeeze his hand. Lila slid across the scant distance between her and Spencer and wrapped herself around him.

"I'm not going to fall apart, Lila," he said, his voice wry and sounding hollow to Lila, who was hearing it through his chest wall now, resting her head against his heart.

"I know. Oh, I know. But you don't have to say it. Because I know that, too."

"So you do." Spencer was silent for a moment, rubbing Lila's back with one hand, clasping her shoulder with the other. "Did you also know that Dad fell apart after Mom died, and married a woman who was her opposite in almost every way?"

Though she'd guessed as much, Lila shook her head.

"She wasn't an outright bitch, but she was damn close. At least she never had a child of her own, and Dad protected the inheritance he'd wanted for me from her. I wasn't sorry when she died, except maybe sorry that her shallow life was enough for her when the world has so much more beauty and love in it. Even if it's not always obvious."

"Is that why you collect art?" Lila asked, pulling back enough to look into Spencer's eyes.

"Partly, I guess. Dad started that. I decided to add to it, to build something other people could enjoy, too."

"What do you mean by that? Are you lending pieces out?"

Spencer chuckled, looking over Lila's head before he brought his eyes back to hers, and brought his fingers up to ruffle her curls.

"Nothing that impressive. But I'm building the main 'house' for display. I live in the garage—what looks like the garage. That surprises you," he said, a wry smile crossing his face, and Lila knew it wasn't really a question. She shut her mouth, which had been hanging open.

"Yes! I had no idea."

"'The Sun' blabbed it like I was building an actual art museum."

"I don't read any newspapers if I can help it," Lila said. "I've seen 'The Sun' in the grocery store but I've never picked it up. But isn't it an art museum? Because it sounds like an art museum."

"Technically, maybe. I'm not charging admission. I'm not a professional and I certainly don't have a staff or whatever else comes with a real museum." Spencer sounded defensive, looking over towards the fence. Lila turned long enough to see Sunny there, nipping away at the grass, and then brought her eyes back to Spencer.

She put her hand on his cheek and turned his face back towards hers.

"It sounds fantastic," she said, letting the words deliver their import softly, rather than with the volume they deserved. "And all this time, I thought you were building some monstrous mansion ... do you know what I called it? I'm embarrassed to say, in my head, I thought of it as ... the 'Taj Spencer.'"

Spencer snorted.

"It's not all that grand," he said, placing his hand over hers. "But I appreciate that you can fuck up with assumptions, too."

"Screw up."

"How long did it take before you gave up on teaching Kristen some manners?"

"Oh, her! She's beyond help."

"What if I am, too?" Their hands were clasped now, fingers interlocked, and the feeling that was becoming as familiar to Lila as the touch of an object's embedded memory—but a thousand times more appealing—was spreading from their hands across and through them both.

"I don't mind. I'm not exactly perfect myself."

"As long as you realize that," Spencer drawled, letting go of Lila's hand to wrap her completely into his arms.

Lila let herself be drawn where she wanted to be, and even stopped short of delivering a playful slug against Spencer's shoulder.

Though his next words almost made her reconsider her non-violent approach.

"You know, I haven't seen the red bra ON you yet ... "

"I knew it! I knew you saw my laundry!"

"How could I miss it? It was awfully tantalizing, and there you were, acting as if you didn't know ... "

"I didn't know, that was the day the propane ... oh!" Lila shook her head. "You're teasing me. I wish you'd just ... "

"Just what?" Spencer's voice dropped from light to sultry in an instant, and Lila allowed herself to answer honestly.

"Just shut up and kiss me."

Spencer did.

23: Aftermath

It was after lunch that harmony shifted abruptly into discord. From Lila's simple question about what Spencer had said to Sheriff Hoffman about how he'd found James' body—"Very little," he responded tersely—they had progressed to arguing about what Jake should know about James' death.

"Kristen would agree with me," Spencer said, frustrating Lila anew, because she knew he was right.

"Oh, so you and Kristen are best friends now?" She intended to tease, but it didn't come out quite right and Spencer frowned at her across the kitchen.

"I just don't see why you would want ... Jake to know about ... "

"It's not that I don't want Jake to know! That's not the point. He's your brother. He deserves to know."

Spencer sighed, and shrugged.

"It's not like the truth is pleasant in this case, Lila."

They stood glaring at each other, a chasm between them even though they were not far apart physically. And while Lila's baser emotions were as inflamed as Spencer's seemed to be, she also wanted to hold him, to communicate with certainty that the irritable storm they had just sparked was only passing ... it was not here to stay.

Though she moved a bit stiffly, Lila forced herself to bridge the distance between them and once she had, she hugged Spencer tight. Spencer's immediate, reciprocal embrace helped dissipate Lila's residual frustration. Thunder followed her to wrap himself around both of their ankles, as if he, too, were participating in the calming contact.

"I know. But it's not as if you really think that not knowing is better, either."

Spencer didn't answer right away, but Lila knew she'd made her point at last.

"You're right," Spencer said finally. "But he doesn't need to know about you—about what you can do." The edge came back into his voice then, and it frightened Lila all over again. "What? What did I say? You tensed up; do you want to tell Jake?"

"I ... " Fear of speaking straddled Lila's other, memory-inspired fear, superseding it.

"Look, Lila, if you ... "

"No. It's ... Spencer, it's ridiculous, but ... please understand, it's not that I think ... it's just ... the memory of seeing your ... of seeing Nell ... at the hands of James ... "

Now it was Spencer's body that went still. It happened so suddenly, so certainly, that Lila released her hold on him, realizing with horror that he'd reached the very conclusion she didn't want him to find.

"You think I ... " Spencer began, words laid out rigidly, brittle to the point of snapping.

He didn't need to finish the sentence. They both knew what Lila feared, rational or not.

"NO!" Lila threw herself back at Spencer, as Thunder mewled and skittered away. Spencer opened his arms to Lila, but they didn't tighten around her body and Lila faltered, stammering over her words worse than before, desperate to get them out. "No, no ... but the memory, it ... I can't think clearly ... I don't believe that you'd ever, don't believe ... but the memory, it gets into me, it's almost ... almost like I lived all of these things myself, not just Nell and A. B. and James and you, but ... everything I ever ... everything I ever picked up, it piles up, it buries me, it's like I don't even know who I am anymore, sometimes ... and I ... I ... "

"Tell me," Spencer said, securing her against him again. Lila let out a sob of relief, relaxing into Spencer's body completely, feeling the incredible solace of Spencer holding her up when she would have collapsed without him.

"N-n-n-no. It's t-t-too much for me; it's too much for anybody."

"Tell me, Lila. Tell me what it's like for you. Let me be there for you—with you—as much as I can. Like you were there—like you are there—for me."

Lila wasn't sure she could speak, so immense was the intensity of emotion that throttled her then. At first, the words barely eked out, but Spencer would caress her along her spine or squeeze her shoulder with his hand and from those small assurances, Lila would find the strength to expel another phrase, another sentence.

And when he didn't step back, when her stories didn't turn his muscles rigid, when it seemed as if he truly was able to absorb the scenes that had fascinated and thrilled Lila, along with the ones that had horrified and terrorized her ... the words came faster to Lila. The transferred memories stacked up more quickly than she could recount them, each waiting for its chance to escape her lips, to rejoin the ethereal realm from which it had been first extracted.

Waiting for Lila to tell how she had experienced them, in addition to how they were originally formed.

Spencer listened, holding Lila the whole time, compelling her with his touch and his willing presence to release the burden she'd always assumed to be hers alone, even when it overwhelmed her and forced her to her Wyoming hideout to restore what little balance she could find.

When Lila's words slowed and the backlog of oppressive, absorbed memories became manageable again, Spencer began to plant small, soothing kisses in her curls, and then on her forehead.

In the sweet silence that Lila was finally able to absorb again, the sounds of birds chirping and a touch of breeze flickering in through the window reached her.

"If you hadn't come here," Spencer murmured just above her head, "and if you hadn't heard the door, we wouldn't be together now."

Lila gasped, not wanting to think of that, but knowing that this facet of her experience was as absolute and real—as complete and genuine—as the rest.

"If Nell hadn't loved that stove so much, and if A. B. hadn't loved her ... " she added.

" ... and then hated the stove after what happened to Nell ... to my mother ... and loved ... " Spencer's voice cracked, but he went on, "and loved me, too ... "

The words didn't need to be spoken, not really. Lila and Spencer had stumbled together into the bittersweet realization of how past sorrows can lead—all unknowing—to future joys. They'd understood that, of course, but Lila thought they both needed this reminder. Just as they needed to acknowledge together that past pain can and must yield to future happiness.

To present happiness.

"I'm so glad to be right here, right now." Lila said, on the edge of crying all over again.

"You sound glad," Spencer sniped, and this time Lila did punch his shoulder. "Hey!"

"I am glad, you dummy. If it took the awfulness of the past to get to this moment, and if it takes a lot of bumbling about and making mistakes to ... "

"Not big mistakes," Spencer smiled at Lila when she looked up at him. "Don't hit me again."

"No," Lila sniffed, and kissed his neck, making him groan. "Not big mistakes. I reserve the right to correct your language and smack you as needed, but I promise not to be mean about it."

"And can I smack you as needed?" The wicked twinkle was back in Spencer's eyes, and he delivered a playful slap against Lila's backside as he spoke.

She frowned at him, but couldn't hold the grimace, and Spencer's smile broadened.

"I just wish ... "

"If wishes were cat food, Thunder wouldn't ever be hungry again," Spencer said, and Thunder meowed. "I'd say he's agreeing with me, but he sounds like he's half-starved, the big baby." Lila raised her fist, faux-threatening, and Spencer captured it, opened it, and kissed her palm, making her jump. But Spencer's expression mirrored what Lila knew was on her own face as he raised his head. "I wish, too. I do."

Lila rested against Spencer's shoulder again then, savoring with every breath they shared the supreme comfort of his arms around her, the sparkling delight of his body against hers. And into the loveliness and fragility of that oddly blissful moment, Thunder sneezed.

"So. How about you feed the bottomless pit over there?" Spencer asked, jerking his head in Thunder's direction.

"And?" Lila raised her eyebrows, focusing Spencer with a steely glare even as she raised a hand to gently press against his cheek.

"And I give Ja- ... and I give Brother Jake a call. What? It's progress, right?"

"It's progress," Lila allowed with a nod and a smile. "For both of us."

"I don't remember much, you know," Spencer said, still holding Lila. She tightened her grip on his body, knowing what he was talking about. "It was always bits and pieces. But I never remembered ... when you were touching the door, I remembered holding that gun ... just holding it ... and pointing it ... "

Lila pressed up as hard as she could against Spencer, and he took a jostling step.

"Hey, now, are you trying to knock me over? So you can have

your way with me, I hope?"

Lila sighed, meeting Spencer's gaze and wink with a frown.

"I can't talk about it for long, Lila. I can't think about it for long. I wish you didn't have the full memory of that night. I don't, and I don't want it."

Lila let go of Spencer then, but framed his face with both hands before he could step away.

"I know. But I do have it. And love is why. Because A. B. loved Nell so much, and loved you so much, and loved Ja—Brother Jake ... that's why it all got stuck in the door. And A. B. loved James, even though he hated what James had become."

Lila watched the emotions chasing across Spencer's face, one after the other, as he absorbed her words. When he bent to kiss her, the intensity of the moment blazed up like synchronous pyrotechnics.

"Love?" Spencer said at last, brushing the word on Lila's lips with the lightest of breaths, the softest of voices.

Lila responded in kind.

"Love."

And as Lila and Spencer maneuvered themselves into the bedroom, shedding clothes as they went, Lila had but one fleeting thought of Thunder, who surely would choose to convert wishes into cat food, if he could.

Later, as Lila lay wrapped in Spencer's arms, she considered not the events of many years that had managed to lead up to this moment, but only this moment. Her neck had a crook in it, and her left arm was a bit numb, but she'd never felt better.

The wind whispered through the window, skittering over her skin on its way to Spencer's. Thunder was nestled near their feet, purring so hard that the vibrations were tangible through Lila's toes, and the sound of it was mingling with that of the pines dancing outside and the slow, steady pace of Spencer's heart underneath her ear.

Beautiful music.

The scent of Spencer's chest was all strength and warmth, masculinity and security. Lila inhaled deeply, and savored the conflagration of sensation around her, lingering in particular on the feeling conveyed through each of her fingertips, splayed across Spencer's skin. Lila shifted her hand, just a half inch or so, and smiled as Spencer's heartbeat picked up.

"Insatiable," she murmured, the sound of her voice fitting in to the melody of the late afternoon seamlessly, as if it belonged there.

"Is that a problem?" The lazy rumbling of his voice sent a surge of passion through Lila.

"Not at all."

"Insatiable," he groaned, and cupped his hand at the base of her neck, pulling more urgently when she raised her head to meet his seeking mouth.

"Ow," Lila said on a gasp when they broke apart. "My neck ... it's ... "

Spencer interrupted her with a chuckle.

"Let's change sides. You're a bit chilled, too."

"And you'll be my windbreak?" Lila said, aiming for sultry but sounding breathless even to her own ears as she shifted up and over Spencer, saw his eyes light up as she moved.

Thunder grumbled and jumped down to the floor of the cabin, which should have depleted the mood, Lila supposed, but somehow didn't.

"I'll feed Thunder first," she said, placing one foot on the floor.

Spencer grabbed Lila's wrist before she could step away,

tugging her back down to the bed, lavishing her with kisses and more, his hands on her body conveying both the potency of his desire and the totality of his love more assuredly than fragile words ever could.

And Lila, who had been afraid of her sense of touch for longer than she could remember, both absorbed the message Spencer was sending her through his touch, and reciprocated it through her own.

Without fear.

The moment was of one of inexplicable truth, undeniable power ... and indefinite duration.

"I swear I just heard that cat sigh," Spencer said eventually, neither dodging nor flinching when Lila raised her fist. Instead— while she was right there, right then entrapped in the brilliant emerald wells of Spencer's eyes—Lila was the one who cried out.

"Oh!"

"What? Your neck again?" Spencer reached out for her, but Lila eluded him. She grabbed her cell phone away from its charger so fast that she snapped the connection, forgetting to unplug it, and then she dashed back into the bedroom and snatched her shirt-robe off of its hook.

She stood out of Spencer's reach, shrugging into the shirt, and then texting with focused madness.

"What?" Spencer was bemused, still propped up in Lila's bed. *In our bed.*

"Just a minute! I've got it!" Lila spared a moment to wave her hand at Spencer. "After all these years, I've got the name for this place!"

Lila turned the phone towards Spencer as soon as she finished typing, and watched his face as he read. The smile that spread over his face when he reached the last three words, the name Lila wanted Lou to place onto the prepared archway marking her land, was just what Lila hoped she'd see. She smiled, too, as their eyes met.

When Spencer's eyes slid from Lila's face to trace down the opening of the shirt she'd not finished buttoning, his expression shifted. Lila turned with a giggle, pressing "Send" as she did.

"Fine. I need to step outside anyway," Spencer groused.

Lila placated Thunder with strokes and murmurs as Spencer dressed, and then when he left the cabin, retrieved Thunder's bowl. She was just about to fill it when her phone buzzed.

"PERFECT!!!" Kristen responded. "itll be done in 2 wks! ill have a surprize for you 2 then 2."

Thunder yowled as Lila was puzzling out Kristen's last sentence.

"All right, all right! I am sorry, you know."

"Mrrrow," Thunder mumbled, when his mouth was full of kibble at last.

"Don't talk with your mouth full, young man." Lila said, giving the cat one last pet from head to tail. The cat changed his vocalizations, and Lila stared. "You probably shouldn't purr with your mouth full, either! How is that even possible?"

The screen door sounded its alert, and Lila turned, straight into Spencer's arms. She was still beaming, but meeting his eyes, she saw that he had turned serious again.

"What?"

Spencer held her eyes, and slid one hand underneath her shirt, pressing the small of her back in that delicious, possessive-but-tender way of his.

"Do you want to tell ... Brother Jake? About what you know, and how you know it?"

Lila considered, keeping her eyes on his, not trying to hide—because she didn't need to hide now.

"I don't think it needs to be common knowledge, but I think it would be easier to explain if we just told him the truth. All of the truth. Do you want to tell him ... about what happened and how it happened?"

Spencer kept his eyes on Lila's, letting her see his concern, how it was made of both darkness and light.

As we all are. But more light than darkness, especially the two of us together.

"I don't want to, but I can manage. I just don't want you hurt."

"You believe me. You're with me. Whatever hurt I have—and I will have some in life, we all will—it'll be okay as long as you believe me, and ... "

"And I'm with you." Spencer squeezed Lila tighter against him as he finished her sentence, and it took her breath away. "Count on it, Lila."

"I am counting on it," Lila said, and they kissed to seal the deal, while Thunder continued to purr as he ate his dinner behind them.

"Is he purring? While he's eating?" Spencer asked, peering around Lila. He still held Lila to him, still proclaiming his love to her through his touch.

"He is. Silly cat."

"Do you think he'll want to visit my place someday?" Lila's eyes fluttered from the cat back to Spencer's face, heart skipping in anticipation again. It had been happening rather a lot lately! "I'll get him a litter box."

"I'm not sure how well he'll travel, and I don't have a carrier yet, but I think it would be great to visit your place."

"It's really not much bigger than yours," Spencer said. "Your place is actually better, aside from the lack of running water. Not that I really miss that, except for showering with you."

Lila grinned.

"Have you ever had a sun shower?"

"A what?"

Spencer's eyes were twinkling wickedly by the time Lila was

halfway through her explanation, and he detached himself from her side just long enough to check the forecast on his phone.

"Looks like a clear day tomorrow!"

Lila shook her head and tried to look stern.

"Don't you need to be working on fences and collecting art?"

"Well, I ... "

"And setting up a time to talk to The Shepherd and Brother Jake?" Lila caught an escaping laugh with one hand. "Kristen would say that sounds like a bluegrass band's name."

"Good god." Spencer said, biting off the words even while his eyes smiled at Lila. "It sounds like an hideous reality show, that's what it sounds like."

"A show about what?" Lila hugged Spencer closer, inhaling his scent, savoring the feeling of his body against hers, warm and solid.

"High-plains sheepherding," Spencer said, his answer so matter-of-fact that Lila laughed again.

"Of course. And I'm sure it would include a lot of censored 'bleeps.'"

"I have a feeling I won't be watching much TV in the future. Not that I watched a lot before."

Lila was so engrossed in the sound of Spencer's voice, deeper and more personal than ever by virtue of the fact that she was hearing it with her head so near its source, that she didn't answer immediately.

"You should take up reading."

"You know, that's not a bad idea." Spencer tucked one hand under Lila's face, turning it up to look at him again. "And I have a confession."

"A confession?"

"More of a story."

Lila tipped her head, confused.

"Not too long ago—maybe two months?—I was out with

333

Sunny, to tighten a few gates, naturally. I rode up to that one just before yours and there was a book there."

"A book?"

"Yeah, sealed in a plastic bag and tucked up underneath the loop wire. And there was a note ... "

"From A. B.," Lila said, connecting the dots.

Spencer nodded.

"'Our neighbor writes good stuff.' And the book was ... "

" ... *A Paltry Beacon!*" Lila said the words with Spencer, and was promptly caught in that awful space between smiling and crying. Spencer kissed her softly, relaxing her enough to let the tears fall.

And the smile, tinged with sadness, to nevertheless blossom.

"I read it."

"And what did you think?"

"I liked it so much I thought I might start collecting books."

"Really?" Lila's voice trembled on the single, inadequate word.

"Really." Spencer said, his thumb tracing the path of Lila's tears, his own expression a blended slurry of old sorrows and new happiness—new understanding. "I returned the book the same way I received it, and he left *Desert Deluge* for me next. A. B. was a crafty old coot!"

"A good crafty old coot," Lila said, shaking her head. "He was determined to throw us all together somehow, wasn't he? You and me, and Jake too. Willing me the cows, giving you my book ... I wonder what he'd make of ... "

"Of us 'getting together' ... in the Biblical sense?"

Lila snorted inelegantly.

"Yes, that." She seized Spencer's hand, where it still lingered against her cheek, arresting his caresses. "We ... there's something ... I've never, not with anyone, felt this way ... "

"No, neither have I. And Lila, I'm not jealous of Jake. I'm protective of you, and I can be abrasive and obnoxious ... "

"And more!" Lila could not resist adding.

334

"And more," Spencer agreed. "But I'll get used to having a brother again. And it'll never be like A. B. and ... James. Never. I don't even drink."

"You don't? No, of course you don't."

"No alcohol, no guns ... I'll have to insist that you keep my secret, or someone will show up and revoke my right to wear a hat."

"You have to keep that hat!"

"Agreed. How else would I let a certain lady know that I knew there was something special about her, even when I first found her ... "

"Yes, I wasn't at my best," Lila said, shaking her head.

"You ARE the best," Spencer murmured, emblazing his next kiss so thoroughly onto Lila's lips that she could feel her legs shaking.

"I've got you," Spencer told her, sparing only a moment to tell her so.

I've got you, too.

Lila would have to wait to speak the words out loud, but it didn't really matter: she knew Spencer knew.

24: Here & Now

Wyoming had been drying for nine days straight on the Sunday when they gathered to raise Lila's archway. Lou brought the materials up using his work truck and a flatbed, and Kristen flitted about, taking pictures from every conceivable angle, at every innocuous step in the process.

"Kristen, all I'm doing is digging a hole!" Lou protested early on.

"But you do such fine fucking work, my dear," Kristen responded, clicking away.

Lou shook his head. He tried once more to object, when Kristen was photographing him lining the front-facing portion of the post holes with sheet metal.

"What's that for?" Lila interrupted.

Lou sighed, and Spencer answered for him.

"Keeps the hole from crumbling when the pole is being lifted."

"Thanks," Lou said shortly. "Sorry, Lila, but I just want to get these poles up! It'd be easier with the Cat, but I left it with Stick in Casper so he could finish prep work on our job for next week."

"These for the backs?" Spencer asked, holding up two more pieces of sheet metal, bent at 90-degree angles.

Lou responded with a nod, and Spencer tossed one piece to Jake, bending to insert the other along the opposite side of the hole nearest him. After watching Spencer, Jake did the same with his piece.

"Nice!" Kristen exclaimed. "I got that! Men at work, I like it."

At that, Jake let loose with one of his infectious giggles, and

Spencer rolled his eyes dramatically at Lou, eliciting a weary grin.

"What's next?" Spencer asked, as Lou stood.

"Assembling the arch," Lou said. "And I'll need everyone to help with this part."

With Spencer helping to direct the others—taking part of the burden of addressing the group from Lou, something Lila knew Lou's employee, "Stick" did on the job in Casper—they worked together more easily. They loosely assembled the flattened "U" shape of the arch on the ground, aligning it with the post holes into which the treated bases of the supporting poles would rest, and then attached two more smaller poles to the archway with rope.

"For lifting the main structure," Kristen told Lila, before she could ask. "It's basically a pulley system to make this all easier and safer. Lou drew me a picture last night."

"Did you keep it?" Lila asked.

"Hell yes! I can make you a copy, too. See, now those divots—I gotta get some photos, but—those divots near the main post holes, that's where the pulley-poles will be based ... wait! Hold still, I need a photo of that!"

Kristen dashed off, leaving Lila with Jake.

"Do you know what all of the shorter posts are for?" Lila asked.

"I think just temporary supports as we lift the thing. The ladder, that's for tightening the upper beam at the end—that one I know."

"Hmm," Lila said, wishing she had Lou's picture to explain the entire process in detail.

"I'm not the best one to ask about this," Jake grinned. "When Lou said this would be easier with 'the Cat,' Kristen had to explain to me that meant heavy equipment, not an actual cat! Occupational hazard, I guess."

Lila laughed out loud, drawing Spencer's gaze. Her heart

caught in her throat as he smiled without hesitation, tipping his hat to her and waving to Jake before returning his attention to Lou.

The ghosts of the past were, it seemed, officially at peace now.

"Okay, we're going to get started lifting!" Spencer called.

"Now we'll see what those posts are really for!" Jake said, gesturing to Lila to precede him.

The four-foot posts were, as Jake had surmised, temporary supports, providing a break in the lifting process and also an opportunity to check alignment as the structure was being elevated into its sentry position as guardian and welcome to Lila's long-unnamed property.

While not perfectly synchronous in execution—"He's not used to working with a bunch of amateurs, after all," Kristen wise-cracked at one point—Lou's plan did work, and quickly, too. When the archway was fully standing, even Kristen was pressed into temporary service, extracting the sheet metal that had protected the main post holes.

She kicked a bit of dirt in the general direction of one of the holes with the air of one performing a great service.

"Okay, now that I've done the hard part, you boys come finish filling these in. I have photos to take! Posterity and all that good shit!"

Lou approached with his level in hand.

"One more check before we fill these in and tamp the dirt down," he said, waving Kristen away. She made a face, and he grinned at her.

"You'd think you could trust ME!"

"You'd think," Lou replied, grabbing the finger Kristen flashed at him and kissing its tip lightly. "It's my job, Kristen."

"I know, I know. Go do it, then!"

Max Huxley arrived just after Lou finished tightening the upper beam, as the group was gathering around the cooler Jake had brought for a drink of water. Max parked his immense, dual-wheeled truck in the lackluster shade of a half-dead pine tree and barreled up to them, clutching a paper-wrapped bottle.

"I brought whiskey! Woulda come sooner, but I didn't have no interest in gettin' put to work," he said, with a wink and a grin for Kristen, who speared him with a lance-like glare.

"I'm pregnant!" she announced, hands on hips.

"Wonderful! More for the rest of us," Max said, waving the bottle around at the loose half-circle of spectators.

Kristen redirected her steaming line of sight at Lila.

"Who is this human Muppet?"

Max burst into laughter, and introduced himself to Kristen before Lila could intervene.

"You're quite a pip, young lady! Max Huxley, The Shepherd, at your service, I'm sure."

"Oh, so you're A. B.'s drinking buddy? I might have known. Kristen Rush, and that's my husband Lou. The big guy."

Max winked at Kristen, shaking her hand with overt enthusiasm before making his way to Lou to slap him hard on his back.

More the middle of his back than his shoulders, which was about as high as he could reach, Lila observed. She turned her face to Spencer before she grinned too broadly.

Kristen was still watching, after all.

"Quite a group," Spencer said, catching the hand that Lila extended and pulling her into a hug. "Kristen is looking slightly less murderous now," he added, lowering his voice.

"I AM NOT!" Kristen shouted.

"Jesus, did you get super hearing to go with your super sense of smell?" Spencer responded.

"Yes, it comes free with pregnancy, apparently, along with super nausea when I smell whiskey!"

"Now darlin'," Max said, clasping Jake's hand on his way back to stand by Kristen, "don't you worry 'bout that. We'll all stand downwind from you when we drink." He promptly licked his thumb and held it up, making a great show of checking the direction of the wind.

Jake burst out laughing, and even Kristen couldn't retain her resident-evil stare in the light of Jake's contagious good humor.

"Brother Jake has a way with people," Spencer observed, still holding on to Lila as snugly as she was holding on to him.

"He does. But you have a way with me."

Spencer's answer was to embrace Lila all the more closely.

"Good god, you two, get a room," Kristen sniped, but the smile she flashed Lila was entirely genuine.

"How long before we hang the sign?" Spencer asked Kristen, all pretend innocence.

"We can wait as long as you want," Lou replied, coming up next to Kristen to capture her in his arms.

"Oh, you," Kristen grinned.

"I don't know about you, Max, but I'm definitely feeling like the odd man out here," Jake said, stepping closer to the regrouping party, Max by his side.

"Now see here, whippersnapper, I've got my own lady friend, so don't go gettin' any ideas."

"Max!" Lila laughed.

"If you're talking about Dottie," Jake said, leaning on his shovel and directing his smile fully on Max, "you'd better watch yourself. I've seen the way she looks at ME."

"Oho!" Max crowed, beaming at Jake's comeback as if he were a proud uncle—and Lila supposed he was, in every way but blood. "Bring it on, boy, bring it on. Dottie'll love every minute, and I'll love it when I win her over!"

The group was relaxed in a way that made Lila think of A. B., with his deliberate movements and soft speech. From disparate personalities and disjoined lives, they had come together in this moment, at this place, for a unified purpose ... in a combined relationship. And if true friendship didn't define all lines of this human structure, it at least there was a strong potential bolstering their current affiliations.

Lila looked at Spencer, whose eyes were glittering as the sun caught those green facets under the brim of his tipped-back hat. Spencer and Jake had gone with Max to visit Nell four days ago, and while it had been a difficult visit—Nell was only a fragment of the loving woman she'd been—it had, as Lila had hoped, set the foundation for healing.

Lila's memory of the Spencer and Jake, one on either side of Nell's bed, each holding one of her hands, was a powerful vision. It was both heavy and light, but Lila had felt love lifting light to the forefront then.

She felt it now, too.

"Your mama, I tell you, she'll have a smile now when she finally passes, knowin' her boys are both back on their land, back knowing one another," Max said, his voice husky, looking from Jake to Spencer and back again.

Lila returned to the conversation with a start, but found she had nothing to add to it.

Silence fluttered down over them then and in the space left by their voices, the Wyoming wind sang as it rippled across the grasses. Birds chirped backup, and somewhere out of sight, a cow bellowed out, punctuating the quiet without truly interrupting. Lila liked to think that it was #225 who—along with a few "friends"— had joined Spencer's herd just yesterday.

The day would be a warm one, Lila thought, her head resting on Spencer's shoulder with ease she could not have imagined mere weeks ago.

Perhaps a good day for an afternoon shower.

"So who's got cups?" Max said at last, his perkiness managing to sound entirely natural, even after his last comment.

Lila realized she was smiling again, and as she looked at the others, found them to be doing the same ... even Kristen, whose eyes were wetly bright with unshed tears.

"Damn Muppet," Kristen bristled, turning her head and bustling off towards Lou's truck. "Remembers the booze, forgets the glasses to go with it."

"Hey, now, this bottle's perfectly capable of bein' passed around!" Max shouted after Kristen.

She yelled back, "Heathen!"

"I like her!" Max announced, bumping Lou on the arm. "You're a lucky man!"

"Thanks," Lou replied. "I agree. And so would she, if ... "

"Oh, she agrees!" Kristen said, turning back for just a moment. "And when are you stupid mortals going to learn *I can always hear you?*"

Laughter flooded out, a blended, musical sound that mimicked the motion of the grasses in the wind.

"Can I see the sign now?" Lila asked Lou, overwhelmed by the simple perfection of this complex moment.

"Sure!" Lou grinned, waving her towards the flatbed, still attached to his truck. As Lila and Spencer started walking, hand in hand, Lou called out to Kristen, "Kristen, Lila wants to see the sign!"

"Adam Spencer, make yourself useful and run these cups up to Max The Shepherd Muppet!" Kristen shouted.

"She's going to make a hell of a mother," Spencer whispered in Lila's ear. "Ha! She didn't hear that!"

"NOW!"

Lila chuckled, and relinquished Spencer's hand. He tipped his hat, winking, before dashing off to do Kristen's bidding.

Kristen was unwrapping the bundled metal sign when Lila met her at the flatbed, reaching out to help hold the unwieldy package as Kristen worked.

"It must be five feet long!" Lila exclaimed.

"Just about," Kristen said, smiling. "Lou traded Mercy Lainor over at Mercy Metalworks to have it made."

"He shouldn't have; it must be worth hundreds!"

"Oh come on, Lila, Mercy probably would've done it for free, considering who it's for, famous fucking author that you are," Kristen's smile was so broad it threatened to strain muscles. "There! It's perfect, isn't it? The work, the name ... you took your sweet time, but you did it right."

Kristen stepped next to Lila and squeezed Lila's shoulders as they stood there, just looking at the words. Lila leaned over the wrought metal lettering, caressing the hard, cool words that would soon heat in the brilliant glare of the Sun.

"I'll be right back, okay?" Kristen whispered in Lila's ear, with one more press of her arm across Lila's back.

Lila nodded, her fingers still flickering, but her mind lodged in stillness, aware of each breath she took—not individually, but unified, part of the tapestry of intermingled lives that had led to this ... that would, with luck and hope, lead on to countless moments unknown: each precious, burgeoning with limitless potential.

"Lila."

At the serious, single word, Lila turned, and Kristen laid a large, wrapped package in the arms that Lila automatically stretched out.

"Kristen! What did you do?"

"You'll love it. Well, I hope you'll love it. Wait a second ... Lou! I'm giving Lila her present!"

Lila gripped the edges of the flat, rectangular object, feeling the smoothed planes and edges of a frame underneath.

"One of your photos, Kristen?"

"Maybe. Just wait a minute, the boys are coming. No, Max, you idiot, leave those cups over there! Gah!"

"Careful now, boys," Max was saying to Jake and Spencer. "If you spill this fine whiskey, you'll be driving over the Big Horns to get me some more from the distillery!"

When the men joined them, Lila sat on the edge of the flatbed, next to her beautiful archway sign, and slid a finger underneath the seam of wrapping paper.

"God, I hope you like it!" Kristen hid her face against Lou's chest. "Tell me when it's over. If she's smiling, tell me that. Otherwise ... "

"Shh," Lou murmured. "She's turning it over now ... "

"Oh!"

Lila stared down at an 11x14 image composed primarily of waving grasses, on which the focus was skillfully honed. And there was Lila herself, just right of center, in front of the fence line that was softly fuzzy in the background ... on top of Spencer, kissing him with abandon.

"What is it?" Spencer said, circling around Lila to see.

"That day ... " Lila began, words forsaking her again.

"Oh, THAT day."

Lila and Spencer shared a significant look, and then Lila remembered that Kristen was still waiting for a response.

"Kristen! Kristen, I love it!"

"I love it, too," Spencer said, taking the photo from Lila as she hurried to hug the worry from Kristen's face. "I'll show it, if Lila agrees."

"I agree! Oh, I agree, it's gorgeous."

"And just out of focus enough to prevent the camera from melting," Kristen said, returning Lila's hug hard. "I'm so glad! I've been worried."

"You shouldn't worry, about anything," Lila said, pulling back and picking up Kristen's charm necklace in her bare hands.

"Holy shit," Kristen said, "you weren't kidding about that mute power Spencer's got."

"Speak up, kids, not all of us got this ability to hear every little thing!" Max called out from his stand upwind of Kristen.

"*She likes it!*" Kristen shouted. "Oh, come on over and see for yourself; I'll watch where I stand."

"I'll hang the sign now," Lou said, reaching past Lila.

"Need any help?"

"No ... on second thought, if you could just hand it up to me after I get up the ladder," Lou said, nodding at Spencer.

"Sure thing!"

Lila picked up the sign, its lettering glinting in the sunlight, so that Spencer could lay the photo in the canvas wrappings that had previously cocooned the sign. The words were heavier than she'd expected, and much as she loved the sign, she was glad when Spencer relieved her of it. When Lila lifted her eyes from the lettering—backwards now, so Spencer would be handing it off to Lou in the proper direction—she met Spencer's gaze, meshing in such a seamless way that she knew he was thinking just what she was thinking.

Yes, it would be a good day for an afternoon shower, but here and now was the most amazing place and time to be.

"I'm ready!" Lou called, and Spencer moved and extended the sign up to him.

"Got it?" Spencer said, letting go of the sign only when Lou nodded.

The loops above the letters of the sign slipped easily into the open hooks that awaited them. Lou climbed higher on the ladder to close the hooks, setting the sign into a gentle sway.

"'Here & Now,'" Max read aloud. "I'll drink to that!"

"Lush!" Kristen cried.

"I'll drink to that, too," Max responded, and raised his glass. "To 'Here & Now,' long may it last."

"That doesn't make any sense!" Kristen said. "No, Lou, wait ... one more shot!"

"One more shot!" Max bellowed. "Another round!"

"It makes sense to me," Lila said to Spencer, smiling at him as laughter swelled around them.

"Me, too." And Spencer winked and tipped his hat before catching Lila up in his arms again.

Acknowledgements

While imagination and hard work are critical to the crafting of any tale, this story in particular would not have been possible without the support, encouragement, and proofreading efforts of many people beyond the author. In concentrated effort to keep the list of acknowledgements shorter than the novel itself, I am selecting only a few for special attention here:

Jayne, daughter and the only Wyoming native in our family ... you stood in Lila's place for the photograph behind the cover design and you've always adored the telling of tales! I hope you enjoy this one, too.

Dean, husband and wearer of many hats ... now you have to read this *whole thing* and determine which parts you infiltrated.

Gary Ruhser, father and author (www.amazon.com/Gary-G.-Ruhser/e/B00GKRQYJS) ... thank you for your encouragement, proofreading, and the gift that keeps on giving (ISBNs).

Jean, mother and poet ... thank you for your support, proofreading-plus, and for your enthusiastic disgust at not being *first* to finish beta-reading.

Janis, sister and friend ... you are my hero.

Tracy, who made sure that Sunny was everything a good horse should be.

Heidi, a woman who accomplishes more in the average weekday than I could manage in a week of Sundays, and you still read the whole thing!

Janette, for beta-reading above and beyond the call of duty, and for helping to inspire the character of Kristen.

Fred Dye, who developed my cover concept from sketchy beginnings to the compelling final presentation that only a true artist can deliver. See more of Fred's work at freddye.com.

Chris Garrard, who reads it all and keeps coming back for more. And who is a soon-to-be published author in another genre entirely (manning.com/garrard).

Amy Lauren, a genuine, talented artist. While Lila, being a fictional character, has only worked while listening to Amy's music within the confines of this novel, you and I are fortunate to be able to listen any time we wish (amylaurenpiano.com).

Karen, another source of inspiration for Kristen and the first person to say to me, "I wish you'd write a novel." You may well have helped to create a monster!

Kay Rutherford, patron saint of strong women and accomplished author (kayrutherford.com).

Theresa, who said, "That sounds like the beginning of a novel!" If you hadn't said so, I might never have believed it, too.

Julie, first to finish the beta-version (I was so glad you couldn't stop reading at the parts you indicated).

The incredible and creative women of the La Crosse Women Writers and Women Writers Ink (WWInk)! I found my writing voice in large part due to the warmth and welcome of the La Crosse Women Writers. We've all come a long way together, and I am excited to see where we will go with one another—and with WWInk (wwink.org).

All of the brave volunteers who offered to read the beta-version of Lila's story ... I greatly appreciate your willingness to read the half-polished version!

Most importantly, thank *you*, the reader! Writing must be satisfying for a writer to pursue it at odd hours and odder locations, but it is not truly fulfilling without the sharing of the tale.

About the Author

Gayle C. Edlin is a technical writer by coincidence and a creative writer by choice. She lives with her husband, daughter, three cats, and one dog in ordinary chaos and daily delights. Ms. Edlin also takes thousands of photographs each year with geekish dedication.

Find Gayle C. Edlin online:
gcedlin (Facebook)
@gcedlin (Twitter)
gcedlin.com (Website)
gayle@gcedlin.com (E-mail)

www.ingramcontent.com/pod-product-compliance
Lightning Source LLC
Chambersburg PA
CBHW020223180626
46810CB00006B/2027